Tapestry of War

JANE MACKENZIE

Allison & Busby Limited
12 Fitzroy Mews
London W1T 6DW
allisonandbusby.com

First published in Great Britain by Allison & Busby in 2018.

Copyright © 2018 by JANE MACKENZIE

A CIP catalogue record for this book is available from
the British Library.

First Edition

ISBN 978-0-7490-2299-0

Typeset in 11/16 pt Sabon by
Allison & Busby Ltd

The paper used for this Allison & Busby publication
has been produced from trees that have been legally sourced
from well-managed and credibly certified forests.

Printed and bound by
CPI Group (UK) Ltd, Croydon, CR0 4YY

This story is dedicated to the myriad people whose lives and endeavours threaded together, weaving victory into the tapestry of war

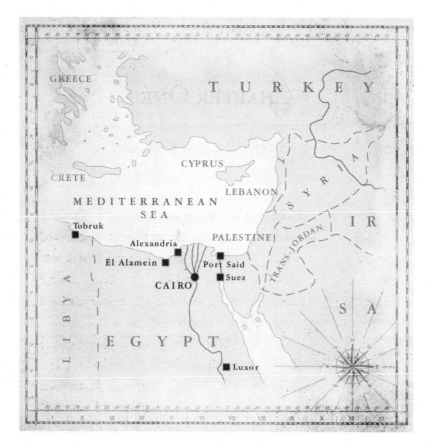

Egypt and Neighbouring Countries During World War II

CHAPTER ONE

Alexandria, June 1941

It was just after dawn when Fran saw the body. She had set out from home in the pitch-black, as soon as she heard the all-clear sounded. She hadn't known quite where she was going, but she was restless and hot after lying awake listening to the anti-aircraft guns, and the house seemed stuffy and confining despite its high ceilings.

She headed as so often before along the Corniche in the direction of the town, drawing in the sea air, shaking her head to clear her frustrations. The sky was indigo, and the sea on her right was inky black, and as ripples of fire began to snake across it she slowed her rapid pace and stopped to watch. Within what seemed like minutes the sun had risen over the waves, both sea and sky lightened to silver and violet, and to the east all was bathed in shades of orange. The sea barely moved, and all was still from here to the horizon. It was hard to believe that all night the anti-aircraft guns had been blazing against the Luftwaffe's bombs.

Fran leant against the railings and breathed deeply, sucking in the smell of the ozone on the warm breeze.

The beach was so busy during the day, especially at weekends, and it was wonderful to see it like this, deserted, becalmed in a bubble of early morning peace. Her eyes strayed to the left, past the breakwater, where the dark sand was taking on shades of gold. It was then that she saw something in the shadows of the breakwater, right down by the water's edge.

It was too big to be a normal piece of flotsam, and for a moment Fran wondered whether it was a piece of debris from a ship, or a floating mine washed up onto the shore. But then she spotted a white shirt, and with a jolt she realised the form was human, a body lying huddled in to the breakwater as though for shelter.

It was strange how long it took her to move. The almost drugged silence of the morning seemed to have made her sluggish, and her brain and her body couldn't quite work together. Eventually, though, she moved along by the railings until she reached some steps, and with her hands clenched made her way down the beach.

She forced herself to approach the body, but when it moved she gasped and took two steps back. It had only been an infinitesimal movement, but suddenly this wasn't a corpse but a living person lying in the sand. His white shorts and shirt were dry too, so he hadn't been washed up here, but had come down the beach from the Corniche. Was he simply asleep, drunk, perhaps?

She didn't want to touch him, but as she stared from her withdrawn space she spotted dark spots in the sand leading away from the man. They were blood, she was sure. This man had been injured.

She mastered her fears and bent to him, turning him with

difficulty. He groaned but didn't wake up. Her first thought was surprise at how young he was; her second that he must be French, from the insignia on his matelot's shirt. The group of French navy men whose ships were impounded here in Alexandria were a familiar sight. They maintained loyalty to Vichy France, but had claimed neutral status, and roamed the town pretty freely. What had this one done to put himself back into the war?

The front of his shirt was covered in blood, and he'd brought his right hand up to hold his chest. Inchingly Fran eased it away to reveal a slash in the shirt and an ugly-looking wound beneath, just below the heart. It was bleeding still, and the sand where he had lain was soaked with blood. How much blood could you lose without dying? Fran didn't know, but the enormity of what she was seeing terrified her. She remembered hearing that you should strap wounds tight by tearing up people's clothes, but couldn't figure out how she could remove his shirt. Frantically she pulled off his shoes and socks, and stuffed the socks clean end first into the wound, then she pulled off his belt and eased it around his chest to hold the socks more tightly. It seemed to cut into him cruelly, and the socks dug into the wound. Could she rip his shirt? She grabbed at the edge where the shirt had been slashed and pulled at the blood-soaked fabric. It gave fairly easily, and she kept on ripping until she had a patch of clean cloth that she placed next to the wound, sitting the socks as cushioning above it before resecuring the belt.

Then she rose to her feet and looked up and down the still deserted beach and out to sea. Where were the fishermen who ought by now to have set sail from the Eastern Harbour? There was nobody, just nobody.

The camps of Greek refugees were nearly a mile away nearer to the town, and she would lose too much time going in that direction for help. The quickest might be to run to the British Consulate, which was just half a mile or so away. There would be guards there even at this hour, and there was transport. Or should she just chance going to the nearest house and hoping she could wake up the local residents?

It was while she was thinking this through that she spotted a man out running on the Corniche. He was too far away, surely, and he would never hear her from where he was, but she called out, and when the runner didn't turn she called louder. 'Help! *Au secours!*' She waited, preparing to go up the beach herself in search of help, but when she gave one more rather desperate cry he turned, and stopped, staring down the beach at her. She waved, and called again. 'Please help me!' He was European, she was sure, and would understand English.

The runner looked around for the steps, and within seconds was next to her, looking down at the young Frenchman, and then back up at Fran.

'What on earth has happened here? Are you all right?' he asked quickly, panting slightly.

Fran responded gratefully to the urgency in his voice. 'I was out walking and spotted him. He was just lying huddled here. I think he must have been bleeding for hours,' she said, and her voice came out ragged. 'I tried to stop the bleeding . . .' She trailed off, looking down at her own clothes, spattered with the young man's blood.

There was relief in the man's face. He was British, but not English – Scottish, perhaps, or possibly Irish? 'I thought perhaps that you had been injured too,' he said. 'So we've got a casualty from last night, it seems.'

'From last night?'

'Yes, some of these French navy fellows were out on the town and got attacked by Free French troops. There's not much love among the fighting French for those who've chosen capitulation to Germany.'

'But he's a long way from the town!'

'Yes, he must have been chased.' He felt the young man's pulse and grimaced. 'Well, if the blighter's not to peg it now I'd better get help. He's lost more blood than any man should. Are you all right yourself, Miss . . . ?'

'Miss Trevillian, Frances Trevillian. Yes, I'm fine, don't worry. Do go and get help quickly.'

He held out a hand to her. 'I'm Jim MacNeill.' He checked the makeshift dressing she had made. 'This is good and tight,' he said approvingly. 'You'll be all right staying with him? Are you sure?' The words were more routine than truly concerned, and she liked that he didn't treat her like a weak female. She'd had enough of that recently.

'Yes, yes, I'm fine! Please go!' she urged him. 'I'll stay and keep the dressing tight. He may wake up, too.' The Frenchman had shown some signs of stirring since she'd begun manhandling him, and she didn't want him to come to and find himself alone.

MacNeill nodded, and ran off up the beach. Fran sat down with her back to the breakwater and eased her patient's head on to her lap. Don't die, she willed him, pulling out her handkerchief to wipe his rather clammy brow. Then she leant her head back against the breakwater and closed her eyes.

Her father would be back at home having breakfast by now. Her unstated destination in heading this way along the Corniche had been the British Boat Club, where the civilian yachtsmen who acted as spotters for Naval Command during air raids would by now have moored up and gone off to enjoy their weekends. Fran had been so mad last night at not being allowed to join them, just because she was female. Thank God, in retrospect, for if she hadn't been so frustrated she wouldn't have been here this morning. All that mattered now was that this young man shouldn't die.

She cradled his head. Where had her runner gone to? He seemed to have been gone for ever. She looked out to sea, trying not to give in to her fears. He is *not* going to die, she told herself again.

She looked down at him again, and his eyes were open. A surge of hope ran through her. She smiled, reassuringly she hoped, and spoke to him in French.

'Well done, you woke up! You'll be fine now. We've got an ambulance coming, and we'll have you in hospital soon in a comfortable bed.'

His eyes didn't register anything, and she wondered whether he was hearing her, but she carried on anyway, talking to him about anything and everything. She eased his head into what she hoped was a better position, and asked if he was comfortable. He gave an infinitesimal nod.

'*Merci*,' he said, in what was almost a voice.

She smiled at him in relief. 'Don't thank me!'

He would be a couple of years younger than Michael, she thought, just a teenager. She was only a few years older herself, but with Michael she always felt more than her years, and with this baby-faced boy she felt like a mother.

Who cared what side he was on? He wasn't fighting with the Germans, just trying to obey his own government by remaining neutral. To the Free French fighters he was to be despised. They were heading off to risk their lives in the desert while he sat out the war in comfort, and if you had asked her yesterday Fran would have agreed with them. But had he deserved a knife between the ribs?

By the time help came he had lost consciousness again. The first to arrive was the Scotsman MacNeill with two first-aiders from the consulate. They brought with them proper dressings and a stretcher, and by the time the ambulance arrived they were already carrying their patient up the steps to the Corniche.

Fran followed behind them. Their professionalism excluded her, and she watched rather impotently from the fringes. The young boy looked small and vulnerable, strapped into the stretcher, his face stripped of all colour.

'Is he going to be all right?' she asked a burly British forces ambulance man.

'He'll be right as rain, miss,' was his reply. 'Better than he deserves, weasel of a collaborator getting himself into a fight on a Friday night.'

'But he isn't even carrying a weapon!' she protested. 'He isn't allowed any, remember.'

'Hah!' was all the ambulance man replied, but Jim MacNeill frowned at him.

'Miss Trevillian saved him, remember. I think she has a right to care about his recovery.'

Fran turned to him thankfully. 'Can I find out how he gets on? We don't even know his name.'

He nodded. 'I'll find that out, don't worry, and if you can give me a contact number I'll make sure you get a call.'

'You can call me at the *Alexandria Journal*,' she told him. 'I'm the assistant editor there.'

He raised an eyebrow, but other than that said nothing. It was the ambulance man who spoke.

'Do you want to come with us, Lieutenant?'

So the Scotsman was an officer. 'Are you an army man, Lieutenant?' she asked him.

'No – navy,' he answered. He smiled at her. 'That was good work you did this morning, Miss Trevillian. If it's all right with you, these two' – he indicated the first-aiders from the consulate – 'can take you home in their car, and I'll go with the ambulance to see where our friend is taken to, and to follow up who he is. You'll be wishing to change, no doubt.'

Fran looked down at her filthy clothes, and her bloodstained hands, and agreed. 'I could do with a bath,' she acknowledged. 'Thank you for coming to my aid, Lieutenant MacNeill.'

'It's my pleasure,' he answered, in that soft accent of his. 'I agree with you, you know. Whatever side you are on, a knife in the ribs is no way to fight a war.'

Chapter Two

It was tough to go to work that morning, but it was only a half-day, being Saturday, and Fran plodded through it, using her time to write a piece about yesterday evening's battle between the rival French forces.

The *Alexandria Journal* was housed in a narrow building in the old town. It was a weekly paper targeted at all of the expatriate and business communities, one of two main English language papers that vied for readership with each other.

Fran had been writing the occasional piece for the paper for some years now, but things had changed when the *Journal* lost half of its staff at the outbreak of war. There had been three Italian employees who had been placed in internment alongside all Italian males when they became the 'enemy'. Then the one full-time English reporter had left to work for the Foreign Office in Cairo. So the ancient editor, Tim Jeffrey, had invited Fran to join the paper full-time, and she had found her place in a man's world, splitting her time between managing the office, liaising with the printing press, editing the work of the outside journalists, and writing the weekly editorials with Tim. It suited her rather vigorous spirit to have a lot of variety in her life, and to be busy. And that they were, for sure, since with so many old staff now gone those who remained were spread very thin.

The *Alexandria Journal* was never going to rival the daily Cairo papers for off-the-press news, but the paper's unstated goal was to keep the communities of Alexandria together – no easy feat when the city was so cosmopolitan. There were several nationalities living side by side here, and their home governments held some very different positions in the war.

'No anti-French propaganda,' Tim told Fran when she started. 'And let's be clear that most of our Italian community here don't deserve what is happening to them. There are lots of people being badly bombed here who have nothing to do with this war, and somehow we've got to write for them. Tell the truth, as far as we can get hold of it, and let's tell the human story too, of what people are doing to help each other and our troops here in Alexandria.'

It was all very well, Fran thought, and she could understand the need to boost morale, and not inflame a delicately balanced community, but people weren't stupid. Things were going disastrously just now in the war, and pretending otherwise would fool no one, and the British were so often wrong in how they managed things here in Egypt. Everyone knew it, and many resented it.

A lot of the time, when reporting on local events or the disastrous price of cotton, the newspaper looked not much different from its pre-war years, and for people nervous about their futures, routine reporting was reassuring. But Tim's instructions left her some leeway to delve into a good story, and she did so whenever she could.

No anti-French propaganda, Tim had said. That was because so many of the community here had links to France, by education, by birth, by friendship. But she could challenge what Naval Command were doing with the French navy here in Alexandria. The Brits had interned the French ships, but were paying the men on board them a salary, and leaving them completely free to roam the city, to socialise and spread whatever propaganda they wanted. That was the problem, wasn't it? One day hopefully France would take up arms again against Germany, but meanwhile a lot of these men were known to be doing everything they could to undermine the Allies, insidiously, through negative talk and leaks about Allied movements. Surely giving the men so much freedom would lead to more and more raging battles like last night's, more anger, more knives in the ribs? It was a subject that needed debate.

Fran was aware that she wrote differently that morning to how she would have written a week ago. The young French matelot was always on her mind. She fretted over how he was doing. Had they given him a transfusion? What did you do other than that for injuries like his? And she found herself wondering about the young matelot himself. Where was he from in France? How did he feel about his treatment by the British? Had he goaded the Free French, or had they attacked unprovoked? She needed his point of view, and she wanted to see him again so that she could ask him.

She ran her questions past their new trainee, a fresh high

school graduate named Asher. 'He didn't look much older than you,' she told him. 'Do you see the matelots out and about when you go out for the evening?'

'Sometimes,' he answered, 'but to be honest I spend more time playing football than out on the town. They don't have a football team, I do know that! Was he badly hurt?'

She nodded. 'Pretty badly.' She pictured the young man as she'd seen him last, grey as the morning mist, strapped helplessly to the hospital stretcher. Had he been back at home in France maybe he too would have been playing football instead of roaming the streets. Asher came from a close Jewish family, and went home each night to his mother's kosher cooking. The matelot was living by contrast in a pretty tough man's world.

'He'll be fine, you know, Miss Trevillian,' Asher said. 'I don't think they'd have lied to you about that.'

She smiled rather wearily. 'I hope so. I'd like to see him.'

'You'll visit him in the hospital? Can I come too?'

She smiled again at his enthusiasm. 'You can tidy this paperwork first, young Asher! And pop that envelope down to the print. Then we go off for the weekend. We've got a couple of days to worry about the article before the paper comes out. It's a good job, because I'm beyond writing any more today. I'm dead on my feet.'

She left the office for once at the same time as the rest of her staff that lunchtime. She made her way home on the tram and, finding both her parents out, ate a quiet lunch prepared by their cook Ahmed, and then headed gratefully for a long sleep.

* * *

18

That evening they had been due to attend a garden party given by the city's most distinguished Englishman to welcome new naval personnel to Alexandria. The party, though, had been put back until the following afternoon, because the air raids had become so much more frequent recently, and it was becoming difficult to do anything out of doors in the evening. Blackouts meant you couldn't open up the house to the outside, and the few tiny candles allowed made gardens gloomy places after dark.

Instead, therefore, the Trevillians invited their nearest neighbours for cocktails, and for a couple of hours they sat outside under the light of the stars, and watched the light display created by yet another evening of raids. Bombs never fell out here among the villas of the wealthy. The Germans concentrated their fire around the Western Harbour, where the navy had its ships. Houses downtown had taken bad hits, but here you could sleep in your own bed, and the noise of the raids was more bothersome than threatening.

The noise meant you had to speak up, but Fran was happy just to sit back and watch, letting her parents and the Eatons talk amongst themselves. She was both weary and restless at the same time. Her experience of this morning was too raw in her mind for her to take much from an evening among middle-aged people she'd known all her life, chatting about the relentlessly familiar just as she'd heard them do for years.

And yet she wouldn't have had the energy this evening to seek out any of her own friends, and there were precious few of her own age group left in Alexandria anyway. It suited her mood to sit back on a cane chair with a glass in her hand and nothing required of her. She swilled her gin lightly, letting the ice clink against the glass, and listened with half an ear.

'The war has destroyed international markets for Egyptian cotton,' Bill Eaton was complaining. 'There's nothing to trade any more, and we'll soon be closing the stock exchange for lack of business.'

Fran raised a private eyebrow, unseen in the gloom. Her father had a small smile on his face, and she waited to see what he would reply.

'Are you worried that we'll all be ruined for the want of a few cotton futures, Bill?'

Bill Eaton almost harrumphed. 'Ruined no, but things aren't what they were.'

'No,' Alan Trevillian replied. 'The economy is struggling, but the British have bought up all the cotton from the last harvest. We'll survive.'

'At rock-bottom prices!' Bill Eaton protested. 'They say old Minton has lost everything.'

Alan Trevillian looked sceptical. 'I rather doubt that. Minton will have taken the bulk of his fortune out of the country. It's the small cotton farmers who are really suffering.'

Bill Eaton merely grunted. Egyptian peasants weren't his concern. Fran looked across at her father, catching his eye, and he winked at her. She grinned over her glass. Her father was on good terms with his neighbours, but he was on a different plane to them, and to so many of the narrow Brits here. He was a far-thinking man with a generous view of the world, and a wry eye always open to its absurdities, and she loved him.

He was approaching fifty years old, but might have passed for ten years younger, with just a hint of grey touching his dark hair, and not an inch of spare flesh on his lean frame. He could be Italian, Fran thought, with his brown eyes and skin, and he had passed the same colouring on to her. It fitted very well in this cosmopolitan city, where the mix of French, Italian, Greek, Arab and Jew had created a unique commercial hub found nowhere else in the world.

And Alan Trevillian, brought up here in Egypt, the son of an eminent irrigation engineer, lived Alexandrian life to the full. He spoke four languages, drank endless cups of Turkish coffee over business each morning in the cafes by the stock exchange, and had an impressive network of friends and contacts across all of the city's communities. The wealthiest financiers respected him, and those who worked for him held him in high regard. But above all he loved Egypt, loved it and cared about it and all of its people.

In contrast, Fran's mother Barbara was more typically English in style, fair and neatly elegant in a restrained style, holding herself at a slight distance from the more exotic ladies of Alexandria, in their make-up and Paris fashions. She supported her husband loyally, but had built her own life among the British women of Alexandria. Since the desert war had begun, sending floods of helplessly injured soldiers to the city's straining hospital, Barbara and her friends had manned kitchens, run clubs, and held weekly events for servicemen in their homes, in a very British demonstration of unity.

She was the calmest, most unfretful of parents on the outside. Standards of behaviour had to be maintained, but only insolence had brought down severe penalties when

Fran and her brother Michael were growing up. Michael was the apple of Barbara Trevillian's eye, the one who could get away with almost anything, and now that he was in the desert army, Fran occasionally glimpsed the worry that hid behind her mother's British sangfroid. But never a word was spoken except to wonder mildly whether he had enough socks, and to regret that he was missing their cook's most prized dishes.

As they drank their cocktails that evening, Fran studied them all and thought how individual was the life that Egypt offered them. The bombing raid came to an end and they sat on for a while, allowing themselves some brighter lamps as more drinks were served. The evening air was balmy after the heat of the day, and a pleasurable breeze circled around them. Their servant Mustafa set out freshly prepared snacks on a low table between them, hot chicken on skewers, roasted almonds, and little plates of cinnamon-spiced pasta. He moved almost silently between them, and an easy hush settled on the company.

Soon the Eatons would head home, and Fran would seek her bed. She hoped that there would be no more air raids that night. Sometimes they had none, other times two or three, and there was no rhythm to them, except that they had got so much worse since the Germans had overrun Greece, and now had their planes stationed on Crete, just a couple of hundred miles away in the Mediterranean. Alexandria was the Allies' Naval HQ, a natural target, and things were unlikely to get any better.

Her father would not be on the yacht patrol again for at least a couple of weeks, and tonight he would sleep. Fran hoped that she would sleep too, but above all she hoped that her young French boy was sleeping in his hospital bed, that the Free French who had poured such anger on their countrymen had now been moved on from Alexandria, and that everyone else was safely under curfew on their ships. The night felt peaceful now, and Fran hoped that the same brief calm could give them all a full night's rest.

CHAPTER THREE

The Trevillians drove to the Osbornes' pillared, colonial-style home the following afternoon under a blazing sun. It was within walking distance of the Trevillians' rather smaller villa, but in her heels and the heat not even Fran suggested they should go on foot.

They found a space on the sweeping drive, and were ushered through the galleried hall by a servant in traditional dress, joining a noisy throng in the main reception room, where the French windows had been thrown open along the full width of the room to the verandah and the sweeping lawns beyond.

Sir Anthony Osborne was standing just inside the room greeting guests. He gave the Trevillians a warm welcome, and stood talking to Alan for a moment, inevitably about the state of the stock markets at the Bourse.

Sir Anthony's wife was standing just a short distance away, immersed in a group of ladies. She waved to Fran and her mother, and within moments Barbara Trevillian had been absorbed into the group.

Fran wandered on through the room. She wanted to find a senior naval official this afternoon, to give her a comment about the French navy for the piece she was writing. She scanned the room, looking for anyone above the rank of lieutenant commander, but there weren't many uniforms inside here. She took a drink from the tray proffered to her by a waiter, and then eased her way towards the verandah, where she had spotted Lucie Carsdale. It was slow progress, because she had known so many of the people here since taking her first steps, but finally she made it outside.

A number of Fran's childhood friends were now married, and many had left Alexandria, but one exception was Lucie. She was half-French, a petite whisper of a thing with striking copper hair and a lightning smile, and far more wisdom than most people credited her with. Native wit, Lucie called it, saying with a wry smile that it was all that had saved her from being expelled from her French finishing school. Fran loved her dearly.

She was chatting in French to a woman Fran knew vaguely, the wife of a local French businessman, Gustave Lalique. The Frenchwoman didn't usually come out with her husband, or at least not to events dominated by the British community. Didn't she have an uncle who was somebody senior in the Vichy regime in France? Fran would have loved to ask her about the street fight, just to see her reaction.

She didn't get the chance, though. In Lucie's warm, Gallic presence the woman was chatting happily about her daughter, who attended ballet classes with Lucie's younger sister. But Fran's arrival stopped the flow of her chatter so abruptly that it was almost comical. The look of misgiving the woman gave her made Fran wonder whether the woman had read her thoughts. Fran greeted her in French, and gave her sweetest smile, but after the most formal of greetings the Frenchwoman made her excuses and left, disappearing indoors.

Fran watched her go, and then raised her eyebrows at Lucie. 'I seem to have had a strong effect on Madame Lalique.'

Lucie held up both hands. 'And that surprises you? I'm not sure Céline Lalique wants to feature in your report of this party!'

Fran was dismissive. 'As though I would report on this event! I doubt it would be of interest to our readers, and anyway I'm under orders not to feed people's prejudices about the British elite!'

'Does Céline know that? I don't think so. I think her husband is doing some good business with British merchants, which will be why he's here today, but underneath it all he's up to his neck in collusion with pro-Nazi collaborators. It's what *Maman* says, and she avoids Céline Lalique if she can. And you know, *Maman* knows everything!'

Fran pictured the aristocratic Angélique Carsdale, with her distinguished connections back in France. 'She certainly does!' she agreed. 'Well, if your mother rejects Céline Lalique, then I won't worry about her snubbing me! Anyway, I've just written a leader for the paper this week that will make her more wary of me than ever. Let's consign the woman to the dustbin, and tell me who you've seen here today. Any young people we know? All I could see were the parents' friends inside, and it's mostly their generation down there too, in the garden. Have you seen anyone else?'

Lucie shook her head. 'Not yet. I was relieved to see

you arrive, I can tell you. It's ironic, isn't it? Our own boys all have to leave and fight somewhere else, or go into government service in Cairo, and in their place we get a whole lot of naval men we don't know, who have been removed from their own friends and transplanted here.'

Fran smiled, but it was all too true. Her own brother was one of those who had departed, after all. She let her gaze idle over a group of young officers in dress whites standing under the shade of a rather out-of-place willow tree, which the Osbornes must have brought in from England. There was a separate bar and refreshment table set up just by the tree, with its own waiter, and the officers seemed to be making good use of it. Lucie leant against the balustrade next to her, and followed Fran's gaze. Suddenly she gave a gasp.

'What was that I just said about not knowing any of the officers? Fran, that's my cousin down there! It's Tony! Tony Harding – he's a second cousin, from my father's family.' She leant precariously over the balustrade and waved towards the group. A couple of officers looked up curiously at them, and then a third, who gave a yell, and raced up the lawn towards them.

'Lucie! I wondered whether I would run into you today.' The young man enveloped Lucie in a huge hug, and then stood her away from him. 'I haven't seen you for ages. When were you last in England? It must be at least four years ago! You're looking great, cousin!'

Lucie was gazing at him in his crisp white uniform, looking utterly stunned. 'You look a bit different yourself, if I may say so! But, Tony, what are you doing here? We didn't hear anything about you coming to Alexandria.'

'I'm not sure we knew ourselves until quite recently. The family know I'm somewhere around the Med, but they don't know exactly where. But as soon as we landed, and I realised we were going to operate from here, I knew I'd catch up with you. Are your parents here today?'

Lucie nodded enthusiastically. 'Yes, somewhere, I don't know where exactly. Were they indoors, Fran, when you came through?'

Fran shook her head. 'I didn't see them.' She smiled at the young officer, and Lucie hastened to introduce them. He was a good-looking man, perhaps a couple of years older than Fran, dark-haired in contrast to his cousin, but with equally striking blue eyes. He greeted Fran courteously, but had no eyes really for anyone except Lucie.

'So if your parents aren't inside they must be out here.' He looked along the verandah, and then down to the lawn, where knots of people stretched around the corner beyond their view. You couldn't see everyone from here, no matter how hard you scanned. Tony turned back to the two ladies.

'Miss Trevillian, will you join Lucie and me on the lawn?' he asked. 'That way I can introduce you both to the chaps who've travelled out with me, and then we can have a look around for Lucie's parents.'

'Why of course!' Fran concurred, and followed as Lucie dragged her cousin eagerly down the verandah steps.

The little group of officers opened up as they approached the willow tree to reveal three more young men. They were gathered around a more senior officer whom Fran knew, who had visited a few times at her home.

'Hey, chaps,' Harding declared. 'Did I tell you I have family living here in Alexandria?' He looked at his senior officer. 'Sir, may I introduce my cousin Miss Carsdale, and Miss Trevillian? Ladies, this is Commander Aldridge.'

Fran smiled. 'The commander and I have already met. How do you do, sir?'

'I'm well thank you, Miss Trevillian.' He shook hands with Fran, and then with Lucie. 'Miss Carsdale, I'm delighted to meet you. So this young man is your cousin? Well, he's very lucky to have family here for when he can get ashore, though I'm afraid we'll be keeping him pretty busy.'

The three other officers had stepped back a little while the commander was speaking. He turned to them now, and waved a rather lazy hand towards them. 'May I introduce you ladies to the rest of this motley crew?' He indicated the men one by one. 'Miss Carsdale, Miss Trevillian, allow me to introduce Lieutenant Moore, Lieutenant Blake and Lieutenant Fielding, three of Harding's companions in the fleet. And where's MacNeill?' He looked around, and called to a man with his back to them, over by the bar. 'MacNeill, come and be introduced, man.'

Fran gave a start of recognition. The man had exchanged sweat-stained running gear for dress whites, but even before he turned she knew that this was her Scotsman from the day before, sandy-haired, solid and with the blue eyes of the north. So he was one of the new men brought in to replace those lost in the battle for Greece? It was logical, and why shouldn't he be a colleague of Lucie's cousin? It was to be an afternoon of surprises, it seemed.

'I've already met Lieutenant MacNeill,' she said to the commander. He looked surprised.

'Already?' he said. 'That was quick work, MacNeill!'

Lieutenant MacNeill came forward, flushing slightly. 'It

was Miss Trevillian who saved that French navy fellow on the beach yesterday, sir. I just happened to be out running, and was able to fetch support.'

'Is he all right, then?' Fran asked, as the lieutenant shook her hand.

'Remarkably so, by all accounts,' the commander told her. 'There were other casualties of that battle, you know, but he was the most serious. So, you found him, Miss Trevillian? Well, well.'

'Not only found him, but bound up the wound as well,' MacNeill said. 'He was close to bleeding to death.'

It was Fran's turn to blush. 'I'm so glad he's all right. I've been worrying about him.'

'I was going to get a message to you at your newspaper tomorrow,' the lieutenant assured her.

His mention of the paper reminded Fran that right now she had before her the senior officer she'd been hoping to buttonhole this afternoon.

'Is Naval Command planning to change policy now, Commander, to stop the Vichy crews from circulating freely around Alexandria?' she asked.

Commander Aldridge gave her a look that showed he knew exactly what she was up to, and deflected her question with practised ease.

'It's always regrettable when troops brawl in the street,' he told her. 'But as for who should be allowed where, you're asking me questions above my pay grade, I'm afraid.'

'You don't think it is provocative to our Free French allies? Isn't this kind of conflict inevitable if you keep up the status quo?'

He gave her his most charming smile. 'I don't think

anything, Miss Trevillian, as I'm sure you know. I do understand why your newspaper would be interested, but I'm afraid you've come to the wrong man! Now, if you'll excuse me, ladies, I see the commodore has arrived, and I should go and say hello. Stay sober, gentlemen, and I'll catch up with you later.'

Good for him, Fran thought, as he made his measured way across the lawn.

'You didn't get far there, Fran!' Lucie grinned at her.

Fran laughed. 'I think it would take more than me to dent the commander's poise.' She turned to the five officers. 'But tell me about you, gentlemen. Have you all just arrived here, then? What do you think of Alexandria?'

It was the one called Blake who answered. 'Alexandria is wonderful, Miss Trevillian, a real pleasure to discover.'

Lucie's cousin Tony dug him in the ribs. 'He means the bars, of course!'

Blake grinned his agreement. 'And the beaches! We've come directly out from Liverpool, you see, and we've been stuck out at sea for nearly two months, so it's great to have arrived and to be able to spread our wings a bit.'

He hailed a waiter, and took a drink from his tray. 'The beer is good too! And as for this' – he gestured to the lush gardens around them – 'well this is something else!'

He nearly knocked over the tray as he spoke, and blushed and muttered an apology to the waiter.

Lucie giggled, and took a glass from the tray, which the waiter had deftly saved. Fran looked at the men more closely. They were all in their twenties, with Lieutenant Moore the youngest, she thought, and MacNeill looking to be the oldest. Of them all, Lucie's cousin Tony was the best-looking, and the most assured. He had the look of someone who had always succeeded, and she thought he had probably gone to public school as well. He would do well here in Alexandria, where money and class were equally valued.

He was chatting now to Lucie, commenting on the heat, and asking if it got much hotter in July and August. When Lucie spoke of temperatures over a hundred degrees Fahrenheit, he looked a bit shocked.

'It's not the daytimes that are the problem,' Lucie was explaining, 'but the nights, when the breeze falls. It can be hard to sleep. But somehow by day it never seems that bad. People from Cairo come here in their droves in summer, because the air is so much fresher here with the sea breezes, and of course you can always throw yourself in the water to cool down.'

'It's going to be fun sleeping below deck,' MacNeill said drily.

'Don't worry, MacNeill.' It was Tony Harding who replied. 'If the air raids keep up like they are at the moment we'll be constantly on duty, and you won't be sleeping at night anyway! And then before you know it we'll be at sea.'

'Do you get long to settle in before you are put on full duties?' Fran asked.

Lieutenant MacNeill shrugged. 'Who knows? We've been given shore leave for the moment, time to settle in, but it won't be for long. We lost nearly twenty ships in the Greek debacle, and twenty thousand men, and they're desperately short on operations. They haven't brought us here to sit around in the harbour.'

His words sobered the rather festive feel to the gathering,

and made Lucie grab her cousin's arm rather compulsively. Even in the shade of the Osbornes' willow tree the war intervened. Her French matelot came back to Fran's mind.

Just then Lucie spotted her parents across the lawn and dragged Tony Harding off to greet them. Fran turned to MacNeill again.

'Do you think you could arrange for me to meet the young Frenchman we saved yesterday?' she asked. 'Is it possible to visit him in hospital?'

'Of course, Miss Trevillian, you'll be keen to see for yourself that the boy has come to no lasting harm. His name is Robert Masson, and he's in Ward 3 of the military hospital. It isn't a critical ward, and anyone can visit, I believe, or would you prefer that I take you?'

She shook her head. 'No, not at all! My mother does voluntary work at the hospital, and I've done a fair bit of visiting myself.'

'And you'd rather interview him without being monitored?' His placid, pragmatic tone belied the glint of humour in his eyes.

Fran acknowledged the hit. 'Perhaps! Do you blame me?'

'Not at all, but I know how my commander feels, so I'll be very glad if you go along on your own! I didn't get much reaction from him myself, but then I'm a British officer, and the enemy. Perhaps you'll fare better.'

'You've visited him, then? Didn't he want to thank you?'

He smiled. 'I'm not sure he needs to thank me for anything – it's you who saved his life. If nobody had spotted him there for an hour or so more I think he would definitely have bled to death. I did think you might be going to visit, so I told him how he was saved. As I say, I hope he'll be pleased to meet you, but do be prepared for an element of wariness. After all, he was attacked by his own countrymen, ones who have made themselves our allies.'

'I know.' Fran sighed. 'It's what I want to write about, because it's so complex and sad. I will try to get his side of the story, but I'll only write what's fair and balanced, I promise you.'

'Believe me, Miss Trevillian,' he said, sincerely, but with a twinkle in those blue eyes, 'I don't doubt it for a minute.'

Jim MacNeill was right when he said the young Frenchman would be wary. Fran took Asher with her to the hospital the next day, so that there would be another young man, one who wasn't British, but even with the support of Asher's friendly, open presence the visit wasn't easy. Robert Masson was out of his narrow bed in the crowded ward, and was sitting up on a chair. He was pale but composed, and received them with all his guards up, as one might greet a visitor to be treated with courtesy but without ever forgetting that this was the enemy. He might have a baby face, but he was no baby, she realised. This wasn't a young boy who'd been led into error by senior officers, but a committed Pétain supporter who believed that one day France would rise up again, but that meantime he owed loyalty to his country's leaders.

'My family are farmers,' he told her in one of his few frank comments. 'We believe in hard work and patriotism. France is a neutral country now in this war, and as such we deserve respect.'

He thanked her for saving his life. How did he feel about those who had attacked him? Fran asked. He closed up and wouldn't answer. She left him alone with Asher, who tried to interest him in his local football team, but young Masson wasn't a footballer, it seemed.

'We got nothing at all by going to see him,' Asher lamented as they left the hospital.

'On the contrary, we've really seen for ourselves how hardened the positions are between the different French forces. Isn't it amazing what different choices people can make in the name of patriotism?' Fran said. 'We've got material for an article, but I think we'll accept that he doesn't really want to know either of us! He's alive, though, thank goodness, and one day he may be on our side again.'

She shrugged rather sadly. 'Let's get back to work, Asher, and I'll stop thinking that because I've saved someone's life he's automatically going to be my friend.'

CHAPTER FOUR

Fran spent some time over the next few days reflecting on the encounters at the Osbornes' garden party. Meeting this group of men through Lucie's cousin was very different from previous introductions Fran had had to officers in Alexandria. It was much more informal, and you felt you had a chance of actually making some friends. She hadn't realised until Sunday how much she needed some friends. She missed Michael, and all of their friends who had left Alexandria. It was all very well having work and family, but there was a gap in her life, which was perhaps responsible for some of the frustration she had felt recently.

She'd made a point on Sunday afternoon of trying to find out more about these officers newly out from England. Their backgrounds fascinated her, and they each had a very individual story.

Tony Harding was a man very like those she had grown up with, assured and easy. He had joined his father's London law firm straight from university, and clearly moved in the best circles. The others were mostly of the same mould, with Blake and MacNeill standing out as men who came from more ordinary backgrounds.

These two were radar and communications specialists, both with physics backgrounds, MacNeill as a teacher, Blake in research. You could feel the common bond between them. They were equally passionate about their science, and equally open about their modest roots, but proud nevertheless of where they came from. And although economical in conversation, Fran discovered in each of them a vein of dry humour, which managed to be self-deprecating and confident at the same time.

What had taken them into physics, Fran had dared to ask? Curiosity, was Blake's answer, from having grown up next to the Royal Observatory in Greenwich. His father had been a clerk there, and thankfully the scientists had allowed his young son George to run pretty free in all but the most sensitive areas. By the time he was twelve he'd known he wanted to follow in their footsteps.

MacNeill's story was completely different. 'It certainly wasn't an exposure to technology that took me into physics,' he told her. 'I come from Islay, and we still don't have electricity on the island, or at least not the civilian population. We learnt our physics from the blackboard at school, and the island produces more clerics than it does scientists! But I had a great maths and physics teacher, who told me it was the future, and thankfully I believed him.'

Oof! That was a gulf that was hard to bridge. Islay was an island off Scotland, that much Fran knew, but she wasn't sure she could pinpoint it on a map. No electricity? It made his island sound like one of the villages along the

Nile Delta, where the Egyptian peasantry scraped a living from the earth with only their donkeys to help them.

'Wow!' was all she could say. 'Now that is remote!'

He had nodded. 'It has a population of just a few thousand, and hardly anyone goes there except the odd whisky connoisseur. But it has a great community spirit, and it's the most beautiful place on earth.'

The pride in his voice was striking.

'And until the war you were a teacher there?' she asked.

'No, I've been teaching for years on the mainland, but I go back as often as I can. My father still works in the whisky business there. He's one of the most expert tasters on the island.'

'Isn't the war stopping whisky production, though?' It was Blake who asked. 'Didn't I read somewhere that the government wants to keep the grain for food?'

MacNeill grimaced. 'They've cut production at the distillery by over eighty per cent already,' he agreed. 'My father still has work, or he did when I last heard, because the younger men have all gone away to the war, but it's a real worry. The distillery is his life, especially since my mother died. I haven't had any news for a while. It's my sister who writes, and she has been away from Islay finishing her nursing studies.'

There was worry on his face, which came from a different world, one that was very far from Alexandria. A remote little island off the coast of Scotland, where people made whisky for a living. Fran would have loved to explore further, but the Osbornes' garden party wasn't the place to ask too many questions. Lucie's parents had joined the group, and their unexpected family reunion dominated the rest of the afternoon.

Lucie's father had thrown out an invitation to all four officers to play tennis at the weekend, and to sail if they wished in a dinghy regatta at the yacht club next Sunday. It had immediately been clear that neither Blake nor MacNeill had ever played tennis, but MacNeill had admitted to being a good hand on a boat.

Regardless, though, their response had been equivocal. They didn't yet know their orders. Alexandria might be their hub, but the navy ships were far more often at sea than they were in harbour. Fran couldn't help hoping, nevertheless. Weren't these men new, and still being briefed? Would they really be going to sea so soon? She hoped not. She wanted to see them again, particularly her helper from Saturday morning. She found him quietly intriguing. He was a man who knew who he was, and where he came from, and she wanted to know more about Islay.

She would have felt a little less hopeful, however, if she had been able to read the letter that Jim MacNeill sealed up to send home the following day.

I so hope that you and Catriona are both well, he wrote to his father.

I've now arrived in Alexandria, and you wouldn't believe the temperature! When I wrote to you from Mombasa it was a reasonably pleasant seventy-five degrees, but here it's eighty-five and sweltering. Things have been quiet since we arrived, and most of the men are loving the beach, but you can imagine that with my fair skin I have to be careful.

Alexandria is a nice enough city, nothing spectacular, with some scruffy backstreets, but it is saved by its waterfront, and some fine buildings like the Opera House and the Cecil Hotel. There's not much evidence of Ancient Egypt left here, but we did walk to Pompey's Pillar and its Sphinx the other day, only to find them covered up and protected against the air raids. There are a couple of very grand palaces too, and some wonderful exotic plant life. I was hoping to smell jasmine for the first time, but apparently its period of flowering is over. The bougainvillea is stunning, though.

What with that, and the flies, and the smells (mainly all right – just street foods, which we're not supposed to try), it's a long way from Islay! There are all kinds of nationalities here too, from all over the Mediterranean, the latest being a flood of refugees fleeing from Greece since Jerry occupied the country. There's a shanty town of them camping on one section of the beach, poor devils, waiting for the people here to find them somewhere better to stay.

All the different nationalities have their own restaurants, and they are good and really cheap. Every time I eat out, or even buy bananas or oranges, I think of you at home, and the rationing. There's every kind of food available here. But the most striking thing about this place is the amount of money there is. From what I can see everyone is trying to make money, from the hawkers in the street who run after you and try to sell you pens and watches, to the other end of the scale – the fellows who make huge fortunes selling cotton futures at the stock exchange.

Among the British community, all we seem to meet are bankers and brokers, and all of them live in rather splendid villas out by the beaches, surrounded by Arab servants. Apart from a few exceptions, the women all seem to do good works, and make tea for the troops, which is ironic really because when they're at home they don't lift a finger. It's colonial life at its best! People have been very kind, but I don't think they have a clue how most people live.

By the time this letter gets to you, hopefully Catriona will have graduated and be a fully fledged nurse. Now there's a real job, one which requires true commitment. The way this war's going there will be endless need of her skills. Hopefully your own skills are still in use at the distillery too, Father, although I fear they may have stopped production completely by now.

I am hoping daily for a letter from you both with your news. As well as this letter I'll also send you an airgraph tomorrow, which will arrive much faster – I wouldn't want you to have to wait three months to know where I am! But I did want to describe Alex a bit, which is why I am writing a full letter as well. Airgraphs are handy, but the amount of text you can get into one small page doesn't give much scope for description.

I'll try to get a photo as well to send with this letter – or at least a couple of postcards of Alexandria so that you can see the Corniche and the beach, and

*an antiquity or two. Who knows, some of the rich
bankers and their wives may even feature in them!*

It was a rather sober man's assessment of Alexandria, a
description targeted at a different world back home. But
this was definitely a letter that Fran wouldn't have wished
to have seen.

CHAPTER FIVE

Islay, July 1941

The War Ministry wanted to take over Fergus MacNeill's little cottage in Bowmore. It was the bombshell that was waiting for Catriona when she got home to Islay. He looked older, somehow, this father of hers, the thickset man who had walked through life always at a measured pace, but who could cut peats and stack bales all day without ever tiring. He had lost some of that steadiness, and there was a grizzling of the hair, a gauntness around the eyes. Why was it always the eyes that betrayed any fragility?

And he was thinner. The old stillman's widow Flora Campbell and other women from the village would bring him soup from time to time, but other than that he seemed to live on nothing but porridge.

'I've been taking his ration book and putting his allowance in his larder,' old Flora complained, 'but he gives his butter away, and his sugar, and goodness knows what besides. He maybe needs to take a dram or two less,' she continued, after a little hesitation. 'But you'll see that for yourself, Catriona.'

Fergus insisted that he was fine, and eating well. What could be better than porridge? he asked. Wasn't that what islanders had lived on for centuries? When Catriona's mother had been alive he'd loved her baking, and the mutton stews that cooked on the stove top all day long. He'd lost interest in food since her death, and though he hadn't moved a single picture or ornament, somehow the house had a forlorn look as though its key components had simply wandered off.

Catriona set about tidying up the old newspapers, and threw open the doors to the July sunshine, and made a pan of his favourite split-pea soup with a ham bone wrested from the butcher. She made his favourite beloved girdle scones, and served them with some of her mother's gooseberry jam, carefully preserved in the larder. It all brought a smile to his face, and he sniffed appreciatively at the smells when he came into the house, but it didn't remove the little knot that seemed to have formed permanently between his eyes.

It was all about the distillery, of course. Poor Islay, which had once had nine working distilleries making the purest of Scottish malt whisky, had already been decimated by one world war, and then by the Depression, and by the loss of American markets during prohibition. For as many years as Catriona could remember, her father had worked only part of the year at the distillery, and the rest of the time had gone fishing, bringing in Loch Indaal flounder, and cod and whiting. But with his skills honed over forty years in the business, there was no one more important when the distillery was working.

And in recent years things had been getting better, and

the American market had been returning. When Catriona had left for her nursing training in Glasgow three years ago, the Bowmore distillery had been working harder than she'd known it. Then came the war.

At the beginning of the war things had looked as though they might not change too much. The young men were called up, of course, and her father and others among the older men threw themselves into the fishing to take their place. The distillery kept plugging on, intermittently. The government had completely closed the big distilleries on the mainland, because the grain they used was needed to feed the country, but here on Islay the pure malt whisky was made from barley, much of which they grew themselves, and they weren't a drain on the nation's scarce resources. They had hoped to be left alone, but now their crops were being removed, other raw materials just couldn't be sourced, no whisky had been produced for months, and the Bowmore distillery offices had been requisitioned by RAF Coastal Command.

And they could no longer fish, or not as they had done before. The once quiet loch in front of their cottage had been taken over by Catalina flying boats. There was something very wonderful about watching them coming in to land on the water, and the children of the village had been spellbound since the first of them arrived in March. Nothing so exciting had happened in Bowmore since the old days of the horse fairs, and the war had brought a new buzz of its own to Islay. There were the men in uniform, vehicles everywhere, the new pier with its barges bringing in goods and personnel, and the electricity station, which had sprung up next to the school. It wasn't going to supply the houses, of course. It was for the camps and the aerodrome, where new concrete runways had been built, and where new planes were arriving all the time. They were here for reconnaissance, searching out the U-boats which were attacking the convoys coming to the Clyde, and the word was that hundreds more personnel were expected on Islay very soon.

Which was where the need for their modest cottage came in, Catriona supposed. She wondered why the RAF needed such a small cottage when there was Islay House standing so grand in its own grounds just a few miles away. But that was unfair. There were already servicemen billeted at Islay House, and in Port Ellen, and all over Bowmore. And since the RAF had taken over the distillery, the MacNeills' home, only yards away, was just the next logical place to be subsumed.

So what was Fergus going to do? It was two years now since Catriona's mother had died, and they had no close family left on the island. There was a cousin living away at Kilchoman, on the west coast, but her father would never go somewhere so remote. He needed village life, a community, his church.

She came into the sitting room that evening to find her father sat listening to music on the wireless, a glass of whisky by his elbow. Was it his second or third glass? He had that sombre look on his face which seemed to settle on him now whenever he was undisturbed.

It was barely getting dark on this July evening, but Catriona lit the Tilley lamp, pushing the pump gently up and down until it flamed. Its gentle hiss was the sound of her childhood, and its warm light was comforting in a way that the bare electric bulb in her nurse's room in Glasgow could never be.

She wanted to speak to her father, and she needed to catch him now, because he wouldn't talk during the evening news. There was no point in beating about the bush. He knew full well what she wanted to talk about.

'What are you going to do, *Daidi*?' she asked him, using the Gaelic diminutive of her childhood to bring him closer.

He took another nip of whisky before he answered. 'I may be able to get a job,' he said finally, as he put the glass down.

'Really?' Catriona was surprised.

Fergus nodded. 'The RAF need a storeman, someone to check supplies in and out of the warehouse.'

'You mean at the distillery?'

'Yes. They're taking on some locals to do civilian jobs. They spoke to me this afternoon.'

'And you'll be able to stay in the cottage?' she asked, willing the answer to be yes.

He looked at her, his expression unreadable. 'Well, not exactly,' he said. 'I think a lot depends on what you want to do,' he answered.

'What I want to do?' She didn't understand.

Her father hesitated, then seemed to take the plunge. 'There'll be vacancies for nurses here on Islay now, and the commander suggested you might want to apply.'

Catriona just stared at him. Did he mean that if she took a nursing post here, then they might be able to keep the cottage? He seemed to read her thoughts, and said in a rush. 'If you and I are both working for the RAF here, then they'll find us accommodation. Maybe not here, because this is so close to their HQ, but the commander says he'll do his best.' He looked at her with pleading eyes.

'If we are lucky, Catriona, we could stay here,' he gestured around him at the little room he'd lived in ever since his marriage. 'But if not, at least we could stay in Bowmore.'

'No!' The word shot from Catriona before she had time to stop it. She saw her father's look of surprise, and tried to compose herself before continuing. This was going to be difficult. 'Listen, *Daidí*, I can't just come back to Islay to work,' she managed.

'Why not? You'll be a great nurse.'

'Well yes, I hope so, and that's the point. The kind of nurse they need here is someone to dress the odd wound and treat routine illnesses, but I want to work with serious injuries. I've been training with a doctor who has done some great work in rehabilitation through massage and other physical therapies, and it's an area that I would like to pursue.' She looked at her father, but couldn't tell whether he was following her. She kept her voice gentle, knowing that what she was saying was not at all what he wanted to hear.

'This kind of therapy can make a real difference to the recovery of someone wounded in battle,' she continued. 'But it isn't something I can do here on Islay. I've trained hard and I want to be of real use, *Daidí*. I'm sure you understand that.'

'You mean you're going to enlist.'

A silence extended between them. Catriona didn't want to answer. Yes, she wanted to sign up. There wasn't anything less brutal that she could say. Her father's next words surprised her.

'Have you heard anything from Jim?' he asked.

She blinked at the change of subject. 'Why no, not recently,' she answered. 'Not since I had his last letter, back in May, and you had one too, remember? He was in Cape Town. Have you received another letter from him since?'

'Yes, from Mombasa. I thought maybe you would have received one too, before you left Glasgow, but with all this happening I forgot to ask you.' Fergus stood up and went over to the dresser, where all such precious items were kept.

Catriona remembered the last letter she'd had. She'd spent the whole of one lunchtime poring over the few lines, which told her just the bare bones of Jim's life, that he was well, got on well with the other officers, that they'd had some heavy seas, but now the sun was shining and very pleasant in the Cape Town winter. Similar temperatures to a Scottish summer! Cape Town, he told them, was a stunning city in a truly dramatic setting. He'd enclosed a postcard showing the beach with the town behind, and Table Mountain as the backdrop, and he'd marked a spot on the beach where he and some others had drunk a beer.

Everything he wrote was upbeat, and there was no talk of where he was going next, or any indiscreet details, which the censor would have removed. It could be India, or the Far East, but before he'd left Jim thought he was going to help protect the Suez Canal. Orders could change of course, and the Cape was on the way to all of these places.

She took the latest letter from her father with a hand that trembled slightly, and leant in to the kerosene lamp to read the tightly written lines. There was no postcard this time, just a brief account of the voyage since Cape Town, which he called 'uneventful', and of their arrival in Mombasa, where they'd stopped for supplies. He described cutting open coconuts and drinking the milk, and seeing a barracuda while snorkelling. To read his letters, she thought, you would think he was on holiday. It all sounded very exotic, and there was never any mention of the war. And he was always in transit. They still didn't know where he was heading.

She looked up at her father. 'He seems to be well, doesn't he?'

A look of impatience crossed Fergus's face. 'Yes, but the key thing is they were heading up the East African coast. That means they were on their way to Suez, like Jim suspected, and on to the Mediterranean. It's where all the action is at the moment, and Jim will have been there for over a month now.'

'We don't know that.'

'Yes we do. It's the most logical thing. Our ships out there are based either in Alexandria or in Gibraltar, and you don't get to Gibraltar via the Cape and Mombasa. So our Jim is in Alexandria.'

'And if he is?' Catriona asked the question as quietly as she could, hoping to calm the tension exuding from her father. Fergus took another swig from his glass before he replied.

'Then he is in daily danger of being bombed out of the water. Jerry is picking off our ships like flies.'

'But the same would be true if he was in the Atlantic, protecting convoys!'

'Perhaps. There aren't many who are in more danger, though. He is not exactly in some safe training placement somewhere. And if you join up too, who knows where they will send you? All the boys who've joined up from Islay are in the desert right now, not a million miles from Alexandria themselves.' He fixed his daughter with stern eyes. 'I don't want you to join up, Catriona. I can't risk losing both of you in this hellish war.'

Chapter Six

They found a body in the loch the following morning. A southerly wind overnight had blown it all the way up from the sea with the incoming tide, and left it on the beach on the other side of the water, by Bruichladdich. The village was buzzing with the news when Catriona went to fetch milk, and a group had gathered to watch from the shore as an RAF barge brought the body alongside the new pier.

The word went round quickly that the body was all bloated, and had been at sea for days, but those who had got close enough said the body had been wrapped by the RAF squad in a canvas sheet, so it would seem that people were just guessing. It seemed logical, though. There had been other bodies reported off the wild west coast of the island, where there was nothing but ocean until you reached America. They were the sad remains of servicemen or convoy passengers who had been torpedoed by the enemy and blown in by the prevailing westerly winds, along with the slakes of oil that soiled the beaches. The bodies didn't normally find their way into Loch Indaal, but this time a fluke of wind had brought its man into the heart of the island.

'Perhaps it's a Hun, and we got his U-boat,' old Flora Campbell suggested hopefully, over the milk.

Catriona wasn't sure it made it any better. Her mood this morning was bleak, and she felt less patriotic than despairing when she thought about the war. She had gone to bed last night without giving her father any answer. Her arguments to him that hospitals were rarely close to battle zones, and that the work she wanted to do was not front-line work, had simply met with shakes of the head, and repeats that he didn't want her to go. After a while she had simply given up and listened to the news with him in silence.

The news didn't help either. Nothing was going right in the war, and all the newsreader could do was stress how valiantly our forces were resisting, and holding out against the Axis powers. Tobruk was being held against Rommel's Afrika Korps, who had it under siege, and Catriona could almost hear the cogs clicking in her father's brain as he imagined Jim's role in trying to break that siege from the sea.

You should be proud, she wanted to shout at him, but she knew that wasn't fair. He *was* proud. He had done nothing but boast for months now about his son the naval officer. The young men from the island had all joined the ranks of the army. Only a few of those they knew were officers, and only Jim was in the Royal Navy. Fergus MacNeill didn't gloat, but he quietly glowed. But until now Jim hadn't been in the field of war, and Fergus hadn't really been afraid.

You couldn't blame him for trying to hold on to his

daughter. His life was being turned upside down, he was only recently bereaved, he was feeling his age. And what was more, if his daughter stayed with him, he might keep his precious home. Here on the island, nobody would think anything but that it was her duty to stay and look after him.

He looked tired this morning, and only grunted at her over a meagre portion of porridge, which was all he would accept. After breakfast he went down to the shore to see what news he could pick up, and Catriona took herself off for a walk, heading up the footpath beyond the distillery. She had to skirt wide round the Battery, because there were anti-aircraft guns in there now, and barbed wire all around, but once past their childhood playground she kept on along the bluff and down to the shore.

She found herself a rock to sit on. To her left, the south, was the ocean that had sent the body in to the loch, and the breeze from it whipped her hair away from her face. To the west, across the water, was Bruichladdich, and in the distance to the north were the Paps of Jura, their peaks standing clear and violet blue against the paler sky. Her only company were the birds, three cormorants perched on a rock, an oystercatcher wading in the shallows, and what could have been terns, or maybe just gulls, screeching overhead.

The light was amazing. There was a delicate cobweb of cloud high up, and the sun filtered through, hitting the white-capped water in silver shards. It was a cool light, temperate and soothing. There were no planes flying, and the activity at Bowmore, though so close, seemed satisfyingly remote.

Tomorrow she would take her bike and cycle up to Finlaggan. In this unusually gentle weather the path through the reeds would not be too wet, and she wanted to hike up the skirt of her dress and walk barefoot to the old ruins, just as she had done with Jim and their friends as children. The flat, blue-green wilderness of Finlaggan was about as far from Glasgow as she could imagine being. There the war would truly disappear.

If she took a job on Islay she would see these waters every day. She stopped her mind thinking, and just sat and breathed, until her conscience told her she should be making lunch, and she made her reluctant way back along the beach, and took the little road this time towards Bowmore.

Halfway along, she passed Miss MacLeod's cottage, standing all on its own by the track. A boggy field ran down from the cottage to the shore, good for nothing but peat, but by the side of the house Mary MacLeod had tamed a space into a vegetable garden. She was there now, on her knees among the carrots, trowel in hand.

Catriona called out a hello, and her old teacher raised her head.

'Catriona!' she bellowed, with her usual gusto. 'I heard that you were home. You finished your training then? *Ciamar a tha thu?* How are you?'

She rose to her feet and made her purposeful way to the fence, brushing dirt furiously onto her aged tweed skirt before holding her hand out to Catriona.

Catriona smiled. '*Tha gu math, tapadh leibh*, Miss MacLeod. I'm well, thank you.' It amused her to be speaking Gaelic to Miss MacLeod. They were both Gaelic speakers, but her teacher would have punished her severely for using the language at school, where they were supposed to speak the King's English. Time had gone by and she was no longer a pupil, but old habits die hard, and she found herself reverting to English as quickly as possible.

'You have a fine garden here,' she commented.

Miss MacLeod shook her head a little mournfully. 'It isn't easy to grow vegetables here, what with the soil, and the wind, but with everything so scarce I feel I have to make an effort to grow some basic things, at least. It gives me something to do as well, now that the summer holidays are here.'

'You haven't retired, then?'

Another mournful shake. 'The young man who was supposed to take my place got called up, and so I've stayed on. I worry that my pupils would be better off with someone more modern teaching them science, but there's nothing that can be done about it.'

Catriona protested. 'You made me want to be a nurse, and my brother want to teach science himself. I didn't have any better teacher in my whole time at the school!'

Miss MacLeod smiled. 'That's kind of you, my dear, although I think your brother got a lot of his passion from Mr Duncanson at Physics Higher Grade. But I do think I may have been able to encourage you somewhat. Tell me, what do you plan to do now?'

'I don't know, for the moment. It depends a little on my father.' Catriona tried to keep her voice neutral, to keep out the guilt, but it didn't fool her teacher.

'He'll be putting pressure on you to come home, of course.' She watched for a reply, and when there was none, she continued. 'Come inside, Catriona, and have a cup of tea. I've been working for long enough, and I'm thirsty.'

Catriona had never been inside Miss MacLeod's house. She followed her with some trepidation into her sitting room, with its high-backed chairs and multitude of photos. At school the children had sniggered sometimes about the eccentric spinster, and her rough, remote house, but inside, the cottage was a very genteel if overcrowded sanctum, not at all what Catriona had expected.

Miss MacLeod disappeared to make tea, and Catriona was left to perch nervously on the edge of a chair, wondering what she could say here without being disloyal to her father. Tea appeared on a fine silver tray, with a matching service patterned with pink roses. And once it had been served, her old teacher took no time getting to business.

'Poor Fergus has been told to leave his house, I've been told. Even if he hadn't, he has been a sad soul living there all alone. So it doesn't surprise me if he wants to have you near him. That is what he wants, isn't it?'

'Yes,' was all Catriona could say.

'Now tell me, child, what would you do if you had a completely free choice? Honestly, now.'

Catriona looked at her, and suddenly found herself telling her all about the last year in Glasgow, when sheer shortage of doctors and skilled medics had opened up opportunities for mere trainee nurses to help with physical therapy and rehabilitation. It was still an emerging field, but with so many people injured, and needing proper clinical intervention to restore physical function, the war was driving new technologies and approaches.

'We can even help with pain management,' she told her

teacher, letting her tea grow cold on her lap. 'We get people walking again, Miss MacLeod, and using their limbs, and even where there's permanent damage we can help restore some function. I've used traction to help a docker whose back was crushed, and after the Clydebank Blitz the hospital was overrun with people left with long-term injuries.'

She stopped, seeing a smile playing on the old lady's face. She felt suddenly a bit foolish at her own passion.

'It seems I helped create a nurse with a real vocation,' were the reassuring words. 'So what do you want to do? Continue to work in Glasgow?'

'No. I really want to work with servicemen. It's what my tutor has encouraged me to do. He has new students coming through whom he can train, and he wants those of us who have already worked with him to go out into the field.'

'To the front, then? You want to enlist?'

'Just because I enlist I wouldn't necessarily be at the front,' Catriona pleaded. 'The hospitals on the front line are for first response, but then they send patients on to more long-term facilities if they need rehabilitation. That's what I've been trying to tell my father, but he won't listen. He says he doesn't want two children in the war.'

'Then why don't you work with the Red Cross? They're opening more and more auxiliary hospitals across Scotland for injured servicemen. Their hospitals are not just for civilians any more, and some are very specialised. You'd get more choice, and you wouldn't actually be in the services yourself.'

Catriona knew about the Red Cross hospitals. Were there any working in rehabilitation? It would be a logical specialism for auxiliary hospitals. And she could stay in Scotland. Would that be enough for her father?

She was full of doubt. 'He has been offered work, you know. My father, I mean. As a storeman for the RAF, and they've told him if I am also employed here they'll give us accommodation. They've even told him he may get to keep the cottage.'

Miss MacLeod looked grave. 'Now they really shouldn't mislead him like that. They'll find you accommodation with someone else, more like. Which won't be much different from him being placed with someone else without you. Have you seen how they have been doubling families up? They were going to put someone in here with me, but my sister is coming to stay instead. She was bombed, you know, in Greenock, and she has been staying with her daughter's family, very overcrowded.'

'He thinks we'll get a cottage,' Catriona insisted.

'And how many empty cottages have you seen around here? Poor Fergus. He just wants so badly to believe it. Tell me, *a'ghràidh*, has your father been drinking at all since you got home?'

The question took Catriona aback, and she lowered her eyes, pinching back tears. Miss MacLeod had never called her 'my dear' before. So was the whole village talking about her father? 'I think he may be drinking a little,' she answered, finally.

'Yes, I have wondered sometimes. Don't get me wrong, child, I'm not suggesting he has a real problem, but if he stays here it can only get worse, even if you stay with him. Tell me, does he want the storeman's job really badly?'

Catriona shook her head. 'He just wants a home, and his family.'

'Well why doesn't he go to Sheila?'

'To Sheila?' For a moment Catriona couldn't even think who Miss MacLeod meant.

'Yes, Catriona, to his sister. Doesn't she live in some fancy mansion? I saw her at your mother's funeral, and she was so worried about your father. Wouldn't she take him in?'

Whew! It made Catriona think. To say that Aunt Sheila lived in a mansion was an exaggeration. She had left Islay many years ago, and married a man from Kilcreggan, on the Clyde. They lived now in a little lodge attached to a big country house just round from Kilcreggan in Cove Bay, and both of them worked for the owners, gardening and keeping house. It was a lovely spot, on the water, surrounded by other big houses, holiday homes of the wealthy merchants of Glasgow. Big, homely Sheila would look after her brother almost too well, if it was possible for him to go there.

But didn't she have evacuees billeted with her from Glasgow? Certainly the big house where she worked had been full of refugees the last time they'd heard. It was worth investigating. Catriona could even ask her father. He had letters from Sheila once a month, without fail.

She looked across at her old teacher with renewed respect, as if respect had been lacking before. It was just a short ferry hop from Kilcreggan to the big towns of Gourock, and Greenock, and Helensburgh. There could be work for her father, better work than a storeman, perhaps. Something that would give him back some sense of self-worth. He would be needed. And there might even be work for herself not too far away. She could visit him often.

Would he go? He would be mad not to, was Miss MacLeod's reply. He wouldn't like leaving, but it wouldn't be for ever.

'Your father is a good man, Catriona. He's worried, and clinging to tenuous hopes, but if someone shows him another way, one which allows you to fulfil yourself too, then he'll let all that go. I'll speak to him. I'll catch him after church tomorrow. He'll listen to me.'

And so he would. Anyone would. Catriona looked down at her cold cup of tea, and in fear of a reprimand she drank it all down.

CHAPTER SEVEN

Alexandria, September 1941

Fran came out of the office and turned onto the Rue Fouad. It was a fine Saturday lunchtime in September, and she was glad to be out in the fresh air, and finishing for the weekend. She would get off the tram a few stops before home, she decided, and stretch her legs for a while before lunch. She headed down the street towards the tram station, fishing for some small change in her bag. As she neared the square she spied Jim MacNeill, sitting at a pavement cafe over an empty coffee cup, lost in something he was reading.

'Lieutenant MacNeill!' she called out to him. 'How are you?'

He started, and looked up from what looked like a letter.

'Why, Miss Trevillian! How do you do?' He rose to his feet and came forward to shake her hand. 'Have you just finished work?'

She nodded. 'And glad of it, believe me! And you're ashore for once. It has been a while since we last saw you.'

There had been various meetings with the lieutenant and his friends over the summer months, mainly instigated by Lucie when Tony Harding was in port. Lucie and Tony's relationship had blossomed into a serious romance, and they sought every opportunity to be together. The officers were rarely ashore at the same time, but over the months Lucie had got at least some of them together from time to time for evenings on the town, and the odd beach picnic. Jim MacNeill had been at these a handful of times.

MacNeill was nodding. 'It's a rare thing these days to get ashore, what with the non-stop supply runs to Tobruk. But Blake is ashore too today, and we're meeting for lunch. I'm just passing time waiting for him. Won't you join me?'

Fran shook her head. 'Oh no, please don't let me interrupt you. You were so engrossed in your letter. Was that waiting for you when you came into port today?'

MacNeill was still holding the letter in his left hand, and he looked down at it and smiled softly. 'Yes. It's from my sister, and I'd been waiting for news. It arrived more quickly than usual, but however long it takes it always seems for ever. But I've finished reading it, so do please join me. Or are you in a hurry? Perhaps you have a lunch engagement?'

Fran was reluctant. He'd seemed so abstracted when she first spotted him, lost in a world far from Egypt, and she didn't want to spoil his moment. But he was drawing a chair out for her, and it would appear rude now not to accept.

'No, I don't have any engagement,' she answered, sitting down. She continued with a diffidence not usual to her. 'But you didn't look as though you needed company when I saw you just now. You were far away, with your family.'

The softer smile came to his face again, and he drew forward a photograph. 'I was looking at this,' he said, and passed it to her. It was of a family group, standing outside a traditional-looking, small house with ivy around its door. There were four people, one of whom Fran presumed was Jim's sister, willowy and fair, a gentle-featured girl with kind eyes. She was finer built than her brother, but the colouring was there, and the eyes held the same steady gaze. She was a nurse, Fran knew, and she looked like the very person you would wish to have by your bedside if you were unwell. Next to her was an older woman, sturdy, comfortably plump, and beside this matronly lady were two men, one who looked much like her, and not unlike Jim, and another who was small and wiry, with a look about him of a garden sparrow. There was something so homely about the picture that it brought an unexpected lump to Fran's throat.

'Your family?' she asked.

Jim MacNeill nodded. 'My sister and my father have recently moved away from Islay to stay with my aunt and her husband on the Clyde.'

'You look quite like your father,' Fran said. She handed the photo back to Jim.

Jim studied his father, and bit his lip. 'He always stands too stiffly for photos, and you'll never catch him smiling. My mother always used to make him loosen his tie, because he does it up too tight, especially for the camera. Uncle Charlie will sort him out, though.'

There was a note of worry in his voice, and Fran didn't know whether to respond. But surely he wouldn't have shown her the picture unless he wanted to talk?

'He looks like a very cheery man, your uncle,' she ventured. She was rewarded with a happier grin.

'Uncle Charlie is a delight,' he agreed. 'He worked as a

boiler man on the Clyde steamers for years before moving to this house, and he's got all the cheek of the boatmen about him. My sister tells me he is keeping my father very busy doing gardens for the rich folk around, and has enlisted him in the Home Guard. Father has put on weight and is happy, Catriona says.'

Fran thought he was speaking to himself rather than to her. She hadn't known that his father was a concern, and she didn't know why he'd moved home, but she wasn't going to pose questions that she had no right to ask.

'And Aunt Sheila is happy because having the family with them means she won't have anyone else billeted on her,' Jim added slowly, his gaze intent on the photograph. 'I wonder how Father will cope with living in a temperance village.'

A waiter came at that moment and Jim came out of his reverie with a jolt and ordered Fran a coffee. 'I'm sorry, I was miles away,' he said ruefully.

Fran shook her head. 'Please don't apologise. Nothing could be more important to you than to know that your family are well and happy. Is your sister as happy as your father in their new home?'

He frowned. 'So-so, I would say. She wants to work in physical therapy, but for now she has taken a standard nursing post locally, at the infirmary in Greenock. It means she can take the ferry across the river each day, and be home each night with my father, but it's not the job she really wants.'

He lifted his head from his study of the photograph, and grimaced. 'It's complicated, this war business. But hey, as a journalist there's one thing Catriona writes that you should find really intriguing. Let me find the passage.' He picked up the letter and scanned it, and then began reading.

The big excitement around here at the moment is that a bunch of Royal Engineers are building jetties and cabins around at Rosneath House, the old Duchess of Argyll's house. It has been empty for a while, so it's logical to use it for something, but they have American engineers helping them, which has roused a fury of local speculation. The REs have to live in tents, but the Americans are living in the big house, and everyone says they have massive rations – chocolate, and fruit, and American bourbon. Not that this will impress you, when you have everything you want out in Egypt.

There have been all kinds of entertainments laid on for them, and the REs have a great band which played for a dance in Cove Burgh Hall last week. I got to dance with one of the Yanks, but I couldn't get any information out of him. He was a great dancer – he had me swinging to Glen Miller, and I was glad Father wasn't there. He would definitely not have approved. Aunt Sheila and other ladies from the village made tea and sandwiches for the interval. I couldn't help wondering what the men thought. I'm sure they would have preferred a beer!

Jim looked up from the letter. 'What do you think of that, then? It's an interesting follow-on from what the Yanks are doing in the Atlantic if they're now working with our own troops to build a base in Scotland.'

Fran was interested. Earlier this month an American destroyer had exchanged fire with a German U-boat in the Atlantic, and speculation was rife that the USA would soon join the war. It was so devoutly hoped for that she could imagine how excited a small community in Scotland would be to have Americans in their midst.

'Engineering assistance doesn't qualify as military intervention, does it?' she asked. 'The Americans could be civilians.'

Jim MacNeill raised a sceptical eye and grinned, and she couldn't help but grin back. She was of course talking nonsense. Any engineers working with the British Royal Engineers must be closely aligned to the military themselves.

At that moment Jim spotted George Blake coming around the corner, and waved to let him know where they were. The lieutenant gave Fran his usual cheery welcome, and sat down with a relieved sigh, dumping his bag on the table, and calling out for the waiter.

'Miss Trevillian was kind enough to join me for a coffee,' Jim told him. 'You'll want a beer, though, I bet.'

'Too right I do! After the last two weeks I need more than coffee.'

A penny dropped for Fran, and she realised that the two men were onshore today because they had just finished Operation Supercharge. According to sources, the Allied fleet had shipped over 6,000 troops into Tobruk in the last two weeks, and had brought out thousands of utterly exhausted Australians who had been holding Tobruk against Rommel's siege for the last months.

'Operation Supercharge!' she uttered, gazing with respect at the two lieutenants in front of her. 'I saw some of the Australians heading off in trucks a few days ago. You got them all out safely?'

George Blake raised an eyebrow at Jim. 'You can tell she's a journalist!' he commented.

'But we've respected the news blackout,' Fran reminded them.

'I should hope so too!' Blake answered, with mock severity, but then relented. 'You know, those Aussies were amazing. They've been on short rations for so long that they're skin and bones. But they joked the whole time as we ferried them on board about who was going to pay for their first beers in the bars here.'

'They'll find enough bars in Jerusalem,' Jim MacNeill commented. 'They're being taken off there for recuperation, and I hope they're soon fit at least to go to a bar. I'd guess it will be months before they are fit for active service again.'

And what about your own part? Fran wanted to ask them, but didn't. Their ships would have gone in to Tobruk by night, under threat the whole time from enemy submarines and planes, working with tense discipline, the urgency of the impending dawn on everyone's mind. She knew that there had been substantial damage to ships during the operation. And similar operations happened all the time in these tight, close waters. She wanted suddenly to hug them both.

'Talking about bars,' Blake was saying. 'What would you say to moving on from here to a more conducive place for a beer?'

Jim MacNeill smiled. 'I'm in agreement with that. I could demolish a beer myself. I'm starving as well, and my stomach's craving something a bit more interesting than the fodder they serve us on board.'

Fran allowed herself to be persuaded, or more accurately towed along in the wake of their thirst and hunger. They headed on foot through the backstreets, seeking out a Greek taverna, which the men declared served the best moussaka in Alex. Two old men sat toothless on little stools as they passed, shapeless inside their cotton jellabiyas, presumably waiting for their own call inside to lunch.

'They don't seem to have much social life, these old fellows,' Blake commented. 'They seem to be waiting out their days in the most listless way possible. One Lebanese chap we got chatting to in a bar told us they are just listening to their bones.'

Fran grinned. 'I think you'll find they're as grumpy and demanding as any old men at home once they get inside their houses. But they live in such small spaces. I think they come out here to get away from the women and children.'

The Greek taverna was simple and clean, and they ate moussaka and a sticky honey cake, washing it down with cheap retsina, which Fran wouldn't normally have drunk, but which tasted surprisingly good. They ate in the courtyard at a metal table, with flies buzzing rather lazily around. A praying mantis stood completely motionless on a windowsill, looking, with its bulging eyes and huge forelegs, like some half-beautiful but half-grotesque ornament. The warmth from the kitchen mingled with the heat of the middle of the day. Around them were people of all nationalities, familiar to Fran, and, she realised, increasingly familiar to the two officers.

They'd had some good nights with the various cultures who made up the wider population of Alexandria, they told her. Greeks, and Syrians, Egyptians of all origins, men whom they met not in the Cecil Hotel but in bars tucked away well behind the grandeur of the Corniche. There were some who turned their back on them. Arrogant, self-serving Brits, you could see them thinking. But others were friendly enough, especially the Greeks, and the bar owners were always pleased to see them.

They had to be careful not to go to bars dominated by the ratings, or army troopers. It was frowned upon to mix, and all the most select bars were for officers only. The Aussies hated that. The British squaddies were used to their 'them and us' culture, and had been taught to know their place, but the Aussies and the Kiwis and the South African troops sometimes invaded 'officer only' bars in protest. Their officers agreed with them.

'One Aussie lieutenant really got angry with Tony one night,' Jim MacNeill told her. 'It's his accent, of course – poor Tony sounds so posh. The Aussie called him a stuffed-shirt Limey, with totally outdated class snobbery, and said if he thought that's what the rest of the Allies are fighting this war for, then he had got another think coming.' He lifted his glass of retsina. 'He was right, of course.'

Blake called for the bill, and the two men paid. Jim took change from his pocket for a tip, but as he reached to put it on the table the Greek restaurant owner came out with a bottle in his hand, and stopped him.

'You pay for your meal, my friend, and that will do. And you'll have a brandy on the house before you leave.'

Jim looked at him with surprise. The Greek unhurriedly

poured out three large Greek brandies, and then continued, directing his words at Jim.

'Your friend that was here with you last time you came, he was here three days ago, and he told me that it was your ship that rescued the caique earlier this month. My wife's cousin was on that boat, and he is very happy to be here in Alexandria, and free with us.'

There was a tangible pause at the table, and Fran caught Jim MacNeill's widened eyes, and George Blake's speculative smile.

'Have you been playing the hero, old man?' Blake asked after a moment.

Jim MacNeill shook his head. 'No, no, not at all,' he stammered. 'I remember the incident. I picked up the caique on the radar when we were out on patrol two or three weeks ago. It was just a routine thing for us. It was the Greek crew who were the heroes. They had risked their lives to bring out five British soldiers who had been hiding in the hills for months since Greece fell to the Germans. The caique's engine had failed, and they were drifting too far out from the Egyptian shore to find their way in.'

'And one of the crew was part of this man's family? Well, then he's a hero, as you say. What do you think, Miss Trevillian?'

Fran could only wonder at the sort of coincidence that surely must only be possible in Alexandria, where the whole of the Greek community was one big extended family. She smiled at the restaurant owner. 'I agree that your wife's cousin is a hero.' She turned to Jim MacNeill. 'But it took you and your shipmates to bring them safely in to harbour. You're all heroes to me.'

'Hear, hear.' It was George Blake who spoke, raising the glass that the Greek had just poured. 'We should drink to heroes!'

Fran raised her glass too, and Jim followed, holding his glass up to the restaurant owner. 'Won't you drink with us too, sir?' he asked.

The man beamed, and poured himself a brandy. Jim reached out to clink glasses with him.

'Please tell your wife's cousin,' he said, 'that it was a privilege to have been able to help. Tell him that what he did for our soldiers was exceptional, and that in this war against evil there are few whom we value more than the Greeks who fight by our side.'

A silence followed, and even the other diners seemed to have caught the mood. Fran felt privileged too, privileged to have been present with these men, and to be part of the extraordinary cultural melting pot that was Alexandria, and which could create such special moments.

Chapter Eight

Alexandria, October 1941

A few weeks went by before Fran saw either MacNeill or Blake again, but she was so busy she was barely aware of it. With Asher acting as something like her personal assistant she could feel some relief in the volume of her work, but she was aware that he needed to see more than just the inside of her office, so she sent him out whenever she could to accompany the outside reporters as they hunted down local stories.

She sent him out with one of their Greek outside reporters to track down the young man from the boat Jim MacNeill's ship had saved, and was pleased to see such a good news story appear in the *Journal*. In a city where so many were secretly hoping to see the Brits fail, the Greeks stood out as firm allies and avid haters of Hitler, desperate to get their country back from German occupation.

In October, Asher was joined at the *Alexandria Journal* by a friend of his from school. Sami Awad was an absurdly good-looking, extremely tall young man with a disreputable smile, who constantly poked and teased his more serious friend into good humour, and led him into office pranks that got by the older women simply because the two were so charming.

Between them they ate up work at a speed that meant that truly all of them in the office, including Fran, could take time for lunch and have decent weekends. This, Fran told her boss, was no credit to him. Like all Brits in Egypt he preferred to hire European staff, and had taken on these two only because he had been persuaded by their influential fathers, and because they were working for absurd wages.

The two were clamouring today to write articles for themselves, rather than just observing, and doing the legwork for others. Fran's article about the US destroyer firing on the German U-boat had excited them beyond measure. America was on the point of joining the war, they were sure, and they produced endless reams of research they'd done to justify more coverage of the subject. Sami had even done a draft article, which was just a bit too wild and optimistic for publication.

'Please don't just reject it, Miss Trevillian,' he begged her. 'You could give me some comments, and I could work on it. Couldn't I?'

Asher was standing behind him. They were going to harass her in unison, she knew, like a couple of young dogs worrying at a slipper until the seams gave way. Well, she couldn't let them write about the Americans, or the war in the Atlantic, but she could let them put pen to paper in more minor ways. She whisked them both off to lunch, treating them to Pastroudis restaurant, and there she talked them gently through a potential agenda for their future as reporters. Her offer that they should cover youth events and take over some of the sports coverage met with distinct coolness, but she persisted. It was only because the paper was so short-staffed that they were already being given the chance to write their own pieces at all, she told them, and from there they could move gradually up to more general reporting.

'Do you know what I don't understand, you two?' she asked them, as they attacked ice cream sundaes for dessert. 'Why do you want to work in journalism at all, when you could do so much better in other professions? If you don't want to go join your fathers in banking, and you're so interested in world affairs, why don't you join the diplomatic service or something in Cairo? I know what a pittance Tim Jeffrey is paying you on the *Journal*.'

Asher frowned. 'I'm not sure the diplomatic service would work very well for us. I'm a Jew, remember.'

Sami laughed. 'And I'm a Coptic Christian! They do tend to prefer good Muslims in the government. But it would be a real bore, anyway. And if I go into my father's bank I'll never get out. No, doing some journalism is good preparation for me. I want to go to Beirut next year, and study law at the American University. Then I'll be off to the USA, you just wait and see! But first the Americans have to come in to the war, and you have to let me write about it!'

Fran waved her spoon at him. 'Have you been listening at all, young Sami?'

'Why yes, but I'm practising to be an advocate, remember?'

Fran laughed. 'And you, Asher? Do you want to go to America as well?'

He shook his head. 'Not on your life, Miss Trevillian.

I'm an old-fashioned Alexandrian, and I look to Britain for my inspiration. Give me the gentle cloisters of Cambridge and I'll be happy. I just have to wait, because my father doesn't want me to travel there at the moment. He thinks I'm safer here.'

Fran raised an eyebrow. 'I hope you don't think you'll be going soon, then! It's not as though we're on the verge of winning this war.'

'I know.' He frowned. 'And for us Jews it will get worse before ever it can get better.'

As they were leaving the restaurant they passed Denise de Menasce, eating at a table nearer to the door. She spotted Fran, and raised an elegant hand in greeting.

'Fran, my dear, how are you? I haven't seen you for an age. And Asher, why my dear young man, how nice to see you here.'

Asher blushed, in as far as his Egyptian skin would allow, and muttered a polite reply. The Menasces were the leading Jewish family in Alexandria, immensely wealthy, infinitely cultured. To middle-class families like Asher's, the Menasces were the aristocracy.

And they were Europeans. They led the Jewish community, but they were leaders also in the entire Western community. Fran thought that Asher had a lot more in common with his comfortable fellow Egyptian Sami, Christian though he might be, than with the Menasce family.

But it was interesting to note how affably Denise greeted him. It set Fran's mind working. Perhaps, after a while, it might be possible to use Asher to report on some of Alexandria's key social events. But not while he still blushed quite so deeply and quite so easily. He needed more of Sami's cheek.

'I'll tell you what, boys,' she said to them as they emerged from the restaurant. 'I may not be ready to let you start writing our newspaper leaders, but this afternoon I'm heading out of town to an inspection of troops. I wouldn't be going, but they've promised that one of Auchinleck's senior staff will be there from Cairo, and our editor wants a British presence from the paper. You can come with me, if you like.'

It would mean taking away from her meagre staff at the office, but she would enjoy their company.

An avid look crossed Sami's face. 'And can I write something?' he shot at her. 'Will you at least read it?'

'You do know I can't abide pests, don't you, Sami? I'll read a short piece, if you like, but don't you go thinking that means anything at all!'

They got back from the desert just in time to close the office at eight. What they'd seen had been a typical formal show for the press, too long and with too little substance, but Sami and Asher were happy, and they'd got the chance to ask some quite telling questions.

It had also been dry work, and the desert had been extremely blowy and dusty, enough to send the two young men scooting from the office looking for a beer before going home. Fran glanced quickly through some papers that had come in during her absence, then attacked her day-worn appearance before heading out herself in search of refreshment.

She was joining Lucie and her cousin Tony for drinks

this evening. She sighed as she looked in the mirror at the dust in her hair, and attacked it with a comb, washed her face and hands, and did the best she could with powder and lipstick. It would have to do for the Cecil. It was an after-work venue, after all, and there would probably be a good few ATS girls in army uniforms. But half-French Lucie would be dressed!

She entered the hotel lounge and saw Tony Harding sitting at a table in the corner, with his arm lying protectively along the back of the sofa behind Lucie. They weren't alone, and as she reached the table two other officers turned and stood, and she realised with pleasure that they were Jim MacNeill and George Blake.

To her amusement, they both looked extremely relieved to see her. 'Good evening, Miss Trevillian. It's a very great pleasure to see you,' George Blake said, bowing slightly over her hand. He cocked his head towards Tony and Lucie. 'I don't mean to give any offence, but Jim and I have been here now for half an hour, and were beginning to think we might have to spend the whole evening playing gooseberry to that pair of lovebirds!'

Fran laughed. 'I'm very glad that I can be of some use,' she said. 'And there was I thinking you were pleased to see me for my own charming company!' She laughed again as George Blake coloured.

Jim dug his friend in the ribs. 'Ignore George, Miss Trevillian. He has just spent the day in the sun, and I think it has got to him.' He drew a chair forward for her, signalling to a waiter as he spoke. 'Won't you sit down? You're the only one of us who has been at work today, and you deserve a seat and a drink.'

'You never spoke a truer word!'

'A gin and tonic?'

'That sounds heavenly.' She flopped into the chair, and the three officers took their seats again. 'So, have you all been on the beach all day?' she asked.

Lucie shook her head. 'Tony and I took a picnic out to Montazah for lunch, but to the gardens, not the beach. It's too windy for the beach.'

'Too cold for my fragile cousin,' Tony teased, but with a smile just for Lucie. Fran could understand why his friends had been glad to see someone else arrive. The relationship between Tony and Lucie grew stronger by the week. When Tony was onshore they were always together, and there was a complicity about them that radiated and excluded at the same time. They were a beautiful couple, and Fran had come to like Tony very much, for the genuinely kind, considerate character that lived behind his sometimes rather over-assured demeanour. But she could imagine that his and Lucie's intimacy might make his bachelor friends squirm a little.

She looked at Blake and MacNeill, and caught a half-grin that passed between them. Both of them had got some sun today, but only Jim MacNeill's fair skin had burnt. He had acquired new freckles over the last three months, and today his nose and forehead glowed with a red that would be sore to sleep with.

He turned to her now, and asked after her work. 'I liked your article about the Greek rescue,' he told her. 'It was very flattering to everyone concerned!'

Fran smiled. 'It was good to have a positive story like that for once, without having to embellish it to make the

Brits look better. I only edited the story, by the way. One of our Greek reporters went out to visit the family. We would have liked to interview the British soldiers whom the Greeks rescued, but they seem to have been redeployed immediately away from Alexandria.'

Jim MacNeill nodded. 'They'll be back with their regiments by now, I would think, after a bit of leave. Probably somewhere in the desert, poor blighters, like your brother. Is he still working as an Aide de Camp?'

Fran nodded. 'What a grandiose name, Aide de Camp! It sounds so important, but I always think ADC is really just the term for someone who runs errands and translates for his superiors! It's the godsend of speaking Arabic and knowing the culture, Michael says, and he assures us that it means he's never in real battle!'

'I can never get over how many languages you people here all speak,' Blake said. 'I was talking to a fellow who had served in India the other day, and he told me that none of the colonials there speak anything other than English.'

It was Jim MacNeill who answered. 'Yes, but English is the only common language in India. Egypt isn't a colony of ours, Blake, and they spoke French and Italian along the North African coast long before we Brits ever came along.'

'That's true,' Fran agreed. 'But it's only the old-timers among the Brits who speak other languages, you know. Lucie's family, for example, and mine. There are plenty who come here and just assume everyone will adapt to them.'

'How very British!' Jim said.

'Speak for yourself, MacNeill. I was really good at French at school!' Tony Harding was indignant.

Lucie snorted. 'The French Tony knows wouldn't buy

him a loaf of bread,' she assured them. 'I've heard him trying to butter up my mother, and it's enough to make you weep.'

'Whereas MacNeill speaks at least two languages, don't you, Jim?' Blake leapt to his friend's defence.

Fran looked at him curiously, and he caught her eye and smiled. 'He means I speak Gaelic, Miss Trevillian. It's the language we use at home. But it isn't much use to me here in Egypt, or indeed anywhere else, as Harding here will remind me, I'm sure.'

Tony Harding grinned. 'It would be all right if you didn't sing in the damn language when you think nobody's listening.' He looked down at Lucie, and said in mock mourning. 'So, my French wouldn't buy me a loaf of bread, huh? Well, MacNeill's heathen language wouldn't even buy you a beer.'

Jim MacNeill kicked him lightly under the table, and called for the waiter. He grimaced when Blake ordered a whisky.

'You'd be better off with a beer than that muck, George,' he said.

Fran was surprised. 'Don't you come from a whisky environment? I thought you said your father was in the industry?'

'Ah yes, but on Islay we make proper whisky, very pure, very peaty, which not everyone knows how to appreciate, especially these fellows. Do you know, Miss Trevillian, they insist on putting ice and soda in theirs?'

'Is that a bad thing to do? I'm afraid my father does the same.'

'And he's quite right, Miss Trevillian!' proclaimed George Blake. 'In the heat of Egypt, how else would you

81

drink your whisky? Ignore Jim, he's a fanatic!'

Lieutenant MacNeill simply smiled. 'I am probably a bit biased,' he acknowledged, in his soft burr. 'Stick soda in your drinks if you must, George. It'll help dilute the rubbish they sell here. Just don't mix it with the best stuff, that's all I ask.'

'On what I earn there's not much chance of that.' George sighed. 'Oh, by the way, Miss Trevillian, Jim and I saw your French matelot this afternoon, or at least Jim assured me it was him.'

Fran looked quickly at Jim, who nodded in response. 'He was scrubbing down decks on his ship,' he told her. 'You'll be interested to hear that Naval Command has finally curtailed shore visits for the Frenchies. They can go into town, but they have curfews now. I think your articles on the issue may even have had some influence.'

Fran was pleased, but doubtful. 'I would say it was the military police who were more likely to have lobbied for the curfew. They were beginning to find it too difficult to ensure peace in the streets, I think.'

'Perhaps it was a combination of the two,' MacNeill answered. 'Either way, it's the right result, I think.'

'Did you say hello to Robert Masson?' Fran asked him.

He made a wry face. 'I called out to him, but he didn't even acknowledge us.'

'Then I think the curfew is definitely the right result,' she said. 'When I think of everything you men are doing for us all, and a little whippersnapper of a matelot can't even be grateful that you helped save his life three months ago, it makes my blood boil.'

'Maybe he didn't recognise Jim.' It was Tony Harding

who intervened. 'Don't boil, Miss Trevillian. It's just too nice to have an evening with all of us together, and we should forget the war for an hour or two. Shall we go and eat somewhere? We may not see you and Lucie for ages, and who cares what one small Frenchman thinks when we have found friends like you.'

Fran looked from him to Lucie. 'Just friends?' she asked, her eyes twinkling.

He answered with a similar twinkle, manoeuvring his arm further around Lucie's shoulders. 'Friends, cousins, call it what you will, my dear. One way or another it makes Alexandria a very special place to be!'

Chapter Nine

Alexandria, December 1941

Over the next three months there were more evenings with the naval officers, invariably organised by Lucie. There were others who joined them, but their core became Blake and MacNeill, who would be there when they were in town, and Tony, of course, who was always there, since the evenings were organised around him being in port. Tony and Lucie grew closer and closer, and at an evening dinner at the Carsdales', Fran was amused to see how Lucie's father teased her about wedding plans.

Fran wondered at times what her brother Michael would think of the new relationship when he next made it home. He and Lucie had grown up together, and so had always taken each other for granted, but since Michael had been away in the desert he and Lucie had developed a more adult, appreciative relationship on his visits home. You couldn't have called it dating. They had just seemed to be more aware of each other, and there was a little tension between them that had never existed before.

That would all be finished now. What had existed,

or half-existed, between Lucie and Michael was nothing compared with what had flowered between her and Tony Harding. They had everything going for them, every certainty of success, and Lucie talked with endless pride about Tony's studies, his achievements, his future career. But he too was proud, Fran thought, proud of the style and sparkle and vibrancy that characterised Lucie, of her common sense, of her loyalty and values. Any slight bombast in him could be checked by the merest raising of her eyebrows, always accompanied by a softening smile.

Blake and MacNeill continued to look on them as you might a couple from Mars. They too could check Tony's occasional nonsense, but they did so in much pithier terms, giving no quarter. They were both so different from him, but they were friends, fellows in combat, and they had a manly bond that remained flatly embarrassed by the overt affection on display between Tony and Lucie.

The two men continued to fall on Fran with relief, and she grew closer to both of them, learning more about their families, and the niece who had been born to George just a few weeks before, and whom he didn't expect to see for years. No one now believed that this war would soon be over, and it was a conscious act of faith on all their parts to believe that it would be won at all.

When their little group was blown apart it came with all the suddenness that war could inflict. Fran was in the office talking to Tim, her editor, when his secretary stuck her head around the door.

'I'm sorry,' she said, 'but there's a call for Fran that seems to be very important.'

Fran was surprised. Who needed to call her so urgently?

'Do you want to transfer the call here, Maria?'

The secretary shook her head. 'It's a private call, Fran, and the lady sounds rather distressed. I think you might want to talk to her in your office.'

'It's not my mother?' It was an immediate fear, always lurking, that something had happened to Michael.

Maria shook her head. 'I think you should come,' she said.

It was Angélique Carsdale, Lucie's mother. 'Fran, *chérie*,' she said, and her voice sounded deeper, more French than usual. 'Lucie asked me to call you. We . . . we have had some bad news. About Tony. There was an attack on his ship, and it has been sunk. Tony has been reported missing.'

Fran didn't quite understand. 'Missing?' she repeated. 'You mean no one knows where he is?'

A pause on the other end of the line, and then Mrs Carsdale continued. 'That's not what they mean, when they say someone is missing. They mean he is probably dead. You see, there were other ships of ours nearby, and they picked up all the survivors. There was no sign of Tony.'

It was astonishing how slowly Fran's mind was working. She didn't seem to be able to get it functioning. 'But they haven't found a body?' she said.

'No. That's what Lucie keeps saying. But, Fran, we can't really build up hope from that. The ship was torpedoed, and about half of the crew have gone down with her.'

So he had been blown to smithereens? Or had he died trapped somewhere and trying desperately to get out? It can't be true, was what kept going round in Fran's mind.

That dinner party at the Carsdales' had been only last week, and all had been well.

'How is Lucie?' she managed to ask.

'Distraught, of course. But she wanted me to phone you. Apparently, Tony's friend, Lieutenant MacNeill, is one of the survivors. He is in hospital. Lucie wanted you to know.'

Fran's fingers tightened around the telephone. After a moment Mrs Carsdale spoke again. 'I don't think he is seriously injured, Fran, but Lucie can't go to see him, not in the state she is in. She thought maybe you could go. I believe you have all become friends, *n'est-ce pas?*'

'Of course.' Fran's brain was beginning to work again, very reluctantly. Tony was dead; Jim MacNeill was injured. She'd been writing a lot about the war at sea for the last few weeks. The fleet had been more successful for a while back in the autumn, and Admiral Cunningham had grown bolder – pushed, it was said, by Churchill. Churchill had accused Cunningham of being too cautious, and declared that if the army lost in Africa for want of naval support, then the navy would never be forgiven.

But the Germans had reacted by diverting a whole fleet of U-boats into the Mediterranean. They were beginning to pick off navy ships in a way the Italian submarines had been unable to do on their own. In November they'd sunk the *Ark Royal* off Gibraltar, and it had been international news. Would the loss of a small destroyer be the same? Not to the rest of the world, Fran thought.

She managed to ask Mrs Carsdale if they knew where Jim was. He was in Alexandria's military hospital, it seemed.

'Tell Lucie I'll go right away,' she said. 'And Mrs Carsdale?'
'Yes?'

'I'm so terribly, terribly sorry, for all of you.' Her voice failed, and she replaced the receiver.

The hospital was bedlam. It received some of the most serious desert casualties, the men who were too badly wounded, too sick to travel further. A convoy had just come in, and there were men lying all around on stretchers, being processed by two nurses and a man in army uniform. They made no noise, these injured men, except for one who whimpered gently as he was moved.

Fran stood rooted for a moment, appalled. This was ten times worse than when she'd come to interview the young Frenchman. Then the reception area had been clear, the hospital had smelt just as you would expect, of carbolic soap. The smell of these stretchered men initially made her shrink, and then she pulled herself together. Jim MacNeill was somewhere inside here. She had no ward number this time, but there must be a part of the hospital reserved for British navy personnel. The reception desk was knee-deep in people, and impossible to approach, but there were three women of about her mother's age serving tea from an urn in the corner. She didn't know them, but they looked British. She spoke to one who was carrying two mugs of tea to some men sitting up on stretchers.

'Can you help me? I've been told a friend of mine is here. He's a lieutenant in the navy, and he was brought here after his ship went down.'

The woman gestured with her head towards a corridor. 'Down there, my dear. Go to the ward at the end of the corridor and ask. If he's a navy man, they should know where he is.'

The bedlam calmed as she went down the corridor. People came purposefully in and out of rooms to either side, and she caught sight of rows of beds, trolleys, nurses standing over patients, a normal hospital scene except for how many beds were squeezed into each space.

She stopped when she got to the end. There was an office to one side with its door open, and inside was a woman who looked like a sister, or a matron, her nose deep in paperwork. She looked up when Fran knocked at the door.

'Can I help you?' she asked, when she saw Fran's civilian attire.

Fran nodded. 'I'm looking for a Lieutenant MacNeill, James MacNeill. I think he was brought here two nights ago, but I don't know for sure when.'

Sister/Matron looked her up and down. 'This isn't visiting time,' she said, discouragingly. But she ran her finger down what looked like a list of patients, and stopped when she reached a name. She looked at the watch fob that hung from her uniform.

'If you wait a few minutes the doctor will have finished his rounds in Ward H, and you can see the patient briefly. You can find out what he needs, if anything, and then you can come back in proper visiting hours.' Her voice was austere, but as Fran nodded, gripping her bag more tightly, and prepared to step back out into the corridor, the woman relented somewhat.

'Don't worry about your friend,' she said. 'He's going to be fine. He has concussion, and has been rather confused, but we will be discharging him as soon as possible.'

A nurse came in at that moment, and Sister/Matron consigned Fran to her care. The nurse was younger than

Fran, and much less intimidating. She led Fran up a flight of stairs, and stuck her head through the door of the ward, scanning for the doctor no doubt, then beckoned to Fran to follow her.

The men in this ward didn't look too bad. Some were sitting by their beds in their hospital blues, a few were sleeping, and in a bed towards the end Jim MacNeill was sitting up, looking rather blankly before him. He was white as a sheet, as though the blood had been siphoned from his body.

Fran was suddenly hesitant. Would he think it odd of her to be visiting? Don't be stupid, she told herself. He has just lost half of his shipmates. She walked slowly through the ward, and up to his bed.

He saw her when she was a few yards away, and his eyes widened a little. 'Miss Trevillian!'

She gave a nervous smile. 'I seem to visit this hospital only when you are involved!' she joked unconvincingly. 'How are you?'

He looked bemused, but after a moment he gave her the automatic answer, 'I'm fine.' There was something immobile about him that was disconcerting. She drew up a chair and sat down.

'I've been told I can only stay for a few minutes,' she told him. 'But I can come back this evening, and I'll bring my father. Is there anything you need?'

'Not really,' he answered, listlessly. 'I don't think I'll be here long. They've told me I can be discharged if I have somewhere to go, and I'm just waiting for someone from the base to come in, to see where they're going to send me.'

'Discharged?' Fran was shocked. He looked far too unwell to leave hospital.

He managed a wry smile. 'There are people who need this bed much more than I do. We have some convalescent rooms at the base, if they are available, or they may send me to some other hospital out of town.'

He moved slightly in the bed, and winced. 'It's only bruising,' he said, seeing Fran's face.

Did he know about Tony Harding? Fran wondered. Or any of the others who'd been drowned? He would have asked, if anyone from the base had visited, but if he'd been concussed and asleep, then maybe he hadn't seen anyone yet. She hoped he wouldn't ask her. He looked so dejected, and weary, and kind of dazed. Was this what shock looked like?

He reached for his water glass, on the table by the bed, and found it empty. Fran took it from him, and went to look for an orderly or someone to fill it. She found the nurse who had brought her up the stairs.

'Lieutenant MacNeill tells me he may be discharged,' she said. 'Are you sure he's fit? He can hardly move.'

The nurse was definite. 'He needs convalescence, not acute care,' was her answer.

'Does he need professional nursing?'

'To change his dressings, yes, but mainly he just needs rest.'

'But can he walk?'

'Oh yes, he doesn't have any injuries that will stop him walking.'

Fran was thinking hard. 'Could we take him home to my family? If we had a visiting nurse? My mother volunteers here, and has training in first aid.'

The nurse shrugged. 'I don't see why not, though you would have to consult Matron. A home environment would probably do him a lot of good.'

'I need to speak to my parents,' Fran said, but she was sure of their consent, and felt suddenly excited. More than from his injuries, Jim MacNeill would need to recover from his trauma, and his loss. At their home he would have peace, unlike in some convalescent hospital.

'I'll come back this evening with my father,' she said, and took the glass of water back to Jim.

CHAPTER TEN

As it happened, the Trevillians brought two men home from the hospital. Just down the ward from Jim was a young sub lieutenant, Len Rudland, who had gone into the water with him. Fran's mother was not going to leave him in the hospital alone to be shipped off goodness knows where, so she had scooped him up along with Jim, and the two of them now had adjoining rooms in the guest wing of the house. They had their own verandah, where they could sit out in the middle of the day, and could receive visitors, or play cards together, or simply doze their days away.

Barbara Trevillian's initiative in bringing a junior officer home with Jim MacNeill helped him greatly. It gave him someone to care about, and to be responsible for. He was taking command, and the young man Len gradually lost the scared eyes he had brought with him from the hospital.

In the evenings the two men joined the Trevillians for dinner, and would sit talking afterwards over coffee.

They learnt that Len came from a farming family in Wiltshire, that he was an only son, and his father was banking on him taking over the farm after the war, that he had a girl back at home whom he'd known all his life. He was shy, and rather intimidated by his surroundings, so they had to tease out his personality, but he had a sweetness about him that made you want to adopt him.

They talked about Pearl Harbour, the great news of America's entry into the war, and how quickly they might see US troops in Africa, and tentatively Fran's father spoke about what was happening at sea, keeping it impersonal, waiting to see whether the men wanted to talk about what had happened to them. They never quite made it, though, to broaching the two men's reserve, and Jim never mentioned Tony, though he must know he was dead.

On 15th December it all got worse when another U-boat attack sank a cruiser, the *Galatea*, off Alexandria. As news came out of the tragedy, Fran saw Jim's face set very hard. Over four hundred and fifty men were lost, including the commander whose flagship she was. How many of Jim's friends had gone this time, Fran wanted to ask, but she couldn't.

Only strict orders from the nurse kept Jim from moving straight away back to the base. He would be of no use to anyone, the nurse told him, and he owed it to his colleagues to rest and get better. What did he think he could do that an able man couldn't do better?

It silenced him, but for two days he didn't come out to dinner, and Len was the only one who joined them, tongue-tied without his mentor. Then Lucie came to visit.

Fran was at work when Lucie and her mother came, and it was Barbara Trevillian who received them. Wisely, the older women left Lucie to go into the guest wing on her own, and had tea while they waited. They waited for an hour, and then Lucie came out, bringing Jim with her, silent but at least present.

That night was exceptionally mild for December, and Fran took her coffee out into the garden after dinner. Shortly afterwards Jim joined her. She was sitting on the verandah wall, leaning against a pillar, and he came and stood behind her, and lit a cigarette. She stayed silent, listening to the crickets. If he had come out here, then he must have something to say.

'I've been wondering for the last two weeks how Lucie was getting on,' he said eventually.

'And how did you find her?'

'Bereft, wounded, bleeding. Tony would be so devastated to think that he has done this to her.'

'But he didn't do anything to her! Poor Tony didn't mean to die!'

'I know, but her grief is a direct result of getting involved with him, isn't it?'

'You mean they shouldn't have become close? But Lucie doesn't regret what happened to them!' Fran knew this, as certainly as she knew Lucie.

'No, but *he* would, if he knew.'

Fran thought through what to say. 'But, Jim, do you think Tony's parents are grieving any less than Lucie is? Or his brother and sister? Dying causes grief to everyone you care about, and if you don't want that to happen, then you would have to alienate your entire family. Tony didn't choose to die. He could have been lucky, and he and Lucie could have been grandparents one day. So then, if they lost a child, would that mean they should never have got together?'

He was silent.

'Did you men ever talk about dying?' she continued. 'My brother has told me that before one operation they went on, he and his mates each put some money behind the bar in the NAAFI, and the agreement was that if any of them didn't make it, the others would get drunk on their money.'

He gave a half-laugh. 'Tony used to joke that if he bought it we would finally have to start buying our own drinks! He used to buy too many rounds, saying that he had better means.'

'So maybe you should buy some drinks for him.'

He looked a question. 'I don't understand.'

'I mean, you should get your friends together, and go to the Cecil Bar, and then to every bar you used to go to with Tony, and have a drink for him in every single one.'

He laughed again. 'There are rather too many.'

'And you're still a crock, so don't do them all, then, but choose the ones he liked best. Surely George Blake would go with you?'

'No,' he said, and she was disappointed. She had hoped she was persuading him. Then he continued. 'George Blake is away, I know, and I wouldn't want to take anyone else. No, I tell you what we'll do, we'll take Len with us. He needs to get out, and he was on the ship too.'

'We?'

'Why yes. Won't you come?'

She looked at him in surprise. He lit another cigarette, and blew a trail of smoke.

'It would please Tony if you would,' was all he said, and then, irrelevantly, 'Are we only eight days from Christmas? It's too late for me to send an airgraph to the family; I'll have to send a telegram. It will give them the fright of their lives, because until they open it they're bound to think it's from the War Office, telling them I'm dead. But I should have sent an airgraph two weeks ago if I wanted it to arrive for Christmas. I don't want them thinking anything has happened to me.'

'Well it hasn't, has it?' she said, and bit her lip. This sensitive, troubled Scot was getting under her skin.

He twisted his face. 'No, not this time! Scotland one, Jerry nil, for now.'

The night out for Tony took place on the Saturday. By then the British fleet in Alexandria was reeling from yet another blow that nobody could quite believe. In the early hours of the Friday morning Italian frogmen had somehow swum through the harbour defences and placed limpet mines on the hulls of the two battleships that were the emblem of the fleet. The explosions looked likely to put the ships out of action for months. Two of the frogmen had been captured, the others were at large somewhere in Egypt. You couldn't hide the damage. The world's press wanted to know more. It was a disaster for the navy, and for the people of Alexandria it was the most exciting thing to happen for years.

What daring, and brilliance! Italians all over the city were celebrating, and the Egyptians were laughing up their sleeves. It was said that when the *Ark Royal* was sunk, King Farouk had cracked open the champagne. So what must he be doing today, to celebrate Britain's humiliation?

Then the next day news started coming through that Force K had been destroyed. The small team of ships based in Malta had hero status with the men here in Alexandria. They had been having spectacular success against the supply convoys Rommel depended on. But now the word was that something catastrophic had happened to them. Fran spent hours at the office that Saturday checking news wires.

She wondered whether this latest blow would pull Jim back down, but it was Len who seemed to feel it most.

'We don't have a fleet left! It's all gone!' Len mourned, and there was a worrying edge of hysteria to his voice. Jim heard it.

'If we've lost Force K, then that's hellish,' he agreed. 'But don't jump the gun, Len. We don't actually know yet what has happened. If we've lost the ships, the Americans will supply us with more. I just hope we haven't lost too many men, that's all.'

Len made to speak, and Jim held up his hand. 'And as for our ships here in the harbour, we'll get them repaired. What really matters is that here in Alexandria nobody died, Len, nobody died!'

Would he still want to go out on the Saturday evening? Fran asked him, and he said yes. 'We'll beat those bastards, Fran, you wait and see! I'm not going to retire to my room again. Now we've got work to do.'

That same gritty anger could be felt in all the naval officers they met that night. The talk in town was of nothing but the disasters, especially the humiliation of the harbour raid. It wasn't a good night to be a navy man in Alexandria. Even the British army officers were gloating.

'We've got Rommel on the run back to Libya, and what are you navy fellows doing? Letting his Eyetie pals swim into your damned harbour, that's what,' an army lieutenant foolishly told Jim.

Jim was taking none of that. 'What are we doing? We're sinking their supply vessels, you bloody fool, which is the only reason Rommel is retreating. He's got no more fuel, and no more food, thanks to my comrades who died out there yesterday. You bloody army wallahs have got damn all to do with it!'

It was fighting talk, but Jim was hobbling on a stick, so there was nothing anyone could do to him. The challenge won, Jim led Fran and Len defiantly out, and took them to bars Fran had never seen before. The two men kept Fran protectively in between them, 'to hold them up', they said. And by the time two in the morning came it was true, and neither man was steady on his feet. In the blacked-out streets they stumbled more than once as Fran eased them back towards the car.

'We ought to have one more for Tony,' Jim slurred.

'Who's Tony?' Len replied, forgetting completely the original point of the evening.

'God man, you know! One of the ones we lost.'

Fran rolled her eyes. 'You two have already had a drink

for practically every man who was on that ship with you. It's time to go home.'

She got them to the car, and eased the two awkward bodies into the back seat.

'Pair of cripples,' quipped Jim, and Len fell into giggles.

Fran slipped into the driver's seat, and drove cautiously home through the dark streets, the lights of the car covered so that they only vaguely lit the ground in front of them. She was dreading getting the men out of the car when they got home, and was immensely relieved to see her father coming out of the house as she slid into the drive.

'I think they may need some help,' she said to him, as she opened her door. Jim pushed open his own door, and sobered when he saw who was there.

'Mr Trevillian! Sorry, sir. It's been a bit too long since I had a night anywhere,' he said, apologetically.

Alan Trevillian laughed. 'I couldn't be happier, Jim, to see you fellows letting your hair down. I'm just glad you took Fran along to take care of you!'

'Shouldn't have taken her to Alberto's bar,' Jim said, remorsefully, the defiance that had kept him going all evening fizzling out in a rush.

Alan took his arm to help him straighten up from the car. 'You'll do fine,' he said, approvingly. 'And so will my daughter. Fran is a reporter, remember. She sees and hears a lot more than any of us imagine.' He smiled at his daughter. 'Did you have a good time, chick?'

'It was interesting,' she answered. 'Especially when the army met the navy.'

Len emerged from the other side of the car. 'Bunch of idiots,' he muttered.

'The navy or the army?' Alan asked drily. 'On second thoughts, don't answer that! We're all for the navy here, and right now I think I'd better get the navy to its bed.'

CHAPTER ELEVEN

The Clyde, December 1941

What a winter they were having! What was it about this war that it should bring them such cold, wet winters, one after another?

Catriona cycled too often through both rain and hail to take the ferry to work. On dry days she loved the fifteen-minute crossing in the dawn light. The wind tossed your hair, and the Clyde never stopped moving. There were ships anchored everywhere, and in the central channel there was an endless procession of tugs, and puffers, and navy ships from all over the world, troopships heading out with their fresh cargoes of young soldiers, convoys coming in from the Atlantic carrying fuel, and food, and supplies, with their accompaniment of corvettes and destroyers, which had protected their passage. There was an Australian ship one day, with its troops all mustered on deck ready for arrival in Scotland. They had a band playing, and the troops waved and cheered as they passed the ferry, which tooted its horn.

When it was raining the crossing was a different affair, and the passengers huddled together for shelter under whatever cover they could find, the men cupping their woodbines in their hands to keep them dry. From the ferry terminal in Gourock there was another cycle ride to the infirmary, where Catriona worked days and nights in her squeezed team, getting her satisfaction from being needed, as one of the few really well-qualified nurses on the military ward. They saw mainly naval casualties, men who had been injured by machinery, by falls, occasionally by the impact of enemy fire, often with burns, or open wounds turning to suppuration.

It took too long to get the men here, very often, and there were no antibiotics to give them. Catriona had heard that the Canadian hospital up the road had antibiotics, but there were none here. Why are we so far behind everyone else? she railed inside, but there was no one to answer. There was no money, that was the real answer. Across the Atlantic they had everything. Here they got by as best they could. So she cleaned the men's wounds, gave painkillers, and hoped to God they wouldn't get septicaemia.

'Canada's a member of the Commonwealth, isn't it?' she asked one of her patients in frustration one day. 'You'd think they'd share some of what they have.'

He looked at her, a bit bemused by her question, and then replied stoically, 'One of their seamen stole my girl a couple of months back. Is that what you call sharing?'

She laughed. That was an answer of sorts.

She saw her American again that day, on the ferry home, the same American she had written to Jim about, whom she'd danced with at the Burgh Hall. You didn't often meet any of the people working round at Rosneath on the Gourock ferry. They had their own launches, and when they had time off they usually went over to Helensburgh. As she pushed her bike on board he recognised her, and came over to talk. And, lo and behold, suddenly he was in uniform.

'It's my dancing partner!' he said, grinning broadly, and then spotted her clothes. 'Hey, you're a nurse! That's amazing.'

She raised her eyebrows. 'You have a uniform too, it seems! I seem to remember asking you at the dance whether you were joining the war, and you said no. You were going to be home with your wife and children for Christmas, you told me.'

He grinned again. 'Well, I decided to try Christmas here instead. Don't you want us in the war?'

She smiled. 'My father had his first whisky for months when he heard about Pearl Harbour, just to celebrate. Did you know all the time, these last months, that you were going to join?'

'We in the military knew that we wanted to. But it took the Japs to convince the American people. You'll be seeing a lot of our ships arriving on the Clyde soon, and a lot more men.'

'Are they coming to Rosneath?'

'Well, we'll have more construction engineers for now. We've some building still to do.'

'How are you managing to build in all this rain?'

'With difficulty.' The American laughed. 'One of our boys has designed us a coat of arms, since we're here in Britain. Do you know what it is? A duck with an umbrella and gumboots! But we're not complaining – we're getting on in spite of the weather. We're happy enough, and the natives are very friendly! Aren't you people having another dance round at Cove very soon? We've received an invitation, and you'll see us all there, in uniform this time. We find it pleases the ladies,' he said, and winked.

'You don't find our dances tame?' Catriona wanted to know. 'The next one's on a Saturday, so it will finish before midnight, because you can't dance on the Sabbath, and you'll get the same tea and sandwiches we gave you the last time.'

He smiled. 'We carry our own supplies, don't you worry.' He tapped his hip significantly. 'Though I must say, we do wonder what you guys do on Sundays around here.'

'Nothing,' Catriona laughed. 'Church, and a walk, or some reading – preferably the Bible! I'm always glad when I have to work.'

There was a jeep waiting to pick him up at the ferry terminal. They were so impressive, these Americans: they had cars, and fuel, and long cigarettes, which they tapped out of soft packets. He insisted on dropping Catriona home, and threw her bike in the back of the jeep, ignoring her protests that it was out of his way, reminding her that he was a happily married man with no designs on her virtue.

She didn't protest too much. It was a luxury not to have to cycle home in the blackout, even though it was only a couple of miles. The water to her left even showed a touch of silver where a hint of moonlight filtered through the clouds. When they reached Aunt Sheila and Uncle Charlie's she tapped him on the arm, and he told the driver to stop. He looked curiously at the little lodge by the quiet roadside.

'Do your family live here, or up there?' he asked, pointing

past the lodge to the shadow of the great house behind.

'Here,' she answered. 'My uncle and aunt work for the owners of the property.'

'This is some area,' he said, gesturing back to the stretch of Victorian mansions behind them, with their long drives and the magnificent views their merchant owners had paid to own. 'Old money,' he remarked.

'Not that old,' she answered. 'These houses are from the last century only. It's where the families who got rich during the industrial revolution came to run away from the dirt of Glasgow.'

'Nice area to live, though. Kind of peaceful.' He gave his signature grin. 'Like I said, perhaps a bit too peaceful sometimes! I'll see you at the dance then, Miss . . .'

'MacNeill, Catriona MacNeill,' she supplied. He shook her hand.

'Captain Ron Martin, at your service.'

'Thank you for the lift, Captain Martin.'

'You're truly welcome, ma'am, the pleasure was all mine.'

He was at the dance, and there seemed to be more American officers than ever. The local girls were delighted, as the quality of dancing was so much better among the Americans. And the local men were equally delighted, for the visitors supplied them with liberal nips of bourbon every time they went outside. There had never been a dance where people disappeared quite so frequently into the cold, and by the time the interval arrived, the men dived into the sandwiches, but very few were interested in the tea.

Catriona danced with Captain Martin, and with anyone

else who was dancing, and wondered why the dancing kept getting livelier, until one of the GIs offered her his flask. She smirked, but refused, because she was working early the next day.

She worked nearly every day in December, including Christmas and Hogmanay. Christmas had never really been a holiday in Scotland, but Hogmanay was different. Aunt Sheila made shortbread and clootie dumpling, full of dried fruit saved from their rations, and though Catriona missed most of the festivities, she came home one evening to find about fifteen people squeezed into their tiny front room, singing to the accompaniment of an energetic accordion. Uncle Charlie, a fine baritone, was leading them all in Harry Lauder songs. This was the Clyde, and Harry Lauder was the local hero, living just three miles away from here, and a dozen voices nearly drowned out the accordion with 'Roamin' in the Gloamin', and then 'I Love a Lassie'.

Catriona found an inch of space next to her father. He normally disliked Harry Lauder for the kitsch view of Scotland that he had touted around the world, but tonight he applauded Uncle Charlie as the song came to an end.

'Are you having a good time?' she asked him. He put his arm around her.

'They're a good crowd, *a' ghràidh*,' he answered. 'It's not the same as home, but these are good people.'

It was a bad time for nostalgia. Jim had sent them a telegram, carefully planned to arrive at Christmas, but with a message wishing them all the best when the new year came. '1942 will take us one step forward,' he'd written, 'and we'll keep taking steps until it is all over.' Their father had read it and cried.

Catriona tucked her hand under his arm. 'Have you sung them a Gaelic song?'

'Yes, with Sheila, a duet, and they loved it.'

'So they should. You always did sing beautifully together. Will you do another one for me?'

'Oh, I'm not sure. They're rather enjoying all singing together at the moment, and the people down here don't know the Gaelic songs. Won't you sing? You know some sweet songs in English, and your mother always loved them.'

She didn't want him thinking about her mother. 'No thanks, *Daidí*. I'm dropping on my feet, and need to go to my bed. Why don't you sing us a Burns song before I go? Everyone knows the words to them, and they can sing with you.'

The idea pleased him, and he sang them 'A Red, Red Rose', followed by two others. The crowd loved them, which brought a happy smile to his face. Catriona gave him a hug, and tiptoed away.

She found Aunt Sheila in the kitchen, cutting cake and making tea.

'You should have something to eat before you go to bed,' she told Catriona. 'You'll no' have eaten anything this evening, I'm supposing?' She looked over at the stove. 'Did you see the soup?'

Catriona nodded. 'I did, but do you know, I'm too tired to eat anything proper. Could I have some cake? It looks amazing.'

'Jessie Bailey brought it with her this evening. She's a wonderful baker, and she gets fresh eggs each week from her brother – you'll no' find any egg powder in *her* sponge.'

Sheila cut a large slice, and gave it to Catriona. 'Eat, child. Jessie will be delighted.'

Catriona sat at the kitchen table, and accepted a cup of tea to go with the cake. 'Dear Aunt,' she said. 'You're an angel.'

'Have you had a hard day? No, don't bother answering. It's written all over your face how tired you are.'

Catriona yawned. 'I am tired. It's because I'm not getting any time off, and it's a long day with all the travel.'

'Yes, that journey adds nearly two hours to your day.' Sheila looked hard at her. 'You're no' getting the kind of work you want to do either, are you?'

Catriona sighed. 'No, I'm just firefighting. But to do anything different I'd have to move away.'

'Well, and couldn't you?'

'With the Red Cross? Yes, I could, if I volunteered, but it would mean leaving Father.'

Sheila finished arranging the slices of cake on a plate, and began to load teacups on to a tray. 'Your father? Och, he'd be all right! Charlie has him so busy he doesn't have time to dwell on things like he used to.'

'You think so?'

'I know so, and he'll be even busier as the better weather comes in. It's a new year, Catriona. Why don't you see what you can find for yourself, and have done with that hospital, and that journey?'

Catriona examined the tea leaves in the bottom of her cup. What was it Jim had written? 1942 is another step forward. Why did she always need someone else to tell her to move forward? Her old teacher first, and now her aunt had told her, and she was right. Her father was what held her back, of course. But now that he was here with his sister, keeping Catriona by his side was a wish, rather than a necessity. She'd told him she wouldn't enlist, but she could work in any number of hospitals around Scotland.

The tea leaves gave her an answer. She could go away now.

Chapter Twelve

Alexandria, Spring

1942 is another step forward, he'd said. For Jim it meant taking little steps, cautious steps, and allowing himself to finger the right to happiness. For Fran it felt much simpler.

The regular bombings of Alexandria continued, but otherwise there was a strange lull in the fighting. Rommel was regrouping and taking in supplies, which could now freely cross the Mediterranean, for the Allies had no fleet left to stop them. The Allied army hunkered down around Tobruk, while at sea German U-boats cruised freely all along the coast, laying mines everywhere. There was no problem seeing Jim that spring, for what was left of the navy hardly ever left port.

So she did see him. They found wilderness things to do together, driving out to the sunset in the desert, or navigating the marshlands on Lake Mariut, to the west of Alexandria. Mariut, or Mareotis, as the Ancient Egyptians called it, was a haven of light and cool waters, full of reed beds and wading birds, where fishermen poled their boats into hidden villages tucked in behind the mudflats.

'Do you think the fish he is catching are direct descendants of the perch his ancestors fished in old Egypt?' Jim asked on one visit. They had pulled their boat up on to the shore, and were lying in the spring sunshine, quietly watching one of the fishermen through the reeds, a timeless figure in his long cotton robe, holding himself so still in his shallow craft that he didn't even disturb the nesting birds as he poled himself forward.

'Perhaps,' Fran answered. 'There was a lot more water in the lake in ancient times, and it was much fresher, they say, less brackish. It stretched westward almost to Libya, and to the east it was linked to the Nile by a canal. All around here were plantations of olive trees, and vineyards. They say Cleopatra had a garden here, and used to sail on the waters in her barge. Or her slaves did for her!'

Jim looked again at the fisherman. 'Well, somehow I don't think this fellow's forebears were slaves. He looks far too dignified.'

Fran smiled. 'The noble Egyptian! It's a lovely old image. I certainly don't think the boats have changed much since Ptolemy. But the lake is gradually drying up, and the stocks of fish are growing smaller, and of course the suburbs of Alexandria are growing. I always worry that one day the villages here will become part of the city, and these fishermen will disappear.'

'Oh no. To become yet more street traders, do you think? That would be tragic.'

At the end of the lake was Abu Sir, home to one of the wonders of the ancient world. Fran took Jim to the beach there, where you could swim in complete privacy in the arms of Ancient Egypt, with the Temple of Osiris and the ancient lighthouse watching over them from the ridge behind. Jim declared this his favourite place, saying that the sands were whiter even than at Mombasa, and the sea more aquamarine. 'The tropics with antiquity,' he called it, although the water temperature in March was far from tropical.

Fran and Jim picnicked on the beach, and Jim carried her into the water on his back, ignoring her howls as her legs hit the cold water.

'Nobody swims in March!' she protested.

'And why not? You've gone soft, miss, from living too long in the sun!'

'I'll have you know I was at boarding school in England!'

'Hah! In Devon! That's almost tropical compared with Scotland.'

'Yes, but you don't swim in the sea in Scotland!'

'Swim? What do you mean, we don't swim? Of course we do! As children we spent all summer swimming, and just a couple of years ago I went in at New Year.'

'Yes, but surely not every family has a history of madness?' Fran asked, then howled again as Jim dropped her bodily in the water.

They took George Blake with them, and Len, who had become a regular companion. In company, though, Jim was less free. In their private world under the sun together she could watch him grow wings, and loved it every time he gave her the gift of his smile, the deep laughter that would spring from him when he forgot his reserve, but when they were not alone Jim remembered the war.

It wasn't too bad with just these two easy-going friends on the beach, where nothing seemed too serious, and they explored the temple together, looking for traces of Cleopatra's tomb, and Jim was vociferous that he had found it. But when they were on show in Alexandria Jim could be almost stiff, with a multitude of personal guards in place. Any hint of congratulation from anyone about his conquest of Fran was enough to silence him. He didn't disengage, but he took a small step back.

'They're trying to crown us, like they did Tony and Lucie,' he said to her once, when some South African officers they knew raised a toast to them one night.

'Oh Jim, no! Tony and Lucie have nothing to do with it!' she answered him, frustrated. 'These men are a long way from home, there's a war on, the world is in turmoil. Can't you just accept that they're glad to see someone happy?'

He shrugged, but he had mentally drawn away.

He got annoyed too at the snobbery of Alexandria. 'I wasn't raised like you,' he told her, when she wanted to attend a party and he didn't. The picnics and lunches and cocktails of the privileged elite continued unabated here, but what to Fran seemed mostly like laudable defiance in the face of war, to Jim looked like overweening arrogance.

Acceptable defiance, to him, was going out to a restaurant, or to the Excelsior cabaret, where officers on leave from the front could let their hair down, and everyone was treated the same way. He wasn't against having fun, but he didn't like the private, exclusive gatherings that Fran had grown up with. And he was more comfortable with servicemen, Fran realised. They spoke the same language, and faced the same challenges. He had a tendency to undervalue men who weren't in the war.

'I think you just don't know how to appreciate people

who are different from you,' she said one time, when he had really annoyed her. 'I'm not saying you're rude. You behave like the perfect British officer, but you hold people away. Take last night, for example, when you were introduced to Salim Mansour. I could tell that you found him too ornate, too manicured, and you didn't like his urbane style, but Salim is a big patron of the arts, his wife is Belgian, he is a hugely well-travelled Lebanese, and they met at the Sorbonne, where he gained a first-class degree. He has a gift for making money, but he spends it on charitable causes, and it is said that his money and influence brought a group of dissident artists out of Syria last year when the Vichy regime there had arrested them for spying.'

She flicked a lock of hair off his forehead, and kissed where it had been. 'All I'm saying is that there is more to him and his kind than their expensive watches and fancy ties, if you would give yourself a chance to talk to them. The ones I have trouble with are the stiff old Brits in their colonial cliques, standing aloof from people like Salim because he's an Arab. You wouldn't want to become like them. The best of Alexandria is its cultural mix. The worst is its love of money, but my father's friends include all nationalities and all incomes. He raised me to understand all of them, but it's just that the rich throw more parties!'

'And your mother? Does she appreciate all the nationalities as much? And all the incomes?'

Fran tensed. Since Jim had started taking her out her mother had been meticulously polite to him, but a good deal of the warmth she had shown him as a pet patient had subsided. Jim was right to suspect that he wasn't quite rich enough or upper-class enough to appeal to Barbara

Trevillian as a suitor. What was charmingly original in a young Scottish officer visiting her home – his soft accent; his remote, rural childhood; his love of his culture – was less appealing now. Fran had challenged her one day, and her mother had said she didn't know what on earth Fran was talking about. Things had been a little frosty since.

'My mother isn't as cosmopolitan as my father,' Fran answered, defensively. 'She goes with him to his parties, and hosts his dinners, but she's happier in a smaller circle. It's as much an issue of confidence as anything. But she has a really kind heart, Jim, you know that.'

She looked at Jim and he seemed to read the appeal in her eyes. He drew her into his arms. 'I do know, don't worry. I'm not likely to forget how good she was to me when I was injured. She has her issues with people who are different from her, and it would seem that I do too. We're both stuck in our own prejudiced grooves. Bear with me, Fran, and I'll try to be as easy and comfortable in this society as your father is, and as you are.'

Lucie came out with them one night. She had emerged from isolation a few weeks ago, pale, but with a new hairstyle and lipstick, and had thrown herself into Alexandria's social life with a frenetic determination that wasn't always convincing. She dragged them dancing, and drank too much champagne, and danced indiscriminately with several army officers from a party of Australians on leave from the desert.

Jim had just returned from an ill-fated, rather desperate expedition to try to relieve Malta. Their diminished fleet had done a heroic job against all the odds, getting four hugely important supply ships safely into harbour. But a formation of German dive-bombers had flown in to Malta by the morning light and sunk all four supply ships before they could unload. The island was no better off, still starving slowly, and two thousand navy crew had returned to Alexandria grindingly frustrated.

'Tony should have been with you,' Lucie mourned, clinging hard to Jim as they left the nightclub.

He wrapped her coat around her shoulders, and guided her down the steps as they emerged into the blue dark of the blackout. 'Tony *was* with us, Lucie,' he answered gently. 'All of the men we've lost are always with us.'

She began to weep silently, letting the tears roll unchecked down her cheeks. 'I've had too much to drink. I promised *Maman* I wouldn't, too.' She took the handkerchief Jim offered her, and dabbed woefully at her face. 'When will it get easier, Jim?'

Fran saw Jim's face grip hard. 'I don't know, Lucie. We're all waiting.'

The air raid warning sirens sounded as their taxi drove them away from town. They dropped Lucie at her home, and Jim saw her to the door, then the taxi carried on to Fran's home.

'You be quick, *Khawaga*,' the taxi driver said, as he drew into the drive. 'Air raid coming.'

'You'll be fine, man,' was Jim's impatient response. 'I'll see the lady into her house.'

On the doorstep, Fran reached a hand up to his cheek. 'Stay over, Jim,' she urged. 'You're not on call tonight, and your room is always here. Then the driver can go straight home.'

Jim shook his head, and she saw the set of his jaw, and knew he had withdrawn again, stung by the memories of Tony.

'I'll get back to the base; I may be needed early tomorrow.' He took hold of her hand, and kissed first it and then her with a sudden fury. 'Will you call Lucie tomorrow?'

She nodded, and he kissed her again. 'Thank you, Fran. You're wonderful,' he said, and headed quickly back to the car.

CHAPTER THIRTEEN

Lucie was quiet and sobered the next morning on the phone. 'I'm sorry, Fran,' she said. 'I was going to be so good.'

Fran put a smile into her voice. 'You *were* good,' she assured her. 'In fact, I've never seen you dance so well. It was an excellent band too. Even Jim danced well, which is something I don't always see, believe me. He forgot all about his two left feet!'

Lucie laughed a little mechanically. 'Thanks, Fran. Are you at work? Would you like to meet for lunch?'

'Why not? It's Saturday, and a half-day. I'll meet you at Pastroudis, shall I?'

Lucie agreed, and Fran replaced the receiver, and turned without much enthusiasm to the pile of paper on her desk.

It didn't feel good to be British in Egypt just now. The British ambassador had humiliated King Farouk, and in doing so had alienated all of her father's Egyptian colleagues, even those who weren't great fans of their feckless king. The economy was in tatters, inflation soaring, the poor of

Cairo and Alexandria were marching against the shortages in the markets, and students were taking to the streets in support of Rommel.

And meanwhile the British GHQ in Cairo wanted the English language press to be nothing more than propagandists for them, and spewed out unconvincing stories that they wanted to see reported verbatim. Every victory they scored seemed to be overstated, and every strength of Rommel's army was downplayed. When the whole Allied army was actually deeply disillusioned by its own generals, and admired Rommel ten times more, toeing the British line became terribly frustrating.

It was certainly frustrating the two boys at the *Journal*. 'Have you heard this song, Miss Trevillian?' Asher said to her that morning, and began singing in a slightly wobbly tenor: '*Bissama Allah, oria alard Hitler.*'

Fran shook her head. 'In heaven Allah, on earth Hitler,' was what the words meant. It was a nasty song, which overtly linked the Islamic religion to the Nazis. It was anti-Jew, anti-liberal, pro-repression.

'Who sings that?' she asked. 'No one in Egypt, surely?'

'They are beginning to,' he answered. 'It comes from Palestine, of course, where else?'

Fran sighed. The Palestinians were turning against all Jews as the war went on. Too many Jews were being allowed into Palestine according to the Arabs; too few Jews were being allowed into Palestine according to the Jews. And no one else wanted Jewish refugees; Britain was refusing them, America was too. Reports were filtering out of Poland and Russia of mass killings of Jews, but nobody in the press was reporting it, which angered

Asher, and Fran felt all the weight of his youth, his ardour, but overriding all that, of the censors. 'Don't inflame' was the *Journal*'s mantra, and even if they wanted to, they wouldn't be allowed.

The general air of frustration at the *Journal* sent Fran looking for something meatier to report in this week's issue. There was a rumour coming in today that Admiral Cunningham was to be relieved of his command. Jim had said nothing about this, so it was to be assumed that it had been kept very secret until now. Or had Jim been instructed not to speak of it?

Whatever the case, if Cunningham was leaving that was serious news. 'ABC', as the navy called him, was an exacting, testy individual. He wasn't always popular, but he was respected and trusted. How could they be thinking of moving him at this critical time in the Mediterranean?

Fran got on the phone, hoping that one of her contacts might be willing to talk. By lunchtime she had gleaned that the news was correct, and the word was that he was being sent to some strategic post in Washington. Tim, her editor, hazarded that Churchill was sending him off deliberately. There were always rumours of rows between the two men, and ABC had been heard to mutter at a dinner once that the 'Great Man' was insufferable, interfering, and a bully.

This was a story that she wanted to write without censorship, either from Tim or from anyone else. Probably, by the time the paper came out the news would be official anyway, but Fran wanted an angle on the story, some detail, some dirt, if there was any!

So it was in combative form that she left the office that

lunchtime. It was probably just as well, she thought wryly, that it wasn't Jim she was meeting for lunch, but gentle, apolitical Lucie. She found her already seated at a small table set away from the window. She paused to say hello to some friends of her mother's, and then made her way to the table. Lucie stood up, and Fran kissed her on one cheek. She'd been pale last night, but today she looked completely washed out, even in the poor light of this dark corner.

'You look amazing, Fran,' she said, and her smile was as wan as her face. 'I don't know how you do it – a nightclub and then work in the morning, and still you radiate energy.'

Fran wondered how to respond. What could she say that would give Lucie back her own radiance? Nothing, of course; the answers weren't that easy. Anything you could say would be trite – you look wonderful yourself, you're doing so well – anything you said like that would be so evidently false.

She decided on a different tack completely, a very direct one, since she had Lucie to herself for once.

'How do you feel now, when you look back on your time with Tony? Do you wish it hadn't happened?'

Lucie didn't blink, but she took her time replying. 'No,' she answered, eventually. 'I just wish he hadn't died.'

'Do you mind me asking?'

'No,' Lucie repeated. 'What I mind is people pretending nothing has happened, as if we never existed.'

The waiter brought menus, and Lucie studied hers without interest. 'There are even people who tell me how fortunate it was that Tony and I weren't together for very long, that because of that I'll get over him quickly.' She closed the menu and put it down, and there was a touch of bitterness in her voice as she continued. 'It's as though it wasn't important. A trifling, passing affair.'

Fran nodded. She could imagine half of their acquaintances saying just that. Lucie was young, war took people away so fast, and of course it was true that Lucie would eventually get over her loss, and find someone else. But it was cruel and unjust to belittle that loss.

'I always thought that you and Tony were a *couple*,' she said. 'What I mean is, you fitted together, you matched, and you seemed to know it immediately.'

Lucie's face lit up. 'You saw that? It was what I felt, all along. You can't explain that to people. I can't even explain it to myself, because it wasn't that we were both musicians, or loved sport, or shared any special hobbies or anything. It wasn't that. We just seemed to understand each other. Do you know, I don't think we ever even disagreed – not once!'

She spoke with an animation completely at contrast with her earlier deflation. Tony, she explained, had wanted them to marry, so that if anything happened to him they would at least have had that experience. He'd gone too soon, she said, and her face dropped again, but then she launched into a eulogy about him that carried her through their main course.

Fran had never known her friend so volatile, so mercurial, and she was almost frightened to speak for fear that her mood could plunge again just as quickly. But talking about Tony seemed to act as a purge. When the waiter reappeared with the dessert menu Lucie took it and looked a question at Fran.

'I think we should, don't you? I've been rattling on, and it does me good to talk about Tony to those who are prepared to listen, but I'd like to hear about you over dessert. You know, Tony and I always thought that you and Jim would make a good couple.'

Fran bit her lip. 'Good, yes; a couple, not yet,' she answered.

They ordered ices, and coffee. 'Not a couple?' Lucie asked. 'I don't quite understand. Of course you're a couple.'

Fran sighed. 'Your relationship with Tony was built on hope and confidence. Mine with Jim is built on hesitation and fear.'

'But you don't know what fear is, Fran!'

'Not me. It's Jim. That's why I asked you if you regret what happened between you and Tony. Jim thinks you must, and he believes the risk of him being killed means he shouldn't be in a relationship. He *is* in one, and it matters to him, but he resists all the time.'

'You wouldn't have thought so to see him dancing yesterday.'

'No.' Fran nodded in acknowledgement. 'Nor would you think it when we sail together, or go to the beach, or the desert. He forgets himself, and his worries.'

'And you don't think he'll forget himself more as time goes by?'

'Perhaps. But there's so much danger around, it reminds him all the time.'

Lucie winced. 'And last night I reminded him again,' she said, remorsefully. 'Oh Fran, I'm so sorry! I wept all over him about Tony. Oh help, I have to stop drinking!'

Fran smiled at her. 'That was just for bravado,' she said. 'You're being very brave getting out and about again, but do you think maybe you're trying to do too much too soon?

It has only been three months, after all. Aren't evenings out a bit of a trial, sometimes?'

Lucie nodded. 'They are, but then sitting at home listening to the air raids is worse. *Maman* wants me to go out, and Daddy tells me it's what Tony would want.'

'He's probably right,' Fran acknowledged.

'Yes. Tony and I did talk about what would happen if he died, you know. We weren't completely unrealistic. Well I told you – that's why Tony wanted to get married. But the one thing he always did say was that I should get back out and find myself someone new if he wasn't here. He made me promise I wouldn't go into a nunnery!'

The waiter arrived with their ices, and Fran took up her spoon and waved it at Lucie. 'A nunnery is one thing, but forcing yourself to go out is another. Did you enjoy last night?'

Lucie shrugged, and shook her head rather forlornly. 'I didn't like what it did to me, either, or how I felt this morning.'

'Come to the beach with us, Lucie,' Fran said. 'Come out by day, when we're doing more active things, and maybe both you and Jim can do some forgetting.'

Lucie nodded. 'I'm doing more and more hospital work, too. I like being able to give something back to those boys from the front. It makes me feel closer to what mattered to Tony, and yet while I'm there I'm so busy I don't think about him. I'll be all right, Fran, honestly I will. I'm going to stop beating myself up, and find some balance.'

'You've always had the gift of balance,' Fran said.

That made Lucie wince again. 'Not recently. But it'll come back. Can I talk to Jim, Fran, and tell him how happy I am to have had my months with Tony? He has to understand that the broken me that you've been seeing isn't the real Lucie.'

'You haven't been broken.'

'No,' said Lucie. 'That was the wrong word. Being loved doesn't break anyone.'

CHAPTER FOURTEEN

Alexandria, May 1942

Jim had received another letter from his sister in Scotland, a letter that did more than anything else to bring a smile to his face. Catriona was working in a hospital for amputees, a residential centre of excellence where servicemen were given new limbs and taught to walk and move again. And she loved her new job.

Jim had had an airgraph a while ago from her, a short letter telling him this longer one was wending its way out by sea. So he had known about her move, but here was the description he craved of her life, and she had included a coloured postcard of the hospital, a grand old stately home given over to the nation. You could imagine battle-scarred amputees learning to live again there, and either walking or wheeling themselves through the beautiful grounds. The postcard showed rhododendrons and azaleas in flower all around a grand lawn, criss-crossed by paths that would invite you to stroll.

The letter was dated 27th February, and talked of bitter cold frosts, chilblains, and problems heating the wards, but Catriona's enthusiasm had come through undeterred. Now in the middle of May those azaleas and rhododendrons would genuinely be in flower, and with the postcard in their hands, Jim and Fran could imagine Catriona right there out on the lawn, working with her patients, hopefully in warm sunshine.

Fran was keenly regretting that her life when at home in Britain had been restricted to the English south coast, dividing her time between school and her father's various relatives. It all seemed so limited now, and she realised that she had never even travelled north of London. Jim told her not to be silly.

'My sister hasn't ever been outside Scotland, as far as I know. She knows her own world, and you know yours, plus you know all of this.' He waved a hand, encompassing the town around them.

But Fran felt it, nevertheless. She had found Islay on the map, at least, and she had unearthed an old guidebook to Scotland in the library, full of retouched plates of flowing rivers and majestic stags on mountainsides, and of kilted pipe bands parading in Edinburgh Castle. She showed it to Jim and he laughed.

'That's just the kind of book that gets published for the upper-class visitors who take in Edinburgh and then the Spey Valley for the fishing, and to shoot grouse,' he told her. 'People who think they are following in Queen Victoria's footsteps. Not so many of them make it across to the west coast. It's a touch more rugged our way!'

'You don't wear kilts or play the bagpipes?'

'Actually, we do. Islay has produced some very fine pipers. Some of them may even be in that picture!

But it's a very restricted view of what we do. It's the landowners' view. First, they forced the people off the land to make way for sheep and their hunting moors, and then they created this aristocratic view of Scotland. The Englishman's idyll.'

Fran raised an eyebrow. 'And what about you in a kilt? Would that be an Englishwoman's idyll?'

He grinned, and gestured at his legs, golden brown below his knee-length shorts. 'It's all about the calves,' he said. 'Mine are a bit hairy, but there's lots of good muscle there, wouldn't you say? Skinny fellows look daft in kilts, because their legs look like sticks, and they don't have any hips to sit the kilt on. It needs to swing!'

'You mean you have to be built like a rugby player?'

He shook his head complacently. 'Not at all, *a'ghràidh*. You just have to be built like me!'

They were eating cheap Lebanese mezze at a favourite restaurant, under a parasol in the shade. Jim had just come back from a week-long radar update course in Haifa, and he had the red patches he always got when he'd had time out in the sun. He never seemed to 'weather' so that the sun no longer burnt. He just lost a bit more skin, and grew more freckles, and his eyes became bluer, if that was possible.

Fran was desperately relieved that he had been on his course this week, and not on one of the three destroyers that had tried to get to Malta. The idea was to try to put some kind of defensive fleet back onto the island, but it had failed, and only one of the destroyers had survived.

Jim had been safe, and for now no one was talking of taking him away from Alexandria. If they based him on Malta, when would she ever see him again? She pushed her share of *kibbeh* towards him, as though by feeding him she could keep him in Alex.

This evening she was going to introduce him to Michael. Her brother hadn't been home for nearly a year, but tonight he would be in Alexandria, bringing some papers or something from Cairo. Her mother had spent two days preparing his room, but had been prevented from ordering up his favourite dinner at home.

'He'd rather we all went to Baudrot,' her father had said, and her mother had reluctantly agreed.

So Fran made her way straight from work that evening along the Rue Fouad to Baudrot, Alexandria's premier restaurant. Fran always felt the restaurant encapsulated her father's style: chic, cosmopolitan, assured, and with that little buzz that ensured that it was never boring. It had been her brother's favourite place from childhood, and his haunt from the moment he started working with his father and had his own money.

Fran was met at the door by the Levantine maître d'hotel, a man who had known her for many years.

'Miss Trevillian!' he said in confiding tones, as he gestured to a waiter to take her hat. 'Your parents and your brother are already here. How happy you must be to have your brother at home! I've placed you in the alcove so that you can be quite private.'

She thanked him, and followed him into the restaurant, where he pointed out their table. Her brother and mother had their heads together, but as Fran approached Michael looked up.

'Fran!' He leapt to his feet and took her in his arms.

He hadn't changed. She'd wondered whether the war

would have aged him, but he was the same joyful, slightly puckish character he had always been, with perhaps more sinew, more wiry lines, but the same very youthful quality of mobility and life.

You could see why he would have been adopted by his senior officers. Michael made friends with everyone, and was infinitely adaptable, socially adept. He had never wanted to go to university, and had put his undeniable character strengths to good use in his father's brokerage. His language skills, like Fran's, just went with his Alexandrian life, but they were undoubtedly of major use in the desert army.

Fran sat next to him, on the other side from her mother, and gave him her broadest grin.

'Smart uniform, squibling! Is it meant to make you look grown-up?' She used her childhood name for him: the squibling, her little firecracker.

He smiled. 'The stripes are the only things that stop the squaddies calling me "boy",' he admitted.

Michael was two years younger than her, five years younger than Jim. The same age as young Len, thought Fran. Towards Len she always felt protective, but she had never felt the need to protect her brother. They had sparred on very level terms all their lives.

They ate together, just the four of them as so many times before. 'If you knew what awful tripe we get to eat out at camp!' Michael said, as he dug into lobster thermidor. 'I try not to think too often about Baudrot!'

He'd had a night in Cairo on his way to Alexandria. 'A decent hotel, a proper bed, and a long bath,' he sighed happily. 'You wouldn't believe how wonderful that is. The sand in the desert gets into your underwear, and rubs its way into every possible orifice.'

He shot an amused look at his mother, who had raised an eyebrow. 'Ears and nostrils, and under your nails,' he added quickly. 'That kind of thing.' Fran choked.

'There is new underwear waiting at home for you,' their mother said, unruffled. 'I thought it was maybe the only thing you could take back with you.'

Alan Trevillian laughed. 'That and half a case of food and drink your mother has made up for you,' he added. 'You'll tell us tomorrow what you can actually carry with you, Michael.'

'Decent soap,' was Michael's answer. 'Food yes, drink no – we have a mess, and don't miss out on drink. I've brought an empty suitcase on purpose to take back some decent eats for the boys.'

Jim joined them for coffee. He'd refused an invitation for dinner, saying that Michael had only one night with his family, and the least that he could do was to give them an hour or two on their own. He'd been right, Fran thought, and it was a delicate touch. But at least Jim had accepted to be introduced. Fran wanted Michael to know and value Jim in the way her father did, and as the two young men started talking it was clear all was going to be fine.

They'd steered clear of talking about the war until Jim's arrival, but with two men in uniform at the table the subject couldn't be avoided. The whole world was waiting for Rommel to make a move, and German broadcasts were assuring Egypt that Rommel would soon be at the Nile Delta, telling the Allied troops that there was nothing they could do, and the people of Malta that the Royal Navy would never reach them. The BBC told a different story, but the two officers here this evening knew that the war was on the brink.

'Can you hold Rommel, do you think?' Jim asked.

Michael shrugged. 'We know where he is, what reinforcements he has, what he's capable of, and he knows everything about us, I'll swear – all our positions, our equipment, our supply situation, the lot. All of our communications leak like sieves, on both sides. My fear is that this acts in his favour rather than ours. He's the one who's going to act, and he can make his strategy in his own time, with all the information at his disposal. All we can do is prepare as best we can and wait. Will we hold him? I think so, because we must. But all this bombast and arrogance, which says we're going to walk all over him, is dangerous. We need to be more afraid, I think, if we're to take on Rommel properly.'

Barbara Trevillian looked very grave, and Alan gestured to a waiter to refresh her liqueur. The men took more cognac, and Alan offered cigarettes.

'You fellows in the navy have good information, don't you, about what the Germans and Italians are doing?' he asked.

Jim hesitated, and Fran wondered whether he was supposed to talk about intelligence. Eventually what he said was nothing secret, though, just a dire summary of what should be evident to the world.

'Knowing enemy movements is the most useless thing in the world if you are powerless to stop him,' he said. 'Michael is right about us underestimating Rommel. Every time we have so-called "beaten" him, it has been because he was cut off from his supplies. It has been our main strength, the fact that fuel and equipment for our forces come safely up from Suez, whereas Rommel's Afrika Korps depended on supplies coming over the Mediterranean. While our ships could take out their convoys Rommel was always stretched. But now we can't do anything. It's down to you guys, Michael.'

A mood settled over the table, not of gloom, but of quiet reflection. Fran lifted her glass and studied the light from the candle through the amber liquid, reflecting little darts of light through the crystal. They would win, she thought. It was inconceivable that they wouldn't. There was just too much to lose. She looked over at her brother.

Please don't be part of what we lose, squibling, she thought, but kept her thoughts to herself.

Chapter Fifteen

Scotland, May 1942

Catriona had been working with a casualty from Egypt that morning, a veteran of the desert war. Granted he was a soldier, not a navy man, but just being with him brought Jim closer too.

'He works out of Alexandria?' Corporal Wilson asked her. 'That's a tricky game. Damned skilled stuff, hemmed in on all sides. They supported us all along the Libyan coast, shelling Jerry from the sea, and they took a lot of hits themselves.'

He'd been at the hospital for some time now. He was one of the lucky ones, if you could call them that. When he arrived here he had lost his leg below the knee, and had a worrying wound that had ripped through bone and muscle in his upper arm. A surgeon in the field had made a clean amputation where the leg had been blasted away, and had made a valiant effort to save the arm, setting the bone and removing shrapnel. The nurses on the long journey home on the hospital ship had then kept everything clean, had dressed wounds, and had given him precious rest, wheeling his bed out onto the decks to feel the sun and the wind. But it had been nearly three months since Wilson had moved anywhere of his own accord, or had been completely out of pain.

He carried a stoical face, covering all his fears with endless supplies of stories and jokes, keeping some especially colourful ones for the orderlies, but when you caught him off guard he looked weary and grim. Like most of their arrivals, fears for the future gnawed at him.

Catriona watched with respect as the visiting surgeon, who had himself been at the front in the First World War, took men like Wilson in hand. Colonel Mount understood the hardship and horror they'd been through, and spoke to them in terms that were matter-of-fact but reassuring – a man's compassion, without flowers. He would talk them through their injuries, placidly telling them what exactly was going to happen to them.

He would operate on Wilson's leg, he explained to him, cutting away a bit to leave him with a good stump onto which they could fit an artificial limb. You could see Wilson's fear at first, then you saw it dissipate as the explanation continued.

'You'll keep your knee, and the stump will give you good control of your artificial leg. Once you're up and about even your friends won't know you've been injured.'

And the arm? Was he going to lose his arm? Wilson wanted to know. Colonel Mount shook his head.

'No, no, we'll save your arm, don't worry.'

'But I can barely move it! It's practically useless,' Wilson fretted.

'Ah yes, but you can use it a bit, can't you? And that

is where Sister MacNeill here comes in. I need to have another look at it while I have you on the operating table, and I'm confident we'll get the whole thing looking a bit more normal inside. Then once the wound is knitting together again, Sister will work with you to get your muscles moving. You'll have exercises to do, and gradually you'll see that your arm gets stronger. You may never be an arm-wrestler or a weightlifter, but you won't be an invalid. Believe me, Corporal Wilson, you've come out of all of this pretty well!'

Two months later Wilson was learning to use his wasted arm, and waiting for his stump to be ready for a limb. He couldn't use crutches yet, so they couldn't send him home to rest, but his family came to visit, a young, scared-looking wife and two small boys who looked around them with awed eyes, wary of the father they hadn't seen for nearly two years. The hospital found them a room, and they stayed for several days, and by the end of their visit the boys were climbing all over their father's wheelchair, and retrieving his bowls during a competition on the lawn. Catriona found time to talk with the wife, a girl from Manchester, and to reassure her that her husband would lead what qualified in these times as a normal life. There was always time at Dunmore to talk, and it was part of the healing process.

There were many cases less able than him, men who would never walk again, men who had lost both hands, men with their minds blasted away, who looked vacantly at Catriona as she tried to get their limbs moving.

These were the saddest cases, but the spirit at Dunmore was amazing, and the men found endless ways to fill long hours. An assistant nurse from the Voluntary Aid Detachment reported helping a patient one day into the latrines, only to find a row of men, all balancing on one leg, engaged in a competition to see which one could urinate highest up the wall. And the pranks one could play with bedpans seemed endless. But unlike other places where Catriona had worked, even Matron didn't get angry, or at least not for long. There was no shouting at Dunmore, only results.

It was a place you could care about. It wasn't that she hadn't cared about the patients at the infirmary, but there hadn't been the same stout heart among the struggling staff, or the time you needed to invest in patient recovery. Dunmore was a place of long-term care, where patients left, then returned for more education, and you followed them right through as they picked up their lives.

Not that she'd seen anyone fully rehabilitated for now. Catriona had only been here for just over three months. She was among the newest of the quickly expanding staff, sharing a room in one of the hastily constructed huts that housed the growing needs of Dunmore. Her roommate had been there only a month or two longer than her, and was an Edinburgh girl called Celia, with an endless fascination for the latest films. Together they went at least once a week to the cinema, avoiding by common consent the goriest films of war in favour of comedies with Arthur Askey and Alastair Sim, or the Hollywood romances of Ingrid Bergman and Rita Hayworth.

And whenever she could, Catriona made the two-hour journey back by train to see her father. She tried to go every two or three weeks, and would bring back her aunt's home baking to share with the staff. It was a satisfying life, and one that felt complete.

It would have been hard to say when she began to feel an itch for more. It had a lot to do with working with Duncan McIlroy. Duncan was a sculptor, a man of Glasgow, who dressed like a bohemian, but who had in fact been an army officer, one of Dunmore's first patients in the war. He had lost his hand at Dunkirk, and said that the greatest stroke of luck he'd had was that a place like Dunmore was on his doorstep.

With his artificial hand he'd thought about giving up sculpture, he said, and had dabbled in painting instead.

'I was useless, though,' he said, with his characteristic laugh, 'and it soon dawned on me that all I knew how to do was either fight or sculpt, and I was pretty poor at fighting.'

So he learnt to use his new hand to hold and steady, his real hand to do all the feeling, the shaping, the carving. The way he curved that hand around an emerging head carved from a piece of dead applewood cut down in the grounds reminded Catriona of how you would touch a child. He would often close his eyes just to feel.

And now part of his mission was to show the patients at Dunmore that you could still work with wood and other materials without two good hands. He came three times a week to give classes, and had a fully kitted out workshop, which had been paid for by subscription from the Glasgow art world.

Men who pre-war had worked in factories, or as labourers, or even, in one case, down the mines, laid all their prejudices against sculpture aside when they entered Duncan's workshop. He insisted on first names, swore like a trooper, and refused to wear a tie, but he made them think about contour and lines, and to work with apple, and cedar, and great lumps of oak.

'He understands wood,' one of them told Catriona one day. 'I've been a joiner all my life, and was thinking that I'd have to give that up completely, without my hand. But I had an uncle who was a cabinetmaker, which is finer work and lighter. My mother still has one of his tables, a beautiful piece. I'm beginning to think I could do the same.'

'You've got a convert,' Catriona told Duncan.

'I'd like to think I've got more than one,' he replied, mitigating his words with a self-deprecating smile. 'They won't all go on to work with their hands, but I hope at least they'll realise that fine work is within their grasp.'

'You give them confidence. It's the best follow-on I could imagine to the work I do. I can get their muscles working, but you give them a reason to work.'

'Why, it's very sweet of you to say so, Sister. Where does your lovely accent come from, if I may ask?'

Catriona blushed. 'From Islay,' she answered.

'Islay! I love Islay. I did some work before the war for the Morrisons of Islay House. Do you know Morrison?'

She shook her head. 'Know the laird? Socially you mean? No, the Morrisons are well above my touch, I'm afraid.'

'An obscene amount of money!' Duncan agreed. 'They're the kind of people who think they have a God-given right to run this country, without any feeling for ordinary people. But the house is beautiful, and they wanted a piece for the garden, so a colleague from the Glasgow School of Art recommended me. A Socialist can work for a Conservative, he told me, and I was pretty short of money at the time!'

It struck Catriona that she didn't know any socialists, or hadn't done until now. She had come across some strident trade unionists among her patients in Glasgow when she was a student, but none of them spoke like Duncan McIlroy. Thankfully it seemed that he found her island roots as mysterious as she found his artistic world intriguing, and over the spring months she spent increasing amounts of time in his workshop, drinking tea by the little coal stove, and studying the students' work, and his own finer pieces on the shelves above.

The place was becoming an irresistible draw, and she found herself looking forward to Duncan McIlroy's thrice-weekly visits with an uncustomary impatience.

Chapter Sixteen

It had been the end of April before Duncan invited her out. They took the train into Glasgow, and went to a jazz bar Catriona had never seen, in a backstreet behind the station. It was a fug of smoke, with a tiny dance floor, a long bar, and seating arranged around the wall into booths of leather benches. This wasn't swing, or the big band jazz Catriona was used to, but an intimate style of music, with a female singer whose seduction, quite clearly, was aimed wholly at the men.

A few couples were dancing, but Duncan led the way directly to the bar, where two men were stood drinking beer. They looked at Catriona appreciatively.

'Duncan, you old devil, how are you doing?' one asked. 'And, who,' he continued, 'is this luscious young lady?'

Catriona was glad of the darkened room as she blushed slightly. Luscious wasn't a word in her family's vocabulary. But if she ignored the choice of word, wasn't the sentiment well due? She had taken trouble over her appearance this evening. She had piled her long blonde hair high on her head, and wore her highest heels with a slender blue dress and her newest coat. The dress was one she'd had before the war, which she'd shortened to match current styles, but she'd done the job well, she knew, and she was aware of looking good. Take the compliment, she chided herself, and gave the man her most composed smile.

'Don't drink the beer, McIlroy, it's dreadful,' the other man told Duncan, as he drew a stool forward for Catriona. Duncan gave her a questioning glance.

'What shall we drink, Catriona? Cocktails? It would go well with the music, don't you think?'

She shrugged rather helplessly. 'Whatever you suggest,' she said. 'I don't know much about cocktails. Aren't they rather expensive?'

'Yes, but when you're broke, being a bit more broke doesn't matter! And anyway, it gives our barman here the opportunity to disguise whatever rubbish he has in stock, and to present it as something drinkable.'

There was a daredevil flippancy about the men that was very attractive, and which made a change from the long daily routine of Catriona's life. She let herself go into their irreverent conversation. One of the men was a lecturer at the university, a historian who had been too old for the draft. The other, Catriona realised with a jolt, was a conscientious objector. Something must have shown in her face when he mentioned it, because Duncan quickly took her to task.

'Don't start thinking David has chosen the easy option,' he warned her. 'He has chest problems, anyway, and probably could have escaped the draft on medical grounds, but as it is he's been put to work in a shipyard, in a welding unit, which plays havoc with his lungs. He could have had it a lot easier. I know loads of military men who have lives twice as easy as David's.'

The man called David gave a rueful smile, and gestured towards Duncan's artificial hand. 'I'm not sure military life is that easy, given the evidence we have of Duncan's injury,' he said, 'but it's nice of him to defend me. I couldn't have faced killing anyone, Miss MacNeill, but I am contributing to defending us from Hitler in the best way I can. There are more people fighting this war as civilians than there are in any of the forces. But I don't want an easy ride, and I can put up with what the job does to my lungs. It's my choice. And anyway, they could have sent me down the mines!'

He was right, Catriona realised. She herself was fighting this war as a civilian, and never doubted her contribution. And working in the shipyards was a reserved occupation. It was just thinking of Jim that made her blink. He'd given up his own reserved occupation in order to enlist, and he was her model.

'What did you do before?' she asked, curiously.

'Part-time artist, part-time shoe salesman! I'm still an artist, and I'm doing a series of paintings of the shipyard, which I think are rather good. It's the men I like to paint. They wear their labour in every line of their faces. They're so bloody tough.'

'That's how I feel about the patients at the hospital,' Catriona commented. 'They carry so much with them, and their faces speak to you, but they have a kind of tough pragmatism that you just want to honour.'

David nodded approvingly. 'Duncan has spoken about that. He's done a head of a man based on one of your patients, which is one of the finest things I've seen.'

144

Catriona looked at Duncan, curious. She hadn't seen any head in his workshop.

'It isn't actually any one person's head,' he explained. 'I've been doing it at home, away from the men, and it's an amalgam of the impressions they leave with me. But I wouldn't bring it to Dunmore, because I wouldn't want them to recognise any part of themselves, or to think I'd been fingering their souls without permission.'

Catriona could only look again. There was even more to Duncan than she had suspected. She picked up her glass and sipped at the cocktail, which tasted fruity, but with a powerful kick. Nights out for her in the past had involved either the cinema or dancing, and she had never spent an evening like this, in conversation with three free-thinking men in a smoky bar. It was not a part of her education that her family had provided for.

She spent a lot of the evening just listening, as the conversation ranged over threatened strikes, banned of course during wartime, and the fate of a theatre production that the authorities had considered not uplifting enough to be staged at this difficult time of the conflict.

The singer continued to croon, but the men ignored her until much later, when the others left, and Duncan pulled Catriona onto the dance floor. She had drunk far more than she could remember doing before. She'd kept up with the men, more or less, and her legs felt shaky under her. The music was slow, Duncan's grasp of her was tight, and she leant on him for support. The very closeness was intoxicating. She could feel his artificial hand hard on her back, a strange sensation, while the other hand curved around her just below the waist. He could have been sculpting her, and she loved it.

'Did *you* ever think about refusing the draft?' she asked into his shoulder. She'd wanted to ask the question all evening.

He nuzzled her hair, and tightened his grip. 'No, I was too cowardly,' he murmured, bizarrely. Then he laughed, a little drunkenly. 'My father was a sergeant in the First World War, and even though he admitted it was hellish, he was incredibly proud. He wanted his son to be an officer in his old regiment, and I complied. And then – bingo.' He held up his artificial hand.

The bitterness in his voice was unmistakeable, and Catriona was silenced.

'Just dance, sweet Sister,' he said, after a moment, and she let herself go into his arms.

They had other evenings out. Duncan took her to the Grosvenor Picture Theatre to see *The Hunchback of Notre Dame*, which made a change from the romance and comedy she watched with her roommate. He took her back to the jazz bar, where there were always two or three artistic types spending their money. And they found a tea shop nearby Dunmore where they could go after they finished work, and where for sixpence you had a sweet bun and strong, sugary tea. Catriona was endlessly surprised by the man's sweet tooth.

Duncan was beguiling, with his probing intelligence and endless creativity. He was planning an exhibition of the patients' work at Dunmore, and the adeptness with which he coaxed the Dunmore fundraisers to find extra cash for his work was breathtaking. Catriona felt like a plodder in comparison as she went about her regular daily work.

From three afternoons a week at Dunmore Duncan was now working four, and he would appear at lunchtime in his workshop, ahead of the afternoon session, and wait for Catriona. When the unsettled weather allowed, she would wangle sandwiches out of the hospital kitchen, and they would find somewhere private to eat them in the grounds. There was a laburnum tree in full bloom, which drew them time and time again, and they would spread a rug underneath it and forget work for a while as they ate.

The news from Egypt was disturbing. At the beginning of June, Rommel's army attacked the Allies and within a week he had taken Bir Hakeim, and was advancing on Tobruk. The BBC continued to spout confidence, but every day brought more bad news.

No news came of the navy, and what they were doing, and Catriona fretted for Jim. She would have liked to talk about her fears, but Duncan was not the right person to talk to. He could be wonderful with the servicemen he worked with, but he talked about their futures and their abilities, never about their pasts, and references to the ongoing struggle were met with a nod, then a slick change of subject.

What had happened to Duncan at Dunkirk? It seemed as though Catriona was never to know. The subject was off-limits, as was his private life, his family. Catriona told him about her father, the loss of her mother, the home from home that was Aunt Sheila's.

'That's nice for you,' was his answer, and then he made her laugh with an anecdote about his lecturer friend and a mad student. She accepted his evasions for some time, but eventually she had to ask him a direct question.

'Are your bar friends really more important to you than your family?' she demanded, irritated one lunchtime by just such an anecdote.

He gave her his most charismatic smile. 'My "bar friends", as you call them, are people who choose me for what I am, for my outstanding intellect and my unrivalled charm. As you do, sweet Catriona! The existentialists will tell you we all remake ourselves every day by what we do and who we are. We don't need roots, we just need now.' He pulled her to him, and the last thing she saw before he kissed her was that impish smile.

He challenged every conventional belief instilled in Catriona over twenty-two years on Islay. Instinctively she felt he was wrong, that your roots did matter, like they mattered to the laburnum tree, or else where would the flowers come from? She had the feeling with Duncan that he constantly slipped through her fingers. He set her nerves tingling, and he was making the sun shine in this month of June, but she held back from giving herself to him completely, for with Duncan you never felt quite sure.

Tobruk fell, after all. The BBC announced it as a strategic defeat, but gravely reported huge losses among our troops. Rommel would advance on Egypt now, and the BBC spoke of our troops retreating to regroup and prepare for battle again.

And meanwhile news came out of a convoy getting through to Malta from Gibraltar, bringing fuel and supplies to the beleaguered island. There wasn't much on the wireless about it, but in the newspapers Catriona found more details. There had been two convoys trying to get to Malta, one from Gibraltar in the west, the other from Alexandria in the east. The one from Gibraltar had suffered huge losses, and only two of its six merchant supply ships had reached the island. The one from the east hadn't made it at all. Four of the merchant ships had been sunk, and four of the navy ships which had been guarding them, and others had been badly damaged. The remainder of the fleet had returned to Alexandria, the news said. She could only imagine in what state they had arrived.

She didn't know the name of the ship Jim served on, though she knew it was a destroyer. Did they change ships all the time? He never talked about such things in his letters, but three of the lost ships had been destroyers.

Catriona refused an evening out with Duncan. If she couldn't talk about Jim, then she couldn't go. The staff and patients at Dunmore stood close, though, and she buried herself in her work.

And then the call came from Aunt Sheila. She must have gone up to the big house she worked for in order to make the call. An orderly came into the ward, and tapped Catriona gently on the shoulder.

'There's a call for you, Sister, in Matron's office. She said to come and find you immediately.'

He gave her a compassionate look, which filled her with dread, and she ran for the office. Matron ushered her inside.

'It's not as bad as you think, Sister,' she said, handing her the receiver, and then she eased herself out of the office, and closed the door behind her.

'Catriona?' Aunt Sheila's voice came through rather disembodied.

'What is it? What has happened?' Catriona blurted, without preamble.

'It's Jim, *a' ghràidh*. He has been wounded, badly wounded. We got a telegram this morning.'

It must be serious. They wouldn't send a telegram for a flesh wound. He must be critical.

'They haven't said what's wrong with him,' Aunt Sheila said, answering Catriona's unspoken question. 'All the telegram says is that he has been seriously injured.' Her voice rose uncontrollably. 'How could they do that, Catriona? To send us such a brief sentence, with no detail? You can imagine how your father is – he's beside himself with worry, and doesn't know what to do.'

'I'll come immediately,' Catriona said. 'Don't worry, Aunt Sheila, Jim is made of strong stuff. Tell Father I'm on my way, and that Jim will be all right.'

She wanted so badly to believe it, and above all she had to make her father believe it. There would be another telegram, she was sure, as soon as there was any better news to give them, or . . . but there she stopped thinking. Jim would get better.

How could she get more news? She thought of all the names he'd given her of fellow officers in Alexandria. George Blake was a name that came to mind. Was there any way she could get hold of a naval officer at a base in Egypt? You would go through the same channels as you did to reach Jim, surely? Her pulse racing, she went off to ask Colonel Mount.

CHAPTER SEVENTEEN

Alexandria, June 1942

It was only after the fleet set sail that Fran had known something huge was happening. They left by night, of course, the resident fleet from Alexandria harbour, plus a mass of ships brought up from India and even further afield to make a major convoy.

The jungle drums had reached the paper a few days before that a large number of ships had passed through the Suez Canal, but the ships had headed east for Haifa, keeping out of the way, and no one had suspected that such a major attempt to reach Malta was being planned.

All eyes were on the desert instead, where the news was terrible. Rommel had outsmarted the Allies completely, skirting round their supposedly impregnable defences to attack them from behind. The word was that the Allied army was being torn apart.

The first of the defensive posts, Bir Hakeim, had been held to the last by those same Free French soldiers who had battled so angrily with the Vichy French in the streets of Alexandria. Alongside them fought rebel Italians and

Germans who were also fighting for freedom against their own governments, and they must have fought desperately, Fran thought.

Soon after the post fell, German radio announced that the soldiers they had captured did not qualify to be treated as prisoners of war. God only knew what was happening to those poor men now.

Confused reports came back from the desert after that, all bad, and many Alexandrians began to pack their bags. Rommel was coming this way, said half the population. No, our boys still hold Tobruk, and Rommel will outstrip himself, said the rest. And meanwhile, whether you wanted to leave or not, you got no sleep, for the air raids pounded merry hell not only out of the harbour but also out of the city every night. What were the Germans trying to do? Fran wondered. Were the bombings just intended to exhaust the citizenry, to prepare them for submission? If this continued much longer there would be no city left for Rommel to conquer.

Fran was sitting wearily in her office, looking at the latest communiqués from the front, when George Blake came with the news about Jim. He took command of her panic, took her car keys from her, and drove her to the hospital, repeating again and again the same reassurances.

'He's not dead, Fran. He's made of stern stuff. You know Jim, he has enough guts to see him through anything.'

Fran said nothing, her eyes fixed on the road, railing silently against the lunchtime traffic that made their journey so slow.

If the hospital had been busy when Fran was last here in December, now it was shambolic, overrun with casualties, with all but the most critical cases being moved out to the tented medical camps outside the town. In the corridors Fran and George made way for men on crutches hobbling out to waiting transports. But as Fran stood over his narrow bed it was clear there would be no moving Jim.

He lay frighteningly immobile, propped slightly to one side, his head, torso and arms swathed in bandages. His eyes were covered too, and all that showed that he was alive was the slow rattle of his breathing, a rattle that terrified Fran because it sounded so shallow. She had heard talk of a 'death rattle', and as she looked down at Jim's broken body tears sprang to her eyes.

'What happened to him?' she breathed, and it was the first time she had spoken since they left the office.

'He was on the *Airedale*,' Blake told her. 'It was attacked by more aircraft than I've ever seen in one go, German and Italian, and they planted so many torpedoes in her hull that she had to be evacuated. Two of our ships took off all the crew, but there were a lot of wounded, especially in the radar room, which went on fire.'

'So these are burns?' she gasped, her eyes fixed on the mass of bandages.

'I don't think so, Fran, or at least not all are. You need to speak to a doctor to get the full story.'

He pushed her gently into a chair and went off to find someone. It was a naval doctor who came back with him, and it was clear Blake had told a mini lie about who she was.

'Miss Trevillian,' the doctor said, 'I'm told that Lieutenant MacNeill here is your fiancé. I'm very sorry that you should have to see him looking like this.'

He gave her a smile, which Fran thought sympathetic but not pitying. She leapt at this with a flame of hope.

'He looks bad, yes, but is he all right, underneath all this?' she asked.

He drew up a chair, and sat down facing her. He gave her the same compassionate smile. 'I think to say he is all right would be to underestimate his situation. Lieutenant MacNeill has a number of serious injuries, and it is perhaps the accumulation of them which makes his case a little complex. The blast in the radar room smashed his ribs, and left him with a messy chest wound. That is why you see him lying on his side. We have cleaned out his wounds and placed a tube, which is working right now to drain away any fluids.' He pointed to a tube that came out from underneath the heavy bandaging on the chest, and adjusted one of the bandages a little so that it sat more firmly.

He continued in the same measured tones. 'He also has head injuries, including a cracked skull, and there we don't actually yet know the extent of any damage. Don't get too upset that we have partially covered his eyes. That is just because his eyebrows were scorched. His sight is not under threat.'

His matter-of-fact manner helped Fran, and she drank in the information. But she was still terrified.

'Lieutenant Blake told me there might be burns,' she ventured.

'There are indeed burns,' he answered, simply. 'They are not severe, though, and they are mainly on his arms and shoulders. His face was largely untouched, which is a blessing.'

'So is your main worry the head injuries?'

He nodded. 'Yes. The chest wounds could cause complications, it must be said, but we have a lot of experience of handling them. Head injuries are more challenging, for many reasons. From where the skull trauma occurred, which is low down by the ear, I am cautiously optimistic that there won't be long-term brain damage, but I must repeat, that is a very cautious estimate.'

A nurse came over and spoke his name at that moment, and he looked up, nodded, then excused himself and moved away.

'You don't expect him to die?' Fran managed, before he left.

He looked at her rather gravely. 'I am not God, Miss Trevillian, to be able to tell you that. Your fiancé is very ill, and the next few days will be critical. But if I were forced to give an answer, I would say that he has a decent chance.'

Poor George Blake was mortified that he had been in service in Alexandria for the same amount of time as Jim, but had so far come through unscathed, while Jim had been injured twice, this time so seriously. If he could, he would have spent his days by Jim's bed, but not only would the navy not have allowed it, the hospital wouldn't either.

Fran had to accept visiting just twice a day to sit over the sleeping figure. He never moved. It would have been so much better had he moved. She didn't know whether he was in some kind of coma because of the head injuries, or whether his sleep was drug-induced. She had no more time with the doctor, and the overstretched nurses found time to tell her daily that he 'was as well as could be expected'.

And she didn't know what to do about Jim's family.

George found an old letter from Jim's sister, which had the address where she and her father were staying in Scotland, and Fran hesitated over writing to them. They would have had a telegram from the War Office, she was sure, that would have worried them terribly, but what could she tell them that was any better? The likelihood was that Jim would never again be the same man who had left them last year. The thought made her feel sick, and she would squeeze her hands tight until they hurt, just to stop the tears.

She trudged on through each day, turning up at the office because she didn't know what else to do. On 22nd June, just five days after her first visit to Jim, the *Journal's* staff sat together to listen to German radio as they announced that Rommel had finally taken Tobruk.

'It has for so long been a thorn in the flesh of German troops on the road to Egypt, but Tobruk is now ours,' the German announcer said, in weighty tones that emphasised the magnitude of the moment.

Tobruk, Churchill's declared unbreachable fortress, that so many had lost their lives for, holding it for months under siege last year. And now it was gone, in the most humiliating of losses. In one day, 35,000 Allied troops had surrendered, and what was left of the army had retreated over the border into Egypt. The Allies, the broadcasters said, were in complete disorder, and the Afrika Korps was chasing hard on their heels. 'Where is your army, Churchill?' crowed the Germans. 'Where are the generals who can stand against the Desert Fox? Now we will stretch our net from one end of the Mediterranean to another.'

Asher was distraught. 'What's the matter with you British?' he yelled at Fran. 'All your useless propaganda telling the world how wonderful you are! Now nothing stands between Rommel and Alexandria.'

Fran didn't know what to say to him. 'We still have an army,' she countered. 'It's not as though Rommel has a clear stroll across the desert in front of him. They'll stop him, Asher.'

'Just as they've stopped him so far, perhaps? I have to see my father!' Asher flung out of the office in tears.

'I'll go after him,' Sami said. 'God knows what his family will do now. They'll need to leave, if those damned fascists are on their way.'

He ran out and down the stairs, and the rest of the staff looked at each other helplessly.

'We need to check all the news lines,' Fran said. 'It's all very well for the Germans to claim they've got our troops on the run, but surely we will regroup and form a new position?'

Where was Michael, she wondered, in all this fray? Had he been at Tobruk? Or had he made it to Egypt? Was he a prisoner now, or would he be joining Jim among the casualties at the hospital? Everywhere were questions, and there were no answers, or at least not the answers you would want to hear.

'Are we going to be able to bring out an issue this week?' she asked Tim. Poor Tim looked scruffier than ever, the sleeves of his unironed shirt rolled up, and his tie pulled loose. He had taken off the eye shades that always made him look so like an American pressman from the 1930s, and was leaning back in his chair.

'Of course we are!' was his response. 'Alexandria still stands, and until some Kraut closes this office my newspaper is still the best in town. We've got more news than ever, and I'm going to write the front page myself! Yannick, get on the phone to the Bourse and see what they're saying, and Maria, can you find out which of our outside reporters are still in town and ask them to get out on their beats? We need some live material of our own, not just what the press associations are sending us.'

This made Fran smile for the first time that day. 'Defiant to the end, huh, Tim? Well, you'd better get working on the editorial now, because it won't be me who writes it.'

'You're quitting?'

'No, not at all. I'm staying with you, but I also have a very sick man in my life. You can do the writing, since you're so fired up, and I'll add what I can. I'm struggling to share your enthusiasm, and the prospect of Rommel walking all over Alexandria makes my blood run cold. And right now, I have an appointment by a hospital bed.'

CHAPTER EIGHTEEN

George and Len were both sitting by Jim's bed when Fran arrived, talking in low voices. As Fran approached, a nurse stopped, and Fran thought she might be about to object to the number of visitors, but then she moved away, too busy to remonstrate.

'He has been awake,' Blake told Fran. 'I got that out of the sister.'

'When?' Fran felt a surge of excitement.

'I don't know, and I don't think it was for long, but from what she told me, the chances are that Jim isn't actually completely out of it all the time. He has his eyes closed, but he can maybe hear us. Whether he can understand, or knows who we are, is a different matter.'

The bandages around Jim's face had been pulled back now so that you could see his eyes properly. He had no eyebrows, and the skin of his forehead had been burnt, Fran knew. But his eyes were untouched, the delicate skin of his eyelids only slightly pinker than normal.

Fran crept closer to the bed, and stroked the skin at

the top of his cheek, staying away from the bandages.

'Jim?' she said. 'Jim, my darling, you're going to be fine, the doctor told me. Stay asleep, my precious, and let all of this heal. We're all here, and we're batting for you.'

She could have sworn his hand twitched, and she reached out to hold it, taking care not to disturb the tube that was taped to his wrist.

'He's going to be all right,' she announced, and for just this moment was sure it was true. But he must surely be better sleeping, under all the painkillers, rather than moving at all. She held his hand steady to still him, and when he didn't move again she turned to George and Len.

'Did you have trouble coming here today?' she asked. 'Aren't you on full alert at the base?'

George nodded. 'Some of us have had specific permission to come here. There are a good number of our men here, and Len and I offered to check on several of them. But I'm not sure we'll be able to come again. We're waiting for orders.'

'What's happening, George?' she said, and couldn't keep the anguish from her voice. 'What the hell's happening? Do you have any information? Is Rommel on his way here?'

He shook his head. 'I wish I knew. You probably have better sources of information than simple sailors like Len and me here. Our men will be re-forming new positions right now, you can be sure of that, but they've taken one hell of a pounding. It makes me mad to think how they've been let down by the army commanders. Our generals are a bunch of incompetents, if you ask me, and one decision after another has been wrong. Our losses have been terrible.'

Fran flinched. 'My brother is out there.'

'I know.' His hand came out to cover hers, and Len pulled his chair in closer. She could feel their support in waves.

She turned back to Jim to hide her tears, and stroked his cheek again. 'Jim will get better, though,' she said, willing herself to believe it. 'Jim is going to get well.'

George fished in his pocket and brought out a piece of paper. 'This arrived for me at the base, Fran. I wanted to show you.'

Fran took it from him. It was a telegram, and as she read it her eyes widened. It had been sent to George Blake from Jim's sister Catriona in Scotland, and had been stamped received at the base yesterday. The text was brief.

'We would be grateful for any information about Lieutenant James MacNeill's medical condition. Yours, Catriona MacNeill.'

'Jim must have mentioned you in his letters to his family, George,' Fran marvelled. 'How wonderful that his sister found you. Have you answered her?'

George shook his head. 'I wanted to see Jim again first. Today I think there is at least something positive that can be put in a telegram. If I get time I'll write an airgraph as well, with more detail, and get it sent away so that she receives it next week, to follow the telegram. I can give her more details in an airgraph.'

Fran nodded. The short letters, which could be photographed and sent quickly by air to Britain, were available only to service personnel.

'It would be great if you could,' she said. 'Jim's sister is a nurse, and will understand his case better than we do, I don't doubt. I've been thinking about his family. If I had news that my brother was wounded, I would be desperate to know more.'

'So, if George sends a telegram today, will you send another with more news later, if things get better?' It was Len who asked this time. 'In case we're out at sea?'

Fran choked a little. 'Of course,' she said. 'God, this is awful, isn't it?' She gestured to the room around her, with its desperately ill men. 'Will the Germans treat these patients properly, do you think, if they reach Alexandria?'

'Jerry doesn't harm wounded men,' George Blake assured her. 'But don't despair, Fran. I may have had a rant about our generals, but our boys will dig in now, don't you worry. Rommel won't make it to Alex.'

Fran tried to believe in that utterance over the next few days, as angry queues of desperate customers formed around the banks trying to withdraw their money, and all trains out of the city were packed with families heading for Cairo and Luxor, from where they could flee to the Sudan, or Ethiopia, Palestine or Syria.

The Allied forces were being driven back further and further, they heard, and at the newspaper they followed both the official and the unofficial news, knowing that by the time the next paper came out, the situation would probably look dramatically different from anything they could write.

Asher and his family had gone. Sami said they were going just as far as Luxor for now, if they could get there. They had shuttered up their house, leaving behind everything except what they could carry.

'We took their most valuable possessions for them, to

keep them safe in our house,' Sami told them at the office. 'They'll come back, I know they will. They'll be able to come back soon.'

At home, Fran's mother had begun to fray under the stress of not knowing what was happening to Michael. She lost her temper with Fran one day, when she came back from the hospital talking about Jim.

'Enough talking about Jim MacNeill,' she ordered her. 'What about your own brother?'

Fran took a shocked step backwards. 'But, Mummy, Michael isn't injured!'

'How do you know? He could be out there in need of us right now. Or he could be . . .' Her face contorted and she couldn't continue. It was Fran's father who intervened.

'Until we hear anything there is no bad news,' he said, very gently. 'And you know Michael has nine lives. Babs, my dear, you brought Jim MacNeill home here yourself in December. You care about every injured serviceman, I know you do, and you know how much Jim means to Fran.'

Barbara Trevillian burst into tears. 'And what if he's a vegetable? Do you still want Fran to cling on to him then?'

Fran felt the blood leaving her face. 'How could you be so cruel?' she asked simply, and left the room.

Her father found her later. 'Your mother has gone for a rest,' he told her. 'She's been working at the railway station all day in the heat, serving food and tea to the troops, and she has overstrained herself. Don't mind her, chick. She does care about Jim, I promise you.'

Fran bit her lip. 'Does she?' she muttered, sotto voce, and turned her head away. Her father's arm came round her.

'He's making progress, you told me.'

163

She leant in to him. 'Yes, but it's terribly slow. What if he does end up with permanent damage, Daddy?'

'Then you'll do what's right for you and for him, chick. But Jim MacNeill is made of sterner stuff than that.'

The two of them ate together, and he made her drink some brandy, and the following day she went back to the hospital, and Alan Trevillian went to work as normal at the stock exchange, where entire fortunes were being lost by fleeing investors. A pale-looking Barbara Trevillian went back to serving tea, the very act of which had become an emblem of defiance. One thing was agreed: the Trevillians were not leaving Alexandria. Fran would not leave Jim, and Barbara would not leave when each day might bring news of her son.

Lucie phoned Fran one morning to tell her that she, her mother and her little sister were among those planning to leave. 'Daddy is insisting on it,' she said, 'because he thinks women and girls will be in danger if Rommel's men reach here. *Maman* has agreed because of us. We're going to Luxor, but if things blow over we'll be back very soon. I hate leaving when I know you can't. It seems so cowardly, but there's no arguing with my father when he's in this mood.'

'Good luck with the trains,' Fran joked, rather hollowly.

At home they now took the air raids more seriously, and had moved downstairs to sleep, Fran and her mother carefully polite to each other, each with the stress lines etching themselves deeper under their eyes. No bombs hit Ramleh suburb, but as Fran drove through the area around the Western Harbour, with its bombed-out buildings, and the sandbags built up around those that hadn't yet been hit, she felt that Alexandria would never be the same again.

On Monday 29th June, Rommel overran the port of Mersa Matruh. Again, in the office they listened to the news, and this time it was the British-controlled Egyptian radio broadcasts that were the most frightening. 'Egypt will be defended to the last,' one broadcaster announced in portentous tones.

And just as people were digesting the news, as the announcer had hardly finished speaking, the biggest shock hit the city. Its citizens watched stunned as the whole Mediterranean fleet sailed out of the harbour, and headed east towards Haifa, running away from the danger zone. The British had abandoned Alexandria.

Fran sat by Jim's bedside, and hoped he hadn't heard any news. He was frequently awake now, gazing out at the ward with eyes that didn't seem fully to understand what was happening to him. He could talk too, short, painful little sentences, although his speech was frighteningly slow and slurred. None of his bandages had yet come off, but the doctor told Fran that his chest wound was particularly gratifying.

'It has drained very well,' he said, with satisfaction, 'and now the wound can close, and the ribs can knit together. His breathing is still painful, and of course there is severe bruising, but bruising won't kill him.'

To Fran he seemed to be in too much pain. Every movement made his face muscles contract, and the bandages on his arms and shoulders seemed to chafe him terribly.

'Are your arms sore?' she asked him, in the slow, clear voice she had learnt to use. He nodded.

But none of the medical staff worried about pain. One day, a kind nurse tried to allay her fears.

'None of his pain comes from anything we don't already know about, miss, and it will get better with time. It's all just about healing now.'

'The burns on his arms must be dreadful,' Fran fretted. 'He gets no peace from them.'

'What matters more now, though, is his mind,' the nurse said.

'His mind is fine,' Fran protested. 'The doctor told me that he could make a full recovery.'

Nobody was going to tell her that Jim had permanent damage to his brain. That was unthinkable. All Jim needed was time to recover, and to be out of this pain. And he mustn't know that his fleet, his closest friends, had sailed away from Alexandria and left him here with only the wounded for company.

CHAPTER NINETEEN

Alexandria, 1st July

It was 1st July and Rommel was sixty-six miles away from Alexandria. Fran met her father in the afternoon outside the Bourse, where trading was suspended, and they walked together arm in arm to the harbour and looked east, where just a mile away a pall of smoke hung over the British Consulate.

The building wasn't on fire, this was a bonfire that had been lit in the grounds, and the consular staff were burning all their documents. Fran had driven along there in the morning to check out the strange stories coming in to the newspaper, and had found heavy-duty vehicles waiting to take the consul and his staff and families away as soon as the burning fest was over.

'So where are you all going?' she asked Nigel Marsh, the deputy consul, a stiff, formal man who had arrived in Alexandria just a year before. 'Are you heading for Cairo?'

Marsh shook his head. 'Oh no, there's no point in that. They're evacuating the embassy staff from Cairo too. No, we'll get a ferry across from Port Said and head directly along the coast towards Jerusalem.'

'All of you?' she asked. 'You're not just talking about women and children, then?'

He looked a bit shamefaced, and pulled himself rather straighter. 'Instructions are to evacuate completely, in case we diplomats should be caught and interrogated,' he told her. 'I admire those of you who are staying, but you civilians should be all right, after all.'

'And you don't think you're giving completely the wrong message? You, and the navy, and all of the other officials who are running away? The Afrika Korps aren't in Alex yet, and we need to make local people believe that they won't make it.'

He gave her a reproving look. 'The navy left because of the increased level of bombardment. I am sure you would not, any more than the rest of us, wish the Allies to lose our fleet, Miss Trevillian. They haven't gone far, and they'll be bombarding Rommel soon, you mark my words.' He moved away from her physically, as though to remove himself from her questioning. 'I think to talk about us "running away" is irresponsible, young lady, and I do hope you won't consider printing any such inflammatory words. We are taking sensible precautions, that's all.'

As he spoke, a grey flake of ash landed on his nose, and he brushed it away impatiently. The ash was falling like gentle snow all around them. Fran had already heard some wag today calling this 'Ash Wednesday'.

She thanked the deputy consul rather ironically for his assistance, and drove back along the Corniche and into town. The streets were deserted, and businesses all closed up. It was quiet as Alexandria never was. Fran stopped

outside a row of shops, where
notices had been pinned to the
Rommel' they said. It was chilling
hardly be surprised. Who would blame
welcoming in Rommel? His propaganda
more effective than ours, Fran thought, with
bonfire and the highly obvious escape vehic ... y
visible to the whole of the city.

The hospital when she got there was strangely calm. A
nurse was taking Jim's temperature, and took the time to
talk for a moment.

'It doesn't seem as busy as usual in the arrivals area,'
Fran commented.

'No,' the nurse acknowledged, with a frown. 'We had
an isolation truck arrive this morning, with some dysentery
and malaria cases, but other than that we haven't had
a convoy. They must all be going to the desert hospitals
over by Suez.'

'But isn't this the hospital for the most serious cases?'
Fran asked.

The nurse nodded. 'For those who normally can't travel
as far as Suez, yes. But right now, those hospitals are safer,
aren't they? The further away the better!'

She fixed a deliberate smile on her face for Jim as she
spoke again.

'We'll be all right, though, won't we, Lieutenant? I can't
see Rommel making it to Alexandria, can you?'

Jim shook his head, slowly, but with marginally more
force, Fran thought, than yesterday. 'See off the bugger!'
he muttered, and it seemed to Fran that his words were less
slurred too. 'Want a gun!' he continued.

169

…e smiled again. 'I don't think it will come to … Rommel's stuck out in the desert, and in any case, we're not too much in favour of guns in the hospital! But I'm glad to see you still have the fighting spirit. I'll leave you with your fiancée now.'

She left them, and Fran slid into the chair by Jim, and took his hand. 'She's very attractive, your nurse,' she said, grinning at him. 'They seem to keep the best-looking nurses for the naval wards.'

He smiled back, and she could have sworn the little movement was almost natural, unlike the sort of rictus he had managed some days before. 'Fiancée,' he said. 'I like that.'

Fran blushed. 'That was George. He introduced me as your fiancée so that they would give me full access to you when you first came in here.'

He said nothing for a while, and then commented, even more slowly, as though it needed thinking about. 'Haven't seen George.'

'I think he's quite busy,' Fran replied, using the same bright tones the nurse had used. 'There's a war on, you know!' She mirrored the deputy consul's own words. 'He's probably out bombarding Rommel's troops from the sea.'

'Rommel's close.' The words were an affirmation rather than a question. Fran nodded.

'He's in Egypt, but they say Auchinleck's forces have stopped him for now.'

'Auchinleck's a donkey.'

Fran grinned. 'I'm glad to see that your navy prejudices are as solid as ever, sweetheart.'

She saw him looking at the water glass by the bed, and

raised it to his lips. He drank awkwardly, and some of the water dribbled down his chin. She wiped it away, and then kissed him, because she didn't want him to think about it. She looked into his eyes for a moment, and he seemed to understand far too much. He managed another smile, and her heart tumbled over.

She talked on about inconsequentials for a while, and lingered until his eyes gradually closed. Tiptoeing away she found her fingers were again digging little pits in her hands. The Afrika Korps mustn't march into this hospital. They would throw all these men out into tents to make way for their own casualties.

With her father that afternoon she stood by the harbour and watched as yet more ash fell nearby them, coming this time from outside the Admiralty buildings.

'I thought the staff of Naval Command had all left when the fleet sailed away, all apart from the guards, and they won't have entrusted the guards to burn their precious documents, surely?' she commented.

Alan Trevillian shrugged. 'They probably sent some bureaucrats down especially from Cairo. I don't suppose they'll hang around for long! I can't see why everything has to be burnt. Couldn't they lay on a vehicle to take the stuff away? There must be an awful lot of documents, that's all I can say, and they're going to be missing a lot of information if they beat Rommel, and all come back here to start again!'

He shook his head, and smiled at his daughter. 'So tell me, chick, is Tim still furiously writing text for the next edition of the paper?'

'Oh yes! He's as sure as ever that the enemy is going to get trounced. The latest intelligence we've received says that Rommel has stopped at El Alamein, goodness knows why, when there's nothing there, but Tim will have us believe it's because he has outrun himself, and exhausted his troops, and that he has no more supplies.'

Her father snorted. 'He can get supplies in through Tobruk now, any time he wants them. It's his new German port, just over the border. He'll be regrouping and bringing in fuel, that's all.'

Fran looked at him in surprise. 'You sound as though you think he is unstoppable,' she said. 'I've never heard you talk like this before.'

'No, I don't think he's unstoppable. But we've all heard too much facile rubbish about how easily we're going to beat Rommel. That kind of reporting has been rather discredited, don't you think?'

Fran smiled. 'It's Tim's way of coping. He doesn't want any of us to run away.'

'Well there he's right. It's a strange kind of behaviour, this scramble to leave. Either you bundle everything you can into a car and head out into the desert, leaving your house to be taken over and all your principal belongings to be looted if Jerry moves in, or you stay here and take your chances, and the same may happen anyway. But you've avoided the panic, the disruption, and you've shown some belief to the locals.'

'We could all be interned, though,' Fran mused.

'We could.' Her father tucked her arm more tightly into his. 'If it hadn't been for Jim, I'd have tried to get you and your mother away, I think. But as it is we'll sit it out, shall we, and trust that our boys still have something to show Rommel? Shall we go and see if the Cecil Hotel is still serving a decent beer?'

The shops all around the square were closed and shuttered, but the Cecil Hotel remained open, and was doing a brisker trade than ever. There were a number of army officers in the bar, passing through Alexandria on official business, which no one was discussing, but whatever it was didn't seem to be stopping them from downing cold beers.

'Do you know we stopped a bunch of Eyetie women at the city checkpoint?' one was telling the bartender. 'They were heading out into the desert to look for Rommel, carrying gifts of cigarettes and fruit! Bloody fools! We should have interned them alongside their husbands. You can never trust an Italian.'

'The gyppos are just as bad,' another replied. 'They're all plotting against us, and just waiting for Rommel to arrive to sell us all down the river. You'd better watch out, you fellows who've decided to stay, or they'll be murdering you in your beds.'

Alan Trevillian remonstrated. 'That's the kind of talk that's creating panic,' he said. 'Don't you army fellows want things to stay calm in the city?'

'I'm not sure that what we say has really changed anything much,' the first officer commented drily. 'The panic is on anyway. I heard that someone was killed this morning in the crush to get on the Cairo train.'

'Yes, and the queues for the banks have reached a mile long. There'll be deaths there soon too, you mark my words.'

Fran left her father arguing with the officers and crept out into the silent streets, heading for the post office. She didn't know if it would be open, but the banks were, and the post office should be. She wanted to send a telegram to Jim's family while she still could.

Jim was so much better, and no one any longer talked about a risk to his life. The War Office would presumably send a telegram to update the family at some point, but it wouldn't be done while the current panic continued. And if Rommel did reach Alexandria, Fran herself might not be able to visit Jim. That thought was the biggest among all her worries.

But for now she wanted to tell the MacNeills that Jim had smiled, and was talking, and that his chest was healing. Don't think about the long-term future, and all the possible permanent damage – today was all that counted. She heaved a sigh of relief when the post office was open, and went inside to compose a message of comfort, from Fran Trevillian, a friend.

CHAPTER TWENTY

Scotland, June 1942

The sun was emerging weakly after yet another downpour as Catriona and her uncle crossed the Clyde on the ferry. For once Catriona gave little attention to the constant movements of boats and ships around them. More personal concerns weighed on her, for her father had left home yesterday morning and hadn't returned.

Catriona had arrived home two nights ago to find him sunk in misery.

'Jim's gone,' he said to her again and again, and nothing she could say would make him believe otherwise. He insisted that the telegram they had received, in all its baldness, was just a prelude to the next telegram, which would tell them that Jim was dead.

He wasn't too wrong, really, because they all knew of other cases where the first telegram was followed by a final one telling of the person's death. Only serious injury warranted a telegram at all, and it was exactly that baldness, that lack of information in the telegram that was so difficult. It left you in a frightened vacuum.

Catriona told him what she'd done. 'I've sent a telegram myself,' she said. 'Remember the man Jim mentioned a couple of times in his letters, his friend George Blake? He's a lieutenant operating out of Alexandria, the same as Jim. Well Colonel Mount helped me to send him a telegram asking for more information than the War Office have given us. If we knew more we might be less afraid.'

'If your telegram gets to him!' her father objected. 'It depends on the man being alive, and from what I can see he's more likely to be dead, or injured like Jim. Have you read the newspapers? They lost most of their ships in that stupid convoy. What are they thinking of, sending our men into such danger? They should hang the commanders, that's what they should do. Bunch o' numpties!'

Nothing Catriona could say would persuade him that most of the ships escorting the convoy had actually returned safely to Alexandria, and that there was no reason to assume, just because Jim had been wounded, that all of his fellow officers had too. Fergus just continued to shake his head, and Catriona began to doubt herself whether her telegram would ever reach Lieutenant Blake. Her father's mood was catching.

The following morning Fergus took himself off early from the house. 'I've a wee bit of shopping to do,' he muttered. 'And I need to get the heels done on these shoes.'

'Are you going across on the ferry to Gourock? Would you like me to come with you?' Catriona had asked, but he had simply shaken his head. It was clear that he wanted to get away, to be alone, and she understood his restlessness. So she let him go, and he didn't come home.

'He'll be having a drink before catching the ferry,' Uncle

Charlie had reassured his wife that evening. 'You know how he hates the fact that there are no pubs here in Kilcreggan. He'll be back before dark, you wait and see.'

But it got dark late in June, and by the time the sky did begin to darken the ferry had made its last journey for the day, without Fergus. Catriona cycled to the ferry pier to wait for it, hoping to see her father's steady gait coming down the ramp, and when he wasn't among the passengers she was tempted to hop on to the ferry for its return journey. But then she would have no way of getting back to Kilcreggan, and what could she do on her own to look for him over in Gourock? She cycled back to the house and spent a sleepless night tossing and turning, wondering if her father had just missed the ferry and was now stuck outside for the night. She worried more about her father than about Jim, strangely, but then Fergus was here, and her concern. Jim was in other people's hands.

Aunt Sheila the next morning was wringing her hands, imagining Fergus lying in a hospital bed. Uncle Charlie made an effort to reassure her.

'He'll be in a bar,' he told her. 'We'll find him in a bar.'

Catriona tried not to think at all, but she and Uncle Charlie set off to find him, and the first places they would try were the pubs of Gourock.

There were American troopships tied up by the quayside in Gourock. The word was that GIs were swarming all over England and Scotland, training, preparing, not yet in action. Strangely, though, the Americans in Kilcreggan had quietly disappeared. They'd finished building their facilities, and then sometime during the spring they had left, just as they had arrived, without any explanation at all. The Royal

177

Navy had taken their place at Rosneath House now, and they didn't issue the same invitations to drinks and dinner at the mess. The stir the Americans had created in the small community hadn't always been welcome, but their lavish, genial generosity was sorely missed! Catriona wondered occasionally what had happened to Captain Ron Martin, her dancing partner.

She wasn't thinking about him this morning, though. She followed Uncle Charlie as he led her up the slipway from the ferry, scanning from right to left in the vain hope that her father might be in the queue about to board for the return journey. She didn't know the pubs of Gourock. They hadn't been on her radar on her journeys to the infirmary when she worked here.

'Do you know where we might find him?' she asked her uncle.

He laughed. 'I worked on the river for long enough, Catriona, and I knew all the bars in those days! Don't start worrying too much about your father. A drunk man is usually looked after, and he is most likely in the nearest bar to the ferry.'

Was that so? Catriona looked at her teetotal uncle with new eyes. His words gave a dimension to him that she had never imagined. She followed him meekly up to the main street.

They found her father immediately, just as Uncle Charlie had predicted, in the bar directly in front of the ferry terminal. The Victoria Bar, it was called, and Catriona had passed it every day on her way to work without ever registering it. At ten in the morning it was almost empty, with just three or four men leaning against one small corner of a huge circular bar. The place stank of stale smoke and stale beer, and it made Catriona want to leave the door open to the fresh air outside.

Fergus MacNeill was hunched over a glass of colourless liquid, which might have been gin. He didn't even look up as Uncle Charlie approached him. Catriona hung back, her gut wrenching as he finally turned and she saw his sunken eyes and lack of expression. He certainly wasn't thinking about Jim right now, or indeed about anything, and in that measure you could say his trip to Gourock had succeeded in its object. It was Catriona who felt the grief, more and more the longer she looked at him.

Uncle Charlie kept his face cheerful as he put an arm around his brother-in-law. 'Hey there, big man,' he said, in kindly tones. 'You didn't quite make it to the ferry last night!'

Fergus looked at him impassively, his face not so much vacant as unreadable. He didn't say a word, and it was left to Uncle Charlie to continue.

'We've a chicken pie cooking for lunch today as a special treat for your lassie here. I can't remember the last time we ate chicken! You'll no' want to miss that, Fergus, or your daughter's visit either, will you?' He picked up Fergus's jacket, which was hanging from a chair behind him, and then he gestured to Catriona to come forward. She put her arms around her father's neck, and kissed his forehead.

'Shall we go, *Daidi*?'

She took the jacket and helped her father to put it on. Uncle Charlie pulled some change from his pocket and paid the barman, an older man who could have been the landlord.

'We took care o' him,' the barman said. 'Ye could see

something bad had happened tae him. Joe here gave him a bed for the night when we could nae find out where he lived.'

Catriona smiled at him, her eyes welling up. 'Thank you,' she said. 'Thank you so much.'

The landlord shook his head. 'No need tae thank us, miss.' He was looking at Uncle Charlie as he continued, 'You'll get him haem now.'

Charlie nodded, and reached out a hand to put some money also in the hand of the man called Joe, who had saved Fergus from sleeping rough last night. He murmured his thanks, and Joe nodded, without speaking. None of the men at the bar had spoken in the entire time they'd been in the pub, and Catriona wondered whether they would be staying there all day, and whether more lively company would come in at lunchtime. And would there ever be any women? It felt somehow unlikely. She tucked her arm into her father's, and led him out of this rather sad, sombre male world into the sunlight outside.

Nobody spoke to her father about his truancy. The fresh breeze on the ferry seemed to wake Fergus up, and he mumbled his thanks as they helped him into Archie's taxi at Kilcreggan pier. Back at home Aunt Sheila took charge, and disappeared with her brother and a pan of hot water, coming back to announce that he'd washed and shaved, and that she'd left him to sleep for a while.

'We'll have lunch a little late,' she suggested, 'so that Fergus can be with us. We need something cheerful on the wireless, and no news of the war while he's around, mind. You've to say nothing! I've hidden the newspaper as well.'

She looked over at Catriona. 'How long can you stay

away from work, *a' ghràidh*? I think it would help your father if you can be around for a wee while.'

Catriona nodded. 'Matron told me to stay away for as long as I need to, and Colonel Mount was even more forceful. I have patients I need to work with, but others can fill in for me for a few days. I want to wait and see if we get a reply to my telegram. It would change everything if we got some better news.'

'Had you heard that they are converting Knockderry Castle into a hospital? The word among the people working there is that they are preparing it to be a recuperation centre for the Free French navy.'

Catriona held up a hand as though to ward off her aunt. The castle was just a short hop up the road from Aunt Sheila's, and had been requisitioned some time ago, though until now nobody had been sure for what purpose.

'Aunt Sheila, I've just begun the most worthwhile job I could wish for. I'm not going to leave it to come back here and live. I've already taken care to work no more than a couple of hours away, so that I can come home regularly. Don't force me to come back to some small backwater hospital where all I'll see are rest and recuperation cases!'

'Whisht, Catriona! Who is suggesting that? But don't some of these small hospitals have visiting staff? The doctors visit, don't they? And maybe they would be interested in a visiting physical therapist. Your father commented last time you were here that we never see you for more than a night if we're lucky, and very often it's just for the day, once a fortnight or more. I was only wondering whether you could continue where you are, but spend a day a week at Knockderry, so that you're here for a couple of nights?'

Catriona blinked. Aunt Sheila seemed to have been making substantial plans in her absence. Right now, her aunt was twisting her hands slowly in that way she had when she was feeling hesitant or unsure, and she must have built herself up to talk to Catriona about this.

Catriona took her time over answering. 'You're rather making assumptions there, don't you think, Aunt Sheila? I suppose that if the Red Cross are going to be running Knockderry, then there's a possibility I could be split between the two, because they are the people who employ me at Dunmore. But we don't know what kind of patients will be here, whether they'll have physical therapy needs, or anything! And I don't know whether my bosses at Dunmore will feel that I can do my job there in fewer days. It's hard to imagine, somehow. I'm stretched at work already, and the hospital is expanding.'

Aunt Sheila persisted, in apologetic tones. 'Will you enquire, at least, *a' ghràidh*? This escapade of your father's has frightened me, I'll not hide it from you, and even if Jim does get fully better, I know how much Fergus has been pining for you since you left us.'

Catriona could feel the claws of her family reclaiming her and pulling her back home, and a feeling of claustrophobia swept over her. But she knew that wasn't what her aunt wanted to do. Sheila knew how much she was asking, she understood Catriona's desire to do proper work, in a serious post, and it was just her fears for her brother that were playing on her.

Fergus was frail, almost like Catriona's nerve-damaged patients were frail. Was it just losing her mother that had done this to him, or losing his home, or the fear of losing Jim? Or had the whisky weakened him, so that now whenever there was a problem he needed a prop? Well, she understood patients who needed a prop, didn't she?

'Let's wait,' she answered her aunt, eventually. 'Let's see if any news comes, and then how Father is, and then, if we think it's necessary, I promise you that at least I'll ask.'

Chapter Twenty-One

Scotland, July 1942

Who was Frances Trevillian? The question tickled Catriona's interest all the while that she worried about Jim.

There had been news from Alexandria, and gradually the family had begun to believe that Jim was going to recover. His friend Lieutenant Blake had sent a telegram, which they'd received just one day after Fergus had been found in the Victoria Bar. It had been brief, but said much more than the War Office had done. Jim had head and chest injuries, but was stable in hospital, and an airgraph would follow.

The airgraph had duly arrived, and had given more detail of Jim's wounds, and Catriona was able to reassure her father that the injuries didn't sound life-threatening. She kept to herself all the risks she could read through the bland sentences, and just hoped that no complications would arise to turn her words into a lie.

The woman called Frances Trevillian's telegram had arrived just a few days later, and this time the news was definitely better. When her father read that Jim was awake and talking, Catriona could see belief returning. Catriona was interested in what the telegram didn't say. There was no mention of moving Jim, which gave an indication of how serious his injuries must have been. Her brother had suffered severe trauma, and recovery would no doubt be slow.

Her biggest fear, which she discussed with Charlie and Sheila, but never with her father, was that he might be taken prisoner. Nobody could be unaware of that danger, as Rommel marched into Egypt, and the grievous, desperate battle of El Alamein began, but in Fergus's mind his son was already on a ship home, heading back round the Cape as so many of Catriona's patients had done, to be brought to Britain for recuperation. He hardly followed the Egypt campaign now that his son was not in combat.

Catriona, though, followed it daily. The Allied defensive position at El Alamein seemed to be holding, and the news told of reinforcements being shipped in, new troops, new tanks, new artillery, with all the supplies they needed to defeat Rommel and send him back to Libya. All the news was bullish, and you could almost hear Churchill talking behind every broadcast.

Back at work, though, she heard more measured responses. Her desert campaigner from Manchester, Corporal Wilson, was near to going home now, and Catriona was helping him to master walking naturally on his artificial leg. They walked through the grounds of Dunmore together, testing his control on tarmac and on softer grass. And they spent time working on his arm muscles. Catriona wanted him to leave here with the maximum possible use of that all-important arm, which still hung by his side, with no real lifting strength. He could use his hands well, and had a good grip, but his upper arm muscles would never fully recover. He had learnt to prop his arm on the table when seated, and then he looked normal, handling a knife and fork just like anyone else, and even writing quite normally.

Catriona took him down to Duncan's workshop, to see what he might be able to do in the way of woodwork, and Duncan taught him to hold a huge lump of wood tucked in the crook of his bad arm, while he used his good arm to fashion it. It was interesting how Duncan deliberately chose the biggest piece of wood he could, as though to prove to Wilson what he could do with that damaged arm, rather than what he couldn't do. Detailed, tabletop work would have been too easy, Catriona thought.

With Corporal Wilson she talked about what was happening in Egypt. Four weeks after Jim had been injured, in mid July, the battle of El Alamein was still raging, and the newspapers reported that Rommel had no more supplies, and no more fuel, and that the Allies now had everything on their side. If that was the case, how had they not been able to push him back?

Wilson shook his head when she asked him. 'They underestimate Rommel every time,' he told her. 'I can't see how he can win, when he has come so far into our territory, but he's clever, is the Desert Fox, a wily devil, and he's fighting brilliantly with the last of his resources.'

They were in the workshop, and Duncan was collecting everything that Wilson needed to work on his project. Duncan never talked about the war, so Catriona was astonished when his voice came from behind them.

'Did you see how they sent the Kiwis to break through Rommel's lines?' he asked. 'And then nobody came behind them to support them? So the poor bastards were stuck behind enemy lines, cut off from everyone, and had to fight it out on their own. What kind of organisation is that? Our idiot generals think they just have to make a decision and it happens, as though the enemy isn't going to react. We've got a bunch of blockheads in command, and they don't care how many of our men are slaughtered while they wander around like headless chickens making their pathetic mistakes.'

The anger coming from him was palpable, and Catriona held her breath, because surely this was rather too raw to shoot at Corporal Wilson, when he'd been injured in just that same desert war. But interestingly, Wilson replied very mildly.

'It's easy to criticise,' he said simply. 'I agree that we don't have the best tacticians in charge, and lines get crossed, and you get an order from one commander to do one thing, then another from elsewhere to do something else. But I think that they too get conflicting orders, from London, and from Cairo, and all the places where people aren't actually seeing what's happening on the ground. And then sometimes things go wrong, and there's nothing you can do about it. Those New Zealanders you're talking about who got stuck out on their own, it was because the anti-tank units who were supposed to support them lost their way in a minefield. That's bad command, if you like, but it's not at the level of the generals – it's the commander of the armoured brigade who made the mistake and, who knows, they probably had a sandstorm to contend with. It's a shame for the poor Kiwis – they lost a lot of men for nothing, but it's the sort of thing that happens in the desert. Believe me, we got used to it. The main thing is, we have to beat them. I'm a basic soldier, but even I know that. For the sake of my children, and everyone else's.'

Catriona watched to see how Duncan would respond. It was really unprofessional to behave emotionally with the patients, and his outburst from just now had astonished her.

'This particular battle will end in stalemate,' was all he said, finally. Then he raised an arm in capitulation to Corporal Wilson, and forced a grin. 'It won't be us who have to finish the job, anyway. What we should be looking to finish is this shelving here. I want to show you how to make a joint today.'

Duncan waited for Catriona to finish work that day and dragged her off for a very basic supper at the local cafe. They drank strong tea, and he apologised rather cursorily for his flare-up from the afternoon.

'I wouldn't have said anything at all if you hadn't already brought up the subject of El Alamein with Wilson,' he said abruptly. 'I thought you nurses never spoke about the battlefield to your patients?'

Catriona raised an eyebrow. 'Do you think that all of our patients stop thinking and reading when they come in here? It depends on the patient, but Corporal Wilson has always liked talking about what is happening in North Africa. He says it makes him feel closer to his friends who are still out there in the desert, and he is handling his disabilities well now. Luckily for you, as it happens, because with another patient your outburst might have caused serious problems.'

Duncan flushed. 'I know. I'm sorry. But we did some good work after you left. He's a good man, that one.' He stabbed at the fishcake on his plate.

'What's eating you, Duncan?' Catriona asked. He'd been irritable with her ever since she came back to work from Kilcreggan.

'Nothing at all,' was his answer. 'Tell me, how is your brother? Have you had any more news?'

Catriona nodded. She had made it home for a night last weekend, and there had been another telegram from Lieutenant Blake, brief but positive. The simple fact of seeing it had made Catriona feel better, for if Blake had been able to visit Jim then things must not be too desperate in Alexandria. Jim was close to being moved to a recuperative unit, the telegram said, and Catriona presumed that soon they would get an official telegram from the War Office to say what was being planned for him.

'He's on the mend,' she told Duncan. 'There's talk of moving him into a recuperative unit.'

'Will they bring him home?'

'I don't know. My father certainly hopes so, and he was almost disappointed by the latest telegram, because he thought until then that Jim must already be on his way. Jim's friend Lieutenant Blake sent us a telegram, and the last time he followed that with an airgraph, so I'm hoping he'll do the same this time. They take a week or two to get here, but you get a full page of information. We're at the stage now where I want to know what we can expect for Jim in the long term.'

'And what about you in the long term?'

Catriona looked up, surprised. 'Me?'

'Yes, you. Won't you be leaving Dunmore now?'

His tone was defensive, and she began to understand his strange mood.

'No! I have no plans to leave Dunmore.' She shot this back at him as quickly as she could, but she was also aware of having had a meeting just a few days ago with Matron, to enquire about the type of hospital that was being planned for Knockderry Castle. Her words must have come across as defensively as his, and he looked at her sceptically. She reached out and touched his hand.

'Honestly, Duncan, I have no intention of leaving Dunmore. It's true that my father would like to see more of me, so I have enquired about spending one day a week at a hospital closer to my aunt's home. But I would otherwise be here, for five days a week at least. In fact, I'll be here a lot more than you ever are!'

'Are you sure? I know how you are about your family, and what a hold they have on you.'

She had to laugh. 'Are you jealous of my family, Duncan McIlroy? You, the existentialist who believes in living for today, without roots or ties?'

'I believe the only people who should set our rules are ourselves, and that we shouldn't dance to anyone else's tune.'

That gave Catriona pause. Was she dancing to her father's tune, or simply allowing herself to care about other people as well as herself? Catriona thought back to what Duncan had said that night in Glasgow about his father wanting him to join his old regiment, and how Duncan had gone along with it, for lack of courage, he'd said. Did he really resent his father so greatly for that decision? Just because an old man had pride in his regiment and in his son?

If it came to the war, Catriona agreed more with Corporal Wilson than with Duncan, that whatever mistakes the Allies might make, those mistakes weren't criminal and had to be forgiven. Whatever happened, they were in the right, and had to continue, and to win.

There'd been bitterness in what Duncan had said about his father in Glasgow that night, and there had been the same bitter anger in his words to Corporal Wilson this afternoon. Catriona felt so much frustration in dealing with Duncan. Am I such a simple soul, she wondered, or is it that he is excessively complicated? She ate her last mouthful of fishcake, took her courage in her hands, and tackled him full on.

'Duncan, what you said to Corporal Wilson this afternoon, about our commanders being responsible for the slaughter of ordinary men – tell me, do you blame your own commanders for you losing your hand? Were you the victim of some stupid decisions made by your chiefs at Dunkirk? Is that why you are so angry?'

She thought she'd gone too far. Duncan squeezed his fork so hard that his thumb went white. He said nothing, and she studied his frown, wondering what he might say. Eventually he placed the fork deliberately down on his plate, and looked Catriona full in the face.

'I think you may have misunderstood, Catriona,' he said, and his voice was unutterably dejected. 'Remember what I said to you. I was an officer, not an ordinary soldier.'

There was another silence, which eventually Catriona had to fill. 'You mean . . . ?'

'I mean that the stupid decision was mine. I was the cretin, and though I may have lost a hand, because of me fourteen men lost their lives.'

Chapter Twenty-Two

Alexandria, July 1942

Sound travels far over the desert, and you could hear the battle at El Alamein from Alexandria, particularly at night, when the traffic noise stopped, and the city went quiet. People spent their nights on their roofs, watching the flashes of light in the far distance, flashes from explosions and artillery fire. The sixty miles between them and El Alamein seemed to have shrunk to just a short echo across Lake Mariut and the flat sands beyond.

Troops poured through Alexandria, the able-bodied heading for the battlefield, and the maimed and bloodied being brought away. Fran reported in the paper that the biggest casualties were among the Indians, the Australians, the New Zealanders – shocking levels of injury and death given the numbers they sent into battle.

But the panic in the city had stilled, and belief had returned. Rommel's hurtle across Egypt had been checked, and the resources being brought in against him must surely be enough to stop him once and for all.

The navy had returned too. Fran had watched with

new hope as the fleet made its way back into harbour. She wanted to see George and Len and the others again, and she wanted Jim to see them too.

Jim knew about the battle waging so close to Alexandria. He could hardly be unaware. His ward, a navy ward, had been taken over by army men, soldiers who groaned grievously in unhappy sleep, with blasted bodies and missing limbs, who had lost too much blood and too often died.

There was a man lying beside him one day whose body seemed oddly foreshortened under bandages that covered his whole face and head and torso. When Fran went to visit Jim, she found an army lieutenant sitting between the beds, and thought he had come to see Jim. She wondered what had brought him to visit a navy man, but she soon realised that the officer was there to check on the patient in the next bed.

'He's my major,' he explained grimly. 'His jeep hit a mine, and we decided I should come in with him to Alex.'

Jim was propped up a little in his bed, his head carefully cushioned on pillows. He couldn't sit up yet, and was permanently a little groggy, but when he was awake he knew what was happening. The damage to his head, it was all about the damage to his head. He had dizzy spells, flashes across the eyes, trouble focusing, muffled deafness, and that slurred speech, which didn't seem to improve.

Fran gave him her hand, and then looked at the inert shape in the next bed.

'He looks serious,' she said, and then thought how stupid a comment that was. But the young army lieutenant nodded, and seemed to want to talk.

'He's lost his face,' he said, his voice tight. 'It was all blown off. I've never seen anything like it. And he's lost his legs, completely lost them.' He made a fist of his right hand, and dug it hard into his left. 'He'd want to go, you know. I'm hoping he won't make it through the night.'

Fran gulped, but beside her Jim didn't blink. 'Better,' he said, in that slow, struggling diction that had become what Jim was. It was that acceptance of death, that military men had and Fran found so difficult.

'Have you lost a lot of men?' she asked softly.

The lieutenant nodded. 'It's been pretty grim. You wonder where Rommel finds his artillery from every time we attack. The RAF have been decimating his supply lines, taking out the truck convoys coming in from Libya, and yet he still seems to be able to find an armoured division when he needs one. Damned Desert Fox!'

Fran wanted to ask about Auchinleck and his generals. If Rommel could stand against such superior Allied forces, then surely something was wrong with their strategy? But the young man had enough on his plate without being asked to defend his chiefs, so she put her journalist hat away, and spoke with what she hoped was conviction.

'He can't hold out much longer. And you've saved Alexandria, you boys. We owe you more than anyone can say.'

The lieutenant shook his head. 'Not just to us,' he said, with a gesture to Jim. 'The RAF has been amazing, and you navy fellows have been with us too, bombarding Rommel from the sea.'

He looked over at his major, sunk in a drugged sleep, and then spoke very much to Jim. 'He'd say the same, if he could. I'm glad you're here next to him tonight. Hopefully he'll go peacefully, and he won't be here when I come in tomorrow morning.'

'What is his name?' Fran asked.

'Walmers. Henry Walmers.'

Hearing his name made him not an officer but just a man, one of the thousands whose families would be receiving that dreaded telegram in the next few days. Was there a Mrs Walmers, Fran wondered, back at home with young children?

'Major Walmers.' It was Jim who spoke, as though he was searching in his mind for recognition. Then he raised a hand from the covers. 'I'm here,' he said, and in his condition he had no strength for irony.

The lieutenant left soon after. Fran had wanted to ask if he knew her brother, or even her brother's unit, but why should he? There were nearly 200,000 men out there, after all.

Before she left the ward that night, when Jim had gone to sleep, she stood by the wrecked body of the major, and laid a gentle hand on his arm. There was no reaction, and you couldn't even hear him breathing. Jim's breathing had been terrifying when he was first injured, but at least it had been there, an audible sign of life. Fran wasn't a particularly religious person, but she made a sign of the cross over the man before she tiptoed away.

When she came in the next day two nurses were busy around the bed, and for a moment Fran thought they had removed the bandages from the major's blown-up face, and came to a halt in consternation, but the man they were tucking in was a new patient, without head injuries, it seemed, a young man who grimaced as they moved him, but who was definitely alive. So Major Henry Walmers was at peace. Fran breathed again, and waited for the nurses to have finished and moved away before she stepped forward.

There was a different officer today sitting by Jim's bed, but this time the officer was there specifically to see Jim. Fran was delighted when she recognised Commander Aldridge, the man who had brought Jim and his friends to the garden party where she had met him just over a year ago.

He greeted her without surprise. He had seen her with Jim on two or three occasions over the last few months.

'Miss Trevillian, how do you do? How is the world of journalism in these troubled times?'

'Reporting on the troubles, of course!' she answered, taking his outstretched hand. 'How do you do, Commander? We've all been so pleased to see the fleet back in the harbour this last week.'

He smiled. 'And we've been delighted to be back in our HQ,' he said. 'We couldn't risk losing the whole fleet to the *Kriegsmarine*, but we didn't go far, you know, and we were always in full combat. But now that we know that Rommel won't make it to Alexandria we can operate from here again.'

'You're sure he won't make it to here?'

Another charming smile. 'Oh yes, I'm sure.'

Fran waited to see if he would say more, but wasn't surprised when he didn't. Previous attempts to get information from the commander came to mind, and she suppressed an inner smile.

'King Farouk seems still to think that the Axis can take

Egypt,' she chanced. 'They say he has his welcome speech already prepared for Rommel.'

One side of the colonel's face twitched. 'Then he may have to rewrite it,' was all he replied. He gestured to Jim. 'Now tell me, Miss Trevillian, how do you find this fellow? He seems to be making a recovery, so much so in fact that the hospital wants to turf him out! We've just been discussing what is the best next move for him.'

Fran looked hurriedly towards Jim. She had thought and thought about what would happen to him. It was inevitable that he would be moved soon – you only had to see the desperate condition of those in the ward around him to realise that he would not be left to recuperate here. But he could only sit up in bed in careful small movements, supported the whole time, so where could he be taken?

'I've been recommending to Lieutenant MacNeill that he should go back to England for a period of rest. We have excellent medical facilities on our hospital ships, and he would be well cared for, and then when he gets home he would have the best neurological care.'

This had been a recurring bad dream for Fran, that Jim would be shipped home, and that she would never see him again. She looked to see his reaction.

Jim was shaking his head, as minimally as he could. 'No!' he said, 'They will put me in an office job. Please! Don't want to leave the fleet.'

His diction was better, surely, than yesterday, though he spoke slowly? And these were full sentences. Was it the need to impress his senior officer that had sharpened his speech?

The commander looked sceptical. 'You're a long way from

being able to rejoin the fleet, Jim.' He might almost have said, you'll never rejoin the fleet. It was written on his face.

But Jim still shook his head. 'Don't send me home.' His voice slurred a little more, and the commander frowned.

'We don't have anywhere suitable to send you locally, Jim,' he said.

Fran was thinking furiously. 'Has the surgeon here made any suggestions, Commander?' she asked. 'I don't mean to interfere in naval matters, but I have heard of men recuperating in Jerusalem, for example, and then being able to return to Mediterranean duties when they were fit again.'

Commander Aldridge's lips twitched. 'You wouldn't have personal reasons for your suggestion, perhaps, Miss Trevillian? It is true that there are options that do not necessarily involve returning all the way home, but in order to justify sending Lieutenant MacNeill to a closer facility I would have to be quite sure that he could return to service here.'

'And couldn't he? You manage the whole Eastern Mediterranean from here, don't you? Operations in Greece, and Cyprus, and Syria are all run from here. You have important communications facilities here at Naval Command. Couldn't Jim contribute to managing those operations once he has recovered, even if he isn't fit for a while to go back to sea?'

She saw that the commander was preparing to answer her, his brows knitted, and she launched herself into further speech.

'Commander Aldridge, only yesterday there was a desperately ill officer in the bed next to us here, a major who was blown up at El Alamein. He isn't here today, and I presume that's because he has died. All around us people are dying. Well, Jim nearly died too, and yet he's here against all the odds. And all he wants to do is serve. Can't you help him, one of your most loyal officers? Please? It would give hope to all of your men to see him being cared for as one of them. It's the spirit that you all fight with, surely?'

Jim's friends were in her mind as she spoke, but she stopped herself from saying any more, knowing that she had already outreached herself. She watched the commander for his reaction, and caught Jim studying him equally intently. The commander looked from one to the other of them, and shook his head, not negatively, but more in resignation. Then he placed a hand on Jim's shoulder.

'It would seem you are a lucky man, MacNeill,' he said. 'You have found yourself a very powerful advocate. Very well, Miss Trevillian, I will speak to the surgeon here and see what can be done for Lieutenant MacNeill without sending him back home. Get yourself well, MacNeill, and then we'll see what we can do with you. I'll try to find you something useful to do here at the base. And meanwhile I'll send some of your friends to visit you tomorrow. We have a few of their ships in the harbour at the moment.'

He rose to his feet, and held out his hand to Fran. 'Do you want a little piece for your newspaper, Miss Trevillian? Have you heard that Admiral Cunningham has been made a baronet in recognition of his services here in the Mediterranean? It was announced in the King's Birthday Honours List, one of the highest honours awarded. I don't suppose old ABC is particularly impressed himself, because he has no time for honours, and for pomp and ceremony. We all remember his cutting remarks about all that, don't we, Jim? But it is finally some recognition of the tight and complex battle we've been fighting against all the odds, and of the sacrifices men like Jim have made. So, it would be good to tell your readers, and to focus on the good news, my dear lady, and all will be well with Rommel, I can assure you of that!'

He gave her another smile, and a small bow, tapped Jim on the shoulder one more time, and was gone. Fran was left smiling at Jim like an idiot, and when she was sure no one was looking she leant down and gave him a long kiss.

'They're not going to send you back to England!' she breathed. 'Oh Jim, I love you.'

'I love you too,' he replied, and she could have sworn there was no slurring at all in his words.

Chapter Twenty-Three

Alexandria, August 1942

The strangest hiatus had come over Egypt after the weeks of battle. Among the British there was an odd assumption that Rommel would never break through now, but others couldn't understand what on earth had been gained by four weeks of attack and counter-attack. Twelve thousand Allied troops were dead, and not a foot of territory had been shifted at El Alamein.

But the Egyptians who had been so quick to hang out German flags were equally quick to put them away again, and there were reports that Mussolini, who had been waiting in Libya to ride triumphantly through Cairo on the absurd white horse he had used on previous occasions, had returned to Italy in fury at Rommel's failure to make the final push.

Rommel would attack again, nothing was surer, but for now both sides seemed simply exhausted, the first flush of battle was over, and for a few weeks people could pick up their lives.

Jim had been gone for nearly two weeks now. Fran's

hope that he would go to Jerusalem had been dashed. She could have visited him there, but instead he had been taken off in a hospital ship to Cape Town, nearly eight thousand miles away. He might as well be in England, for all the communication they could expect from him, but George Blake told Fran the decision was the right one for Jim and for them all.

'It's quite normal for our wounded to be sent to South Africa to convalesce,' he told her. 'It's a place of peace in the Empire, easily accessible for our ships and with the perfect climate for convalescence. Jim would have found the overland journey to Jerusalem very difficult, anyway, whereas the hospital ship they took him off on is a converted passenger liner, five-star, all comforts! The hospitals in South Africa are five-star too, and it's their winter right now. It has to be good for Jim to get away from this heat.'

'How can you be sure they'll send Jim back here from South Africa, and not send him on to England when he's better?' Fran asked, refusing to be reassured.

'Because if they'd wanted to do that they'd have sent him straight home in the first place,' George explained, speaking slowly as though to a rather dense child. 'Stop worrying, Fran, and help us make the most of a week or two without being on full alert. I want to go out to Montazah, and Lucie says she'll come with us if you do.'

Lucie had returned to Alexandria, along with most of the Brits who had fled, and there seemed to be a determination among everyone to make the most of this period of temporary calm. Fran went with them to Montazah, but she found it vaguely irrelevant to be going to the beach just now, when the war seemed to be hanging in the balance.

Asher hadn't returned. Fran spent a lot of time wondering what had happened to him, but even Sami didn't have any news. The international press had finally picked up this summer on Jewish reports of systematic extermination in Poland and Russia, where the Germans were marching Jews out of their villages and machine-gunning them into giant pits. Perhaps a million people had been killed so far, it was thought.

Fran reported the story in the *Journal*, but wished she could have Asher with her, railing, angry, to focus all of them on the enormity of what they were hearing. Where could he have gone with his family? Were they still in Egypt, or had they fled further afield?

August arrived, and with it came Winston Churchill. He flew in to Cairo from Gibraltar, and news stories buzzed around of the fireworks he was lighting among the chiefs of staff. He was furious, it was said, that Rommel hadn't been finished off, and within a week he had sacked Auchinleck from his post.

The announcement came on a Saturday, and Fran was scanning the Sunday newspapers the next morning to see what other journalists were saying when Michael suddenly appeared at the house. He walked in unannounced as they sat over their Sunday breakfast, and his mother came out of her seat so fast that she knocked it over. As he stood smiling at her in her dining room she threw herself into his arms and cried.

Michael had been given leave while his commanding officers were in Cairo fawning over Churchill. But he'd been around the whole political camp until yesterday, and was fizzing with news.

'What fun it has been!' he told them all, as he sat down and took a sweet pastry. 'You know that Churchill went out to see Auchinleck at his camp? Well, poor Auchinleck couldn't have made a worse impression on old Winston. He received him in his shabby old tent, and gave him a breakfast that had flies buzzing all round it. Churchill may like to think he is one of us, but he's actually very much the grand old man, and he doesn't like being covered in sand, sweat and insects! It seems Auchinleck told him he needed at least eight weeks before he could fight Rommel again, which went down like a ton of lead. Churchill never listens, they say, especially when he's grumpy. And then, after the meeting with Auchinleck, Churchill went off to visit the Desert Air Force camp, and the RAF delighted him with a slap-up lunch they had brought over the desert from Cairo, prepared and served by Shepheard's restaurant with silver service on the beach! You can imagine what the RAF boys had to say about Auchinleck. They have no time for the army at the best of times, and they blame Auchinleck for the whole of Rommel's advance.'

Alan Trevillian laughed. 'I'd say Auchinleck got no more than he deserved. But how do you think Montgomery will fare in his place? He's never even seen the desert, has he?'

Michael shrugged. 'Montgomery's an unknown quantity, and they say he's a nasty ferret of a man, but who knows, maybe that's what we need. We certainly don't need more of the same old command. We've all had enough.' He drank off the last of his tea, and his mother immediately filled his cup.

'Can we go to the beach, do you think?' he asked. 'I've only got a couple of days, and I really want to unwind. It hasn't been much fun this last while.'

You couldn't extinguish Michael's buoyancy, but there was a drawn, tight look about his face that was new.

'You look exhausted,' his mother said.

'We're all exhausted,' he answered. 'Auchinleck was right about that, at least. Who the hell fights a war in the desert in July? It's been unbearable, and the men couldn't have continued any longer. We've had dysentery and malaria as well, just to add to our problems.'

'But eight weeks? Do you agree that you can't fight for eight weeks? What if Rommel attacks again?' Fran asked.

'Well he will, of course, but not straight away. His troops are in far worse shape than ours. I doubt we'll get eight weeks, but we'll have time to see Montgomery in place, and then let's see what he can do.'

They called Lucie, and the whole family went to the beach, picking her up on the way. They went to their beach hut at Sidi Bishr, and spent a Sunday afternoon over a picnic. In the relief of seeing her brother Fran finally relaxed, and lay in the shallows for most of the afternoon, imagining Jim in his bed on the ship, perhaps wheeled out to enjoy the breeze on deck.

Behind her the old friends Lucie and Michael had challenged each other to races in the waves, Michael giving Lucie a head start, but always managing to catch her. Lucie's laughter came to Fran across the water, with a simple, unforced happiness that had been missing for too long.

Alan Trevillian was due to take his yacht out again this evening on the night patrol of the harbour, and normally Michael would have been only too keen to be with him as crew. But tonight he would be happy with a comfortable bed. Perhaps they could go out for a drink first with Lucie. They would talk childhood rubbish, and tonight Fran would sleep without dreaming about Asher, or even Jim.

Her hair floated in the water, and the waves lapped at her body, but her face was beginning to burn in the August heat. She looked up the beach to where her parents were relaxing in the shade. Her father had closed his eyes, she was sure. She should seek out the shade herself, she knew, but she didn't want to move. She rolled over on to her front, and propped herself up on her elbows.

Out at sea a navy ship went by, a minesweeper off on patrol towards Port Said. The war was always there, after all.

CHAPTER TWENTY-FOUR

Scotland, August 1942

Catriona approached her first day at Knockderry Hospital with some misgiving. A small convalescent centre staffed mainly by unqualified VAD nursing assistants was not where Catriona wanted to be. But her matron at Dunmore had assured her that Knockderry was keen to have the help of someone trained in physical therapy, and it had been arranged that she would work there each Monday, which was when the Free French Navy's own doctor also visited. They could then work together.

It also meant she could spend Sunday with her father, and she'd spent yesterday walking with him along the loch side, trying to take his mind off the news that Jim wasn't being sent home. They'd finally received an official telegram telling them that Jim was being transferred to Cape Town to convalesce, and Catriona was sure this was good news. If Jim's condition had been really serious, they would definitely have brought him back to Britain.

'They'll send him back into that Mediterranean,' Fergus muttered. With his island accent he always extended the word 'Mediterranean', so that it had about eight syllables and sounded like a place of doom. Catriona couldn't help smiling, but she reassured him nonetheless.

'No one will put Jim back on a ship in a hurry,' she told him. 'He had too many injuries. Wait and see, perhaps they'll send him back here later, once he's better.'

They were all early risers in Aunt Sheila's household, and there was even a breakfast prepared for Catriona before she cycled off in the early mist the few hundred yards to Knockderry. She was curious about the castle. It stood on a rock high above the neighbouring mansions, an overdecorated Victorian pile with fanciful round towers and pointed conical roofs. It must have been some merchant's idea of a nobleman's castle, but compared with the other, gracious houses that lined the loch, Knockderry was dark and ugly.

She pushed her bike up the steep drive and round to an elegant lawn and garden. Here you could see why the house had been built up on the rock. The views across the water were quite stunning. The mist masked the other shore, but Catriona was sure that on a fine day you would see for miles. The patients must have that view too from their wards. It would help with recuperation.

Matron was on the wait for her, and as Catriona leant her bike up against the wall she came out of the building and extended a firm hand. She was a good-looking woman in her fifties, perhaps, who measured Catriona with clear blue eyes and seemed to like what she saw.

'Sister MacNeill, I'm very glad to meet you,' she said, with a carefully professional smile.

'Thank you,' Catriona replied. 'I'm very pleased to be here.'

'Not as pleased as we are, believe me! We have a number of patients who will benefit a lot from your expertise.'

'Do you?' Catriona was curious. 'I've been wondering. I thought this was more a centre for rest and recuperation.'

'In part, yes, but we receive patients all the time who have been discharged from the infirmary and who have some challenging recovery issues.'

So there would be patients like those Catriona had cared for at the infirmary herself? Those with the terrible injuries from shelling and accidents at sea? The matron gave her a tour, and there were indeed men with multiple fractures, muscle damage and mobility issues whom she could really help.

It wasn't usual for a matron to be so welcoming and friendly to her staff, but Catriona thought that in this instance Matron was particularly pleased to have her. The rest of the nursing staff whom she met on the tour were all VAD nurses. These nurses did invaluable work, but had been co-opted for wartime service in time of need, and had only basic training. To have a full sister on the staff, even for one day a week, would be of great help to the matron, and it meant that Catriona would be treated with respect.

It was strange to be surrounded by French speakers. At the infirmary she'd nursed just a few Frenchmen, but here they made a community, and those who were the most able cared for the most unwell. There was a hum of French around her all the time, and Catriona tried to rake up the language she had learnt at school.

'Do you speak French?' she asked the matron.

The lean, wiry woman laughed. 'Not more than a few words. The hospital has only been open for a few weeks, and I haven't had time to learn yet! But the men have been based in Scotland for quite a long time now, and you'll find they have learnt some English, if only in the pubs and shops. Some have become more fluent than others, of course, and when necessary they translate for each other.'

The place had the comradely feel of Dunmore, but there was a subtle difference here. These men were not crippled, and she would not be preparing them to make the most of their lives as civilians with lost limbs. Every one of these young Frenchmen would be going back into active service. They did work like Jim's too, escorting convoys across the dangerous waters of the Atlantic. And it was Catriona's job to make them fit to put their lives in danger all over again.

The building was less intimidating inside than out. The panelled, corniced, high-ceilinged rooms had been converted into homely, practical wards. They needed to feel homely, of course. It struck Catriona, just as it had back at the infirmary, that these men, some of them merely boys, didn't have homes of their own to go to. They were self-imposed exiles, fighting in the hope that one day they could return to a liberated France. It made her feel a heavy sense of responsibility towards them, and she no longer thought of this as a waste of a Monday.

'Dr Roman will be here soon,' Matron told her, as they made their way to her office. 'He comes over from the base at Greenock, of course, and he often has a patient or two to see there before he takes the ferry.'

She pronounced the doctor's name with the emphasis on the second syllable. A French doctor, then? It was great to think that the Free French base had a doctor of their own, a countryman who could talk to the men in their own language. He would know their histories too.

But when Dr Roman arrived he was a complete surprise. He came into the office full of apologies, a huge man in his late thirties, perhaps, with a mane of dark hair blown about by the wind, and as soon as he spoke Catriona realised that he wasn't French at all. He had an accent that could have been Russian or Slavic, but which Catriona realised suddenly must be Polish. A Pole? Among the French? Did he speak French, then, or just get by in English?

He was talking volubly to Matron, and his English certainly was fluent, if heavily accented. There was an outbreak of gastric flu among the officers at the base, he was explaining, and he had almost not come today for fear that he might bring the virus with him. 'But I have taken all precautions, and one part of my work cannot stop because of another, really it cannot.'

He turned to Catriona. 'So, you are our new physical therapist! Welcome, Sister, welcome! We need you, really we need you!'

A VAD nurse came in just then with tea for them all. Dr Roman added three sugars to his, and then looked at Catriona with a rather rueful smile. 'I take too much sugar, when there is rationing for everyone, but if I cannot have coffee, then I must have sugar with my tea!'

And then he whisked Catriona off with him to watch him do his rounds. He half-shambled, half-gambolled around the wards, with a retinue of two VADs and Matron behind him. It was clear to see that his once weekly visits here were of immense importance, and it was equally clear that the men both knew and loved him.

He spoke good French, as good as his English, Catriona

thought, and probably equally as unpredictable. He spent a long time with each patient, and from what Catriona could understand he knew in detail what had happened to each of them, what jobs they all did on the ships, even where they came from in France. He was like a great big avuncular bear.

As they moved from bed to bed Catriona made notes on what was needed for each patient. There was one patient who was recovering from chest wounds like those Jim had had. Catriona spoke to the doctor about instituting a programme of chest exercises, which would help prevent long-term breathing problems and deformities. Dr Roman listened intently, and thanked her.

'It is something the VADs can do when you are not here?' he asked.

She nodded. 'I'll begin today, and show the VADs what I do.'

He smiled at her, a big, generous smile. 'Already we are learning from you. It is wonderful! You know, I am a paediatrician by specialism. I don't have any surgical training, so here I just do my best, but what we have here is a team, and good hearts. You will add your heart to ours!' Catriona hid a smile, and the round continued.

By the end of the day she did indeed feel as though she had joined a family. She wanted to go back to school, though, to improve her French. She set off on her bike to catch the ferry back to Dunmore feeling exhausted but content. Tomorrow she would see Duncan, and since the weather was fine they could picnic at lunchtime under their tree. He would be able to tell her more, she was sure, about the Polish forces in Scotland. She knew that a whole group of Poles had decided to continue fighting when the Germans had taken Poland. Hadn't they been among those evacuated at Dunkirk? Duncan might not want to talk about that, but he must have come across some Polish troops at that time.

They were exiles too, therefore, like the Free French, and she'd heard of whole Polish regiments being set up in Scotland. There had been a group of them in Helensburgh, hadn't there, just another ferry ride away from where she was now? She wanted to know more.

She arrived at the quayside as the ferry was preparing to leave, and just managed to cycle on before it left. She would be in time for the eight o'clock train, and would be back at Dunmore in time for a reasonably early night. The light tonight was magnificent on the Clyde, and with the long summer evening she might even be back before it got dark.

As she wheeled her bike further along the ferry she spotted Dr Roman in front of her, holding a rather ancient-looking scooter. She called a good evening to him, and he turned with a smile.

'Why, Sister MacNeill, you are heading where?'

'Back to my main job,' she explained. 'I work at Dunmore Hospital with servicemen who have lost limbs.'

'That is wonderful. So you are a real specialist?'

'I'm not sure I would call myself that. I have the standard nursing diploma, but I had a tutor who was interested in physical therapy, and who trained his students in his methods. It became a particular interest of mine, but I worked as a general nurse first at the infirmary, with some of your patients. I've only actually been practising as a physical therapist for a few months.'

His bushy eyebrows rose. 'Really? I would not have believed it! We should thank your teacher. He has taught you the very latest techniques, it seems, and made you a true expert.'

Catriona blushed, as she always did when she received compliments. 'It's just what I like doing,' she protested. Then she let her curiosity pose its own questions.

'You are Polish, Dr Roman, but you speak such good English and French, and you work with the Free French Navy. Have you always been with the French forces?'

He shook his head. 'No, no, I came over with many other Polish officers, and my brother is one of them. We were based in Glasgow when we first arrived. But I worked in France for a few years when I qualified, when I specialised in paediatrics. They trained me, you see, and so I learnt French. And then in Glasgow I met Commandant Langlais at a French gathering. He commands the Free French base here, and he asked me to come here to work. We already had Polish doctors with us who could take care of our own troops, but the French had nobody. So I left my comrades and came to Greenock, and here I have been for over a year now.'

'And your brother?' Catriona didn't want to pry, but he was speaking without any hesitation, she thought.

'Oh, Alfons? He is still with the regiment, near the border in your Lowlands. But all that they do at the moment is routine duties and training, so he is bored, and I am busy, so I have the better place.'

'But you see him sometimes?'

'Yes, Sister MacNeill.' He pulled his scooter upright as the ferry pulled into Gourock and the people in front of them started to move. 'I see enough of my younger brother to remind me that I am Polish! And I have my friends among the French navy who have made me feel like one of their own. I am a lucky man!'

They pushed their two-wheeled vehicles up the slipway, and Dr Roman stopped to say farewell.

'Goodbye, Sister. Until next week. And thank you again for thinking to come to Knockderry.'

'It has been a good decision,' she said in reply. 'It is a lovely hospital and I think I'll be very happy working with you. I just wish I spoke better French.'

'Ah, but we will teach you! I have some books if you would like them, and then the patients can help you to learn. It will be good therapy for them.'

He mounted the ancient scooter and gunned the pedal three times. The engine started up with a protesting rattle and a puff of smoke.

'This scooter is like us Poles,' said Dr Roman, raising a final hand in farewell. 'It keeps running on nothing, but it won't give up!'

Chapter Twenty-Five

They had never had a French serviceman as a patient at Dunmore, and Catriona was inundated with questions all the following morning from her fellow nurses. Were they handsome? Were they as charming as everyone said they were? Catriona could only laugh.

'They're quieter than the patients here,' she told them. 'They chat amongst themselves, and joke around, but they don't seem to give cheek to the nurses like our lot. Maybe it's just the language barrier.'

She had a busy morning catching up with what she'd missed yesterday. There was a promise to take on another nurse with her training, especially since the hospital was expanding, but Catriona thought that kind of help would be a long time coming.

She snatched just half an hour with Duncan at lunchtime, and they sat in his workshop rather than under their tree. She'd brought over lunch on a tray, a potato pie with powdered egg, which was even worse than usual.

Duncan was waiting for her, and pulled her fiercely

into his arms. 'So, my little island girl, what did they do to you yesterday?'

'Do to me? Why nothing, dear Duncan. What did you think they would do?' She grinned up at him.

'You never know with those Frenchmen!'

'That's what the nurses thought! You're all ridiculous! They're a bunch of boys, mostly, a long way from home.'

'No glamorous officers?'

She laughed, and pulled herself away. 'Hundreds of them! Now, stupid, shall we eat before this stuff goes cold?'

As they ate she asked him about the Poles. He seemed very happy to talk about them, though she was careful not to mention Dunkirk. She had dropped that subject after his pained revelation. It was too much of a no-go area.

'There's a Polish army camp near my parents' house,' Duncan told her. 'My mother bakes for them, and invites them to tea, and all the local girls go silly over them at dances, because they dance so much better than we Scots, and look very romantic in their uniforms. Is your doctor like that?'

Catriona shook her head. 'Hardly! He must be nearly forty, and he's a big untidy sort of man. But he's very sweet, and very dedicated. He says he came over with his brother, and their unit was stationed here in Glasgow, but that now his brother is in the Borders. How many Polish troops are there here, do you know?'

'In Scotland? Well, there must be at least ten thousand of them. You remember when the whole of the Scottish 51st Highland Division was captured in France? Well, the Poles formed a division to replace them, and came up to guard the Scottish coast against invasion from Norway. I think that's one of the reasons they are so well liked here.'

Catriona was surprised. 'So many? I hadn't realised. I think there are only around a thousand Free French in Greenock.'

'That's a lot for one town, though,' Duncan said thoughtfully. 'The Polish army is spread all along the east coast, and in the Borders, as you say. Hey, do you think the French need a sculptor's services?'

'Searching for business? I thought you had all you wanted here, and needed the rest of your time for your own work?'

'Who knows, maybe I just want to keep an eye on you. It's like I say, those French naval officers have one heck of a reputation!'

It was a comment that made Catriona smile, happy to think her movements mattered to this enigmatic man. She didn't have eyes for anyone other than Duncan, but she didn't mind him being a little uncertain. In the next few weeks she began to see what he meant about her French patients. They were indeed charming, with a finesse often lacking in her countrymen, but they weren't as beguiling as Duncan.

The weather improved as August went on, with a fine spell of sunshine in which they moved every possible patient outside for the day both at Dunmore and at Knockderry. It was good to have some weekend time at home in this weather, and life got more exciting in Kilcreggan as the month advanced because the Americans came back to Rosneath, and this time with a bang.

The locals saw their vehicles and equipment arriving from early August, but the official handover didn't come until later in the month, when a thousand young men suddenly moved onto their quiet, rural peninsula. Catriona wondered whether Captain Martin would return, but it was unlikely, as it was new officers who were moving in, according to the locals who worked at the base. They were delighted, of course. Wages would be higher and conditions more generous under the Americans, and homes all around the peninsula would have chocolate again, and those fancy American biscuit brands.

There were some misgivings among local people, though. This volume of servicemen was way beyond the numbers who had been at Rosneath until now. Catriona's father muttered about the damage so many GIs could do to the local girls, and no doubt many mothers would agree with him. The last time the Americans had been here their naval ratings had not been allowed into Kilcreggan. Would it be the same this time? Uncle Charlie told Fergus not to worry – what on earth could be the interest for a bunch of young GIs on inflated salaries in coming to spend their evenings in a village that didn't even have a pub? They would be happier with the entertainments of Helensburgh.

The officers, of course, could go where they liked, and the village gave a welcome dance for them at the end of the month. Catriona had managed to be home for the Saturday evening, and she and Matron were plotting to take along three of their Knockderry patients, men who were in the hospital more through mental strain than because of physical injuries, and who would benefit from an evening out to take their mind off what was haunting them. Two of them were only what they called '*officiers mariniers*', which she thought was the same as a petty officer, but it pleased Catriona to think of them among the American officers in Cove Burgh Hall. They too, she wanted them to know, could go where they liked.

Even her father and Uncle Charlie would be going to the dance, out of simple curiosity. Catriona wondered whether she should invite Duncan, but somehow a village dance with home-made lemonade didn't feel like his thing, though he would probably be one of the first to find the Americans outside the hall with their flask of whisky! Anyway, to bring him home would invite far too much comment. Dunmore was her independent world away from Kilcreggan, and Duncan needed to stay hidden for now.

She was delighted on the evening to run almost immediately into Captain Martin. 'Why if it isn't my favourite dancing partner!' he said on seeing her. 'How have you been, Miss MacNeill? Still travelling over every day on that ferry?'

'No, I have moved to other posts now,' she answered. 'How do you do, Captain? May I introduce you to Mrs Sutherland, the matron at Knockderry Hospital?' She gestured behind her to where the three French patients, in evening uniforms procured from the Greenock base, were standing rather nervously with two of the VADs from the hospital who had accompanied them there. 'We have brought some of our Free French comrades along with us to enjoy the evening.'

The captain made a flourishing bow to Matron, and nodded his head in welcome to the men. 'Hey, we've heard about the new hospital around here. You're doing great work, Mrs Sutherland, and it's a pleasure to meet you. Have you heard that we are setting up our own hospital too, just up the road?'

Matron smiled. 'We certainly have, Captain. A

state-of-the-art facility built out of nothing in the way only you Americans can manage! You're bringing your own service staff over to run it, I believe? Well, Miss MacNeill and I will be wangling an invitation to visit it, as soon as it's up and running. We're sure it will have equipment and medicines that we can only dream of.'

'Well, you will most definitely be invited. In fact, some of the organising staff are here already. I must see if they are here tonight, but if not, you must come and meet them at Rosneath. You guys need to share, and we're keen to help.'

He moved forward to speak to the three Frenchmen, and within a couple of minutes Catriona saw him make a gesture to a junior officer, who came forward and took the three off to where a group of Americans stood in a corner. Another couple of officers came forward to dance with the two VADs, and once he had seen all this accomplished Captain Martin came back to join Catriona and Matron.

'That was very kind of you, Captain,' approved Matron. 'We've all heard of your American generosity, and it is wonderful to see it in action.'

He made a mock bow, and grinned. 'We aim to please, ma'am. Can I ask you to join me for the next dance?'

Matron laughed. 'Oh no, my dancing days are over, thank you, but do take Miss MacNeill on to the dance floor. I see some ladies from the village over there whom I have been meaning to talk to about some fundraising they have promised us.' She inclined her head with old-fashioned graciousness to Captain Martin and walked purposefully off.

Captain Martin watched her go. 'That's a fine woman,' he said, with real appreciation. 'She reminds me of my own mother a little.' Then he turned to Catriona. 'So, you're working at Knockderry Hospital now? We'll be near neighbours!'

'I'm there one day a week,' Catriona told him. 'My main job is a little further away, and I stay over near Glasgow for much of the week. But tell me about you, Captain Martin. We had been told that all the staff at Rosneath were new this time, so I hadn't expected to see you back on our shores. It's quite a surprise to see you here this evening.'

'Why yes, they brought in a whole heap of new staff, all right, but some of us were brought back because we have skills that are particular to this operation.' He tapped his nose and winked. 'You won't ask me what those skills are, of course! I keep my most important talents for the dance floor.'

He whisked Catriona on to the dance floor as the band struck up a waltz, and glided her round as proficiently as the last time they had danced, when he had shown her how well he could swing. It seemed perfectly innocent, but mindful of him being married, Catriona got one question in as quickly as she could.

'So did you get time back at home between being here?' she asked. 'Did you manage to spend time with your family?'

He beamed at her. 'I sure did! Not as long as I would have liked, but even a week is a blessing right now. The boys change so fast! Thank you for asking, Miss MacNeill. It's kind of you.'

They twirled around the hall, and she learnt that his sons were five and seven years old, and they lived in Colorado, and already knew how to ski. His pride shone out, and the sheer enthusiasm of the man was infectious. Were all Americans like him? Catriona wondered. If so, then their energy would be bound to win the war.

She danced with each of her French patients before the break, when tea and sandwiches were served, and she made sure that the VADs did the same, rather than focusing in on the allure of the GIs. Then at teatime Captain Martin found his way back over to her and Matron and suggested that they might be hungry. He offered them each an arm, and led them over to where Aunt Sheila was serving the sandwiches and pastries. Catriona introduced her, and within a few minutes the captain had invited her and all her family to the American base the following day, for drinks at the officers' mess.

He invited Matron, too. 'Won't you come, ma'am? I'll fish out my medico colleagues and you can talk hospitals to your heart's content.'

Under such siege both of the older ladies melted, and arrangements were made. Captain Martin then moved away, but before he did so he winked at Catriona. 'You'll give me another dance later, Miss MacNeill?' he asked. 'Another waltz, by preference. You're a pretty fine dancer. And don't worry, I'm not making advances, but even my wife would understand that a man needs to dance, and with someone who knows how. Your village here is charming, but it seems to be a bit short on ladies who like to dance!'

CHAPTER TWENTY-SIX

'Going to the base?' was Fergus MacNeill's response to the invitation when he heard about it later. 'What on earth for?'

His sister gave him short shrift. 'I told you, Fergus, we're invited to the officers' mess. It's a great honour, and you'll wear your best shirt. The captain said he wished to thank us for all we are doing to welcome the Americans to Kilcreggan. And he had particular praise for my damson tarts.'

Uncle Charlie looked quizzically at his wife. 'I'm no' quite sure it was your damson tarts that secured us an invitation to their base, my dear, but I have to say I'd give a lot to go and take a gander at what those Yanks are doing round at Rosneath.'

'There will be alcohol, Uncle Charlie,' Catriona warned.

'Well, if the Americans are paying, I may even have a drink myself! I only don't drink because it doesn't much agree with me. It's not some kind of religious objection, you know. Who knows, maybe they'll have cocktails or something I've never tasted!'

'And you'll have a whisky,' Catriona told her father. 'You'll enjoy it.'

'It'll be that awful American bourbon,' grumbled Fergus, but she could see that the idea of some entertainment was beginning to appeal to him. She took care not to remind any of her relatives that they would effectively be in a bar on the Sabbath. If they thought of the mess as some kind of private residence it would pass a great deal better.

They took Archie's taxi round to Rosneath the next evening, and picked up Mrs Sutherland on the way. It seemed strange when they reached the base to have to stop at a checkpoint. The public road went right through the base, and it was a road they knew so well, but the villagers of Rosneath all had special passes now, and the general public had to take a detour around the whole village. Their party had clearance, though, the guard confirmed, already arranged by Captain Martin.

The base was just around the tip of their little peninsula. It had been built all around the Rosneath Estate, the old residence of Princess Louise, Queen Victoria's daughter who had married the Duke of Argyll. She had moved here when she became the Dowager Duchess, and now, after her death, the estate had found another role.

Once past the guards they drove along the coast road past the old house. Uncle Charlie had the front seat next to Archie, and he gave those squashed in the back seat a running commentary on all that he saw.

'They're preparing some kind of mission here, that's for sure. Do you see all those barges tied up along the pontoons? Well, they're landing craft. They use them to ferry troops from ships to the shore. I'd say they're preparing to land a whole heap of troops somewhere. Look at all those jeeps – they must be training to get vehicles ashore as well, on enemy territory somewhere. Well, if the Americans are going in somewhere, they'll be going in big. What say you, Archie? Have you heard anything? You must have come in here a few times over the last few weeks.'

But Archie knew nothing. 'Most of their visitors come over on the base's own boats from Helensburgh,' he said. 'I've only been in a couple o' times since the Yanks came back, the last time a week ago, and most of this stuff was nae even here then. They're sure piling in their equipment.'

The officers' mess was located just past the house and estate, in the old building that had once been the Ferry Inn, long ago when this peninsula still allowed public houses. Now the US Navy had converted it for themselves, and it was serving alcohol again.

'Trust the Yanks to get themselves the only pub in the area!' Archie commented. 'They call it the Princess Louise, and it's real posh, they say. I brought an admiral here earlier in the month.'

Aunt Sheila had bridled slightly at the mention of a pub. To the best of Catriona's knowledge she had never been in one. But when Archie alluded to the admiral she visibly relaxed, and even preened herself at his words, brushing down the lapels of her summer jacket. She relaxed even more as they were welcomed in person by Captain Martin and ushered into the visitors' lounge of the mess. Catriona was relieved, because to the left of the entrance hall she had seen a bar through an open door, but the lounge they took their seats in was more like a sitting room in a luxury hotel. There was a deep-pile carpet into which your feet sank, sofas and easy chairs in very new-smelling beige leather, and a number of small tables with a scattering of cigarette boxes and heavy glass ashtrays. Catriona was sure it hadn't ever looked like this when it really was the Ferry Inn.

Captain Martin saw everyone seated before he took his own chair and waved forward a waiter who had followed them into the room. Was the waiter American, Catriona wondered, or one of the local people employed at the base? She waited to hear his accent, and was pleased when it was local. The level of service, though, was slick as no Scottish service ever was. Peanuts, salted potato crisps and cream cheese crackers appeared on the tables, and within minutes Catriona found herself sitting in front of a long glass of gin and tonic, misted with ice. Even Aunt Sheila's orange juice was served 'on the rocks', as Captain Martin called it, in heavy leaded crystal.

Another officer, a young lieutenant, came in and joined them, and was soon in discussion with Uncle Charlie and Catriona's father. Catriona could hear Fergus bringing up the subject of 'my son the lieutenant', and knew that he would talk happily for hours.

It meant that Captain Martin could devote himself to the ladies. He apologised that none of his medical colleagues were available this evening, but took Matron's telephone number so that an exchange of visits could be arranged.

'You are at Knockderry full-time, Mrs Sutherland? In residence? Does that mean you are not from Kilcreggan yourself?'

Catriona listened as her capable boss melted under Ron

Martin's easy questions. He didn't have the reserve of the Scots, and his candid approach seemed to bring his guests out of themselves. It was helped by the fact that the small sherry that Matron had accepted was subtly refilled without her noticing. They learnt that she had lost her husband during the First World War, that she had brought up two children on her own before returning to nursing, and now had four grandchildren, that her son was an architect seconded to the War Office, that her daughter was married to a ship's captain commanding a large liner, which ran the Atlantic as part of the very convoys that the Free French, among others, were protecting.

Catriona was curious, and, following the captain's example, she allowed herself to be bold. 'And is it because of the Free French that you accepted the appointment to Knockderry, Mrs Sutherland?' she asked.

'Not exactly.' Matron turned confidingly to Aunt Sheila. 'I think you wanted your niece to be closer to you, didn't you, Mrs Graham? Well then, I think we both came to Knockderry for the same reasons. You see, my daughter is on her own in Dunoon with two teenage children, and with my little car I can be with them two or three times a week. My home is in Ayrshire, you see, and just too far away for comfort.'

She then addressed Catriona with most un-matronly warmth. 'But you are right in a way, Sister, because now that I am here I wouldn't wish to work anywhere else. It is special having such a close community of men in one's care who share the same experiences and challenges, and it is even more special working with Dr Roman, because he understands their situation like none other.'

There was a hint of hero worship in her voice, which wasn't evident when they were at work. Was Matron in love with their doctor? After two gin and tonics Catriona was prepared to believe anything.

It was just as the waiter was offering more drinks, and Aunt Sheila was protesting that they ought to leave, that another officer came into the room.

'Ah, Alex!' Captain Martin exclaimed with satisfaction. 'Ladies, this is my colleague Captain Hayden who has been appointed as commander of our new hospital. Alex, this is Mrs Sutherland, Matron at Knockderry, and her colleague Sister MacNeill. We hadn't thought that you would be back in time to meet them.'

Captain Hayden bowed in that peculiarly American way to Catriona and Matron, and then to Aunt Sheila, to whom he was being introduced.

'It's a pleasure to meet you, ladies. I'm so sorry I'm late. I got in half an hour ago, but I found the men listening to the wireless. You'll have heard about events in Egypt, perhaps?'

'Egypt?' Aunt Sheila queried. 'You mean something new has happened today?'

'Why yes, ma'am. It seems that Rommel has attacked again just south of El Alamein. There aren't any details yet, just your usual BBC blurb, but the armies are fighting again, that's for sure.'

He had the attention of the whole room now. The men stopped talking, and Captain Martin laid down his cigarette. The silence hung for a second, and then Captain Hayden spoke again.

'I'm sorry if I've brought you bad news, but I'm not sure

it is bad, really, not now that you've got new commanders out there. Rommel must know how quickly the Eighth Army is being strengthened, and he is desperate to get in an attack now, while he still has a chance.'

'Isn't your brother out there, Miss MacNeill?' It was Captain Martin who asked.

Catriona shook her head. 'He was, but he was injured on a convoy trying to get to Malta, and he has since been evacuated to South Africa to recuperate.'

'I remember that convoy,' the medical officer said. 'It was a pretty heroic attempt, if I remember. Haven't a couple of convoys made it through since from Gibraltar? I know we flew in some American planes to Malta, and there's been enough fuel on the island for them to be quite effective. We've been stopping Italian tankers from getting to Libya to refuel Rommel.'

The whole war seemed to turn on these convoys, Catriona thought. Duncan might bang on about poor strategy, but poor supplies seemed to be even more crucial. Hadn't Wellington said that an army marched on its stomach? There was word that civilian populations in Greece and the Balkans were starving to death as the Germans confiscated their harvests to feed their troops. Fuel and food being fought over, ships, tanks and aircraft being built, and at the front end, lines of men facing each others' shells and guns, trying to justify what it was all for. The world had gone mad, and there didn't seem to be a single corner left where people weren't dying.

Except in South Africa, where Jim was safe. Catriona thought briefly of his colleagues and friends, George Blake and the mysterious Frances Trevillian, who were in

Alexandria. Would the new commanders out there be able to hold Rommel back, as the men here seemed to think?

Tonight Catriona decided that these issues were not for her to worry about, and, as Captain Hayden settled down to talk to them about their hospital, she ignored her aunt's disapproving eyes and accepted another gin and tonic, ice and all.

CHAPTER TWENTY-SEVEN

Scotland, September 1942

Aunt Sheila predicted that Catriona would suffer the next morning, and she was right. She cycled to work in the early morning with her hastily packed bag strapped to the bike, and hoped that not too many complex new cases had arrived since last week, and that the VAD girls had kept up the therapies she had prescribed last Monday.

She did the rounds with Dr Roman and the team, but by mid morning her head was splitting, and she went looking for aspirin in the dispensary. There Dr Roman was preparing medication for a new patient, and he looked at her with sympathy as she took down the aspirin bottle.

'Is this for you, Sister?' he asked. 'I did think this morning that you didn't look your normal self. Are you feeling unwell?'

She raised rueful shoulders. 'Not so much unwell, Doctor, as suffering from the after-effects of overindulgence. My family was invited to the American Navy Base yesterday evening, and I'm afraid I accepted one drink too many. It's not something we're used to around here.'

His reaction was kindly. 'Ah yes, Matron mentioned that you had all been there, at the officers' mess, is that not so? Well, it isn't pleasant to have a headache, but I do think you probably deserved an evening out, and they say the Americans entertain very lavishly.'

It appeared Matron had recounted their whole weekend to him. 'And you took Laurent, Legrand and Bourdon with you to the village dance on Saturday evening,' he continued. 'Matron tells me that you took special care to dance with them several times during the evening. That was very kind of you.'

'It was nothing. You know, both the villagers and the Americans were very pleased to meet them, and I think they enjoyed their evening.'

'There can be no doubt about that. I've spent a little time with each of them this morning, and they have improved tenfold since I saw them last week. I would take them back to the base with me, but we still don't really have anywhere where the men can be peaceful. One more week, though, and they should be fine to leave here.'

He moved to the basin and poured a glass of water for her. 'Take this,' he said, 'and maybe you would like to sit down for a short while?'

'No, not at all. Please don't pamper me or I'll feel even more guilty! I'm going out into the fresh air, anyway, which will do me good. I want to check on Alain Marcel's leg, and he's sitting in the garden just now.'

'Ah yes, young Alain. Listen, Sister, take a little time with him, if you can. He is our youngest patient, and he has had a very difficult time.'

Catriona looked a question, and he continued. 'He

comes from Alsace-Lorraine, which has always been a disputed region on the border with Germany. When France was occupied the Germans took it back, and Alain's family suddenly found themselves living in Germany. Alain's father was a prominent local politician, and he was interned with a number of his colleagues because he spoke up too loudly against the new laws being imposed.

'Alain was seventeen, and his mother persuaded him to get away, otherwise he might end up being conscripted into the German army. He and a cousin found their way to La Rochelle and got away on a fishing boat, but not before they read that the Germans had tried and executed his father and all his colleagues, and that their families had been forcibly "deported" back to Vichy France. He's had no more news of them, but it is reasonably certain that his mother and sisters are in a detention camp somewhere.'

Catriona's heart clenched. 'What will happen to them?'

Dr Roman sighed. 'Who knows? They will have been categorised as "undesirables", which is one level above the Jews. I think we all know now what Hitler wants to do with the Jews, and there is no sign that France is in any way defending its own. But maybe the Marcel family will survive.'

'But Alain Marcel has his cousin, at least?'

A shake of the head. 'His cousin joined the navy, with Alain, and they were indeed both together, but he was killed in the Atlantic last year.'

Catriona's headache suddenly seemed irrelevant. 'Do you know,' she said, 'of all the patients, he has struck me as one of the most robust and positive – cheeky almost. He always jokes and smiles, and is the first to help serve the others.'

Dr Roman smiled. 'He's a splendid young man. I think the word you have for it is "engaging", is it not? What gives him away is that he volunteers for all the most dangerous jobs on his ship, and has a reputation as a – what do you call it – a daredevil? It's as though he is challenging fate to do its worst, and you know, he is only just nineteen years old.'

'I did think he was quite reckless when he said that he broke his leg climbing the ship's mast in heavy seas.'

'That sounds like Alain!'

'I'll take him out some tea,' Catriona said. 'Would you like some, Doctor?'

'No thank you, Sister. I think I mentioned to you before that there is only so much tea I can drink.'

Catriona smiled, and stepped towards the door, then turned back. 'Tell me, Doctor, do you know as much as this about all of the thousand men at your base?'

He laughed, a deep chuckle of a laugh. 'No, Sister, not at all! I've seen quite a lot of Alain Marcel, because he has a gift for injuring himself, and he is one of the ones I concern myself about.'

'It seems to me that you concern yourself equally about them all,' she said. 'Matron told me so, and I see that it's true.'

She whisked herself out of the room as he laughed again, and stood outside the door kicking herself for having spoken so freely to the hospital doctor. He made it too easy, that was the problem. There wasn't the distance that she had always felt with other doctors. His avuncular warmth to his patients just seemed to overflow in all directions.

She spent the time she had promised with Alain Marcel.

His English was good, and so she tried to engage him about his family. He closed her out. How then had Dr Roman broken through his barriers? Was it because she was female, or was she just too close in age for him to give her his confidence? The men who shared their personal lives with her were those who were missing wives and girlfriends, who were used to sharing their thoughts with a woman. Fathers, too, loved to talk about their children. In contrast, young Alain Marcel was a cagey teenager still, who had lost those he was used to confiding in. Dr Roman, old enough to be his uncle, would inspire more confidence.

She gave up on confidences, and was finishing putting Alain through his paces just as Dr Roman came wandering out into the garden. The doctor always looked as though he was simply ambling without purpose, but Catriona thought that impression was very deceptive. He stopped and chatted to all of the men sitting out in the unaccustomed hot weather, and gradually made his way to where Catriona was just packing up, leaving Alain flexing his muscles painfully.

'*Mademoiselle MacNeill me torture,*' he complained to Dr Roman. The doctor just laughed.

'How can you call it torture to be out in this lovely sunshine?' he answered. He looked across the lawn to the stunning view of deep-blue waters and purple-green hills. 'You are blessed, *jeune homme*, to be in such good hands in such a beautiful place.'

Catriona stood up, and picked up her bag. 'If you didn't throw yourself off ships' masts, Monsieur Marcel, then I wouldn't need to "torture" you.'

'Ah, but someone has to be he who climbs, mademoiselle.

I cannot help it if I am the most athletic and, how do you say, *en forme*? My comrades are all old men. They need me.'

He gave her his most winning smile as he spoke, and she laughed and moved off.

'You will remember to do your exercises, won't you?' she said to him in her parting shot. 'Otherwise you won't be the most athletic among your fellow sailors at all. In fact, you won't be climbing any more masts, ever!'

'For you, mademoiselle, of course,' he replied, and saluted. She returned his grin and left him to the benign company of Dr Roman.

What a weekend it had been, she thought to herself, as she caught the train back to Dunmore that evening. She had danced and drunk gin, and had been treated to American-style hospitality. She'd learnt that they liked all their drinks iced, that they didn't make their own snacks, and that they seemed to have imported everything they ate.

Her bag was stuffed full with chocolate and 'cookies', which were the gifts the officers had given to each of them as they left, in addition to the cigarettes they gave to the men. Catriona had asked Uncle Charlie if he felt at all patronised by the gifts, and he had snorted.

'Patronised?' he'd said. 'The day they can rival your aunt's home baking they can begin to patronise us, but meanwhile I'll accept their factory-made products and enjoy every moment of them!'

Duncan would enjoy them too, and tomorrow they would have lunch together. It was a new thing, this business of having two lives. She wasn't sure how they would work together long-term, but for now it was fun to have the two.

There was this great difference between Dunmore and Knockderry – Dunmore was a major centre, with all the formalities that went with it, while Knockderry was more intimate, more of a family. Much of that atmosphere came from Matron, whom she'd learnt so much more about this weekend, and from Dr Roman, with his special human touch.

She leant back against the hard bench in the third-class carriage, feeling her tired bones. Both of her jobs were equally important, she knew, and she needed to be '*en forme*', as Alain Marcel would say, for her work tomorrow. It had been quite a trip home. She closed her eyes briefly, and looked forward to her bed. Hopefully, she thought, not every weekend would be quite so exhausting.

CHAPTER TWENTY-EIGHT

Alexandria, September–November 1942

In the three months that followed Jim's departure from Alexandria, it seemed to Fran that the whole world changed. He was absent from her life in more than just the physical sense. Each day that passed brought home to her more and more the fact that men like Commander Aldridge, other officers whom Jim had worked with, countless thousands of men out there in the desert, were separated from their wives, fiancées, the women they loved, and had been for over two years.

Those women were continuing their lives, keeping things as normal as possible, and Fran learnt to do the same. She learnt that she had to wait, and in a part of her that she hadn't known before she learnt too to be proud to be part of something so much bigger than them all.

What she desperately wanted, though, was some news of Jim. She'd had no letter from him, despite writing to him almost daily. If he was able, he would have written, and Fran had to battle against the demons in her head that told her that Jim must be permanently brain-damaged.

She threw herself into work, in an office without either Asher or Sami, since Sami left for the American University in Lebanon in August. There was more to do than ever, and she reported non-stop on a war that was moving forward in steady, indelible steps. Here in Egypt, Montgomery turned around the Eighth Army, telling them that there would be no more retreats, but no more rash advances either. He steadied them, and their tanks and artillery were placed in solid, defensive positions, which obliged Rommel to put his forces at untenable risk. When Rommel was repulsed in early September, the message reverberated around the Mediterranean that the Axis could after all be beaten, and when he was sent into his final retreat in November, the world knew that the Afrika Korps had been destroyed as a fighting force.

The *Journal* reported the victory in jubilation, and on 10th November, as Rommel fled from El Alamein, Fran reported in full Churchill's speech in London.

'I have never promised anything but blood, tears, toil, and sweat,' Churchill told the nation. 'Now, however, we have a new experience. We have victory – a remarkable and definite victory. The bright gleam has caught the helmets of our soldiers, and warmed and cheered all our hearts.'

Churchill always did have a dramatic turn of phrase, but this time he sounded genuinely moved, Fran thought, as she typed in the lines. We had beaten Hitler's Nazis, he said, with the very same technical might that he had before wielded against us, and things would never be the same again.

This is not the end. It is not even the beginning of the end. But it is, perhaps, the end of the beginning. Henceforth Hitler's Nazis will meet equally well armed, and perhaps better armed troops. Henceforth they will have to face in many theatres of war that superiority in the air which they have so often used without mercy against others, of which they boasted all round the world, and which they intended to use as an instrument for convincing all other peoples that all resistance to them was hopeless. When I read of the coastal road crammed with fleeing German vehicles under the blasting attacks of the Royal Air Force, I could not but remember those roads of France and Flanders, crowded, not with fighting men, but with helpless refugees – women and children – fleeing with their pitiful barrows and household goods, upon whom such merciless havoc was wreaked. I have, I trust, a humane disposition, but I must say I could not help feeling that what was happening, however grievous, was only justice grimly reclaiming her rights.

If Rommel got through Libya and reached Tunisia he would be met by all the power of the Americans, for they had launched a full-scale assault of the French North African colonies. Within three days of their amphibious landings in Algeria and Morocco the two countries had come over to the Allies, and the French armies were now fighting against the Germans again. Tunisia was their next goal.

Even more emotively for Alexandrians, Eisenhower had

appointed their very own Admiral Cunningham, who had gone over to the USA in the spring to build the naval alliance, as Supreme Commander of the Naval Expeditionary Force. Most of those invading North Africa might be American, but ABC was in charge at sea.

Was this the turning point, as Churchill was suggesting? Things were going better elsewhere too. The *Journal* reported it all, piling good news upon good news. The USA was beginning to make real gains in the Pacific. The Russians disrupted the entire German southern front in Russia. The Germans would not make it through Russia now to Iran and the oilfields they had so desperately tried to reach. Fewer of their tankers tried to cross the Mediterranean, because there was no more oil. Hitler, it was said, was conserving what he had for other fronts.

It had taken three years to get to this point, and some warned that it could take another three to see an end. But here in Alexandria no one cared. The mood was jubilant, and everywhere there were huge celebrations. Fran hadn't been out in the evening for months, but now her parents whisked her out with them to a grand party at Alexandria's largest nightclub, and to a champagne supper at the Menasces'. Fran went along willingly enough. It would be stupid to mope on her own at home when there was so much to be thankful for.

Their navy friends weren't there. They were busy following Rommel along the coast, and just a week later a convoy from Alexandria reached Malta unopposed, laden with supplies. The siege of that valiant island was over at last.

It was not until the very end of November that Fran finally caught up with George and Len. It was a Saturday, and George phoned the office late in the morning.

'What are you doing this evening, Fran?' he asked. 'Could you come out to dinner? Len is free too, and I have something for you.'

There was nothing Fran wanted more. Being with these fellows was the closest she could come at the moment to being with Jim.

'Wild horses wouldn't keep me away, George. Where do you want to meet?'

'Shall we say Alberto's?' He named a scruffy bar in the backstreets, a favourite old haunt of Jim's because the beer was good, and very cheap. It was one of the bars he had dragged Fran and Len out to on that memorable night after his first accident, and he always said he had a fondness for it, because it was the night he had first really fallen for Fran.

'The town is swarming with happy army wallahs at the moment,' George continued. 'We went to the Cecil last night and could hardly even reach the bar. Hopefully at Alberto's we'll at least find a seat.'

'Sounds good to me,' she answered. 'Just make sure you're there before me. I wouldn't want to find myself in there on my own!'

'Don't worry, we'll take you somewhere better afterwards!' he promised. 'We'll be there by seven, so come along any time you like after that.'

She arrived soon after them, though, because she was so anxious to see them. The bar was full of locals, and of a large, noisy group of Aussie soldiers. There wasn't a woman in sight, and Fran slipped through the door as inconspicuously as she could, and made a beeline for the table in the corner where she had spotted the boys.

They both rose, and she threw herself into their arms one after the other. One of the Aussie squaddies whistled, but his mates shushed him, and Fran sat down while Len waved for a waiter to get her a drink.

'How amazing to see you guys!' She couldn't stop smiling. 'I haven't seen you for over a month.'

'We've been busy!' George said.

'Don't I know it! Were you both with the convoy?'

'We sure were!' There was a kind of suppressed excitement about Len in particular that she couldn't quite place.

'So, tell me about it,' she demanded.

It was George who started. 'It was the air cover that made the difference,' he said. 'Now that we've taken the old Italian airbases in Libya our aircraft are able to protect us right along the coast. And they've got new Spitfires on Malta. Those guys were determined we were going to get through.'

Len nodded. 'But our boys were only protecting us from other aircraft, Fran. The enemy fleet never even appeared, and even from the air they didn't find us until we were nearly halfway there. They say the Luftwaffe has mostly left Crete, and they seem to have given up hope of capturing Malta. You should have seen the welcome the islanders gave us!'

'And tell Fran what happened when we got back to base,' George instructed.

He was grinning encouragement at Len, and Fran

raised both eyebrows. 'Well?' she asked Len.

Len blushed. 'Our captain called me in and told me he's going to recommend me for promotion,' he said.

'Oh, that's fantastic, Len! So you'll be a full lieutenant? No more of George and Jim lording it over you! You've obviously been doing some pretty good work.'

He blushed even redder. 'I hope so,' he muttered. 'It's all been about organisation, I think. The captain seems to think I'm good at organising the men.'

'He's a natural leader when he's on board ship,' George agreed, 'Even if he behaves like an ass so often onshore!' He fished in his pocket and brought out an envelope. 'There was another piece of good news when we got back, Fran. I found this waiting for me.'

He handed the envelope to Fran. It was addressed to George at the base, and had come through the Forces mail, stamped as received at the base just two days ago. On the back was marked 'If undeliverable, please pass to Sub Lt L. Rudland'. The handwriting was well known to Fran, and her hand shook as she held it.

'F-from Jim?' she stammered.

'Yes.' George smiled at her encouragingly. 'Open it, Fran.'

'But it's addressed to you!' She scanned George's face, but he merely smiled, and after a moment she slid her thumb inside the envelope and drew out, not the sheet of paper she was expecting, but another envelope. On this was written just one word: 'Fran'.

She took a sharp breath, and looked up at George. 'He wrote to me via you?'

He nodded. 'There was a letter for me in there too, and

he said he thought a letter would get to you more quickly if it was sent directly to the base.'

Fran gazed at the envelope, not knowing what to do. She longed to open it, but she wanted to be on her own when she read Jim's letter. She looked again at George.

'How was his writing? Is he all right?'

He seemed to understand her dilemma, and he reached into his pocket and brought out a slip of paper.

'Here, Fran, read his letter to me first, then you can read your own later.'

She took the sheet eagerly and scanned it. It had been written four weeks ago, when the final battle was in full flood at Alamein, and the handwriting looked quite normal, if a bit shaky. What had he written? She took a breath and began to read.

Dear George,

You seem to have been having an interesting time up there in the Med while I am holidaying here in Cape Town. I'm doing well, and have been given a major exercise regime to get me back in shape. I'm damned lucky, I know, because I could have had much more lasting damage.

My hearing isn't quite right yet, and I get a bit wobbly if I stand up too quickly, and my hands have been pretty unsteady up till now, which is why I haven't written. But I can hold a can of beer, and I'm allowed out now from time to time to wander around Cape Town's bars with some other guys.

Writing is exhausting, so I'll keep this short. Could you give the enclosed letter to Fran. I think it's the quickest way to reach her, and I've never actually known her postal address. Have a drink for me at Alberto's, and tell the bartender there that the beer is much better in Cape Town. I'll be back there before you know it.

Yours aye,
Jim

A flush of pleasure waved over Fran. Jim was himself, not a damaged man. He was getting better, and would soon be back in Alexandria. This letter was written a month ago, and by now maybe he was even on a boat? She stopped herself. That was moonshine, and she knew it, but it didn't matter. She'd waited four months without any news at all, and now she knew that Jim was on the mend she could wait for as long as it took.

She looked over at her two friends. 'I'm so glad we came to Alberto's,' she said. 'Thank you, both of you.'

'We'll go somewhere else now,' George said, grinning at her. 'But I did think it would be fitting to start the evening here.'

'You were right. You know, we should eat at the Greek restaurant Jim loves as well! We'll avoid all the posh spots, and have a good old bar crawl. Or do you want to crack open some champagne to celebrate Len's promotion?'

Len shook his head. 'We'll celebrate that when it's confirmed,' he said.

George agreed. 'Tonight we're celebrating victory and recovery,' he told Fran. 'And you're out on the town with the boys. I think the Greek place sounds perfect, and we'll drink some of that cheap retsina that Jim always tries to convince us is so good.'

'Lead on, then,' she said, standing up and linking her arms through both of theirs. 'If Jim is investigating the bars of Cape Town, then I think we should see if we can do just as well right here in Alex!'

CHAPTER TWENTY-NINE

My darling Fran,

Your letters have been my prop, sweetheart. Without them this whole recuperation period would have been the loneliest time of my life. Everyone here is wonderful, but they aren't you.

I know from your letters that you are working long hours at the newspaper, but in my dreams you are in the boat on Lake Mariut, drifting in the sun, or on the beach at Abu Sir. The beaches here are wilder than those in Alex, so they make me think of Abu Sir. As I get fitter I'm hoping to start swimming again, and one of the hospital visitors is talking about taking some of us to Boulders Beach, where there is a colony of penguins, would you believe.

If you read my letter to George you'll know that I still have some lingering health problems of hearing and balance and muscle control, but I am improving fast. I've set myself a target of being fit to

*leave before the end of the year, and the doc seems
to think that's achievable.*

*I can't write more, Fran, because it still takes a
lot of effort, but I will write again very soon. Keep
your letters coming, please. Each one I receive takes
me further along the road, and closer to coming back
to you.*

With all my love,
Jim

Those were fine, loving words from a dour Scot! Fran
read and reread the letter that night, and kept it with her
every moment over the next few days. She wrote to him
immediately, telling him about the relief and delight of
Alexandrians at being saved from Rommel, and about
George and Len's successful mission to Malta. He would
be so happy to hear that Len was being considered for
promotion.

Write to me at home, she told him. *That way, if
George and Len are away at sea, I'll still receive
your letter. They say they could be spending a lot of
time further along the coast now. Being with them
yesterday brought you back to Alex for one night,
and we had a drink in most of your favourite bars.*

*Rest and get better, my love. Don't charm your
nurses too much with that beautiful accent of yours,
and come back to me soon.*

She wanted to enclose a photo that Jim had taken of
her earlier in the year, in that very boat on Lake Mariut. It

was a close-up of her laughing at the camera with nothing behind her but rippling water, her dark hair a mess of curls. Jim loved that photo. He had offered a copy to her parents, which was framed in the dining room, and she almost sent it to him.

But if he really did leave Cape Town before the end of the year, this letter might miss him. It had taken four weeks for his letter to reach here. In four weeks it would be Christmas. Her father told her he was sure Jim must have the original with him, anyway. They would have packed all his bags when he left on that hospital ship.

So Fran went back to work on the Monday determined to be sensible. And who should appear in the office but Asher and Sami. She'd had no idea that Sami was back at home. And she hadn't seen Asher since he and his family had left Alexandria in June.

She swept on them both in the same way that she had swept on George and Len, wrapping her arms around Asher, in particular, like a long lost younger brother.

'What happened to you? Tell me where you were. I want to hear all about it!' She pulled him and Sami together into her office, and closed the door firmly behind them.

Sami couldn't wipe the smile from his face to have his friend back with him, but Asher was more serious, as always.

'We went to Sudan,' he said, 'and stayed in a hotel until my father could rent somewhere for us to stay. He was always sure we were going to be coming back, and he was in contact with his business partners, even though he was working from Khartoum. I've never seen anyone work so hard to make sure we didn't lose everything. I think he might have lost a lot more, but his partners were always aware that the whole Jewish business community here would turn on them if we came back and found they'd stripped us bare.'

'So you're all right? The family, I mean? Your father's business is fine?'

'The business, yes.' He paused and continued. 'The house didn't fare so well.'

Sami interjected with his usual impetuosity. 'Would you believe it, some fascist sympathisers had been into the house and daubed foul comments all over the walls.'

Fran was horrified. 'Oh, Asher, I'm so sorry.'

He bit down on his lip. 'The bastards wouldn't dare come in the front door and tell us what they think of us, but they're delighted to get in the back and trash the house, and let us know they think we're Jewish scum. Thankfully, everything we had of real value we'd left with Sami's family.'

'And the whole neighbourhood helped you to clean up,' Sami said. 'You have a lot of friends, you know that.'

Asher looked unconvinced. 'In our neighbourhood, perhaps, but what about the rest of Alexandria? And the rest of Egypt? How many friends do we Jews really have? My father wants me to start planning my future elsewhere now.'

'So I can't persuade you to come back to work here?' Fran asked.

Asher shook his head. 'Not unless you'll let me come back for a few weeks only, Miss Trevillian? Would you? I attended some courses at Gordon College in Khartoum this autumn, and my tutor has recommended me for admission to the American University in Beirut in January.'

'You've decided not to wait to go to university in England?'

He shook his head. 'My father is against it while the war is still on, and how many years will it be before it's all over, do you think? Anyway, I've made up my own mind that I want to go to Lebanon. My world is here, and I don't think Jews should be ditching the region just because the region is ditching us.'

Fran looked at him curiously. His words and tone were both tough, but as he finished he gave her a smile, which reassured her.

'So you're joining Sami!' she said. 'That's wonderful news! I think you're right to crack on with your studies. You could lose a lot of time hanging around here, and the university in Beirut has a great reputation. And what about you, Sami? Are you on holiday?'

He nodded. 'We finished term last week, and I got back yesterday to find this creature was home.'

'And how are you getting on?'

'I love it. Beirut is so French, and yet the university is so American. It makes for a fascinating life, and there's so much going on in the city. They're working peacefully towards independence, and it's the most enlightened place in the whole region, I swear to you. It makes Alexandria look like nothing but a money market in comparison.'

He took a quick breath, and continued his flow. 'I keep telling Asher here that he'll have no problems there. And it's a great place to be a Christian. I've never been anywhere before where I am in the majority!'

'And they're preparing the elections?' Fran asked. The Allies had put a Free French government into Lebanon over a year ago, and they had recognised Lebanon's right to independence. Now they were preparing elections to decide their own future.

Sami nodded furiously. 'The university has hosted a number of debates.'

Fran smiled. 'Would you like to write about it? For the *Journal*, I mean?' The furious nodding continued, and she turned to Asher. 'And would you write me a piece about Khartoum, and the Sudan, and what it was like to be there in exile? It's a strong people story that would interest our readers.'

He hesitated. 'I will do, of course, but can I also write about why we weren't allowed into Palestine?'

Fran shook her head, and he sighed. 'Listen, Asher,' she told him, 'I know it must have been hard to be driven from your home, and I care as deeply as you do about the way Jewish people are being targeted, but the *Journal* cannot get involved in any Zionist propaganda.'

He made to protest, and she checked him. 'I'm not saying you're a Zionist, but it's easy to become one when you start getting bitter, and Zionist rhetoric just fuels the anti-Semitism we can all see growing around Egypt. The *Journal* won't fuel problems in this country, and nor should you. You heard Sami, you're going to live in an enlightened cultural centre where people are working things out moderately. It's the perfect place for you to study and learn.'

She saw that Asher was going to argue some more. 'Let's go out for coffee to celebrate you being home,' she said quickly. 'And I'll tell you what, I'll give you an assignment that you could find very interesting. I've heard that the president of the Jewish community in Alexandria is launching an appeal to your community to raise funds for the war effort rather than to keep sending money to fund illegal immigrants into Palestine. Go and ask him why. I'll send you to interview him, and you can be as radical as you like in your questions, but promise me to listen to him, and to write a fair piece.'

'And will you publish it?'

She pulled him towards the door. 'Coffee, Asher! No, I won't promise to publish it, but I'll promise to read it, and if you've written something worthwhile I'll see if I can get it published somewhere. Is that fair?'

He grinned at last. 'Yes, that's fair.'

'That's my boy! And after that you can get out of my hair and go and argue with your university professors instead.'

CHAPTER THIRTY

Scotland, November 1942

The American invasion of North Africa explained everything to the people of Kilcreggan. For two months beforehand the numbers of American troops and vehicles arriving on the peninsula strained everyone to the limits of their patience. What had until now been an operation hidden around the corner in Rosneath spilt over everywhere. Never had so much traffic occupied their roads. And the young GIs were so cocky, too easily sure of themselves. They had no respect for age, residents said, or for conventions.

A convoy of ten huge, ten-wheeled trucks took out part of the Kilcreggan garage forecourt one day as it tried to negotiate a tight corner. Mr Jardine came out raging, waving his fists at them, but the GIs packed into the trucks just yelled at him, 'Never mind, Pop, we're gonna win the war for you. Send the bill to Uncle Sam!'

Mr Jardine was a veteran of the First World War, and was unimpressed. 'Bunch o' damned greenhorns,' was his response. 'Full o' cock and bull, but not one o' them has ever faced a real gun. Whatever they do, they'll make a mess of it, mind what I say.'

But when he went to complain to the base they sent their own men and equipment to repair his fence and shelter. It was more than the Royal Navy would have done for him, his neighbours told him – with them he'd have had to fill in forms in triplicate. He muttered a little more, and then calmed down.

Across at Gourock and Greenock docks there had never been so many ships, and Catriona had difficulty getting home from Dunmore one weekend because the railway lines were clogged with troop trains and freight trains.

'Ye'll just hae to wait,' said a resigned porter to passengers, as wagon after open wagon of a slow-moving train slipped through the Dunmore station loaded with what looked like bulldozers on the front, and crate after crate at the rear. 'Your train'll be along when it's good and ready.'

Were they going to invade France? That was the question on everyone's lips. Surely not, when Jerry had such a stranglehold on Europe, but this was no small operation, that much everyone agreed.

It was the early morning of Sunday 18th October, and Catriona was standing with her bike waiting for the ferry to take her across to Kilcreggan for her day with her father. Would there even be a ferry? The whole of the Clyde Estuary before her was a mass of ships, hundreds of them as far as the eye could see. They were strangely quiet, riding at anchor, and the noise came from motor launches moving between them and the shore, and from men moving around the decks, hailing each other. The quayside was quieter too than it had been for a long time, and she realised that this must be it. These were the ships assembled for whatever operation they had all been preparing for. The sheer scope of it held her silent.

It was the woman standing next to her who spoke. 'Makes you wonder, doesn't it?'

Catriona nodded. For many months now, the Clyde had been the only fully useable waterway in Britain, the only one not subject to constant bombing, and they were used to seeing large convoys gathering here, but this was different. It brought a lump to her throat.

There was a ferryman on the quayside, and Catriona made her way over to him. 'Can the ferry even make its way through that?' she asked.

He grinned. 'There'll be a ferry, dinnae worry, whenever Hamish manages to get through from Kilcreggan. He's already made it o'er there this morning. And if he does nae, you can just walk over, can't you?'

It would almost be possible, Catriona thought, so closely were the ships anchored to each other.

'And this isnae all,' the ferryman said proudly. 'There's a whole fleet of ships sailing in just now frae Belfast, and they're all going tae meet up here. The rest'll have tae stay in the Firth outside the boom, though. There's nae mair space inside.'

The ferry appeared, nosing its way towards the quayside, and a couple of marines stepped forward to check passengers' papers before they embarked. They had a fascinating fifteen-minute trip across to the other side. On the decks of troopships men waved to them, a mix of army and navy uniforms, mainly American, with a few ships flying the Royal Navy ensign, and between the ships darted small supply boats. Alongside the military ships were more industrial-looking cargo ships loaded with all kinds of equipment. And moored closest to the docks were the naval escort ships, which would protect all the others, the corvettes and destroyers and cruisers that had become so much at home on the Clyde. Would any of her Frenchmen be aboard these? she wondered.

It surprised Catriona that civilians were even allowed to pass through here, but then what was there to hide? There could be no disguising such a massive fleet. It must have been gathering for days while she was away at Dunmore. It was visible from all around, and the hills above Kilcreggan would be full of locals wanting to see more. Or would there be guards stopping you from climbing up today?

It was no typical quiet Sunday when she reached Kilcreggan. There were more security checks when they reached the pier, and a cordon of marines preventing local children from approaching the beach, where more marines surrounded some shallow boats. As she set off on her bike Catriona took one last look at the fleet behind her, wondering if it would still be here when she came back this way tomorrow evening.

Her father and uncle were sure the operation was going to invade France, but her patients at Knockderry the next day had other ideas. The Americans might want to invade France, but it was too soon, they were sure. It was their most senior patient by rank, a captain recovering from an appendicectomy, who hazarded the guess that it was North Africa that was to be invaded.

'They have not spoken to us,' he said. 'The Free French

are not involved in this operation. That will be deliberate, because to be honest our presence would antagonise those French soldiers and officers in Tunisia, Morocco and Algeria still loyal to Pétain and Vichy France. But when they see this massive operation they will turn on their German masters, and our people will be with us once again. We will have the whole of North Africa on our side.'

He spoke in rhetoric similar to de Gaulle, which made Catriona smile, but future events proved him right. Press silence held, local people stayed respectfully at a distance, and a week later, after several manoeuvres, the fleet sailed away under cover of darkness. The Clyde seemed deathly quiet afterwards, and there was no movement from the US base. All hatches seemed battened down, and there was no one to ask questions of. But on 8th November, three weeks after Catriona had first crossed the Clyde through that fleet, the first news came in on the wireless of amphibious Allied landings in Morocco and Algeria.

The BBC newsreader spoke of enemy forces in Morocco surrendering within hours on the beaches. Before the invasion even took place, he said, French resistance fighters had neutralised the coastal batteries, and more than one French commander had openly welcomed the landing Allies.

Catriona sat with her family, delaying going to bed so that they could catch the late news. Just yesterday the BBC had confirmed that Rommel was on the run, and now today there was this. The evening news was extended to cover it all, and Catriona was sure the whole country must be listening.

Alamein was Jim's victory, she felt, even though he wasn't

physically there. Whereas this operation felt like their own, born on the Clyde, on their own little peninsula. Operation Torch, the newsreader had called it. Was Captain Martin with them? Catriona was sure he must be.

She found her patients at the hospital poring over the papers the following morning, brought in early by Dr Roman from Greenock. Only an invasion of France could have been closer to their hearts. They were glued to the wireless, too. More news had come in this morning, and it seemed Algiers had surrendered to the Americans within hours, and with hardly a fight. When they heard this a cheer went up throughout the ward where they had all gathered together, and men slapped each other on the backs. Dr Roman had his hand wrung by one after another, and Catriona and the VADs were soundly kissed.

'*Vive les Américains!*' one shouted, with his arm round a VAD nurse. 'And you British, of course, but you will see, these Americans will win over the North Africans more easily than you who have been fighting against them and against France for the last two years.'

'But we haven't been fighting against France!'

'That's not what our people have been hearing. And who bombs our ports, and who sank our ships and killed twelve hundred of our servicemen when they had already become neutral?'

'You dislike the British?' Catriona asked.

'Me? *Pas du tout!* I am a Free French, remember! I work with you! But our people back in France have been told for a long time that the only way forward is to collaborate with the Boche. We have to make people trust us again.'

Another of his colleagues interjected. 'Don't try to

understand us, Sister. We are French, after all!' He caught her up in his arms, and danced an impromptu waltz around the ward hampered only by the plaster on his ankle. He stopped when Matron came in, but even when she caught him by the arm he only grinned.

'You'll do yourself damage, Ensign Lefranc!' Matron reminded him sternly, pushing him into a chair. 'Dr Roman, what were you thinking of not to stop him?'

The doctor was at the other end of the ward, listening to the wireless with the men. He looked ruefully at Matron. 'I didn't notice,' he admitted. 'But today is not an ordinary day, and I do not think that our friend has done himself any real harm.'

He turned to Catriona. 'And as for the British being kept in the background in this battle, I wouldn't worry if I were you. It's about time the Americans did something. After all, the biggest victory at the biggest cost has been in Egypt, and I do not remember that the Americans were at El Alamein.'

'No, but *we* were!' the young Lefranc said, irrepressibly. 'And so were you Poles, *mon Docteur*. The British didn't win on their own.'

Dr Roman's lips twitched, but he pretended to frown. 'None of us will win on our own, *mon jeune*. Isn't that the point?' He looked at Matron. 'I can see that these young men will be insufferable for the rest of the day. I am very glad! It is better than any of my medicines. Shall we leave them to have lunch?'

Catriona and Matron and the doctor left the VADs in charge of the ward, and ate lunch together in the little dining room reserved for staff. Catriona never ceased to wonder at what miracles the kitchen at Knockderry performed with the simple rations they had. There were gifts of eggs and vegetables, of course, from this little rural community, and of fish when the catch was good. Everyone in Scotland had some family member in the war, and as Aunt Sheila always said, hopefully someone was being good to our boys wherever they were too.

But the real reason, she was sure, why the food was so good here was because the patients themselves went into the kitchen to lend a hand. They were gastronomes, these Frenchmen, and they could turn even turnips and tinned meat into something worth eating. Today they had been rather preoccupied, so it was beetroot salad and quiche for lunch, but there was home-made bread, and it was immeasurably better than at Dunmore.

In a previously unknown gesture Matron produced a bottle of her home-made elderflower wine, and offered a glass each to Catriona and Dr Roman.

'This is very good, dear Matron,' Dr Roman said, as he sipped the wine.

Matron almost blushed. 'Not at all, Doctor, but I thought we should do something to mark this special day. Who would have believed we would have two such splendid successes at the same time in Africa? Rommel out of Egypt in the east, and the Americans carrying all before them in the west.'

'Things aren't over, surely?' Catriona ventured. 'The troops still have to go into Tunisia. Will that be easy?'

Dr Roman shook his head over a forkful of quiche. 'No, it won't be easy, because the Germans will have time to send in reinforcements, but what the Americans lack in experience they make up in equipment and numbers, and in determination. They want to make their mark outside of the Pacific. I just hope they won't be too impatient.'

'And then?' Catriona asked. 'If the Allies have the whole of North Africa?'

'Then we move into Europe, my dear.'

'And to Poland?'

'I hope so,' was his simple reply. 'But we still have a very long way to go.'

CHAPTER THIRTY-ONE

The mood at Dunmore when Catriona returned there was equally jubilant. There were so many men at Dunmore who had been in the desert, so many limbs blown off by mines.

'As long as this time we aren't being yet again over hopeful,' was one caveat. 'We've driven Rommel over the border before, and he's regrouped and come back at us.'

But the news was so conclusive, so convincing, that the men allowed themselves to believe. The detail in the newspapers of Montgomery's battle plan, and the way Rommel was now being chased right the way along the Libyan coast, was just too persuasive. They didn't dance around like the French, but their quiet satisfaction showed as they talked about where the war would go from now.

'A walk in the park!' was their disparaging commentary on Operation Torch. 'All the Yanks have to fight are a bunch of Frenchies who will come over to whoever looks like winning.'

But they watched with keen interest, nevertheless. 'They'll

get Rommel in a pincer movement,' one said. 'He'll get reinforcements, but he won't stand against the Americans.'

'About time too!' another muttered. 'Took the damned Yanks long enough to get involved, didn't it?'

A Royal Navy man protested. 'They've been with us at sea for a year now.'

The reply was benignly tolerant. 'They're learning! Couldn't find a U-boat in a million years until we showed them how!'

His neighbour raised a finger to his lips, and gestured to a patient on his other side. But Jozef Gorski showed no sign of understanding. He was a brand-new patient, whose cargo ship had been torpedoed by a U-boat in the Baltic, as the other patients had been quick to find out.

He was the first Polish patient Catriona had seen here, because the Poles had their own Polish School of Medicine at Edinburgh University. This man had lost a hand to frostbite, and was in danger of losing the other. There wasn't much for Catriona to do for him at this early stage, but she stopped by his bed anyway.

She wasn't sure he understood everything she said, but she sat down and spoke to him slowly. 'You're far from your comrades here, Mr Gorski. Is there anyone you know living nearby?'

He shook his head. He looked shrunken in doubt and fear, and glanced frequently at the stump where his hand had been. The other hand was heavily bandaged. He would lose fingers, no doubt, but Catriona hoped fervently that he wouldn't lose it all. To be left without both hands was a serious life sentence. Some of her French patients at Knockderry had done convoys through the Baltic, and they said it was the coldest, harshest place you could imagine being in winter.

It was typical of Dunmore that by mid morning a Polish visitor had arrived to translate for Jozef Gorski. When Catriona passed by his bed later he was chatting away, with new colour in his pinched face. He was too thin, too, Catriona thought, but that would soon be taken care of. She crossed her fingers tightly that they would save his other hand.

It was a great couple of weeks at Dunmore. Catriona was able to sign off several patients who had come to the hospital with major issues. Morocco surrendered, and came over to the Allies, and a French general brought in by the Americans secretly from Vichy France was placed in command of the French African forces. The race for Tunis began, and despite some setbacks the news kept even the most unwell patients in good spirits. Some late autumn sunshine allowed Catriona and Duncan to walk at lunchtimes, and even he seemed infected by the post-Alamein mood.

She quipped him over it, and he answered quite seriously. 'I've never denied that we need to win this war, Catriona. I just wish it could be done with less needless waste of lives and limbs.'

He was in good spirits, because his long-hoped-for exhibition was nearing fruition, and he had taken a group of patients off-site this week to view an exhibition space, which was bigger than anything he'd hoped for.

'We'll show work that is being done now, but also other stuff from way back in the summer, made by some of the men who've left,' he told her. 'I'm even hoping the committee will find some money to bring the men back to see their work on show.'

'Don't a lot of the men take their work away with them?' Catriona wanted to know.

'Yes, but the best has been left here. I asked the men to leave it. What have been taken away are the bookshelves and cabinets and the like, but the exhibition will focus on the sculptures and engraved work.'

They had a night out at the cinema to celebrate, and saw James Cagney in *Yankee Doodle Dandy*, a musical that Duncan would normally have decried but that he sat through this time without complaint. Catriona loved it for its brash, innocent Americanism. It made her think of the Rosneath base, and the warm cheerfulness of the GIs who had been there.

A drink at the jazz bar completed their evening after the film, and Catriona had an American cocktail to stay in the mood. On a weekday, Duncan's friends, the lecturer and the shipyard worker, weren't there, but the singer was the same crooner as the first time Catriona had been there way back in May. The songs were the same too. The familiarity cloaked them, and as Catriona had a final dance with Duncan she could feel all the tantalising draw of him, with the same force as six months ago.

'You're beautiful, my Islay nymph,' Duncan murmured in her ear, and she let herself fold into him.

The mood at Dunmore lasted as the dry weather continued. Moments with Duncan were stolen as he immersed himself in his exhibition, and meanwhile Catriona went home to Kilcreggan every weekend.

Her patients there stayed buoyant, but they were visibly shaken when the Germans retaliated for Morocco and Algeria coming over to the Allies by occupying southern France. For those who were from the north of France, nothing for their families would change. They had been occupied from the moment the Germans overran France. But those who came from the south were anxious. It might have been just a puppet government that the Germans allowed to govern there, but the young men had hoped and expected that their families were less oppressed by their French militia than they would be now by the *Wehrmacht*.

'Things are hardening in France, but at least it will make the French people realise now that the Germans are their enemy,' Dr Roman said to Catriona. 'It will help build the resistance. Now that Morocco and Algeria have switched sides, people all over France will start to dream again, and support for the Nazis will crumble.'

'But what about Alain Marcel's family and people like them?' Catriona asked. 'Won't they suffer even more in their camp if it is run by the Germans?' Alain had left the hospital now, and might well be on a ship out on the Atlantic, ready to do something even more reckless.

Dr Roman frowned. 'It is you who have the right, my dear, and the compassion. I am wishing suffering on people who do not deserve it. As if there was not already enough suffering! I must make a point of going to see young Alain when I get back to the base. He will be so worried.'

Catriona found herself needed more and more at

Knockderry, but less by her father. A letter had finally come from Jim, and had stopped Fergus's fretting. Jim was doing fine, he assured them, and was building up strength slowly. Now that the Mediterranean had become less treacherous, Fergus could even cope with the idea that his son might one day return there. Catriona told him about the poor Polish mariner with his lost hand and fingers, and suddenly Fergus wanted Jim back in Alexandria rather than here in Scotland, where he could find himself escorting convoys through the nightmare of the Baltic Sea.

Catriona thought it more likely that Jim would be kept ashore for some time. Jim wouldn't tell them about any problems he had, but she didn't remind Fergus of that. He thought his son was nearly back to full health.

The community at Kilcreggan seemed very quiet with the departure of the Americans. The hospital staff were still around, with their complement of wounded from the American convoys, but everyone else seemed to have left. Catriona had never made it to see the hospital, but Matron had visited, and had come away awestruck by the equipment and range of medicines they had. They'd been able to borrow occasionally, when they were in real need. No one could say that the Americans weren't generous, and now that most of them had gone they were sadly missed.

It was only by chance at the end of November that Catriona ran up against Captain Martin, almost literally as she cycled away from the ferry one Sunday. He was coming out of the paper shop by the pier, crossing the road without looking, and he sent her bike wobbling over the road as she swerved to avoid him.

'Miss MacNeill!' His face broke in to a broad grin. 'Why I haven't seen you for . . .'

'Two months!' she replied, speaking rather sharply as she realised she hadn't hit him.

He came over to where she was straightening up her bike.

'I'm sorry, I walked right out in front of you. You shouldn't cycle so quietly!' he said. 'Hey, you look real shaken. Can I buy you a coffee?'

Her nerves settled, and she shook his hand. 'It's Sunday, remember?' she said to him. 'The tea shop is closed, and the only thing you can buy in Kilcreggan is the newspaper you're holding.'

'Well then come to the base, and we'll have some real coffee,' he urged. 'I need some sanity, and some female company will do the job! We'll put your bike in the back of the jeep, and I'll run you home later. Do you have any urgent need to get home?'

She shook her head. 'They don't even know what ferry I'm on.'

'Well then, what are we waiting for?'

He gave her his characteristic beaming smile, and she allowed him to stow her bicycle. He drove them to the Officers' Mess, the wonderful Princess Louise, where some of his fellow officers were having breakfast of amazing smelling bacon and eggs.

'Have you had breakfast?' he asked her. 'No, well me neither,' and he ordered food for them both. The bacon was the best Catriona had tasted since the old days of Islay, before the war. It was served with coffee, which she rarely drank, but it was too good to refuse.

All the while she threw questions at him, and now

that their operation had been successful he was only too pleased to talk.

'We couldn't come out into the community before the mission left,' he told her. 'We didn't have time, if the truth be told, but we wouldn't have wanted to answer questions either. You know what? General Eisenhower called our fleet the mightiest assembly of shipping ever gathered together in any port in the world. It needed to be protected, as I'm sure you'll understand.'

'And you didn't go with the fleet?'

'Oh, I did, but I'm a naval engineer, an amphibious landing expert. My involvement was over once the troops were safely landed. I got back here last week.'

'But you didn't bring any of the landing craft back with you? I didn't see any as we passed the shore.'

'No, we'll be winding up this base now, handing it over to some submarine people who want to use it. Not my area, I'm afraid.'

'So you'll be leaving Rosneath?'

He nodded. 'Not immediately, but sometime in the next couple of months. I'm being sent to the Pacific, so if they use this place to prepare for the next invasion it won't be me doing the training. I have to say I'll miss this community. You're fine people, and we've been graciously received. But I won't miss the rain!'

She smiled. 'Well, we'll miss you too, Captain. You've been very good to us in a short space of time. And it has been fascinating to know you and your colleagues. You've brought a lot of colour to our little world.'

'Sometimes a bit too much,' was his answer. 'Our men have treated this area like a playground at times, and if the officers have been able to offset any bad legacy by inviting people in here to see that we can also be quite civilised, then it has been a good move. And it has been nice to meet some families, when we are missing our own. And to have a coffee from time to time with a fine young lady, instead of with this lot here.' He gestured to the other officers in the room, and then continued on a wistful note.

'You have a look of my Carrie, you know. She has the same clear eyes and swinging hair, and you are both women of intelligence. Maybe next time our young officers will be quicker off the mark to appreciate a fine young lady like yourself.'

Catriona laughed. 'I think all of your men have found more glamorous material than a simple island girl at the dances in Helensburgh and Glasgow!'

'Oh, the girls they meet are sometimes too simple, believe me. That's the problem! A girl like you, bright, of decent folk, well grounded, you would know how to handle our boys.'

Catriona raised a rueful brow. 'I have enough trouble handling the one I already have, I can assure you!'

'You have a boyfriend?'

'Why yes.' And then, at his look of surprise. 'He works with me at the other hospital, where I spend most of the week.'

'But he isn't spoken about?' He asked the question as an elder brother might, and when he saw her self-conscious look, he continued with a frown. 'I liked your family, Miss MacNeill, and I would have thought if you felt able to, then you would have told them about your boyfriend.'

Catriona was angry. Duncan represented her

independence, her right to freedom of thought, and she had kept him from her family to preserve that. Hadn't she?

'Thank you for your concern,' she answered, tight-lipped, and then changed the subject. 'Have you had more news about the progress of your troops in Tunisia?' she asked. He looked at her rather thoughtfully for a moment, and then followed her lead.

'They're near to Tunis now,' he said. 'The Germans have massed troops against us, though, so all is not won yet. Have you finished your breakfast, Miss MacNeill? Shall I run you home now?'

There was a rebuff in his words, and now she felt rather ashamed. In what he'd said about Duncan he was speaking with the same voice her father would have used, with the same values, and he meant well. She nodded, and rose to leave. Her coat was brought, and Captain Martin helped her into it.

'Forgive me, Miss MacNeill, for butting in where I'm clearly not wanted. If you weren't so like my wife perhaps I wouldn't have said anything. I should learn to keep my big Yankee mouth shut.'

Catriona shook her head. 'No, I'm the one who should be sorry. As I say, you've been very kind to my family, and you only spoke out of goodness. Don't worry about me, though. Didn't you just say I was well grounded?'

His disarming grin appeared. 'Indeed I did, and I therefore eat my words! Come then, my dear lady, and I'll run you round to your home. Your family must be wondering where you are. Maybe I can invite them here one more time before I leave.'

'I'm sure they would love that,' Catriona replied. A

sparkle came to her eyes. 'One more taste of Yankee generosity wouldn't go amiss!'

His own eyes gleamed back. 'Oh, we have no illusions, don't worry! We'll have to leave everyone with a gift or two, just to be sure that if and when our guys return they get the welcome we hope we deserve!'

Chapter Thirty-Two

Scotland, December 1942

It was a rare thing for a patient to be given a private room at Dunmore. They were reserved normally for people in very special need of peace and quiet. But Colonel Frobisher was given his own room as soon as he arrived.

It drove Duncan mad. 'What makes a man like him so special, for him to get his own room?' he wanted to know.

'He's a senior officer,' Catriona said. 'I think the men would agree that he's better to have his own room. He can hardly muck in with ordinary soldiers, can he? He would make them feel uncomfortable too.'

'He should be in some posh private hospital, then.' He sounded really angry.

'He's a friend of our surgeon, Colonel Mount. They served together in the First World War, and Colonel Frobisher has come here especially to be treated by him. Don't you think that a man who has fought for us in two wars deserves the best treatment?'

Duncan shook his head angrily. 'He hasn't even lost a limb!' he muttered.

'He nearly did. He might still lose his foot if it isn't operated properly, and he's going to need a lot of help to get properly mobile again. My guess is that he will need a walking stick for the rest of his life.'

'Serves the bastard right!'

Catriona stared at him. 'How can you say that? You don't even know him!' She saw his expression change, and said, 'Or do you?'

'I may do,' was all he would say.

He had his most set scowl on, and Catriona knew not to push him. When he got like this he became somebody alien, and could be very hurtful. Catriona sighed, and went back to her work.

Colonel Frobisher's right foot had been trapped under a military vehicle. There were multiple bones broken, and his toes had been crushed. It would be a delicate job for the surgeon to save his foot.

Catriona went to visit him, and found him sitting up in bed, his foot immobilised under a cage. As she entered he put down a sketch he had been working on, a detailed copy of the vase of flowers in the room. A box of artist's pencils lay open beside him, and he had matched the pastel colours of the flowers very exactly. The work was that of a very painstaking man, a man for detail, but he also showed subtlety in his work.

Catriona introduced herself to him, and found him quietly charming in an upright, military manner. He was in pain, she knew, but he showed no sign of it as they discussed his post-operative treatment.

'You'll be able to see a physical therapist at home if you wish,' she told him. 'That way you won't be here too long.'

He smiled. 'Yes, indeed. Colonel Mount has already told me that he'll be evicting me from this room as soon as possible. My wife is preparing a room for me downstairs in our home, and our daughter is coming home to boss me around. She has some medical training, and will keep me thoroughly under control.'

'Well that's very good, and you'll have Christmas with your family, and then when your foot is due to come out of plaster, I am sure Colonel Mount will wish you to come back here so that he can see it for himself. That will be early next year, and while you are here I can set a course of exercises for you. Now, let me leave you to your artwork. It's a lovely sketch you've made, very delicate.'

'Why thank you, Sister. I don't claim to have any special talent, but it makes me look at things properly, I find. It's a hobby that relaxes me.' He picked up the drawing as he spoke, and looked at it with a frown. 'This isn't much good. I prefer to use watercolours, really, and to sketch out of doors. I think I'm better at trees and sky than I am at close-up work like this.'

'I don't agree. You've caught the fall of the leaves and petals beautifully.' Catriona twitched the curtains over to give him better light, and then left him in peace.

Three days later the Colonel's foot had been carefully reshaped and reset, and Catriona came across him on her way through the grounds to Duncan's workshop. He had been wheeled out on to the lawn to paint in the chill winter sunshine. It was too cold for most of their patients to want to be outdoors, but Colonel Frobisher seemed to be made of tough stuff. One of the footrests of his wheelchair had

putting the finishing touches to some sculptures, very free and almost sensual in style. It was, Duncan told her, to be the tactile part of the exhibition.

'And is there a competition?' Catriona asked the men.

A gnarled-looking squaddie gave her a grin. 'Not officially, Sister. But they'll all tell you mine's the best o' the lot here. Or they would if they 'ad an ounce of honesty in 'em.'

There was general derision, and one of the men threw a rag over the squaddie's work as everyone started packing up.

Catriona smiled. 'As you're heading back, you fellows, you can stop and admire another artist at work. Colonel Frobisher is painting a watercolour out on the lawn.'

Duncan had been chatting to one of the men, but at this he turned. He said nothing, but something in his expression made Catriona flinch. He let the men leave, and once he was sure they were well away he headed for the door.

'Where are you going?' Catriona asked in panic.

'To see that bastard Frobisher, of course.'

'Duncan, no!' Catriona ran after him and grabbed his arm, and he pushed her off so hard that she stumbled, falling on her knees. He moved purposefully on, and she followed when she had picked herself up. She reached him just as he got to where Colonel Frobisher was sitting.

'Colonel Frobisher, well, well, well,' Duncan said, with chilling calm. 'What a lucky chance to meet you here.'

The colonel looked up from his painting, and frowned at the young man standing four-square in front of him. You could tell that he didn't know who Duncan was.

'I beg your pardon?' he said, and his voice was rasp

sharp. Then as Duncan continued to stare at him he clicked. 'McIlroy! By God, what the hell are you doing here?'

Duncan held out his arm. 'I lost a hand, remember? I was treated here, and then became their resident artist.'

'That's right, you were from Glasgow, I remember now, and you were an artist – sculptor, weren't you?'

'There you go, you see, you do remember! And do you remember the last time you saw me? Before I was injured, I mean? We were trying to defend the canal, and Rogers got shot and ended up in the water. You left him to drown, Frobisher. Do you remember that?'

The colonel drew himself up as far as he could in his wheelchair, and glowered at Duncan. 'No, McIlroy, I don't remember any such thing. Left him to die? That's rot, and you know it. What I do remember is you getting hysterical. I'd forgotten that since – there's been a war going on for the last two and half years, in case that has escaped you. You were a damned lousy officer, McIlroy, full of illusions and sentiment. The man you're talking about was dead when he hit the water.'

'He was hit in the shoulder,' Duncan spurted. 'He was *not* dead.'

'He was hit in the heart. And we had to retreat, otherwise I'd have lost the whole battalion.'

'We could have spared a couple of minutes.'

'Under fire? Don't make yourself more of a fool than you were two years ago, man.'

The two men glared at each other, Duncan with his feet planted right in front of the colonel's chair.

'You make me sick, do you know that?' he said, and as he spoke his fragile control on his temper cracked completely, and he hit out. Catriona screamed, because she thought he was going to hit the colonel, but instead he caught the easel, and sent it flying, the paint in the palette splattering all over the picture as it hit the ground.

The colonel didn't move. 'Well done, McIlroy,' he said, his voice emotionless. 'That's a fine thing for an artist to do.'

Duncan gave a nasty laugh. 'You call that wishy-washy copying of nature art? It's just the sort of dried-up stuff I'd have expected of you. You have no soul, Frobisher.'

He turned on his heel and marched off back towards his workshop. Catriona stood horrified, rooted to the spot. After a moment she made a movement towards the colonel, and took his hand.

'Are you all right?' she asked him.

'I think it is a little cold after all, Sister.' His voice sounded unutterably tired. 'Would you be kind enough to take me back to my room?'

Chapter Thirty-Three

Catriona got the colonel back inside, and put him into the care of a nurse before she went outside to pick up the easel and the open tubes of paint, which had left bright-coloured spots all around on the lawn. She packed it all up into its box, and gave everything to a porter to return to the colonel. Then she slipped off to her room to change her laddered stockings, and wash her grazed hands and knees. She caught her reflection in a mirror, and hardly recognised the white, gaunt face that was looking back at her.

What should she do? She went through the next couple of days in turmoil. She didn't think Colonel Frobisher had mentioned Duncan's outburst to anyone else at the hospital, otherwise Duncan would almost certainly have lost his job. Who was right? Who could know what had happened in the middle of a battle as the Allies ran for Dunkirk? The only thing Catriona knew for certain was that the colonel was a patient, and had been physically helpless, and that Duncan's behaviour had been so unprofessional as to be unforgivable, and so vicious as to chill her heart.

She avoided the workshop, and stayed inside the hospital buildings, where Duncan never came. Her roommate asked her to go to the pictures, but she made an excuse. She didn't want to go anywhere.

She went to see the colonel again as he was preparing to travel home. 'I wanted to say sorry,' she told him. 'I knew that Duncan McIlroy had some issues over your presence at Dunmore, and I should never have mentioned in his presence that you were painting in the grounds. It never occurred to me that he would behave in the way he did.'

He had recovered his urbanity, and was generous. 'Sister, it is not in the slightest part your fault. I didn't handle the situation well myself, and allowed him to anger me too much. I believe that McIlroy has been psychologically scarred by his short experience of war. It takes some people that way, those who are by nature very sensitive, and McIlroy is, after all, an artist. And he lost a hand. For an artist that must have been a terrible blow.'

'He does great work with other amputees,' Catriona said. 'He is passionate about making them see how much they can still do.'

'Well then, we'll just let him continue doing that, and when I come back for my next visit I will stay indoors, and not trouble his space.'

'You are very kind.'

'So are you, Sister. You took very great care of me the other afternoon. McIlroy or no McIlroy, I had pushed myself too far so soon after surgery.'

'So you'll listen to your daughter a little when she wants you to rest?' Catriona ventured a smile.

'Who knows, Sister, I very well may!'

So she said goodbye, and finished the week, and went wearily home. She hoped that nobody in the family would notice her low spirits, and made the cold weather an excuse for staying indoors by the fire. She felt dog-tired, and couldn't explain why.

On the Monday morning she cycled to work at Knockderry and set about her usual tasks. There were two VAD nurses off with a winter bug, and there was their work to do as well, so she was kept very busy. By lunchtime she felt like a limp rag, and all she wanted to do was to throw herself into an easy chair. She didn't even have the energy to join staff in the dining room, and found herself a corner in a little side bay where there was a chair facing the leafless trees out of the window.

It was Dr Roman who spotted her huddled in the chair as he passed by. 'My dear Sister,' he said to her, 'are you feeling all right? Do you perhaps have this bug that is going around?'

He spoke too kindly, and it overset her. Something popped inside, and the trickle of a tear appeared at the corner of one eye.

'What is it? Sister MacNeill, what is the matter?' He sat down beside her, and took her hand.

She looked at him. 'It's nothing,' she tried to say, but the next moment she was in floods of tears.

'Come to my office where no one can interrupt us,' he said, and led her down the passageway, and into the small, cupboard-like space that held Dr Roman's desk and two chairs. He propelled her into a chair, gave her a large handkerchief, and then disappeared, returning a minute or two later with a glass of water, which he pressed into her hand.

'Drink that,' he instructed, and though his voice was as genial as ever, Catriona would not have dreamt of demurring. Not until she had drunk the whole glass did he smile, and continue.

'Tell me now, then, *chère mademoiselle*, what has happened? I have never seen you unhappy. What has life been doing to you?'

Catriona had pulled herself together, and felt all the embarrassment of her twenty-three years. Her Presbyterian upbringing told her she should be ashamed of falling apart in public, but Dr Roman had no such reserve, and in the glow of his personality she found herself talking for the first time about Duncan, and their problematic relationship, and how hard he was to understand, and she finished by telling him about Duncan's outburst.

'He pushed you over, you say?' Dr Roman asked, but there was no judgement in his voice. She held up her hands, where the marks of the grazes were still visible.

'That doesn't matter, though,' she said. 'What he did to the colonel was much worse.'

He looked thoughtful. 'Do you think so?'

'He was our patient!' she cried out. 'He was in a wheelchair, and had just nearly lost his foot.'

He smiled. 'You are a real nurse, Sister, one made with the heart and not just by training. How did the patient react? Was he as upset as you?'

She sighed. 'At the time he was just as angry as Duncan, and said some pretty harsh things about Duncan's unsuitability as an officer, but when I saw him a couple of days later he was very nice. He said he thought Duncan had been psychologically damaged by the war, that he was unsuited to active service and had been too sensitive to withstand it.'

'That could be true. And how do you feel about that? If this young man has psychological problems, do you think it is your duty to solve them?'

He'd come to the crux of the matter. How did he know that Catriona had been torturing herself for days with worries about Duncan's future? A part of her was appalled by last week, another part wanted to go to Duncan and make him better.

She didn't answer, because she didn't know what to say. Duncan's face swam before her, soft in the dance-floor lighting, with the scent of him close. And then she saw him in his anger, his face twisted, his eyes blazing and ugly.

'Catriona,' Dr Roman was saying, very gently. 'May I call you Catriona? Your boyfriend knocked you over. You have told me yourself that he holds you at a distance. Has he ever given you any reason to believe you can get close enough to really help him?'

She shook her head. Duncan was the sparkling artist, the man with the fascinating, quirky friends, and innovative ideas. He didn't like it when she saw too far beyond that.

'But you care about him?'

Catriona gulped, then nodded. She felt about two feet tall, but Dr Roman didn't seem to see it like that.

'He's a lucky man,' he said. 'But he won't ever realise how lucky he is, even if you stay with him for life.' He sighed. 'I'm not a very good person to advise you, Catriona, and it is not my place either, but I hope you remember in your dealings with him just what you are worth. I think you have been brought up to be too modest – you don't have any conceit.'

She found the choice of word surprising. 'Is it a good thing to have conceit?'

'Well, I may well have chosen the word badly, in my poor English, but you need some *amour propre*, some love of yourself, and you need to make it quite brazen.'

'I don't think I am made to be brazen,' she said. 'Anyway, if people need to have brazen conceit, I don't think you have any either, Dr Roman.'

He smiled. 'No, well that is the penalty of being the oldest son in a large Catholic family! If you ever meet my younger brother who is in the Borders, you will find him very impudent indeed. So much so that I would wish the ladies he meets also to have enough *amour propre* to stand up to him.'

Catriona couldn't help laughing. 'I have heard that the Polish officers around Scotland make many conquests because they are so dashing.'

Dr Roman looked down rather dubiously at his ancient white coat and crumpled collar. 'Not all of us, I'm afraid.'

Catriona laughed again, then broke off as she realised how rude she must seem, but the doctor was twinkling back at her.

'Now that is better, to hear you laugh, my dear.'

'I feel one hundred per cent better, Dr Roman. Thank you!'

'And you'll think about yourself, and not worry too much about everyone else?'

Catriona exhaled. 'Yes, I'll do that. Someone else told me recently that I shouldn't be seeing a man whom I hadn't told my family about. That there must be some reason why I didn't want to acknowledge Duncan. Perhaps he was right.'

The doctor frowned. 'Now that was unfair,' he said, with uncharacteristic severity. 'You are not a child, and have the right to explore a relationship without passing it up for inspection by your family.'

'Yes, but I did think when we had the dance here at Burgh Hall that I couldn't possibly have brought Duncan along, because he would have scoffed at our sedate community.'

'And you knew that for yourself, Catriona, you didn't need your father to tell you, or some other man passing judgement. You've had your own reservations all along about this young man, and now you have even more.' He rose from his chair, and came round the table.

'You'll do the right thing, don't you worry,' he said, and held out his hand. She put hers in it, and he helped her up quite unnecessarily from her chair.

'But don't go worrying too much about a long-toothed colonel who has spent thirty years in the British army either,' he said, and his tone was much more light-hearted. 'It probably did him good to be challenged, and might make him think a little more about the men underneath him. Although, if I know anything about senior officers, I very much doubt it!'

He still had her hand in his, and to her surprise he raised it to his lips and kissed the tips of her fingers.

Catriona blushed beetroot red. 'Is that the gallantry

of the Polish officer we hear about?' she managed to ask.

He blushed a little himself, but then shook his head determinedly. 'No, Sister MacNeill, it is your gallantry that I am saluting,' he said.

Chapter Thirty-Four

Catriona might feel reassured and emboldened by her talk with Dr Roman, but she wasn't sorry not to see Duncan in the week that followed. His exhibition was this week, and he was at the Guild Hall, not at Dunmore. Catriona should have been there too, at least for the opening ceremony, but she had cancelled her request for time off, and left the Dunmore officials to attend on their own.

Matron, resplendent in her best starched collar, went along with Colonel Mount and the trustees of the hospital to the official opening, and coaches were laid on to take along any patients and staff who wanted to visit the exhibition afterwards. Catriona watched them go, and then forced herself to focus on her work.

'We thought to see you at the opening ceremony, Sister,' said the squaddie sculptor on the Wednesday.

'I couldn't get away, sorry,' she lied. 'I'll go along later in the week, don't you worry.'

'Well it's grand, what he's done,' he said. 'I'm a plain English working-class man, me, and I'm the last man

292

who'd have thought I'd be doin' sommat like that, but he makes you get into it, that lad. And he's got areas in that exhibition for the fine joinery work, an area for plaster sculptures, the lot. It means all the men feel involved.'

Catriona bit her lip. She should go. This was the fruit of a year of work for Duncan. She would go, perhaps, later in the week, if she had time. She smiled rather mechanically at the soldier, and made her way on through the ward.

At tea that afternoon the nurses all said the same thing. The exhibition was so good for Dunmore, they enthused, and there were men there with their families who had left the hospital months before. Had she been along? Catriona shook her head.

'But aren't you really friendly, you and him?' one of the nurses asked.

Catriona squirmed. 'We are, of course. I'll be going along, don't worry, it's just that I had a patient leaving today and I wanted one last session with him.'

The nurse nodded, losing interest.

'Tell me,' another nurse said. 'You live out by Rosneath, don't you? Isn't that where you go home to at weekends? Well, did you hear about the baby born in Helensburgh last month? The lassie is a neighbour of ours, and she went out with a GI from Rosneath last winter.'

Catriona seized on the change of subject. 'I don't think Helensburgh gossip reaches us over on the other side of the water,' she said apologetically. 'I suppose there must be a lot of pregnancies at the moment. The girl didn't keep in touch with the GI when he left, then?'

'No, but it's worse than that, Catriona. You see, the GI

was one of them darkies, and the wee laddie came out like milk chocolate.'

Catriona gulped. She didn't suppose Helensburgh had ever seen a black baby before.

'Oh Lordie!' the other nurse said. 'And what did the family say to that?'

'They've been trying to force her to give the baby away. She's just a teenager, and not the brightest lassie, otherwise she'd have dealt with this before the baby was born, instead of just waiting for the bomb to drop when they saw the baby. She's awful confused, the wee soul, and terrified for her future, but even if she gives him away, surely nobody will want him. She's been packed away to her grandmother's for now to hide them both away.'

Catriona could imagine the future for a black baby taken from his mother in Scotland. He would live in an institution, surely, for the whole of his childhood. In London, maybe he would stand a chance, but on the west coast of Scotland he would always be alone. Even in Glasgow he would struggle.

'The family have been talking to those in charge over at Rosneath,' the nurse was continuing. 'The hope is that they may help in some way, perhaps trace the father or something like that.'

Was that what Ron Martin had meant when he'd spoken of the damage his GIs had done, and said that the girls they'd got involved with were often too simple? Was he dealing with this case? Catriona hoped so. She'd seen herself the strong values that guided his actions, and she thought he might fight the corner very hard for a frightened young girl and her baby. She crossed her fingers that he might succeed.

The thought of the young girl and her baby hiding out in her granny's back room gave some perspective to her own problems, but they didn't go away. All week she hovered between going to Duncan's exhibition, and the instinct for flight, for self-preservation. You're a coward, she told herself angrily. You're hiding yourself away.

But she wasn't hiding. She was getting on with her job, in the purposeful world of Dunmore, and if she wanted its security it was for good reason. If your instincts tell you to stay away trust them, she told herself. If she'd taken flight, then she'd headed towards the light, the sane, the normal, and away from something dark that had made her recoil. Never mind that for so long Duncan had known how to make her glow, and that when she remembered those moments she ached for him. However much she might miss him, she was sure that he would not miss her for long. His real passion was his work, and any real cure for his demons would come through his art.

Let him have his exhibition; let it be successful. She was glad for him, deeply glad. But she would not go. Try telling me I don't care about my patients, she dared the world. Or that I haven't done everything I could to help Duncan. If there's one thing I do know, it's that I'm loyal, and do my best. Time off, she decided, would be no bad thing.

The following week was less busy than usual. As many patients as possible had been allowed home for Christmas, and only those who couldn't travel stayed at Dunmore. Even the Polish patient was taken away by some of his compatriots. Duncan didn't come to Dunmore at all, and classes would not resume until after the new year. It was a week to rest, and to decorate the wards with holly, which they dipped in Epsom salts to give it a frosted sheen.

Catriona was working over Christmas, to allow other nurses, those with families far away, to travel home for once. Christmas fell on a Friday, and she spent the day with her patients, in an atmosphere which managed to be surprisingly festive. There was roast chicken for everyone, and even a tot or two of rum punch, which led to some extremely silly games being played on wheelchairs in the corridors. It lifted even Catriona's spirits for a while.

She stayed on later than usual on the Sunday, to give her colleagues time to return to work, and it wasn't until early afternoon that she stepped off the ferry at Kilcreggan and cycled home. Her family were in an unusually festive mood too, just like her patients. They'd had chicken here too, it seemed, on Christmas Day, and her aunt had allowed her men some beer. And, much to Fergus's delight, this evening they were invited to the base.

'Don't tell me you're pleased at the thought of drinking that American whisky again?' Catriona teased him, but she too was pleased. She would see Captain Martin again before he headed back across the Atlantic, and at the same time she could satisfy her curiosity about the little black baby hidden away in Helensburgh.

The Americans had given a party at Rosneath for the local children the afternoon before, pulling out the stops it seemed, before the main part of the base was closed. There had been sweets, chocolate and chewing gum, and a Father Christmas had given out toys. It was doubly special for children who didn't really know much about these

American Christmas traditions, and who hadn't had new toys since before the war.

'You're a wonderful bunch,' Catriona told Ron Martin that evening. 'What a lovely thing to do for our children! They don't get too many treats these days.'

'Do you know what?' he replied. 'Some of our toughest guys here had tears in their eyes yesterday. Christmas ain't easy when you're away from your family, and there's nothing worse than us lot just sitting around here looking at each other. It was a whole heap better to have some kids around.'

And he knew all about the Helensburgh baby. 'We've been doing quite a bit of work on that one,' he told her. 'Jefferson, the father, was killed in the Pacific during the summer, so there won't be any help coming from him, but it's pretty obvious that the kid can't grow up here. We've contacted an American charity, which may be able to help the baby emigrate to America. We've also sent the news of the baby to the man's family. I think they should at least know that their son had left a child, and there have been cases where the families have wanted to adopt the baby. It's all they have left of their son, after all.'

'Goodness, that's impressive. If the boy could go to his own blood it would be great. You've done a lot in a short time.'

He grinned. 'Kind of you to say so, ma'am, but we've done just what we should. Politics would have dictated it even if it hadn't been clear that Jefferson exploited a vulnerable, rather helpless kind of girl back last winter. I told you, we want no harmful legacy left behind here. Our boys will most likely be back, black ones and white ones. We need those dances at Helensburgh for them!'

'And you'll get them! And our more modest dances round at Cove Hall as well, especially if your colleagues bring along their hip flasks!'

'Don't worry, we'll leave careful instructions.' He called a waiter to refill her glass. 'Tell me, Miss MacNeill, am I forgiven for having spoken too freely to you last time you were here?'

Catriona felt her throat clench, as it did every time she thought of Duncan, but she steadied herself, and gave him a determined smile.

'I think you Americans are used to speaking up,' she said, 'but in this case everything you said turned out to be right. I'm no longer with the unacknowledged boyfriend, you'll be pleased to hear.'

He looked concerned. 'He dumped you? No, you dumped him, I'm sure. Well, I hope it wasn't my remarks that turned you against him, but your own good judgement.'

'Let's just say I was exposed to a new side of his character.'

He gave her an acute look. 'I hope you haven't been too hurt, honey,' he said, shedding his formality. 'You're a lovely young lady, and you deserve better.'

She blushed, but then shrugged. 'Nothing too terrible has happened to me, and I've learnt a lot.'

'And you don't want any big brother figure protecting you! You're very right, Miss MacNeill, and I would love to be around to see what happens next in your life. Have fun, little lady, and make sure you break the next one's heart! It's been a real pleasure knowing you.'

He raised his glass to hers as he spoke, and they chinked, a tiny, bonded chink between nations.

'And it has been a privilege to know you, Captain Martin.'

Catriona was more careful this time about how many gins she accepted at the base, and was able to turn out for work the next morning in good form. Something special had happened at Knockderry this Christmas, it seemed, and she cycled to the hospital full of anticipation.

On Christmas Eve, it seemed, General de Gaulle had appeared with an entourage at the Free French Naval Base in Greenock, and had then crossed over on the ferry to visit the hospital. The buzz had gone around the neighbourhood, and Uncle Charlie and her father had been quick enough down the road to see the great man as he left.

Was he as tall as everyone said? Catriona wanted to know. But they couldn't tell her. He'd been seated inside a military vehicle when they saw him. But he had waved.

She would have to wait to find out more from her patients, and when she arrived at the hospital she found the whole place buzzing. They'd had just a couple of hours' notice of the visit, apparently. Dr Roman had come across to warn them, and the nurses and porters had set to cleaning, while the patients quickly finished putting up the Christmas holly. They'd got hold of Dr Roman too, and had put him in the hands of a midshipman who had been a barber before the war. He'd taken him ruthlessly in hand, and the dark, shaggy mane of hair was gone, replaced by a sleek cut.

'It makes him look very handsome, *n'est-ce pas*, Sister?' asked one patient with a wink.

The doctor shook his head at the Frenchman. 'It makes me very cold, that's what it does! You didn't have to do that ferry journey with me this morning. My poor ears in that wind! And all that for your general.'

He did look quite different, younger, and more obviously Polish, with his broad cheekbones and forehead. But his fraying collar was the same, and his shoes needed new heels. Catriona didn't want him to change too much.

'How did you find the general?' she asked him, when they were away from the patients.

'Important, and aware of it,' he twinkled. 'Not a man who likes to be upstaged. Did you hear that de Gaulle's great rival General Darlan was assassinated in Algiers on Friday? The same day that de Gaulle came here?'

'You're not saying he arranged it?' Catriona was horrified.

'Not at all, though I think Free French supporters may have done, and I'm sure de Gaulle isn't too distressed! It must be very convenient for him that he was visiting sick soldiers when it happened, so good for his image, don't you think? He's now the only natural French leader, and I think 1943 could be a very good year for him. Perhaps we'll even invade France.'

1943. Indeed it was going to be a very different year. 1942 had been so positive for so many months, but it had finished hard, at least on a personal level.

Catriona thought back to last Christmas, when they'd received the telegram from Jim, and he'd spoken of them all taking small steps forward. Since then the war had turned a corner. It had been a long year and a very long road, but something major had changed. And for her French patients here the developments had been all positive.

She smiled at Dr Roman. 'And if we invade France, de Gaulle will be leading our Free French all the way! Well, I'm sorry to have missed his visit, but I rather hope he won't come again, for if he has become so very important, and knows it, as you say, then we may have to turn the whole of Scotland out to receive him next time!'

CHAPTER THIRTY-FIVE

Alexandria, December 1942

The sense of relief was tangible as people planned Christmas in Alexandria this year, and there was a determined return to normality. Trips to the desert had to avoid the battle zone because of remaining minefields, but other than that there were no restrictions on people, and no air raids, no hurried running for shelter during nights out. The blackout continued, but some people were even ignoring that now.

Many Alexandrian families planned their holidays in Luxor, but Michael was coming home to the Trevillian household, so they were going nowhere. It sometimes seemed to Fran that she was destined never to leave Alexandria again, but the reason for staying was too good to complain.

The Carsdales were staying too, Angélique Carsdale saying that she and her daughters had already spent enough time in Luxor this year, when her husband had insisted on them leaving in the summer.

'We travelled up there like cattle, squashed into a

train with too many people,' she told Fran's mother. 'And then we hung around for weeks just waiting to be able to come home. Now we have peace here, and I am not moving.'

So Barbara Trevillian invited them for Christmas lunch, and happily it was warm enough to take their drinks outside. It felt very special to Fran. She could remember sitting out in this garden a year ago talking to Jim, in the wake of Tony's tragic death. The Carsdales had then been in mourning for a cousin, and Lucie had been a broken person. Today there was sunshine, Fran had had a letter from Jim telling her he was on his way back from Cape Town, Michael was here, and Lucie seemed to be standing again on steady feet. The war had marked them all, but there was much to be thankful for.

Alan Trevillian proposed a toast to absent friends. They were toasting Lucie's brother, who was away in England at school, and Jim, who was hopefully on a ship right now on his way up the African coast, and George and Len, who were with ships on Malta, but everyone knew that the person they were mainly toasting was Tony, the one they would never see again. Lucie's eyes welled up, but Michael was next to her, and he put his arm around her.

Fran caught her mother watching them, and thought, don't try too hard to couple these two, Mummy; don't read more into a brotherly gesture than is intended. Knowing Lucie as she did, Fran thought that any interest Michael might have was unlikely to be reciprocated, at least in the near future. Lucie might be steady, and laughing, and no longer in darkness, yet she wasn't looking for a man. But

Barbara Trevillian was at her least rational where Michael was involved, and she would dearly love for him and Lucie to become closer.

The whole nightmare of the summer had profoundly affected Barbara Trevillian, but Fran thought the biggest effect on her mother had come from the political changes and the threats to their lifestyle. Barbara wanted her family to be as they were before, and a future she could understand, with her son married to a girl of good family like Lucie, one whom they had always known. And her daughter . . . well she wanted her daughter not to base her hopes and her future on a damaged man.

Fran's father had done a lot of work to change her mother's view of Jim, and she had even come a long way towards accepting his family background, Fran thought. In the face of her daughter's commitment she really had no choice. But to gain Barbara's full acceptance Jim needed a future. A man returning to Alexandria to be given a dead-end office job, and to be 'looked after' by the navy, was a man she would do her genuine duty by, but not one she wanted as a son-in-law.

So whenever Fran showed her a new letter from Jim her mother smiled, because it was the right thing to do, but there was no heart to the smile. Fran remembered it as she raised her glass that Christmas, and remembered too her father's words recently when she'd railed yet again against her mother's lack of support.

'Stop just one moment, chick, and think a little harder. Has your mother ever spoken out against anything you do? Did she try to stop you becoming so involved in the newspaper? Or curtail any of your activities? And didn't she bring Jim here when he was injured the first time? And refrain from interfering as you and he became more than friends, even though he isn't from her world? She's our quiet support, and puts up with a lot from you and me, Fran. We're neither of us always easy to live with!'

Fran disagreed. 'You are! You always keep your calm, whatever happens.'

'Well, perhaps that's just a lack of imagination on my part! Your mother has become more fragile since Michael has been in the desert, and that is because she doesn't lack imagination. She may seem stoical and steady, but she feels things very deeply, and it's only because she loves us all so much that she keeps her worries to herself.'

'She has taken against Jim,' Fran said, insistent.

'She has learnt a new level of fear, that's all. She wants you to have a good life, which is quite natural, and she isn't as sure as you are that Jim is going to be fine. She just wants to hold us all tight. And you wait and see, when Jim finally arrives she'll accept him back, and do what she can to help you make a life together. At the end of the day she'll do it for you.'

Having Michael home did Barbara Trevillian more good than anything. You could almost see her hugging him the whole time, from wherever she was in the room. And she was beginning to relax too, for Michael wasn't going back to the war. His unit had been diverted from the pursuit of Rommel and sent back to Cairo, replaced by fresh troops. They were on leave, and then were being deployed to new

305

duties around Suez, but Michael wouldn't be with them. He had been recommended to join the staff at GHQ in Cairo, and though, like a lot of desert campaigners, he had few good words to say for the back-seat Johnnies at GHQ, he was nevertheless grateful for the contacts this might make him for after the war.

'They seem to think I have a good understanding of Egyptian culture and politics,' he said, preening himself slightly.

'And do you?' his father asked drily. 'Because if you know what's going to happen politically I wish you would tell the rest of us.'

Michael grinned irrepressibly. 'I know as well as you do that none of us will still be in Egypt in twenty years' time, or not unless we do something pretty clever. Which is why I want to target the diplomatic service. I'll be best friends with everyone for the next couple of years, and see where I can find myself when this is all over.'

'You'll never get anywhere,' Fran told him bluntly. 'The top diplomats all went to Oxford together, and belong to the same clubs in London. You didn't want a university education, and you've never spent any time in London society. You're lost already, squibling!'

'Wait and see, sister dear!' was his only reply.

He stayed with them for two weeks, and they took in the new year at Baudrot, eating among a crowd of revellers, taking with them George Blake, who had appeared in town just two days before. Michael and George struck an immediate chord, and Fran was glad to see that her mother was as good to George as she had always been, undeterred by his close alliance to Jim. It was a good job, because George was full of talk about his best friend.

'So, Jim is on his way back, you say?' he asked Fran.

Fran nodded. 'His last letter was sent on 15th December, and he was expecting to embark any day.'

'And he's fully better?'

'Not fully, no. He seems to have some problems still with his hearing on one side, but they say he may have to live with that for ever. It isn't important,' she beamed at him. 'It won't stop him living.'

'Even better,' George commented. 'It may stop him going back to sea. That man is jinxed, and shouldn't be allowed anywhere near a ship! Since he's been away we've been getting convoys through to Malta without a single ship lost.'

'So it was Jim's fault?' Fran protested. 'Poor Jim! He did all the hard work and left you guys to enjoy the fruits of success.'

It was Michael who asked the pertinent question. 'But tell me, Blake, if Jim's not going back to sea, will there be anything for him to do here in Alex now, do you think?'

George wasn't sure. 'There will always be a base here, but they're moving our HQ to Malta now, and basing the larger part of the fleet there. Len and I will be operating out of there from now on, and just calling in to Alex. Malta's the perfect place to manage the Med, slap bang in the middle, and we'll be invading Italy from there before you know it.'

He sounded excited, but it alarmed Fran. 'So they could base Jim in Malta too?'

He nodded. 'It's possible. But he'll be here for a while, I'm sure, while they decide what to do with him.' He saw Fran's crestfallen face, and added, 'Don't start fretting now, Fran, you have no idea yet what's going to happen. And remember, six months ago you thought he was going to die.'

She sighed. 'I know, George, but I just want 1943 to be different, for us all.'

'It already is, Fran, for you at least. Even if Jim is on Malta he won't be at sea, except when he gets leave, and then he'll get on board a ship and be here like a shot. Come on, let's toast Jim, wherever he may be right now.'

'Do you think they'll be celebrating the new year on board his ship?'

'If I know Jim, you can bet on it!'

There was a general light-headedness about the evening, both at Baudrot and afterwards, when Fran, George and Michael strolled the streets of the town and found their way to a nightclub. The people of Alexandria were bidding a relieved farewell to 1942, and were out in force in every bar. Allied troops on leave were everywhere, some rather too drunk for comfort. Michael and George steered Fran quickly past a group of rowdy sailors, three of whom had swapped their uniform hats for Egyptian fezzes. Fran persuaded George not to pull rank and give them a hard time.

'I hope they exchanged those hats, and didn't steal them,' he muttered. 'I've heard it has become a sport for the army troopers in Cairo to knock the Egyptians' hats off, but I didn't think I'd see our navy boys doing the same.'

'I'm sure they made a swap,' Fran said.

'You don't believe that for a moment. I tell you, Fran, if this country throws the Brits out by the scruff of our necks at the end of this war, we'll only have ourselves to blame.'

'Too right, Blake,' said Michael. 'But even if the hats have been stolen, and of course they have, do you think you can restore them to their owners? And your boys have had too much to drink to listen to an officer out on his own. Come on, man, there's nothing you can do. There are a dozen of them!'

'If Jim was here we would take them on,' George muttered again.

'Yes, because he's as mad as you are,' Fran said, propelling him up the street. 'Come on, George, we need to toast Michael's new job.'

'Yes, and I'm paying,' Michael agreed.

George took one last, angry look at the sailors behind them. 'Bloody disgrace,' he muttered, but then allowed himself to be led inside the club. Over champagne he fixed a slightly inebriated eye on Michael, and told him, 'You're welcome to a Cairo post, Trevillian, dealing with those asses at GHQ. I'd rather be at sea any day.'

Michael grinned and raised his glass. 'I salute you. You know, though, when I was in the desert I was useful, but in reality a lot of men could have done what I did. I'm hoping that in Cairo I can in some way offer something new, deal with people differently.'

'And you think you can genuinely make a difference, when your superiors are all so convinced they are right?'

'Well at least I can speak to the locals properly, government departments, heads of service and the like. I'll be at that level, remember, not making strategic decisions. But maybe,' Michael smiled at the waiter as he refilled his glass, and thanked him, 'maybe it's how we deal with the ordinary people that is going to make the difference.'

Chapter Thirty-Six

Alexandria, January 1943

Fran was working in her office when the secretary came in.

'There's someone to see you, Fran,' she said.

Fran looked up, and there was Jim, standing rather uncertainly behind the secretary. Fran had been so deep in the work she was doing that at first she couldn't quite register that it was him. There was a pause, short, but which seemed endless, then she caught her breath. She could physically feel her eyes widening, just like you read in books. She couldn't speak, but her eyes never left his.

The secretary whisked herself out, and closed the door to the outside world, and the click of the door seemed to release them both from their stillness. A smile Fran couldn't control swept right through her, and she managed one word. 'Jim!'

He returned her smile, and made a move towards her, and she came out of her chair, rounding the desk that stood between them. He looked well, she registered, tanned from the South African sun, but then as he moved again she saw a slight halt to his step. She wanted to hear him speak.

'How are you, my beautiful?' was what he said, and it was perfect, because his diction was right, his voice his own. She sobbed, and threw herself into his arms.

They sat for a long time, talking about his journey, Michael's new job, George and Len's new lives on Malta, general catch-up. All the while Fran sat within the cradle of his arm, scanning his face as though she needed to relearn every line.

'And your health?' she finally dared to ask him. 'How is it all going? You look so well.'

'I sound all right,' he agreed, 'although I sometimes find myself searching for the most obvious of words. My mind can go blank too easily. And though I may sound fine, the rest of you don't! I'll always have problems with my left ear they tell me – sound is all muffled. But the right ear is fine. It seems I took all the impact of the blast just behind the left ear.'

He looked down at his hands. 'And I react slowly. I can't catch a ball, because my brain just won't connect fast enough. It's not helped by the problems I have with these.'

'Your hands?'

'Yes.' He reached out as he spoke, and took her right hand in his. He squeezed, and nothing happened. There was no grip. He'd written that he had some problems, but now she could feel it for herself.

'For the moment I write rather painstakingly with a big fat pen, and I eat with special cutlery,' he told her. 'Knives and forks with foam wrapped round them, which I can get hold of, and even so I can't really cut up a steak. It doesn't make me great social material. There are some other residual muscle control problems too, but it's the hands which are the most obvious. I can pick things up with my fingers, but I can't bear down.'

Fran was calculating hard. Her mother would see this as soon as he tried to shake her hand. It would be automatic for Barbara Trevillian to invite Jim to the house, and inevitably he would be under scrutiny. Jim, she thought, mustn't be aware of this inspection. He knew that her mother had doubts about his background, and if added to that he felt any disgust from her at his disabilities he would be so mortified that he was capable of ending their relationship.

There were so many issues with Jim, so many things that made him withdraw from her. Last year it had been the memories of Tony's death, and now, well now the risk was that he would consider himself too damaged to marry her. He and her mother would be in agreement, if ever they started talking about it. They could even end up in the most miserable of collusions.

Fran would need her father's support before she brought Jim to the house. And any invitation must be for drinks only, not for dinner, until such time as he could eat with their full cutlery service. And that time would come. With all the natural ferocity in her, Fran was determined on this.

'What have they told you about the recovery time?' she asked him.

He shrugged. 'It'll come, that's all I've been told. I'm not going to remain handicapped.' He said the words with his old measured determination. 'I have exercises to do, and it's down to me how hard I work. I want to get quickly to the point where I can use radar equipment again. That's the first goal, and it shouldn't be difficult. I can do quite delicate work already, as long as I take my time and focus, and don't have to grip.'

So everything was positive. Everything, Fran thought, as she leant her head against Jim's shoulder, sturdy and muscled as ever on the chair next to hers. Jim could have been dead, and instead he was here, every solid, living, breathing ounce of him.

'So what's next for you here?' she asked him. 'You won't be going straight back to work, surely?'

'Oh no. I have to check in with the medics here, and there will be assessments to go through, and a whole heap of other stuff. When they're satisfied that I can be useful, then I'll no doubt have a meeting with the commander to decide what I'm going to do and where.'

And then maybe he would end up on Malta, she thought, but didn't express her fears. The most important thing for Jim now was to end up in a role that mattered, where he could develop his skills and his future. If that meant he couldn't be full-time in Alexandria, so be it.

'So you're on holiday!' she said instead, grinning at him. 'George had the cheek to tell me you've spent the last six months in five-star luxury while he and the boys won the Mediterranean for you.'

'George can just come here and tell me that in person!' he retorted. 'I may not have full muscle control back yet, but I could down that lightweight idiot with one hand tied behind my back!'

A couple of days later Jim and Fran met her father for a drink after work. Sitting over a beer Jim couldn't look more normal, but he was brutally frank with Alan Trevillian about the issues he was still battling. Afterwards, her father told Fran that he had rarely been more impressed by anyone's resolve.

'That matter-of-fact, positive attitude of Jim's must have been a lot of help to him over the last few months,' he said, admiringly. 'When you think back to how he was last July, it was hard to believe then that he could recover so well. He's worked very hard!'

'So, do you think he'll pass by Mummy?'

'He will because I'll talk to her.' He sounded unusually stern.

'He has trouble with a knife and fork still,' Fran warned him.

'So we'll have him round for drinks, and provide finger food. Your mother may find that a bit strange, but as I say, I'm going to talk to her first.'

'She'd better not snub him,' Fran muttered.

'When did you ever know your mother to be rude to a guest? Fran, trust me.'

So she did, but as she exposed Jim to her mother's mercies Fran bit her lip in fear. Any hint of a snub would cut deep.

Your mother won't be rude to a guest, Alan Trevillian had said, and it was true. Barbara Trevillian didn't exactly gush over Jim, but she was all that was polite, asking him a multitude of concerned questions about the hospital he'd been in, about life in South Africa, about his family back in Scotland. When she asked him about his plans Fran held her breath, because she didn't want Jim to be too blunt about his problems. But Jim had it all under control.

'I'm still a bit of a crock, as you'll have seen, Mrs

Trevillian, but I'm getting stronger by the day, and expect to be back on full-time duties within a month or so.'

'But you won't be going back to sea? Lieutenant Blake seemed sure of that when we saw him for the New Year celebrations.'

'It seems unlikely, mainly because of some hearing problems in my left ear. But I'm fully expecting to resume a full officer's role onshore.'

Jim had the measure of her mother, Fran thought. His performance this evening was so strong that her mother couldn't help but begin to believe again that he had a serious future.

Barbara was smiling at him with more warmth. 'You've paid a price for this war, it seems, but thank God not too high a one. You know that our son Michael is also now in a non-combat role? He has been attached to GHQ in Cairo.'

Jim nodded. 'Fran told me. You must be so relieved, Mrs Trevillian, and proud too. They wouldn't have placed Michael there if he hadn't made himself really valued.'

Jim watched as Barbara glowed, and then continued with a gleam, his soft accent coming out more strongly than ever, with all its charm. 'The war effort in the Med needs good brains behind the scenes,' he said. 'I guess it's up to myself and Michael to provide some of those brains!'

'Steady, tiger!' Fran grinned. 'You're not an admiral yet!'

'Oh, I don't want to be an admiral! I want to prepare for a civilian career in technology.'

Every word he said was music to Barbara Trevillian's ears. There was a hint of amusement in Fran's father's voice as he brought the evening to a close.

'We'll let our convalescent go for now, shall we, ladies?

You've work to do, I'm sure, before you're fit for duties again, Jim. But we'll see you again very soon.'

'You'll come next weekend?' Barbara ventured. 'Michael will be here, and we could have lunch.'

Jim shot a surreptitious look at his hands, and gave a non-committal answer.

'We'll have drinks in town,' Fran said, with decision. 'Michael will be full of how good the bars are in Cairo, and we need to bring him down to earth.'

Barbara raised an indulgent eyebrow. 'Well, if that's what you young people prefer to do, I don't suppose Michael will need much encouragement.'

Fran was to remember those words, again and again. For Michael never made it home again. Just two days before his planned visit, they learnt that he had been on a diplomatic mission with his superior to Algiers when their RAF plane had been shot down over Tunisia. The wreckage had been spotted, small pieces littering the desert, and there was no chance of survivors. Michael's safe job at GHQ had not been so safe after all.

It blew the deepest possible hole in the family, and robbed Fran's mother of all interest in the future. Jim could become what he wanted now: Barbara Trevillian no longer cared.

CHAPTER THIRTY-SEVEN

Alexandria, March 1943

Fran was checking over the newspaper's accounts when Jim came to fetch her for lunch. It was a tedious task at the best of times, but today it seemed especially mind-numbing. Whoever said that work was the best cure for grief had been lying, Fran thought, or at least they hadn't been referring to book-keeping. Proper reporting could absorb her completely, but office tasks seemed to take for ever these days, and she found herself constantly drifting away. So much seemed irrelevant. Only Jim always seemed real, and important, and he warmed her when all else failed.

Today Jim was meeting with the commodore at the base, to learn what the navy planned for his future. It made it even harder to concentrate, and when lunchtime came and he still hadn't arrived at the office she began to chew her nails. By the time he finally appeared the rest of the staff had all gone off to eat, and she was alone. She didn't hear him come in, and was frowning over the accounts when he gave a little cough. She looked up and he was standing just inside the door, a smile playing on his face.

'Do you know how beautiful you look when you're concentrating?' he said.

'Concentrating isn't the word I'd have used,' she answered, ruefully, but she couldn't help but return that smile. It was one of pure mischief, and there was an air of excitement about Jim that was making currents through the air.

'You've got good news,' she breathed, her smile becoming broader. 'I can see you've got good news!'

He nodded.

'Tell me!' she urged.

'I'll tell you over lunch. Come on, gorgeous, I'm starving, and we're going to celebrate!'

It was a victory for Jim to be able to suggest lunch in a restaurant. He had worked so hard in the last two months, and already he could use normal cutlery, and eat without any spills. He could use all his radar equipment too, and control fine instruments. That was the most important. It meant that he had a future in technology. What had the navy offered him? Fran was desperate to know.

Jim steered her out of the office into the spring sunshine, and around to the Brasserie Danielle, a restaurant opposite the Bourse, which was popular with market traders and bankers and which was way above Jim's normal price bracket. He ordered champagne, and shushed Fran's protests. Champagne had been far from their minds for the last two months, but today, he insisted, was different.

'You'd better be about to tell me you have a job here in Alex,' Fran warned him.

'I not only have a job here in Alex, but I have one that is going to keep me at the leading edge of radar technology.'

He couldn't keep the excitement out of his voice.

Fran smiled at him. 'Go on, darling, just tell me,' she said.

'Well, they want to set up a centre to update radar operators working in this region on the latest equipment, and they've asked me to run it. We'll run some sessions on ships, and some in a training centre at the base. I'll have to spend some time in Port Said, because they do a lot of the equipment refits there, but that's not a problem, it's only a drive away.'

Fran glowed. 'Oh, Jim, that's wonderful!'

'I know. I never thought my humble teaching background would end up enhancing my naval career! I really thought that if I wasn't on active service I would stop using radar, but now I'll be constantly ahead of the game.'

'And they won't send you to Malta!'

Fran had never stopped worrying that he would be posted to Malta, particularly since Michael's death. She suspected that Jim would have liked to be at the centre of things again, especially as the Tunisia campaign drew towards a conclusion, and they could start imagining an invasion of Italy.

But this new job answered a lot of his fears that he would find himself sidelined into shuffling paper. Now he would be working with engineers, learning from them about their equipment, and passing on that knowledge to radar operators who were already in the field.

Jim raised his glass to her. 'No, my love, they won't send me to Malta.' He gazed for a moment into the bubbles, and then seemed to brace himself.

'Fran,' he continued, 'the commodore has also suggested that I take the leave that is due to me. I told him I don't need it, having spent months doing nothing but rest, but he insists that I should do something different, not associated with my injuries, so that I come to the job fresh. There are some important meetings next week, but after that he suggests I should go to Luxor for a holiday.'

'A holiday?'

'Yes.' He took a sip of champagne, then continued. 'I want to go away with you, Fran. But before we do that, I want us to be married. I know I'm half-deaf and half-useless, but I'm no longer at any risk of being killed. Do you think, my precious Fran, that you could marry a radar officer with no net worth and an uncertain future?'

Fran had been lifting her own glass to her lips, but she froze, and looked at him over its rim. He waited, watching her, and as she returned his gaze she felt her eyes filling up with tears.

'I thought you would never ask,' she said eventually, her voice catching.

He took her free hand. 'I didn't know whether I would have a future, Fran. I could have died at any time. Well I nearly did die, didn't I? And then, well then afterwards I was a handicapped mess.'

Fran shook her head. 'You were never going to die! And even if you had, or if you'd been permanently damaged, I would rather have known what it was to be your wife first.'

'And your parents? How will they feel?'

A cloud came over Fran, and she sighed. 'Daddy will be happy for us,' she said. 'And Mummy, well . . .'

Jim moved his hand to cover hers more fully. 'It's been a while since I saw her. Is she still as bad?'

Fran bit her lip. 'She still barely speaks, Jim. If I haven't invited you to the house it's because she just can't cope with people, other than Daddy and me.'

'And you think she could cope with us getting married?'

Fran shrugged helplessly, then gave a little, hopeful smile. 'Maybe it will bring her out of herself a little.'

'And it won't worry her if we get married straight away? If we're to use my leave, then we need to get married fast. Would it make it easier with your mother if we wait and do a proper wedding?'

He was watching her anxiously, but Fran shook her head.

'In a way, if we get married quietly it takes all the pressure off her. She will feel Michael's absence less if we do something small. Daddy will encourage her to invite a few people, and that may do her good, as I say, but I'd like to keep things intimate. Just you and me, my parents, and a few close friends. Or just the four of us if Mummy can't cope with more. We're in mourning, and it's a good excuse for not bothering with any fuss.'

She looked at him with her characteristic openness. 'You know, it's your family who probably won't like this – they don't even know who I am!'

She saw Jim flinch, and knew she'd touched a chord. He took a moment to answer her.

'It's true that I haven't mentioned you to my family,' he said. 'Mainly because it would just have raised speculation when I wasn't sure of you. But now I'll send them an airgraph, so that it arrives quickly. I wouldn't want to be married without them even knowing.'

'Well, personally I think your father will hate the idea of our marriage. He would far prefer you to take a good, hard-working Scottish girl whose background he can understand. It's the same problem as with my mother, but in reverse.' She smiled at him. 'Not that I'm going to give you up for that or any reason! I'll just have to win your father around by learning to boil an egg before I meet him!'

Jim smiled back, and took her right hand in his. 'I'm not sure what I ever did to deserve you, Fran. I'm an unpolished physics teacher from Islay, and you . . . well you have so much, and you're so sassy, and fun, and radiant, and strong. You battled for me last year when I was wounded, held by me the whole time I was away in Cape Town, and then welcomed me back despite all the damage to me. I'm not sure I'm worthy of such devotion, but I'll make you a promise. I don't have much, but I can earn, and I'll work all my life to make sure you don't regret this moment.'

Fran placed her left hand over his. 'I won't have any regrets, Jim. Believe me, I will never regret this moment. You're too modest, and I don't think you'll ever realise quite how important you are to me. It's quite simple, really. I can't imagine ever living without you.'

'Scars and all?'

'Yes, my darling. Scars and all.'

323

CHAPTER THIRTY-EIGHT

Scotland, March 1943

It was three months since Christmas, and it had been a long, blustery winter on the Clyde. Catriona had worked her way through it, finding equilibrium as she massaged and pulled her patients into fitness. She still hadn't made her peace with Duncan, not because she hadn't wanted to, but because he wouldn't allow it. She had avoided him for too long, perhaps, while she recruited her strength, and then when she had tried to talk to him later he had simply turned away. She could have sworn he was in a huff, and realised that he had expected her to take his side unconditionally against the colonel. He certainly didn't realise that the violence of his behaviour had shaken her so badly that it had broken something beyond repair. Almost she could have sworn that he was playing hard to get, waiting for her to grovel. What she wanted was to be friends, but if that wasn't possible then she would stay away.

Captain Martin had left too, and Rosneath had become a Royal Navy base again. Before he left, though, he had worked what felt like a miracle to Catriona. The family of

Joe Jefferson, having lost their son to the war, had asked to adopt their grandson. The baby had been moved to a home while his papers were organised, but he would be on a ship heading for New York in the next few weeks, accompanied by an American nurse.

Catriona's heart ached for the baby's mother, because such an adoption was so final, and so far away that she would for sure never see her son again. But Mary, her fellow nurse who had spoken to her about the baby, was much more pragmatic.

'It's a part of the lassie's life that she can put behind her,' she said. 'They asked her if she wanted to be in touch with the family in America, and she said no. The GI dumped her, after all, and she has lived in fear for months. She's too young and too naïve to handle that kind of pressure well.'

'But did he dump her?' Catriona asked. 'He was killed, after he left here. Perhaps he would have got back in touch if not.'

Mary gave her a quizzical look. 'You're too kind, Catriona! He left here in March and was killed in August. There was time to write a letter if he wanted to.'

'Writing doesn't come easily to everyone,' Catriona ventured, and then gave up as Mary shook a very cynical head.

March came in grey and soggy, the kind of weather that you plodded through, waiting for a glimpse of sunlight. From London the weather forecasts were much fairer, but when London's civilian population was taking such a pounding it felt unfair to complain here, where people slept in their own beds every night, and the Anderson shelters went unused. One hundred and seventy-three people were crushed to death one evening in a terrible accident at Bethnal Green Underground Station, where thousands gathered every night to shelter from the bombs. It happened midweek, and the nurses at Dunmore sat together in hushed distress as the reports came through on the BBC. Sixty children were dead, which somehow made it so much worse.

The casualties at Dunmore and Knockderry kept on coming, for the battle of the Atlantic raged on, and they were now sending French corvettes into the treacherous Baltic as well. They hadn't had a bad frostbite case at Knockderry yet, and as they came to the end of the month Catriona crossed her fingers that they might escape without any lost fingers, as the waters of the Baltic warmed for the summer.

She headed home on the last Sunday of the month, and there was a slight lifting in the cloud level as she took the ferry. She bought her ticket from the boatman, and congratulated him on there being no rain. She knew him well after so many crossings, and he was usually cheery when the weather was fine, and as glum as could be when it was wet. He always had some news for her, and she knew when new Australian troopships had arrived, or a Canadian corvette had come in with major damage.

Today there was no need to ask him. He was talking non-stop about yesterday's disaster. The aircraft carrier HMS *Dasher* had blown up just a few miles away, and hundreds of the ship's company had been killed. Everyone hated it when men were killed in accidents. They put their lives at risk so often, and to die needlessly when the enemy was hundreds of miles away seemed such a terrible waste.

Local boats had apparently seen the explosion when a plane hit the ship on landing, and had put to sea to rescue any survivors. Over a hundred had been saved, the ferryman said. Catriona wanted to know where they were now. Were there lots of injured? Would they have been taken to local hospitals? The boatman didn't know.

She made her way home, wondering whether she should be heading in the other direction to the infirmary, where she could offer her services, but it was more likely that the injured would have been taken to hospitals further down the coast. She cycled on, feeling frustrated.

At home she walked into the kitchen to find Aunt Sheila cleaning out cupboards. It was something she did when she was uptight or angry, and she would pull every bag of flour and every tin of peas out and stack them on the kitchen table while she attacked woodwork that was already clean from the last time Uncle Charlie had infuriated her.

Catriona would have liked to tiptoe around her, but there was no room to manoeuvre. 'Hello, Aunt,' she therefore said. 'Have you had a good week?'

Aunt Sheila looked up and muttered. 'Good week? I'll give you good week!'

'Oh dear, has something upset you?'

Aunt Sheila pulled herself upright, and launched into speech. 'Upset me? I'll tell you what, Catriona, you can take that father of yours away with you and find him somewhere to stay in Glasgow. I don't want him in my house any longer! Do you hear me?'

'What has he done?' Catriona could feel the colour

draining from her face. What on earth could he have done to enrage his sister so? Aunt Sheila could fire up at her husband, but she had shown endless patience with her brother since he'd come to stay with them. If she was this angry then he must have shocked her very badly.

'Read this.' Aunt Sheila fished a letter from her apron pocket, and handed it to Catriona. She sank into a chair at the kitchen table and folded open the single sheet. It was an airgraph from Jim.

Dear Father, he had written,
This is a letter I should have written to you some time ago, but late though it may be, I hope you will be happy for me. I have now been given a very nice training post here in Alexandria, and since I am no longer in danger of being blown up I have proposed marriage to a wonderful girl whom I have met here, Frances Trevillian. Fran stood by me all the while when I was wounded, and her family have been incredibly good to me. They are fine people, people whom you would like, and Fran is someone whom our whole family will love, I know. Her father is in finance here, and Fran has lived all her life in Egypt, though she went to school in England. We plan to marry immediately, since being so badly injured has shown me how precious our time is. I will be writing a longer letter to send by sea, and will include photos of Fran and her parents, as well as of our wedding.

Catriona stared for a while at the short letter, and then looked up at Aunt Sheila. 'Frances Trevillian. She is the lady who sent us a telegram last summer to reassure us about Jim, when he was sent to Cape Town,' she said, in wonder.

'I know,' her aunt replied. 'She sounds like a fine lassie.'

A smile came to Catriona's face, and fixed itself there. 'Jim married? And happy! And safe! Oh, Aunt Sheila, this is the best news!'

'Tell your father that,' her aunt muttered. 'Oh, Catriona, why is my brother such a negative man? This letter came yesterday, and he read it and exploded, saying he didn't want his son home, that he could just stay out in Egypt now, and who was this girl anyway? Just some socialite, he said, who would drain his son and look down her nose at his family. I've never heard him rage so much, and when I tried to defend Jim he leapt down my throat and told me that since I've never had a child I could know nothing about the matter.'

Catriona was appalled. Her mother had always told her that it was the greatest grief of Aunt Sheila's life that she hadn't had children. For her father to throw that at her was unforgivable.

'Where is he?' she asked.

'Your uncle took him off to chop logs. I hope he chops off his hands!'

'He would do better to chop off his tongue. Aunt Sheila, I'm so sorry.'

'Well, it's not your fault, child, so don't go apologising,' her aunt said, sounding calmer. 'But poor Jim, after all he's been through, deserves for us to be happy for him.'

Catriona came round the table and gave her a hug. 'Well I am, and you are, and so will father be, once he gets over the shock. He just doesn't like things to change, you know that. If Jim had met a girl in Scotland and courted her, the family would have had time to get to know her, and to plan their wedding with them. It's just fear talking with Father – his comment about her being a socialite tells us that. He's frightened that she'll take Jim into a different life.'

'No doubt she will, but did your father think Jim was going to come back and live on Islay after the war? He has been living a different life for a long time already.'

'But as a teacher he lived a life that father could relate to, and he was still in Scotland. Egypt is just too far away, and too alien, and then, Jim has written to us about how glitzy life is in Alexandria.' She grinned. 'He didn't like it at first, if you remember. He rather disapproved of the glamour. I can't wait to see some photos of Fran and her family.'

'I'm sure she's lovely.'

'Yes, but my dear aunt you would think a slug was lovely if Jim introduced her to you!' She squeezed her aunt again. 'You know what a soft spot you have for my brother! Can I help you put all this back in the cupboard, and will you then let me make a cup of tea? I left Dunmore at dawn this morning, and I'm literally dying of thirst.'

They drank tea together, and toasted Jim and his new bride, and the light came back to Sheila's face.

'I could have killed your father yesterday,' she said, over a tea biscuit.

'So I see! I would have felt the same if I'd been here. But you know he loves you, and he loves Jim – perhaps a bit too much at times, and he sees the whole family through those blinkered eyes of his. He just needs a lot of reassurance, that's all.'

'Well you can reassure him if you want to, but unless he apologises I'll no' be doing anything of the sort.'

'He will apologise, don't worry.'

I'll have to give him the words, though, Catriona thought. She finished her tea, and washed up the cups, and left Aunt Sheila preparing vegetables for lunch as she headed out to find her errant father.

CHAPTER THIRTY-NINE

By the time Catriona left for work at Knockderry the following morning Fergus MacNeill had apologised to his sister, and peace had been restored in the Kilcreggan household. Reminding him about Fran's telegram to them when Jim was in hospital, and the steadfastness she had obviously shown to him, helped Catriona to persuade her father that she must be a girl with a big heart. Catriona also told him stories she had heard about British women in Egypt running tea stalls and free cafes for the troops, just like those that local women here ran for servicemen of every nationality.

'Jim would never fall for a girl unless she was one of us, a good British soul who cares about people,' she told him, and as he got used to the news he began to believe her.

Once a longer letter arrived, with more information and the important promised photos enclosed, then his new daughter-in-law would begin to be more real to Fergus. That letter would take a couple of months to get here, though, so Catriona hoped there would be another airgraph or two before then.

For Catriona, Jim's marriage was the best thing that had happened all winter. She almost bounced into work, and ran into Matron in the hallway, bringing down a swift reprimand on her head. It didn't matter how well you got on with Matron – you could never forget who she was!

Catriona wanted to see Dr Roman. He had become her friend and ally at Knockderry, and they would often hide out to take tea in his office, where they could speak more freely than in front of Matron. He was a man who loved good news, and she wanted to tell him hers.

He hadn't yet arrived, though, so she got on with her work, checking the list of new patients to see what fresh problems might be waiting for her today. She was walking through to check something with Matron when Dr Roman came in. He looked exhausted, and more dishevelled than usual.

'I'm so sorry I'm late,' he said, addressing Matron. 'I spent the weekend in Ardrossan, and only got back to Greenock late last night.'

Catriona stopped in her tracks. 'Were you with the survivors of HMS *Dasher*?' she asked.

'Yes. I went down with another doctor from Greenock,' he said. 'We weren't sure what was happening to the injured, and as it happened they needed extra hands to collect blood, and other basic tasks.'

'That was very good of you, Doctor,' purred Matron.

He held up a hand. 'I didn't do anything very heroic. And once the injured had been stabilised they were all gradually moved off to Glasgow, and some of them to Drymen, I believe. The panic is all over now.'

'How many survivors were there?' Catriona asked. 'I heard there were hundreds killed.'

'Yes, well over three hundred dead, I think. The ship went down in minutes. But they saved over a hundred and fifty men who were in the water. The local fishermen were the heroes – they got to the scene so quickly.'

'And did you work all night on Saturday?' Catriona asked. 'And then non-stop into the evening yesterday?'

He nodded, but then smiled. 'I am fine, Sister, believe me. I have had a few hours' sleep.'

'Maybe you would like a cup of tea,' Matron offered. Catriona smiled inwardly – she was as guilty as Matron of always suggesting tea as the solution to everything, but the doctor had his own strong views about the British cup of tea.

'No, no! I am late, and we must start our rounds. Come, Matron, show me what has been happening here at Knockderry.' He moved quickly to his office, where Matron joined him, and Catriona went on to see her first patient.

All morning Dr Roman kept up his normal frenetic pace, enveloping every patient with his usual energy. It wasn't until just before lunchtime, when he came in to the dining room to join several of the nurses, that he went to sit down, and as he pulled out his chair he stumbled. He didn't fall, but he grabbed the table, and then lowered himself down into the chair, his head leaning forward.

Catriona was behind him, and she stepped forward to grab his elbow, and to hold him as he sat down.

'Thank you, Sister,' he said, in a shade of his normal voice. He lifted his head and it was sheet-white. 'I just had a dizzy spell there.'

Matron stood up and came round the table. 'Doctor, you are exhausted,' she said, and her voice brooked no argument. 'I think you should rest for a while.'

'No, no, I just need a glass of water, and maybe some food.'

'And you will have them, but when you are in your bed.' She gestured to two of the VAD nurses sitting nearby. 'Nurse McColl, Nurse Brown, help Dr Roman up to the Blairmore Room, and see him settled. Doctor, I will personally bring you a cup of hot cocoa. You need some sugar.'

She ignored all his embarrassed protests, and the VAD nurses jumped to follow her instructions. The doctor was helped from the room, and then Matron stalked off to the dispensary, and when the cup of cocoa appeared so did Matron, a paper of sleeping powder in her hand.

Catriona knew a moment of consternation. 'Do you mean to give the doctor a sleeping draught in his cocoa?' she asked, rather nervously. 'A whole one, I mean? Won't that leave him feeling rather too groggy, later on?'

Matron was on a mission, and shot her a bullet of a look, but then seemed to take stock, and poured just over half of the powder into the cocoa.

'This will be enough,' she approved to herself, refraining from acknowledging Catriona's intervention. She placed the cocoa back on its tray, next to a little plate of biscuits, which had been brought with it, and another VAD nurse jumped to pick it up.

'I'll take this myself, thank you, Nurse,' said Matron, at her most magisterial. 'Do continue with your lunch, ladies, or the soup will grow cold,' and as she spoke, she swept out of the room.

The three VAD nurses who were left looked over at Catriona for a lead, unsure how to react, then one giggled. 'Poor Dr Roman,' she said.

Catriona smiled. 'He has worked all weekend, day and night, to help after the ship exploded along the Firth. It won't do him any harm to be cosseted, and to get some sleep. Shall we eat, girls? We need to get back to the wards to cover, don't you think?'

It was four o'clock before Catriona passed by the Blairmore Room on the first floor. It was an old private bedroom from the days of the castle's more glorious past, and had beautiful views over Loch Long to the Blairmore shore across the water.

She eased open the door and peeked in to see if there was anything the doctor needed. He was sleeping, tucked up in hospital pyjamas, and had flung the sheets back slightly as though seeking freedom from what had undoubtedly been over-nursing.

She moved over to check his water jug, and looked down at the well-known features, which looked so different bared in sleep. Elderly people looked older, somehow sunken, when they slept, while her eighteen-year-old patients always looked like children. Some crooked and hid themselves, but Dr Roman lay spread out, with nothing to hide. He seemed younger too, and more fragile, but that fragility wasn't an exposure. He looked fearless, serene, open to the world.

His neck was naked, freed from its worn collar and grey tie, and a few black hairs spilt from his chest under the pyjamas. He was no longer a doctor but just a man, his mother's son. His mother didn't know the work he was doing here, and she maybe didn't even know if he was alive, but she knew her son like this, the simple man, the one who, wherever he was and whatever he did, would somehow manage to take all the horrors of the world and put his arm around them.

Catriona was in awe of him more as he lay there asleep than ever she had been when he was awake. She tiptoed quietly away, and shut the door behind her to protect his rest.

By six that evening the doctor was up and dressed, and looking very sheepish, and above all very groggy.

'You drugged my cocoa,' he accused Matron, but she merely smiled, a satisfied twitch that said, you needed it, and I know best.

Matron and he made a final tour of the wards with Catriona and two of the arriving night nurses, and then Catriona began packing up.

Dr Roman met her in the hall. 'At least you slept well!' she commented, looking at his bleared eyes.

He let out a breath. 'Slept! I have been knocked out, I think! And now I have to drive my scooter! I'm not safe, and there isn't even a good strong coffee to drink here to wake me up!'

'Could I drive it for you? You could be a passenger, and I could take the train home from Greenock instead of from Gourock.'

'Have you ever driven a motorbike?'

'No, never. But is it very different from riding a bicycle?'

'A little! No, I think that is perhaps not a very good idea. I will suggest something else, though; I will drive very slowly to the ferry, and you can cycle beside me, then if I fall you can pick me up. The crossing on the ferry should be windy enough to wake me up fully.'

So Catriona followed him along to the ferry, watching him closely in the gloom as the ribbon of road snaked along the waterside. It was chilly on the ferry, so they huddled together under the covered area.

'This cold certainly chases away sleep,' Dr Roman said, and manoeuvred himself to stand as a windbreak between Catriona and the night.

Catriona shivered. 'So do you think you'll be all right to drive on to Greenock when you get to the other side?' she asked.

'I am sure,' he said.

But as Catriona pushed her bike down the ramp of the ferry she saw the doctor stumble before her.

'*Idiota!*' he muttered to himself as he picked himself up. A passenger picked up the little scooter for him, and he thanked him. He reached terra firma and turned to Catriona.

'I am fine, honestly,' he assured her. 'I just caught my foot on a bolt that was sticking up through the ramp.'

'Maybe, but I saw the dose of sleeping draught Matron gave you at lunchtime. It will slow your reactions for many more hours, I would think. Please let me cycle with you until you reach home. It's only a mile or two to Greenock, and once you're home I'll just take the train from there.'

He looked as though he was going to demur. 'Please,' Catriona repeated, and at this he finally capitulated.

'Damn Matron and her potions! But you're right, my head feels stupidly heavy, and I should accept your company. I'll take the back roads, and we'll take our time.'

He lived in an old Victorian tenement on the fringes of

Greenock's West End, a building of eight flats, which he said had been handed over to the French navy, and which housed a number of its officers. He opened the front door onto the usual tile-lined common entrance hall, and leant his motorbike against the wall.

'Won't you come in?' he asked Catriona. 'I feel I should at least offer you a cup of coffee after your extra cycle.'

She was suddenly shy. 'Your flatmate?' she asked.

'He's away at sea,' he answered. Then he caught her expression, and gave her a reassuring smile. 'Don't come up if you don't wish to, my dear, but I can promise you, you are quite safe.'

She flushed. 'Oh, I know,' she stuttered, and quickly stowed her bike next to his, then followed him up the four flights of stairs to the very top flat.

It was a very compact flat, with a small sitting room leading to a galley kitchen, and two bedrooms leading off the hall. The doctor installed Catriona in the sitting room while he went off to brew coffee, and very soon the most fragrant smell was coming through from the kitchen.

He came through carrying a tray with two surprisingly delicate cups, a milk jug and a sugar jug, all in matching porcelain.

Catriona raised an eyebrow. 'What a beautiful service.'

He smiled rather self-consciously. 'My fellow officers find it a bit ridiculous, but I like to drink from nice china. The coffee is good too, I promise you – having French officers around you can be sure of proper coffee supplies. I don't know where they get it from, it's the entrepreneurs among them who sell it on the black market, but it's available if you are prepared to pay well for it.'

'I don't know anything about coffee, I'm afraid,' Catriona confessed. 'But I'm happy to try it.' She took the cup that was offered to her.

'Don't add milk until you have tasted it,' he advised her. 'It should be drunk black and sweet.'

She sipped the hot, pungent liquid. It was much stronger than anything she knew, but it was so much better than what she had always called coffee that she gave a sigh of contentment.

'Mmm,' she said.

'You like it?'

'I love it! It's kind of bitter and fragrant at the same time. It tastes like a celebration.' She told him about Jim, and his new bride.

'That's wonderful news,' he said. 'I'm just sorry that I cannot offer you a fine cognac to go with the coffee, then we could celebrate properly. I do have some cheese and biscuits, though. I don't suppose you have eaten since lunch, have you?'

'No, and you, Doctor, have eaten even less.'

'You don't think you could call me Pietrek?' was his answer. 'After all, you gave me permission to call you Catriona back in December, didn't you?'

Catriona blushed, but didn't answer.

'I'm sorry if you don't think you could,' he continued. 'You see, for me you have become such a dear friend, someone I look forward all week to seeing each Monday.'

'How true that is!' she said, tingling with pleasure. 'And it's such a rare thing, to have a friend.'

He beamed at her. 'So you feel our bond too, do you? Well then, you do have to call me Pietrek now!'

'Pietrek is a lovely name.' Catriona's voice shook a little, but she took care to pronounce it the same way that he did.

'I don't hear it very often now,' he mourned. 'My French colleagues all call me Pierre.'

'Well that's not very fair. I bet you don't give them Polish names! Why can't they use the name you were born with?'

He laughed. 'I don't mind, I promise you, but I might have known you would come to my support! You are always my greatest defender!'

'Am I?'

'Always!' He gazed for a moment into his empty coffee cup, and then placed it on the table. 'You're a very special woman.'

His voice was no longer jovial. He looked up at Catriona, and then away. 'Have you finished your coffee, Catriona, because if you have I think I should walk you to the station.'

She put her own cup down. 'Are you still feeling tired?'

'Tired? No, I am not tired. But my dear, I think you should go.'

There was no misunderstanding him. Catriona held her breath. He had that same look that he'd had that afternoon in sleep, open and hiding nothing, but there was something more, a kind of yearning, that she hadn't seen there before. She wanted to touch him, or at least to tell him they were in this together, but how to do so? She pulled together her courage.

'Didn't you promise me cheese and biscuits, Pietrek? Of course, I'll go, if you tell me it's what you want, rather than just what you think you should do.'

He shook his head in frustration. 'I should never have

invited you up here. I'm sure I could be your father.'

'How old are you?' she asked, and found herself calmer than she had expected.

'I'm nearly thirty-eight years old!'

'And I am nearly twenty-four! Believe me, Pietrek, you are nothing like my father, and I do not want to go home.'

CHAPTER FORTY

Scotland, August 1943

In the months that followed that evening in Pietrek's flat, Catriona felt that she finally knew why adulthood had been invented. The incomplete and troubled Duncan had disturbed her a great deal, but she realised that he had never quite understood who she really was.

Like Duncan, Pietrek wanted her free and free-thinking, and wanted her to revel in life, but unlike Duncan he also cared about family, and allegiance. He was responsible, caring, an indefatigable worker. He matched her, and he was very quickly and quite simply woven into her being.

They spent so many evenings in his flat, eating his bachelor rations, playing chess and cards, listening to music, talking – always talking. When his flatmate was absent, which happened all the time, Catriona stayed over, but Pietrek gave her his room, and himself moved into the other. He enveloped her body as they sat together, physically so close, and yet held her in a kind of reverence that wouldn't touch further.

How was he still single, a doctor with so much to give,

and such fine eyes? she teased him. So he told her, about the woman he had loved, and the so-called friend he had found her with, and how he had left Poland for France then, to study and to get away.

'And you haven't found someone since? In romantic France?'

'In France all the women want a man more handsome and accomplished than I am, *kochanie*. I am too bumbling and too raw to appeal to them. No, I needed to wait, and find myself a golden lily here in the Scottish rain!'

He told her about his family, all ten of them, his father a shopkeeper, his mother working long hours behind the shop counter, with their eight children running free around the shop until they were old enough to work. It was an image Catriona could relate to. On Islay families were often large, and worked together on the croft or in shops like Pietrek's, the oldest children minding the youngest, in communities where everyone knew everyone else.

Pietrek had been the eldest child, which showed in everything he did, and had taken extra responsibility when his father had died. It was what made him seem sometimes older than his thirty-seven years, perhaps, or nearly thirty-eight, as he kept reminding Catriona. But when he spoke about his mother the years fell off him, and he could look so wistful that Catriona would move in close and place her hands around him as one might a child.

She wanted to introduce him to her family, and Captain Martin's words about Duncan kept coming to her mind. An unacknowledged boyfriend wasn't really your love, and Pietrek was that and more, so he should be known. But her father's reaction to Jim's marriage gave her pause. How would the Presbyterian Fergus react if his daughter came home with a displaced foreigner, and worse, a Catholic?

It took until the summer to make the attempt, and by then Catriona and Pietrek had been together for over four months. Catriona spent the Saturday night with Pietrek after work, and the following morning took the ferry across to Kilcreggan as so often before. It felt like pretence, because her family all assumed that she had come straight from Dunmore, but she had never actively lied. Her routines were so well established that they just didn't ask.

It was almost amusing now how Fergus had accepted his son's marriage. Four months had worked their magic, and a photo of the newly-weds sat in pride of place on the mantelshelf, Jim looking so well after his accident, proudly standing in his white dress uniform with his arm around Fran, a willowy girl, chic and *piquante*, with short dark hair curling over her head. She looked so happy to be with Jim that she couldn't fail to win over his family.

There was another photo of them with Fran's father and mother, taken on the verandah of a house. Some exotic plant, perhaps a jasmine, trailed over the wall beside them, and they looked urbane and almost exotic themselves to Scottish eyes. Fran's father wore a beautifully tailored suit, and her mother a slim-cut dress that could have come from a fashion magazine. The idea of seeing, say, her Aunt Sheila in such a dress boggled Catriona's mind. Her father said nothing, but would come back again and again to study the photo, as though the longer he looked the more he might understand this other world.

'Remember Donny MacRae,' his sister would tell him. 'He worked for years in India, and we've seen photos of him on just such a verandah, and didn't he come back to Islay and just fit back in with us all when he retired?'

'Hah!' Fergus replied. 'He had skin like a dried-up fish from all that sun, and he lorded it over us all for long enough, until he spent all his money on the drink, and had to live like the rest of us!'

But he was soothed, nonetheless, and all his life he had believed in the Empire, and British greatness. Now his son was part of it, and he began to feel proud.

How would he take the news Catriona was coming with today? She waited to launch her subject until lunchtime, when they were seated together at the kitchen table.

'How are things going up at the castle these days?' her uncle asked her. 'Aren't the Atlantic convoys having an easier time of it now? Surely that means you have fewer patients?'

It gave her the opening she needed. 'Not really,' she answered. 'There are still as many casualties on the Baltic runs to Russia, and they seem to be using our poor Frenchmen more and more for those. Pietrek says it's almost worse, because the runs exhaust people so, and they take much longer to recover.'

Her stomach churned as she waited for a response. 'Pietrek?' her uncle asked.

'I mean Dr Roman. You know, the wonderful doctor I've talked to you about, who is such an inspiration at Knockderry. His name is Pietrek, or Peter, if you prefer.'

'You call him by his Christian name?' Aunt Sheila asked, amazed.

'Not at work, no, but at other times I do. Pietrek and I have become very close.'

The table bristled now. 'What do you mean, very close?' her father glowered.

'I mean just that, *Daidí*. Pietrek is someone whom I would like you to meet.'

It was a long lunchtime, and Aunt Sheila's milk pudding sat untouched for a long time while the questions raged over all the issues Catriona had expected, religion, nationality, family, prospects.

'You'll end up a damned Pole!' her father thundered at her at one moment, using a word that for him had a deeply religious meaning. Damned – you are damned.

'I won't necessarily end up anything at all,' she answered him, as mildly as she could. 'Pietrek and I are not married, and he hasn't asked me. We are getting to know each other, as people do everywhere. But I would like you to meet him.'

Uncle Charlie, kindly Uncle Charlie, gave a nudge to his wife, and then said to Catriona, 'And how would you like to do that, my dear?'

Catriona took a breath. 'I thought maybe I could invite him here for lunch next Sunday.'

Aunt Sheila, a staunch Presbyterian, had been as shocked as her brother by the little bomb that Catriona had dropped in their midst, but under her husband's eye she was quicker than Fergus to bring herself under control.

'I think that's a good idea,' she said, after a moment. 'Bring him here so we can see this young doctor for ourselves.'

'Young?' Fergus spluttered. 'Didn't you tell us the doctor you were working with was an older man?'

Catriona sighed. 'He's thirty-seven,' she said baldly.

'Aye, and that's no bad thing, Fergus,' Uncle Charlie

hastened to say. 'Catriona's a girl well older than her years, and one of the young lads left around here wouldn't do for her at all.'

'He's a damned Pole! He'll be taking my daughter away to some heathen village!'

'Not heathen, Father, Catholic!' Catriona said, on an almost hysterical laugh. 'I know he's everything you don't want to hear about, but didn't you bring me up to judge people on their qualities, and not their birth? Won't you at least meet Dr Roman, and talk to him? If you dislike him then, I'll understand.'

'And you'll drop him?'

'No, I'm not promising that, but I'll take your opinion seriously, because you're my father, and I respect you, and Aunt Sheila, and Uncle Charlie. Pietrek will respect you as well, and he has such a high regard for family that he has asked me to arrange this meeting.'

'Hah! That's just flannel, my girl! If you had real respect for where you come from you'd be looking for a decent Scottish man, not some unknown foreigner.'

'Won't you just meet him?' was all Catriona said.

It was Aunt Sheila who answered. 'We'll meet him, *a' ghràidh*. He's a man far from home and family, doing a good job here. I would offer him lunch anyway. He will have to be special, though, if he is to win us over to think he is worthy of you.'

Catriona caught her aunt's hand. 'He's certainly special,' she said. 'Matron is half in love with him, and all our patients adore him, and believe me, Aunt, you will all do so too.'

* * *

To say that Catriona's family fell in love with Pietrek would be an exaggeration, but the lunch passed as well as could be expected, and Uncle Charlie, at least, told them all afterwards that any Pole who could come to Scotland and learn English as well as Pietrek had done, spoke fluent French as well, and was working so hard to help people, was someone worth knowing.

'He speaks a bit stiffly, I grant you, but that's to be understood. And he's got more qualifications than you or I could even dream of,' he told Fergus. 'He could make himself a cracking living in this country if he chose to stay after the war.'

'But he won't, will he? We'll win his country back for him, and then he'll break my lassie's heart and bugger off to where he came from,' was Fergus's answer.

But he didn't say more. His way of handling Pietrek's intrusion into their lives was not to mention him at all. Catriona shrugged, and decided she had done what she could.

There was a problem, too, in that she couldn't refute too strongly what her father had said. For some time now there had been new activity around the peninsula, and this month the Americans had returned to Rosneath. North Africa had been won, our aircraft were pounding Sicily preparing for an all-out attack on Italy, and now, everyone was sure, an invasion of France was being planned.

This would be the big one, the push that would drive the Germans back into their own homeland. Pietrek's brother Alfons came to visit him in Greenock, and told them that his Polish regiment was training hard for an invasion. There was no sign of them moving yet, but they were all waiting for the call. They were going to liberate Europe, and sink their boots into the throats of the Germans for what they had done to Poland. And then they were going home.

'You'll be wanting to go home too,' Catriona said to Pietrek, painfully holding her breath.

He shook his head at her, but said nothing more while his brother was there. Then when they were alone he took her in his arms and they talked.

'You must realise, Catriona, that I haven't actually lived in Poland for most of the last years. I was in France, remember. Now my heart is pulling me back, but not as much as it is pulling me to stay with you.'

'But what about your family?'

'I have thought so much about this, and it just goes round and round in my head. When we finish this, and have our country back, then of course I need to see them, and I don't even know if your country will allow me to stay. I am hoping, though, that I may have choices that people like Alfons may not have.'

That was logical. Pietrek was a doctor with fluent English, where his younger brother was a technician who had only learnt enough English to get by.

'And so you will wait and see?' Catriona asked.

'Not quite. There is one thing I would wish to do, *kochanie*. I don't feel that I can let my little brother go off to France on his own. If anything happens to him I need to be there. The focus of the war will shift away from here, you know, and when the invasion happens I can offer more to Poland by being with our troops all the way to Berlin.'

That was the last thing Catriona had been expecting him to say. Wasn't he needed here? Hadn't he told her that the Polish army had plenty of doctors? Catriona wanted to shout it out, but said nothing. She had wanted to go into the field herself, after all, and had felt so frustrated and aggrieved when her father had held her back. She wasn't going to be the person who held Pietrek back.

She couldn't tell him she was glad, though. It would take her all her time to adjust to the idea before any troop movements finally came. And she couldn't say anything to her family.

'Of course you'll go when the time comes,' she said eventually. 'I wouldn't have expected any less from you.'

'Nor I of you,' Pietrek answered.

That night she wouldn't let him sleep in the other room. 'I need you here,' she told him.

'Catriona,' he whispered. 'How can I marry you when I don't have a country or even a nationality?'

'We'll marry when it's all over, but for now I need you here.'

'You want just to share my bed?'

'No, I want to share everything.'

He held her away. 'You don't think it's too risky?'

'You're a doctor, aren't you? You know what to do.'

'And you'll trust me?'

She held his head in her hands, and looked into his eyes. 'Take me to your bed, Pietrek,' she said.

CHAPTER FORTY-ONE

Alexandria, August 1943

It was very different living in an apartment in Alexandria, close to the restaurants and shops, instead of in the villa a drive away where Fran had spent her childhood. Fran and Jim had no live-in servant, and though their man Alieu came in by day and would leave them prepared dishes if she asked him to, Fran was experimenting with cooking for Jim when they arrived home each evening. The results were sometimes better than others, but it was a new pleasure for Fran to serve food for them both, and Jim seemed to eat anything without complaint.

She didn't yet dare cook for anyone else, though, so when Lucie came around, or George or Len came to stay on their visits to Alex, it was Alieu's food they all ate together. The apartment had become something of a focal point for friends and colleagues, easy-going and informal, where you served yourself, and there was always coffee on tap in the mornings for sluggish young heads.

Michael was always missing of course. Fran wondered if he would eventually become less absent, just as Tony had gradually faded from their daily lives. Tony, though, hadn't been her brother. Lucie made reference to it one day, and showed remarkable insight.

'I saw your mother the other day,' she told Fran. 'It was the first time I'd seen her since your wedding. She was in a group organising parcels to send off to Sicily. She's lost more weight, hasn't she?'

She saw the shadow that crossed Fran's face, and continued. 'You know, it makes me realise what was the real difference between myself and Tony's mother in our bereavement. I don't think any woman can ever really get over losing a child, do you? Whereas I may not have another man yet, but I haven't written myself out of happiness. Your mother seems extinguished, somehow.'

Fran was grateful to her for not mincing her words, or pretending that things were fine when they so clearly weren't.

'That describes her very well,' she said, with a sigh. Sometimes she confused her grief for Michael with her grief for her mother. But then, they were actually part of the same thing, weren't they? And part of the grief was realising that you couldn't make anything better, or take away the pain.

'Is there anything we can do? Her friends, I mean?'

Fran shook her head. 'Her greatest help comes from my father. They have become closer, and spend their evenings together now, just the two of them, without even me at home. He has been teaching her chess, and they seem to have peace, between them.'

'And does she come here?' Lucie gestured to the apartment around them.

'They both do, for dinner, just the four of us.' Fran

found herself smiling, in spite of her pain. 'She has fallen in love with my husband.'

She caught Lucie's look of surprise. 'Oh, he hasn't replaced Michael, not that. But Jim is so kind to her, and turns on that Highland charm of his, very gently, and you can feel her warming up. That cold, pinched look leaves her face.'

'You've got a lovely man, Fran.'

'I know,' Fran answered, then broke off as she choked up.

The beach featured large in their lives that summer. Jim had fitness as his prime objective, and Fran would spend long hours throwing a ball to him, working on his motor skills. They swam too, and picnicked in the sun, doing all the things they couldn't do last summer, hugging a happiness that this damned war made so precious.

Jim was busy at work, and had been doing some combined training with the US navy up at Port Said. The Americans, he enthused, were the future of radar technology. He had worked with a female radar officer too, in a job no woman would have been doing in the Royal Navy, and he loved the fact that the American ships were so much less hierarchical in the way they operated. George teased him that he would be emigrating after the war. Fran told him not to chance fate, because it was far too possible for teasing.

At the *Alexandria Journal* Fran continued reporting on the war. Africa was free of Axis troops, the Allies were preparing to invade Italy, and Churchill was in Canada having talks with Roosevelt. He was to visit Washington too, and Boston, where he would receive an honorary degree. According to the *New York Times* he was the American darling, the hero of the hour, and even his wife Clementine and daughter Mary were given slots on Canadian radio. It made good reading for the Brits in Alexandria, and Fran's boss Tim was a happy man.

Sami was back at the *Journal* for the summer. He had finished his first year at university with top grades, and was riding on a cloud of enthusiasm for all things American, even greater enthusiasm than Jim's. Sami was definitely emigrating after the war. He wanted a master's degree in law from Harvard or Yale, and a career in New York. The only blot on the landscape of his life was Asher.

Asher hadn't come home for the summer. He had started the year in the second semester, of course, and so it was logical for him to stay on to take some summer courses, but Sami told Fran that he attended classes just enough to avoid trouble, and had found some worrying friends.

'I think he just didn't want to come home,' he told her. 'He says that the Jewish community in Alexandria doesn't have any guts, and that he never again wants to stand by while demonstrators insult the Jews, and while his family's home is defiled.'

'So he is with a Zionist group?' Fran asked. 'I thought you said that Beirut is a moderate, open place. Where has he found such friends?'

'Oh, they're there if you hunt for them. I suppose any campus breeds radical opinions, and Asher went looking for them.'

Fran was dismayed. 'So he isn't really studying?'

'Well he is and he isn't. He hasn't failed anything this semester, but he hasn't taken any pride in his studies either.'

His worry was evident. He had been Asher's greatest friend in Alexandria, and clearly fretted at the chasm that had opened up between them in Lebanon. It was inevitable that Asher would explore Jewish issues in his new-found life of freedom, Fran thought, but hopefully he would come through. He was a complex creature, but sensible at the core.

Sami spoke now to reassure himself. 'I'm hoping that being in Beirut over the summer will change how he sees things,' he said, hopefully. 'There are fewer people around, and less political activity, and Asher will shine in class because a lot of those staying on to study are not the brightest students.'

Such hopes were dashed, however, just a few days later. Fran was in her office when she heard an altercation taking place outside. She opened her door to find that the secretary was blocking access to a middle-aged Egyptian in a well-cut suit and fez, who was brandishing a piece of paper at her as he poured out a torrent of words.

'It's your newspaper that's responsible for what happened to my son. I want to see the manager – Trevillian, is she called? She will answer to me for this! You're a bunch of cheap, trouble-mongering hacks, that's what you are!'

Fran pulled her door wide open and stepped forward into the outer office. The secretary shot her a frightened look.

'This g-gentleman wants to speak to you, Mrs MacNeill.'

The man shook his head violently. 'I want to speak to Miss Trevillian,' he said.

Fran moved towards him and held out her hand. 'I am, or was, Miss Trevillian. I was married in the spring, and changed my name. May I help you?'

'Help me? No, you can't help me! You have already done enough damage, Miss . . . Mrs MacNeill. My name is Ammiel Giladi.'

Enlightenment struck Fran. 'Then you must be Asher's father. Please, Mr Giladi, come into my office.'

She stood back and invited him to enter through the door behind her, smiled a reassurance at the secretary, and followed Mr Giladi into her office. Something serious had happened to Asher, that was sure, and she wanted to know what it was.

She ushered him into a chair, and once seated he seemed to lose the power of speech. He just sat, looking down at the clock on her desk, with an expression on his face that was much more disturbing than his angry bluster had been.

'You've come about Asher,' Fran said to him once she'd taken her own seat. 'Won't you tell me what has happened?'

He gripped hold of the paper in his hand, and found his voice. 'He has gone to Palestine to join the Palmach,' he said.

'The Palmach? But don't they fight with the Allies?' Fran asked. Palmach was a militia of Jews from Palestine, which had fought very valiantly against the Germans in Syria.

He shook his head. 'For a journalist you are not very well informed, Mrs MacNeill. The Allies stopped funding the Palmach and disbanded them after El Alamein, when they decided that the Jewish population in Palestine was no longer under threat. But the Palmach went underground, and now they have become a guerrilla organisation.'

He held out the paper. 'Read this, and you'll understand better.'

Fran took what was a letter from Asher. He'd gone to defend the new settlements, he wrote. Britain had failed the Jews, and Hitler was intent on exterminating every last member of the Jewish people. All over the world Jews were being persecuted, and now they needed to bring people in to Palestine by any means possible and make a nation, give the Jewish people a homeland. And every young man of able body had a duty to join the fight.

Fran read the words, and read them again. Her mind felt suspended, and she tried vainly to imagine studious Asher in the wilds of Palestine with a gun in his hand.

'I'm sorry,' was all she found to say, for there didn't seem to be anything else.

'Sorry! I should hope you are sorry. Do you know that until my son came to work here all he wanted to do was study and make a decent life for himself? Who sent him to see Menasce last December? You did, and Menasce talked to him about the clandestine immigrations to Palestine. He gave him some names in Lebanon, and put my son on the path he has now chosen.'

'But I didn't send him to Menasce!' she answered. 'I sent him to your moderates, to investigate their work in raising money in your community for the Allied war effort.'

'Yes, but he sought out Menasce as well, didn't he?'

Fran thought back. It was true that Asher had gone to interview Menasce as well, for balance, he had said, and she had thought that very reasonable. He hadn't come back inflamed, or not that she had seen. But then Asher was a dark horse, and would have known not to report anything illicit that he had learnt from Menasce.

She stayed quiet. There was no point in trying to defend herself against this man's accusations. There had been so many factors that had influenced Asher, but his father needed a focus for his anger. Had he confronted Menasce himself, she wondered, or just come running straight to this office? She guessed the latter. Tackling the wealth and power of Menasce would be much more complicated.

'Do you think Asher was wrong to think he had no future here as a Jew in Egypt?' she asked eventually.

'None of us will have a future here if the Zionists get their way,' was his reply. 'Egyptians are only turning against the Jews because of the whole Palestine issue. We will end up all having to live in separate countries, with young men like my son lined up between us, guns in their hands. I've lived peacefully all my life here, Mrs MacNeill, as my father did before me. I am an Egyptian first and a Jew second. But you have turned my son into a fanatic.'

She could only shake her head. 'I'm sorry you think so, Mr Giladi. I believe Asher knew the Menasce family well enough long before he came to the *Journal*.'

Asher's father waved an impatient hand. 'Of course! We all know the Menasces. How could we not? They are the leading Jewish family of Alexandria. But you sent my son to delve into the man's politics, and you encouraged him to challenge everything he'd been brought up to believe.'

'You think so? Well then, I'm sorry, Mr Giladi.' Fran felt inexpressibly tired and dejected, and wanted the man to leave. She listened for another ten minutes as he unburdened all his anger, and said very little more. She wondered if she should offer him a coffee, but didn't, and when he finally left she sat staring at the wall of her office, feeling an ache in her guts, not just at what had happened to Asher, but at what was happening to Egypt. Nothing was ever going to be the same after this war. Everything had been polarised, and all would continue to be polarised now, of that she was sure.

She was due that evening at a function organised by Lawrence Durrell and his British Information Office to promote a military exhibition to the press. There would be decent wine, and lots of gossip among her press colleagues, and normally she would be looking forward to it. But today she couldn't face the triviality of it all. She left work early and made her weary way home, wanting to see Jim.

With Jim she knew she would leave Alexandria in the next few years, whenever the war ended and his duties were finished. They would make a life in Scotland, or perhaps even in America, if George was to be believed. But what about her father, who had been born here in Egypt and had a whole life invested here? What would he do?

But more importantly, what about the people here who had nowhere else to go? People like the Menasces, damn them, had British or French citizenship and plenty of money safely stashed in Europe. They could stir up all the trouble they pleased, then go wherever they wanted later. But most of the ordinary Jews here were Egyptians, with livelihoods and generations of culture invested here. Many didn't even have passports, and were accepted as Egyptian by goodwill. What would happen to them, and to the companionable neighbourhoods where Egyptians of all creeds had lived for so long equably side by side?

Damn everything, she thought. Damn everything, that's all.

Chapter Forty-Two

Alexandria, November 1943

Nothing more was heard of Asher. The months went by and Fran could only hope that he was still alive, and had found friends, a brotherhood that supported him, no matter how much she disagreed with what they were trying to do. She hated to think of him disillusioned, maybe scared, and wondered whether he would dare to leave and come home if he changed his mind. Just don't become too hardened, Asher, she thought, and above all, stay alive.

Until his disappearance, Fran had coped with the other darknesses in her life, with the constant ache for Michael, and her worry about her mother. Being with Jim was so special that it enabled her to ride above everything else. But Asher's father's visit hit her like a punch in the midriff, and she had trouble pulling herself back up from the ground.

Jim reminded her that she couldn't be held responsible for the decisions of a thinking, independent young adult, but it wasn't just that. It was the madness of the world that was beginning to get to her, the cockeyed, randomly brutal war driving its wedges between peoples, and her fears for what legacy it was going to leave. Suddenly the adventure of her new life with Jim, his enthusiasm for everything and his love for her, were not enough to lift her spirits.

It was at the beginning of November that Jim finally really tackled her. He had watched Fran toying with one of Alieu's best dishes one evening, pushing it around her plate without interest, and suddenly he grabbed her hand.

'Fran,' he said, in his most serious voice, 'do you know that you have become thinner than your mother? You didn't even touch your food when we went out with Len last night. And you haven't spoken a word to me the whole time we've been eating this evening. This can't go on!'

She'd been in a world of her own, nowhere in particular, just the little grey place in her head where her worries about her mother would revolve around, and the niggles of life at work. She was tired and had the beginnings of a headache, and she didn't feel her conversation would be of much interest to anyone.

'I'm sorry, Jim. I'm not feeling too good,' she admitted.

'You need to see Dr Samson.' Jim's words were more of an injunction than a suggestion. Fran looked at him rather blankly.

'I think you should make an appointment tomorrow,' he insisted. 'In fact, I'll make the appointment myself.'

Jim was so rarely prescriptive that Fran was taken by surprise. His tone was tough and unequivocal, and as she looked at him Fran realised that she must be behaving very strangely indeed for him to react in this way. A wave of love for him flowed through her at the same time as a wave of fear. Was she so useless? Was she driving him away? She wanted to cry.

And when she saw Dr Samson, her doctor since childhood, she did cry. He only had to come around his desk and show concern.

'Fran, my dear, it has been a long time since you came to see me. What can I help you with?' he said, and she collapsed into tears.

Dr Samson sat close to her, perched on the edge of his desk. She'd been trying to be too strong, he told her, for everyone else's sake. He'd expected to see her after Michael's death, but only her mother had come to see him. He'd been very happy to learn about her wedding. Was everything all right with her new husband? This question was posed very delicately, and as she dried her tears Fran hastened to reassure him that her marriage had been a wholly positive thing, that she and Jim had a wonderful life together, and that until recently she had felt nothing but happiness at how her life was going, marred only, of course, by the family's grief.

'I just seem to have hit a wall recently,' she told him. 'I'm constantly tired, and I know I'm terrible company. I go up and down like a yoyo, but it's more down than up. Mostly, I just can't be bothered with anything.'

'Have you talked this through with anyone?' he asked.

'Well, Jim knows how bad I am, of course. He's the one who insisted I should come to see you.'

'And your mother? Have you talked to her? After all, you were both bereaved back in January.'

Fran fixed a painful gaze on him. 'How can I? Poor

Mummy has been so unhappy. What she needs is support, not any added worries.'

He looked sceptical. 'I'm not sure you're right, Fran. I think your mother would find it comforting to know that you too are human, and hurting, and that you can be brought down just as she has been. People aren't made stronger by having strong people doing everything for them. They become stronger by helping those around them. And you are the daughter, remember. Your mother's natural instinct is to support you.'

He ignored Fran's gesture of refusal. 'Are you eating?' was his next question.

She shook her head. 'Food just makes me feel sick these days.'

'Yes, I thought you looked a little thinner. So you're tired, and nauseous. Tell me, Fran, have you missed a period recently?'

Fran looked at him, thunderstruck. 'Why yes, but I often do, and I haven't been eating, so I assumed that was the reason.'

He smiled again. 'You've been married now for over six months, my dear, would it be so strange if you were expecting a child? You've had so many other worries that you have perhaps not been thinking about the possibility, but if you are pregnant it might explain some of how you are feeling. Come, let us do a small examination.'

Fran left the doctor's consulting room half an hour later in a complete daze. Until now, her marriage to Jim had been an end in itself for her. All she had wanted was the new life that they shared in their little apartment, the cosy evenings together and with friends, the intimacy of being one of a couple. The cocoon of their little world was too precious, and she didn't want it to change. The news Dr Samson had just given her was like a bombshell. She didn't feel ready, didn't want to be pregnant.

Talk to your mother, he'd told her, and without thinking too hard she jumped on a tram and headed out along the Corniche. It was nearly lunchtime and hopefully her mother would be at home. Jim was training on a ship for the day, and wouldn't be home until the evening.

The walk up to the house was actually nerve-racking. There was a bubble in Fran that needed to be let out, and if her mother wasn't at home it would have to wait. She entered the house without knocking, and called out a hello.

'I'm in the dining room,' an answering voice called back.

Fran found her mother arranging flowers in a vase. Everything about the scene was familiar, even the soft lines that now framed her mother's eyes, and the new grey hairs that sprinkled her hair. Fran was so conditioned to think of her mother as vulnerable, but here in the shelter of her own home she looked quietly serene. She didn't radiate, but she looked peaceful, as though the sadnesses of her life had become, step by step, almost mellow companions. In contrast, Fran felt as though she was at war with hers.

'Why, Fran, darling, what brings you here?' Barbara asked. 'Shouldn't you be at work?'

Fran found her voice wobbling as she answered. 'Mummy, I've just been to see Dr Samson, and he tells me I'm two months pregnant.'

Her mother stood for a long moment without moving, and then came the smile.

'A baby! Why, Fran, that's wonderful,' and then her smile faded as she saw the shadow on Fran's face. 'Aren't you happy, my love?'

Fran shrugged helplessly. 'I don't know.' She brushed her hand impatiently over her face. 'I haven't been well, and I don't seem to be thinking very clearly. Am I ready to look after a baby? I can't even look after myself at the moment.'

She could feel her mother looking at her closely, and forced herself to return her gaze. 'Is it wrong of me not to be over the moon?' she pleaded.

Barbara Trevillian moved forward and put her arm around her. 'Sit down, Fran. You look all in.' She coaxed Fran into a chair, and then sat down beside her. There was a pause, and then her mother started talking.

'Do you know, when I fell pregnant with you I found it completely overwhelming. Your father and I had only been married a very short while, like you and Jim, and Alan had just been called up, after finishing his studies at Oxford. We didn't come out here to live until the war ended, you know.'

The First World War. Fran rarely thought of it, but of course her parents had lived through it, and her father had seen active service in France. Her mother had been pregnant in equally uncertain times, and when Fran was born her father was out of the country. She knew that, had always known it, but somehow had never really thought much about it.

It dawned on her that her mother had lived twice in fear of losing someone to war. Her father had come through the war unscathed, but the wife left waiting, expecting her first child, would have worried constantly.

No wonder she had begun to crack last year, and then to lose Michael when she'd finally thought him safe was just too cruel. Fran had been born in Devon, close by her grandparents' home, so presumably her mother had had some family support. Had they all been close, like the stories you read about the home front during that war?

'Did you live with my grandparents while Daddy was away?' she asked.

Her mother nodded, then gave a wry smile. 'But you didn't get much of a welcome into the world, poor thing, because your Uncle William came home injured just a week before, and everyone was preoccupied by him.'

So not the support her mother needed, then. Uncle William had suffered shell shock, Fran knew, and had suffered repercussions ever since. Why had she never given it all much thought until now?

'We didn't lose William, though,' her mother was continuing. Her face twisted. 'We need to win this war and make sure there are no more wars, so that your baby doesn't get caught up in any conflict ever in his life. It's been enough, all this!'

Fran bit her lip. 'You know, even if we do win the war, life isn't going to be simple, not here at least. Had Michael not died he would definitely have had to leave here to make a career. He didn't believe that, but I'm more sure than ever.'

Barbara sighed. 'Michael was always the great optimist, so positive. It was what made him so wonderful. But I fear you're right, my dear. Your father thinks we'll have a few years, but we know that the nationalists will take over

Egypt one day and that we won't be welcome. Thankfully, Alan will be thinking of retirement by then, anyway. And as for you, you and Jim and the baby will make a new life after the war, back at home.'

The baby. The more her mother spoke about it, the more real the baby began to seem. How would Jim react when she told him? Fran wondered. Her instinct told her he would be delighted, and that it would fit entirely with his burgeoning plans for a life in the USA. Would that upset her mother, to think that they would be so far away?

'Jim thinks his best chance for a career in his field may be across the Atlantic,' she ventured.

'In America?' Her mother sounded surprised, but not shocked. A small frown of concentration came to her forehead, and Fran could almost see her brain trying to process the information.

'He may be right,' she said finally. 'And I can see him fitting in well there. It would be a good place to raise a family too. A young country, full of energy. What your father finds most difficult about the idea of leaving here is the thought of living back in England, where he says everyone is as closed-minded as they are closed in by the weather.'

Fran thought about her mother's life, the friends she chose, even the flowers she had just been arranging, dahlias, which would have been quite at home in her native England.

'But you would like to live in England, wouldn't you?' she asked.

Her mother hesitated. 'I've been in Egypt for twenty-four years,' she replied eventually. 'Not all my life, like your father, but nevertheless, it's a long time. I don't fear the English culture like your father does, but I do see exactly what he means by being closed in.' She smiled rather wistfully. 'You get used to the sunshine.'

Fran took her mother's hand. 'Well, once Daddy retires you can spend as long as you want every year with us in America.'

A gleam of amusement reminded Fran of her mother as she used to be. 'You'll have to make sure you settle somewhere warm, then! It might even help me to persuade your father to retire earlier.'

'California?' Fran suggested.

Barbara laughed. 'California would be wonderful!' She looked at Fran as though to study her face. 'So you've been unwell, you say? Do you mean just with morning sickness?'

Fran shrugged. 'Yes, and tiredness, but I've been depressed too. Dr Samson told me I've been trying to be too strong since Michael's death, and now it's caught up with me.'

Her mother nodded emphatically. 'Your father and I have both said the same. You've been almost untouchable. But, of course, you had Jim, and your new life.'

'Yes, and he has helped me so much.' Fran sighed. 'But at the end of the day I still have no brother.'

'He's still with us, Fran,' her mother said. 'You may not believe that, but I do. I talk to him sometimes, when I'm on my own.'

A little smile came to Fran unbidden. 'Does he give you a lot of nonsense?' she asked. 'I dream about him, and they're always scenes from our childhood, of the idiotic little firebrand who broke my toys and then mended them all the wrong way up thinking I wouldn't notice!'

Barbara chuckled. 'Do you remember him breaking the kitchen window with a cricket ball and ruining Cook's stew? He came out screaming at Michael and nearly handed in his notice! But you're not so different yourself, you know. If you have a boy, I will expect him to be just the same.'

A baby Michael! That would be wonderful.

'And if I have a girl?'

'Then she'll be as beautiful and as clever as you. You know, Fran, they say that pregnancy lasts a full nine months for a good reason. You need all that time to be ready for a new baby, and the changes it will bring to your life. But meantime your life with Jim won't change for a while, and when the baby comes . . . Well, when the baby comes it will bring us all new hope, and a new little life to help mend ours.'

Fran gripped the hand she was holding more tightly. 'Thank you, Mummy,' she said, with a rather watery smile.

Her mother reached a finger to wipe her tears away. 'Are you able to eat?'

'Not much, I just feel sick at the sight of food.'

'Then I'll ask Ahmed to make us the simplest of cucumber sandwiches for lunch. You don't need anything rich. Tell your Alieu the same, or just make food yourself – light food without spices, which doesn't turn your stomach. And take a day or two off work, Fran. Give yourself and the baby a break. Get Jim to take you out to Lake Mariut this weekend. You take on the world's troubles through your work, but you don't need them right now.'

Her mother saw more than you would imagine, Fran thought.

'I thought I was going all wrong,' she admitted. 'It helps to know that at least some part of it, the tiredness and the sickness, was the baby's fault and not mine!'

'Ah, now there, my dear, you have an important lesson to learn, which only time and a cantankerous child will teach you. The baby is never wrong, and mothers are destined always to feel slightly at fault! It will be a lot of fun to watch as a grandmother!'

CHAPTER FORTY-THREE

Scotland, December 1943–May 1945

How could it be that Pietrek was leaving already? Nobody believed that France would be invaded in the middle of winter, but the Polish regiment that Pietrek had chosen to rejoin was moving south to train near to the channel ports, in readiness for the big event. Either Pietrek went with them now, or he didn't go at all.

Knockderry Hospital didn't know what they would do without their doctor. There were fewer casualties, though, and the Free French navy itself was beginning to plan for its part in the invasion of France. Corsica had been liberated by Free French forces back in October, and General de Gaulle had been officially named President of the French Committee of National Liberation. The scent of freedom had blown over the whole of France, and resistance groups were said to be wreaking havoc on their German occupiers, with heavy repercussions for the people of France.

At Dunmore there was no let-up in the volume of British army amputees, who were so often now victims of explosions in Italy, where the Italian government's change of allegiance to support the Allies had only made the Germans more aggressive in their hold on the country. Catriona worked on as ever, and thought that only through work would she see her way to the end of this war.

She spent more and more nights with Pietrek, arriving late by train from Dunmore, and leaving at dawn to be back at work on time, skidding on frozen pavements in the bitterest winter Britain had known for years. They made food and talked as though nothing was changing. Only in his bed did Catriona's desperation show. Nightly she gave herself to him and held him as though the very next day would be the end of everything.

Then he left, and she returned to her shared room at Dunmore, to the routines and the chatter of the nurses, and controlled her ache with a determination that for the next year, or however long it took, she would be equal to Pietrek, and to the challenge of finally liberating them all.

Both of them wrote daily, long letters that were simple diaries of their lives, nothing exaggerated or overdramatic. She told him about her patients, about the films she had seen, and he told her about the training camp, the other regiments they were working with, the frosts and snow they trained in, his brother's latest exploits at a local dance in their English town. But always he finished with the same sentence. 'You are my love, I don't forget you, could never forget you, you are my future, and I will be with you soon.'

In the house in Kilcreggan only her aunt ever asked Catriona about Pietrek. Her father had assumed, with evident relief, that Pietrek's departure meant the end of his 'dalliance' with Catriona. He was more concerned about Jim, and the prospects for his return. News had come by airgraph in time for Christmas that Jim's wife Fran was pregnant, and the baby was due in June. A new optimism sat in the Kilcreggan household, and Catriona's longings had no place there.

The months went by, and D-Day came, and before it did they had a new assembly of ships on the Clyde, greater than ever before, bigger than for the North African invasion eighteen months before. To Catriona it was even more momentous but it was no longer exciting. She knew fear and hope in equal measure, but not the thrill she'd known before when she'd seen the fleet assembling. Now she had someone too closely involved, and this invasion was the key one, that would decide hers and everyone's future.

Pietrek's regiment didn't sail for France until July, when the Normandy beaches had been taken, and the battle for France was in full flood. After he sailed his letters stopped, but Catriona told herself this was normal, and she shouldn't panic just because communication stopped in the heat of the invasion. Pietrek would be at the rear treating casualties, not in the first line of battle.

It was four long months before any letter arrived, and by then it was October, and the nights were growing darker again, wet leaves squelching underfoot as Catriona trod her way around Dunmore. The letter had been written two months before, and had taken its time to find its way to Scotland. Pietrek's regiment had been in Normandy, part of the pincer movement trying to encircle the retreating Germans. They had failed to trap the German army, Catriona knew, but shortly afterwards Paris had been liberated, and they had seen the photos in all the newspapers of General de Gaulle parading triumphantly under the Arc de Triomphe. Had Pietrek been anywhere near Paris? Catriona thought not. The hardest work was being done much nearer to the coast.

So where would Pietrek be now? Towns all along the coast in France had fallen to the Allies, and troops were pushing inland. Would he have had any of her letters? She would have loved to talk to someone about it, but though her aunt occasionally asked for news, concern for Pietrek was Catriona's private domain.

Jim and Fran's baby had been born, a little girl called Victoria Jean. Fergus regretted that it wasn't a boy, which nearly brought him to blows with both his sister and his daughter. But he was pleased nonetheless, for Jean was Catriona's mother's name. All of the Kilcreggan household called little Victoria the D-Day baby, for she'd been born the day after the Normandy landings. Pictures arrived by September, and Aunt Sheila immediately saw all kinds of family likenesses. Most striking was a close-up, studio photo of Jim, Fran and baby Victoria together. The tenderness written on both parents' faces was so striking that it brought a lump to the throat. The picture made Catriona long for Pietrek so much that she hardly dared to look at it.

There were still enough patients at Knockderry to need Catriona's services, but she had reduced her visits there to one every fortnight. It meant she was less often at home, for she put in extra hours at Dunmore, but she just wanted to be busy, and she treated the wounded who arrived at Dunmore from France with even greater fervour, grilling them for news as she once had grilled the injured returning from Egypt.

She followed the Allied army every inch of the way through France and into Germany, never quite sure where Pietrek would be. She had another letter sent by him in October, which she didn't get until after the new year. From its content it was clear he had written several before that she hadn't received. He was in eastern France, and wrote of hard travelling, hard fighting, endless injured. The Red Army had taken Poland from the Germans, but Pietrek worried that they might be even worse masters than the Nazis. Pray for my country, and pray that the Russians heed their allies, he wrote, and then, to finish his letter, 'You are my love, I don't forget you, could never forget you, you are my future, and I will be with you soon.'

In January Catriona followed every report of the Yalta Conference, where Roosevelt, Churchill and Stalin met to discuss post-war Europe. Russia had put their own puppet government in to rule Poland, and Roosevelt and Churchill wanted the government reorganised on more democratic lines. But their very language conceded defeat. The agreement was deliberately vague, conciliatory to Stalin, so vague, in fact, that one commentator said that the Soviets would be able to 'stretch it all the way from Yalta to Washington without ever technically breaking it'.

Over a year had gone by since Pietrek had left Scotland. Since he'd sailed for France she had had only two letters, and there were no more. Would Poles be safe in Germany? How must he feel after Yalta? Write to me, Pietrek, she urged him. But she was sure he had written. Letters just weren't getting through the war zones.

By the spring of 1945 Fergus MacNeill was making noises about returning to Islay. There were no more RAF seaplanes at Bowmore, and he had heard from the War Office that his cottage was now at his disposal again. He had received a rent for the cottage, which had helped him to live during the last five years, but now the rent had stopped, and he wanted to go home, and get back to work. They wouldn't be making whisky, but he could fish, more successfully than he could fish on Loch Long.

'Come with me,' he urged Catriona. 'You need a new life, back at home, away from people who've done you nothing but harm.'

Catriona merely shook her head. She wasn't going anywhere, not while she was waiting for Pietrek. But as the months went by and there was still no letter she began to have the most terrible doubts. Germany was under administration, the occupying Allied forces weren't at war in the same way that they had been before. Nurses at work with loved ones overseas were receiving regular letters, but she had nothing. Aunt Sheila took her aside one day and spoke to her, very gently.

'You do know, don't you, that you are not Pietrek's next of kin? If he has been killed, then no one at the War Office is going to let you know, *a' ghràidh.*'

'His brother would write to me,' Catriona said, her throat clenching. 'Pietrek gave him my address at Dunmore, and instructed him to write to me if anything happened.'

'Could something have happened to both of them?'

Catriona shook her head, tears smarting at her. 'No! Letters have got lost, and they'll be getting lost still! Aunt Sheila, please don't try to prepare me; I don't want to be prepared for anything!'

* * *

On May 8th they celebrated Victory in Europe. They listened to the wireless all morning as the King and Queen appeared in London before cheering crowds, and in the afternoon the whole Kilcreggan community came together, and they had a street party with cakes and sweets for the children.

In the evening they lit a fire on the hill overlooking the Clyde, and all along the river you could see similar fires, on both sides of the water. The night before, the residents around the corner in Rosneath had begun celebrating early, and had lit a huge fire using fuel from the base. The police had demanded that they extinguish the fire since the war was not officially over, and blackout regulations were still in force! A good fracas had ensued, and finally officialdom had admitted defeat and withdrawn. The people of Rosneath had well and truly won the war!

But on May 8th it was all right to light a fire, and they roasted potatoes, and drank whatever beer they could lay their hands on. Finally the five-year ordeal was all over. There was such a general feeling of elation that Catriona couldn't help but share it, even if she had to suppress every fear in order to do so. It was a Tuesday, and normally she would have been at work, but she had hurt her foot, and was stuck at home. They would be having a party at Dunmore too, she was sure.

They even had a telegram from Jim. 'Congratulations to one and all. On our way home hopefully soon.' Fergus danced a jig around the kitchen when he read the words, and another around the bonfire that evening.

'All of our boys will be home soon, you wait and see,' a neighbour said, shaking Fergus's hand delightedly as they toasted their sons with their beer bottles. Catriona could only watch in silence. If Pietrek was alive, then did he have a home to go back to? And if he didn't, would he come home to her? It all depended on him being alive, and Catriona clenched her glass of blackberry wine and made her own private toast, praying for the gift of life.

CHAPTER FORTY-FOUR

Winchester, July 1945

The two letters arrived on the same day, one postmarked Germany, and the other more recently from Winchester. Catriona found them in her pigeonhole at Dunmore when she went for her break, and took herself outside, trembling, to open them alone. She sat on a garden bench in the weak July sunshine and opened the latest letter first, her fingers unsteady.

Pietrek had just arrived in England, having travelled with three seriously wounded soldiers from his regiment. He was fine, uninjured, doctoring others. The relief was so great that Catriona felt dizzy.

'I am staying in a very nice house in Winchester with two elderly ladies, and they have told me that if you can come to visit they will be pleased to receive you too. They have another spare room. Would you be free to come to see me, *kochanie*? Do you still wish to after one and a half years? I am longing to see you.'

Catriona sat transfixed. There was nothing to stop her travelling to England. Nothing at all. She hadn't taken leave for two years, and the numbers arriving at Dunmore had become a trickle compared with a few months ago. An excitement took hold of her that she could barely contain, and she laughed silently into the empty garden, hugging the letter to her chest. Pietrek was fine, and he wanted to see her.

She read the other letter. It had been written in April, and had taken three months to find its way to Scotland. Pietrek had gone from France to Belgium and then to Holland, his division fighting with the Canadian army to cross the Rhine and win their way into Germany. At the time of writing he had been in Holland again, where they were clearing the country of German troops. He wrote of picking up and treating desperately injured German soldiers, the poor men terrified, demoralised and longing for an end. This was so much her Pietrek. She needed to see him so badly that she jumped up and went straight in to find Matron.

She sent him a telegram to tell him she was on her way. She wasn't due home at Kilcreggan for over a week, so she didn't tell them anything. By the following morning she was on a train.

As she sat in the crowded carriage heading south it dawned on her that she was finally going to leave Scotland for the first time in her life. All those ambitious plans to nurse on the front line during this war had taken her no further afield than Glasgow. She'd been so frustrated, and had buckled under only because of her concern for her father, but in the end the world had come to her, in the guise of American GIs, Free French sailors, and one very important Polish doctor.

It was a clear day, and Catriona sat glued to the window

as they passed through the Borders and on into the Lake District. As they neared the industrial area around Preston she ate the tinned-meat sandwiches that the cook at Dunmore had insisted on preparing for her, and then she dozed, her hand gripped tight on her handbag.

The journey seemed interminable, and she changed train three times, but eventually she was boarding a creaky little train at Reading, destination Winchester. Her stomach churned with a mix of excitement and trepidation. Would Pietrek have received her telegram? Would he be free to meet her? She'd dreamt about him last night, and thought about him all day. Would he look the same? And would he be thinking the same things, worrying about her? She took out her mirror and gave a final touch to her lipstick, pulled the comb again through her hair, which had grown longer, she realised, since Pietrek had been gone.

The train slowed down, and she stood up and reached for her old case with clammy hands. A trooper in uniform stepped forward and helped her down with it, then insisted on lifting it off the train and giving it to a porter.

'Thank you so much,' she said, with a smile she thought must look ridiculously timid.

'It's my pleasure, miss,' he said, and the edge of appreciation in his voice gave her courage. She drew herself up and looked round, and there was Pietrek, standing just a few steps away.

It didn't matter how many times in the year and a half she had looked at his photograph. Now that she saw him again in real life after such an absence, he was suddenly a stranger. There was something intimidating about his officer's uniform, too smart, different from the one he had worn when forced to at Knockderry, and underneath his cap his hair had been cropped short. She gazed at him for a moment, unsure, and then he took off his cap, smiled, and gave her a small bow, a touching little gesture typical of him from the past, so different from anything anyone else ever did that suddenly he was her man again. She smiled in a rush of relief, and moved forward as he opened his arms.

Catriona and Pietrek spent five days together in almost wicked indolence. He visited his patients once a day, but as he said, they weren't really his patients any more. He had handed them over, and he was visiting the hospital more to give them company than for anything else. He was waiting for a transport back to Germany, but for now he had little to do.

She stayed with him, or rather in a bedroom far removed from his, in the rambling old Victorian villa on the outskirts of Winchester where he had been billeted. The two ladies who lived there could have stepped out of an issue of *The Lady* magazine, pink-cheeked relicts from a bygone era. One was the widow of a First World War colonel, the other her sister, who had come to stay with her once she was widowed. The house was too big for them, and too difficult to keep up, and the hours they spent in the garden weren't enough to keep it under control, but they were dedicated to the war effort, and grew vegetables and fruits, which were a delight.

They had a soft spot for an officer, especially one as courteous as Pietrek, and plied him, and by default Catriona, with plum, and gooseberry, and rhubarb tarts, and cups of tea with carrot cake, which they served to them in a little sitting room that they reserved for their billeted guests.

'You really must stop charming older ladies, Pietrek,' Catriona told him. 'First Matron at Knockderry, and now two gentlewomen of England. I will always have rivals who want to feed you and nurse you, it seems.'

'They just take pity on me,' he said, 'as you did, *kochanie*.' He bit hungrily into his slice of cake. 'But they are charming, and their carrot cake is descended from heaven!'

He took Catriona to see Southampton, with its massive docks and surrounding residential areas so desperately bombed. Catriona had never seen anything like it, save the damage to Greenock in its single blitz back in 1941. But here the city had been literally pummelled.

'How did people survive such bombing?' she asked Pietrek.

'I imagine many didn't, but just along the road Portsmouth was worse.'

He held her hand, and they walked together through the streets, and he bought her lunch with his saved-up pay. 'They'll rebuild,' he said. 'It's over now, and all will be rebuilt.'

Catriona was doubtful. 'In bankrupt Britain? It'll take some time, surely?'

But it was what Britain needed to believe in now. Elections had been held this month, and although the results had been delayed while votes from forces overseas were brought back, there was growing expectation that Clement Attlee's Labour Party might form a government. Could they deliver people's yearning for new homes, jobs for all, and a new National Health Service, after so many had paid such a high price during the war? Catriona thought back to her evenings with Duncan and his friends in the bar in Glasgow, and could imagine them arguing out the details.

Ordinary people wanted no more to do with the elitist Britain of the past. A new age of egalitarianism was being dreamt of. But it didn't extend to the poor Poles who had fought so valiantly alongside our forces in Africa and Europe. There was growing anti-Polish sentiment, particularly among the trade unions, who said that if the Poles returned to Britain they would take jobs away from returning British servicemen. In Poland the new police state set up by the Russians struck fear into everyone, and the word coming out of the country was that returning servicemen would be treated with deep suspicion, as Western collaborators. And yet the British government was trying to persuade the Polish troops to return home.

Even generous Pietrek was cynical about this. 'They say we'll be safe,' he said. 'They say they have assurances. Well, they had assurances six months ago that Stalin would facilitate democracy in Poland, and look what he has done!'

It hurt Catriona to see him brush away at an imaginary lock of hair – the lock of hair that had hung over his forehead, and that he had always swept back in moments of stress.

'But hasn't the government also said that any Polish serviceman who wants to stay will be given asylum here?' she asked.

'Which government? There isn't a government at the moment, and we don't know who will be elected.'

More than anything, Catriona knew, he was worried about his family back at home. And about his brother, and their comrades back in Germany, in the Allied Occupation

Force. All of them had parents and siblings back at home, some of them also had wives and children, and all of them needed a future.

They left the subject alone for most of their time together. It was just too painful, and too open-ended. Instead they walked in the green fields around Winchester, and toured the cathedral, and drank tea and played chess in their private sitting room. When the time came for Catriona to leave, the elderly ladies insisted on baking a vegetable pie, which could be sliced for her journey, and gave her a large punnet of strawberries.

'It has been a pleasure to have you here,' one told her, when she protested that they should keep the strawberries for themselves. 'You and the dear doctor make a nice couple, and I hope things work out well for you both.'

The note of doubt in her voice only added to Catriona's fears. As she stood with Pietrek at the railway station she fought back tears in desperate gulps.

'It won't be long now, my precious,' Pietrek told her, but she didn't believe him. The nineteen months until now had been so long and hard that she could no longer comfort herself with illusions. There was no way that the occupying forces could leave Germany quickly. There was too much mess to clear up, too many Nazis hiding out, and malnutrition and misery everywhere.

'We think we have shortages here,' Pietrek told her. 'But rationing has kept everyone fed, and children healthy. I wish I could see only well-fed children in Germany, but they are starving, literally starving.'

The Canadian army was already heading home, and

the Polish regiments were being incorporated into the British army. The British were settling down for long-term administration, but would use foreign troops mainly in the early crisis period, Pietrek thought.

'I'll apply to come back as soon as we know what is happening to our regiment, and when I know what my brother wants to do,' he told her.

Catriona thought it would be a year, maybe more, before the Polish regiments were disbanded and could go home, and even longer before they knew what homes they had to go to. She sat on the train, gripping her bag for comfort, and out of the window she saw a poster with the slogan the Labour Party had fought the election on. 'Let Us Face the Future', it read.

I want nothing more, she thought. Just bring us a future we can work for, but bring it for all of us, not just for those the Empire has smiled upon.

Chapter Forty-Five

Islay, November 1945

She was at least getting letters through from Pietrek now, Catriona thought. The chaos was turning gradually to order in Germany, though food rations allocated to local people remained terribly poor. Troops were stationed long-term in towns to provide order and administration, and were supposed to be helping the people, so many of whom had suffered too, ordinary people who had lost sons, been bombed out of their homes, and now were starving, all for a regime they had never properly understood. For the most part our troops understood that an old lady in the street was not their enemy, had never been their enemy, but there was also a feeling that it was Germany's turn to pay. Pietrek wrote of Allied soldiers using their generous army rations to buy German women, then dumping them if they became pregnant. 'All conquerors learn to exploit,' he wrote, and you could feel his distress on the page.

Catriona had come home to Islay with her father. The Clyde, without Knockderry, without the American base, without her French sailors, had become just a place of transit for troops returning home. And at Dunmore the local staff were now sufficient for the patients who remained. It had felt wrong to leave without resolving the stand-off with Duncan, but he was there less often too, and when she did run across him he simply turned his head and marched on into the garden towards his private retreat. It was frustrating and sad after sharing so much with him. He had made her think, taught her to question establishment views, and opened her to her own emotions.

It was Pietrek who had completed her as a woman, but Duncan had taken her a good way along the path. Had she done anything similar for him? she wondered. It was difficult to say. He'd wanted her as a woman, but she hadn't felt she gave anything to his soul. He'd kept that to himself. The staff at Dunmore had given her a small party on leaving, and she had tried to invite Duncan, but he had ignored her notes, stayed away on her final day, and she'd had to give up.

So she and her father had left Aunt Sheila and Uncle Charlie, after over four years of unbelievable hospitality, and Catriona had returned to the island to wait.

Islay too was finding its feet again as a civilian island, cleaning up remnants of the military's presence. Barbed wire and concrete shelters adorned the landscape, but there were good legacies too. The electricity station installed to power the military bases would soon provide electric light to the houses of Bowmore, they were promised, and the RAF had also left behind a fine new pier, which made fishing a lot easier. Electric light was the magic charm that set the locals talking. Everyone who had visited Glasgow, or any major town on the mainland, knew what it was to have power at the touch of a button. Fergus MacNeill said it would be sad when the old kerosene lamps disappeared, but Catriona knew better – he had loved having electricity at Aunt Sheila's.

The magic promise was for some months away, though, so it would be the old Tilley lamps that would welcome Jim and his wife Fran. Jim and his family had arrived back in England a few weeks ago, and had been visiting Fran's cousins in the south. Now they were making the long trek north to Islay, just for a couple of weeks. It wasn't the best season to make your first visit to a remote island in the north-west. Catriona wondered how Fran would cope with the simple life of Islay, and worried that she might despise them all. After their trip north, Jim would have to report for duty back in England and prepare to be demobbed, but he had plans to return to Scotland afterwards. Fran was pregnant again, and Jim wrote that he would like the baby to be born on Scottish soil. Would Fran cope with that? The prospect of the visit made Catriona nervous, but she longed to see Jim, and hoped that a warm welcome would make up for what they couldn't give to Fran.

There was little space in the cottage for three more people, especially people used to their own private lives. Fergus and Catriona therefore took over old Murdo's cottage for Jim and Fran. It had been used during the war to house a couple of officers, but other than that it had been empty since Murdo died in 1938. Catriona spent hours scrubbing it out, and sewed new curtains from a couple of old bedspreads. With some ornaments and a vase of dried grasses the little sitting room looked quite cheerful. Would it be enough to persuade Fran that she could come back to Islay later for a longer stay?

They arrived on a Monday, thankfully in unusually dry, mild weather. Catriona had been helping at the local hospital over the weekend, but she was at home when they arrived. They had a car, and they drew lots of glances as one of the village's favoured sons drew up outside Fergus's cottage. Jim came out first, then opened the passenger door for his wife, who had little Victoria on her knee. He swung the toddler up into his arms, and turning, spotted Fergus, standing nervously by the cottage door.

'Father!' Jim strode up and took his father's hand, holding it tight. Then he did something almost unknown in island culture, and pulled his father to him in a long embrace, holding the child between them.

Fergus said nothing, and Catriona thought that he couldn't find words. He bit his lip on what looked like impending tears, and then reached a hand to touch his granddaughter, stroking her hair. Gradually a smile came to his face, and the little girl gave him a hint of it back. It was understated, but Catriona had rarely seen anything so beautiful.

She watched Fran. She was as elegant and beautiful as Catriona had expected, but more real than her photos, dressed practically in a woollen suit, and she looked less like an empty socialite than Catriona had feared. She gave Fergus a warm, rich smile, and then her gaze moved on to include Catriona in the same smile. There was an appeal in it, and Catriona realised that Fran, too, was anxious to be accepted.

It was going to be all right. Fran was charmed by her little cottage, and for now found the process of lighting lamps and burning peats a novelty. She was much more direct than any young woman would normally be with her father-in-law, very assured, but it was done with such charm that Fergus couldn't take offence. And by his granddaughter he was enchanted. Little Victoria had her mother's colouring, with huge amber eyes and soft brown hair, and at sixteen months old she was beginning to speak, in lisping tones, which Fergus listened to as though each word was a jewel. She quickly learnt to call him *Seanair*, the Gaelic word for 'grandfather', and she would bring endless treasures to show him. 'Look,' she would say, placing the item gravely into Fergus's hand. She was their little victory child, and she was the best walker there had ever been for her age, the best talker. It was Fergus who said so, and no one was allowed to say otherwise.

Jim watched over it all with a happy smile. He had changed, Catriona thought. It wasn't just that he was four years older, a man in his thirties with a family to look after. He had an air of authority that transcended that. He'd always been deep, but now his whole experience of the war, both the good and the bad, had given him new layers.

She said as much to him a few days after their arrival. They'd gone for a walk with Victoria in her pram, and they had strolled along the old lane towards Miss MacLeod's house.

'Is the old lady still living?' Jim asked Catriona, as they neared the house.

'Very much so – she is only in her sixties! She kept on teaching through the war too, until young Martha Beaton graduated and came back here last year.'

'Amazing woman!' He paused, looking around him in appreciation. 'It doesn't change, does it? It was one of the things I feared over the last few years, that I would come back here and find my home all different. But actually the place has stayed the same, and it's we who have changed.'

'Well, you certainly have. You're an international man now, rather than a simple islander.'

'I'm not sure that Islay folk are that simple! But you've changed too, you know.'

'I've never lived any further afield than Glasgow.'

'I know that, but you're different, nevertheless. I love the way you sort Father out, and don't let him browbeat you. He always used to treat you like a little girl. Now he gives you the same respect he gives to Aunt Sheila.'

Catriona laughed. 'So I'm destined to end up as Aunt Sheila? Well, it's true that I want a homelier life, perhaps, than you do.'

'And would you stay on here? Is that what you would like?'

Catriona had written about Pietrek in her letters. Jim knew who, what, had taken over her life in the last two years, and he also knew that he was in Germany. Was he asking her whether she could imagine Pietrek here?

She looked around her, at the boggy peat field to her right leading down to the white beach and the water beyond. It was an ebbing tide, and a green sward of seaweed had been exposed as the water receded. On the other side of the loch there was another line of green, then white, then green again over at Bruichladdich. All you could hear were the seabirds. There was endless peace in the scene. It wasn't as grand a landscape as some of the Highlands, or as tidy and wealthy as Cove Bay and Kilcreggan, and four years ago all she had wanted to do was to leave and find a bigger platform to work in, somewhere to prove herself. But now as she looked at it, she felt a rush of affection, and thought that she could indeed live here, if only she could have her man with her. Would there be a role for a Polish doctor on Islay? He was suited to such a community, but would such a community ever embrace him?

'If things work out,' she answered Jim, 'then yes, I would stay here, or come back here sometime in the future when the right opportunity arose.'

He put his arm around her and she knew he understood. 'What about you?' she asked him. 'Are you going back to teaching? I can't see it, somehow.'

He took time to answer, and a frown came to his brow. Eventually he held up a hand. 'Listen, Catriona, don't say anything to Father, will you, because nothing is decided yet, but when I'm in Portsmouth in a couple of weeks I'm meeting with someone who may offer me a job in America.'

'America?' That was beyond what Catriona had imagined.

'Yes, in New Jersey, for a company who are leading the way in developing television and radio for the consumer market. They have invented a colour television set, and goodness knows where they will go in the future. America will lead the way, though, that you can be sure of.'

Catriona's brain boggled. She didn't even know anyone with a black and white television set, and it was likely to be a long time before one appeared on Islay. But Jim's enthusiasm was evident, and he launched into a description of the kind of work he wanted to do that left her more and more bewildered. The one thing that was patently clear, though, was what this would mean to their father.

'You'll never come home,' she blurted out, interrupting his flow.

She'd cut through his enthusiasm like a knife. His grave look came back into his face, and he stopped walking and leant against a fence post. 'I promise you it won't be like that, Catriona. Travel is getting so much easier. I could never imagine not seeing Islay and you and Father again. Anyway, I'm not emigrating, just hopefully taking a job for a few years, which will build my future, and then I can come back to Britain.'

Catriona didn't believe that. Once in the land of technology and riches, what would bring Jim and Fran back to these shores? She thought of Captain Martin and his fellow GIs, with their easy generosity, confidence and assumption of entitlement. They would like Jim, for his friendliness and his beautiful manners, and for the Scottish heritage they seemed to lap up so happily. But above all they would love him for his competence, and the assurance that had grown on him and that suited him so well.

Jim was still looking out over the loch. 'When will you tell Father?' she asked him.

'When and if things are settled, and I am sure of getting the papers I need to travel. We wouldn't go until after the baby is born, anyway, and we'll come back here as soon as we can, for a longer spell, of course.'

A wry moment came over Catriona, and she raised an eyebrow at him. 'Is that why you were asking if I will stay here on Islay? You want to be sure someone is here with Father so that you are free to leave?'

He looked as though she had hit him. 'God no, Catriona! If I thought that leaving would force your hand in any way I wouldn't go.'

She felt ashamed, and hastened into speech again.

'Ignore that, Jim, it was a horrible thing to say. It wasn't your fault that you were sent off to Egypt during the war, or that Mother had so recently died, or that Father's home was taken away from him. It was normal that I should stay. None of it was anyone's fault, and you paid such a high price for your role – much higher than any I paid for mine.'

She came close and put her hand through his arm. 'From now on, the only reason that either of us needs to live on Islay is if we choose to. Father will be all right now that he has his home back, and the fishing has started again, and there are plans to begin distilling again. Do you realise it has been nearly six years since Mummy died? Even if I am elsewhere, I can come home frequently, and he'll be fine. Just make sure and tell him that you're only going for a year or two, and promise him you won't come back with an American accent!'

CHAPTER FORTY-SIX

Islay and Glasgow, November 1945

The two weeks with Jim's family went by more quickly than Fran could have imagined, and two weeks would never be enough to absorb the shock that was Islay. It wasn't a bad shock, just a world so different that it challenged every sense and every learnt response.

It was beautiful, and wild, and natural, and for someone brought up without mountains, the views over to the hills of Jura were quite breathtaking. The weather stayed mild, and the light miraculously good. You needed the light to capture the kind of special blue luminosity over the waters.

But it wasn't the scenery that challenged you on Islay. Fran had expected to find a poor community, but although people lived with relatively small means they weren't poor. They grew their own vegetables, and caught fish, and kept chickens, and there was more food than in many parts of poor, bankrupted Britain.

What was challenging was the intensity of the little community. Jim's father might have taken a little cottage for them, but it didn't mean you were private. All the cottages gave onto the street, for a start, and then, everyone wanted to see Jim, and to meet his exotic new wife. They dropped in unannounced, without even knocking, strolling through the door calling a 'Hello' as they entered. But no one came empty-handed. There was a pot of home-made jam, a few oatcakes, some peats for the fire, home-grown vegetables, anything, in fact, that the people of Bowmore and beyond could supply from their own homes and gardens.

The men took Jim off fishing, while Fran and Catriona would stroll the streets with little Victoria in her pram. They would make slow progress, because everywhere people stopped to talk. Fran had the impression of a community that worked hard but didn't hurry, where everyone had time for each other, and pulled together whenever one of their own was in need.

They knew perhaps too much about each other's lives, but it was on the whole a kindly knowledge. Everybody belonged, and if you strayed you would be quietly but surely hooked back into the fold. Even the most errant were looked after, and prayed for, no doubt, in Bowmore's lovely round church.

It was a self-sufficient, purposeful life, modest and good-humoured, and it helped to explain Jim to Fran, his anchored sense of identity, that respected everyone but bent its knee to no one, that treated the world with humour but rejected the insincere. She loved listening to him speaking in Gaelic, and discovered his singing voice at an impromptu ceilidh held in a neighbour's house one Friday evening. He had always sung to Victoria, but in the tiny, lamplit sitting room that evening his voice seemed far more haunting, with everyone except herself joining in the chorus of a Gaelic love song.

They would be going back down to England for a while, she and Jim, and her parents were coming over for Christmas, celebrating the fact that you could sail again directly through the Mediterranean, and not take three months to get home from Egypt all the way around Africa.

Her parents were planning to buy a house too. Alan Trevillian had no desire to return to England, to the joyless food and rationing, and to the social restrictions and buttoned-up cultural mores. Pragmatism drove him, though. He hoped to have some more years in Egypt, but he knew they needed to be prepared for upheaval.

Fran had been sad to leave Alexandria, for she was sure she would never return. So many people were leaving. Nearly every European Jew they knew in Alexandria had already left, fleeing the ever-increasing hostility and violence against them. The Egyptian Jews were mostly stuck, but they all saw their futures in Jewish Palestine. Asher's family had already quietly disappeared earlier that year, possibly helped by Asher himself. To be Jewish was bad news in Egypt now, but Christians were not exempt either. All of the European communities were living on borrowed time, and the Brits were the most hated of all.

So Fran's parents would be home, in the middle of the English winter. They would all spend Christmas together at her aunt's home in Devon, and then they would be at a very special wedding, between George Blake and Lucie, the prospect of which brought a rush of happiness to Fran each time she thought about it. Their own best George and Lucie, brought together so slowly as the war came to a close, and Jim was to be best man.

But then Jim wanted to come north again as soon

as he was demobbed, so that the baby could be born in Scotland. It wouldn't please her mother, Fran knew, for she had planned to stay on in England for the birth. Her mother wanted time with her daughter before she left for America. But could Barbara Trevillian come here to Islay? Fran had become so much closer to her mother over the last couple of years, but she was under no illusions: for all her steadfastness and loyalty, Barbara lived in a rather inelastic world. How would she rate this little community, so modest in comparison to everything she knew?

It was Catriona who had the solution. 'Have the baby in Glasgow,' she suggested. 'That way he or she will be born in Scotland, and there are hospitals there that will satisfy all of your mother's anxiety, and decent hotels where she can stay. Then when you come out of hospital you can bring the baby here for a while so that everyone can meet him. You can leave little Victoria here with us, if you want. You've seen how happy she is with her grandfather. Or if you prefer to have her with you, then I can come down to Glasgow too, and look after her.'

'You can't do that, Catriona. What about your work?'

Catriona shrugged. 'I'm only filling in here, as you know. I can leave whenever I want.'

Fran knew that was true. Catriona was a woman in waiting, and everything in her life was in abeyance just now. She would make no professional moves, no long-term commitments, and there was a kind of enduring patience about her that Fran admired all the more because it was so different from her own more febrile nature. It wasn't docility that characterised Catriona, though. She had the strength to stand by Pietrek against all her father's wishes, and would carve a life with him wherever they could, whenever he was free.

Jim had his own reservations about Pietrek too, because of his age, and the complications it would bring to his sister's life to marry a stateless foreigner. He said he hoped that Pietrek was as special as Catriona thought him, for their road would not be easy. Fran, though, had no doubts at all.

'Your sister is as grounded as you are. Trust her to make the right decisions for her life.'

Catriona had told her about Duncan. 'I was so stupid,' she said. 'I fell in love like a silly girl when all the time I had reservations about his character.'

'But you did have those reservations, didn't you? Your innate sense stopped you from leaping in there completely.'

Catriona looked thoughtful. 'Poor Duncan,' she mused. 'He is fundamentally such a decent person, intelligent and thought-provoking. I saw another side of life through him, and he does such good work, but he has been damaged, and I think he already had weaknesses that didn't survive combat very well. He has an exhibition of his own sculptures at the moment in Glasgow, and I have been thinking of going to see it, because I ran away from the exhibition he put together of his patients' work, and I don't think he ever forgave me for it. I think he is manning this exhibition in person.'

'Then let's go together. You suggested a Glasgow hospital, and now Jim has put your local GP on the case of registering us with one, and Jim wants to visit. We'll be there for a day or two, and have to return the car there also. Couldn't you come with us?'

A slow smile came to Catriona's face. 'Now there's an idea! A car ride all the way to Glasgow! I could indeed, and I would love to,' she said. 'It's been three years since I broke off my relationship with Duncan, and he wouldn't speak to me afterwards. I'd like to put the past to bed.'

Fran was agog to meet Duncan McIlroy, and when she did she had a very womanly appreciation of his appeal. He was a handsome man, possibly Jim's age, with a very mobile expression and hands, lots of charisma, and especially lots of talent. When they entered his exhibition he held himself very much under control, but his eyes froze on Catriona. His eyebrows rose, and he set out immediately to charm Jim and Fran, keeping a watchful eye on Catriona's reactions. He gave particular attention to Fran, and she thought he was looking for a trace of envy in Catriona's eyes.

Jim fell in love with his work. 'Is any of it for sale?' he asked.

'All of it!' Duncan assured him. 'I'm not earning much else these days, and I find that for an artist to starve in his garret is a much-overrated pastime.'

'You're no longer doing your workshops at Dunmore?' Catriona ventured.

He gave her a carefully casual look. 'I get some classes, but their numbers are down now that not even the Japs are shooting at us. It's mainly those who've lost multiple limbs who are left, and the shell-shocked, and some who return for ongoing treatment.'

'So you're concentrating on your own work? Well I'm glad. It's worth pursuing.'

Catriona was making a noble effort to be generous and friendly, Fran thought, but it was clear that Duncan had an edge to him that was quite alien to the frank and open MacNeill character.

They toured the exhibition, and Jim picked out a small

piece of wood sculpted in a complex swirl with a fist at one end, which was labelled 'Hard Current'.

'This is beautiful,' he commented, running his finger around it. 'Why Hard Current?'

'Because life has a tendency to bring you around full circle to where you started,' Duncan answered, then smiled, a very beguiling smile, Fran noted.

'Don't get me wrong,' he continued, 'sometimes it's good to find yourself back where you started, especially if life has chucked you along a road you didn't want to be on.' He took the piece from Jim and turned it over to hold the curve in his palm. 'You've good taste, by the way, this piece is one I love to hold.'

'And why the fist?'

Duncan stole a look at Catriona before he replied. 'Because sometimes it's a fist you need.' He handed Jim a sheet of paper from a table behind him. 'These are the prices, but if you want this piece I'll give you a quarter off the price. I'd like to see it go to Catriona's family.'

He strode over to another table, where another small sculpture sat, a bodiless head on what looked like a boat adrift on rough waters. He brought it over to Catriona, and put it into her hand.

'Take this, Catriona, as a poor artist's gift, though it's a strange piece to give to someone as whole as you. I hope you're in calmer waters than this poor soul.'

Fran watched Catriona, who touched the head gently. It was neither male nor female, but androgynous, with fine bones and wild hair. 'I hope we all are now,' she murmured, and then looked up at Duncan. 'Should you really be giving away something as fine as this?'

'If I want to,' was his reply. 'Thanks for coming, Catriona. No husband yet?' His voice was carefully light and teasing.

Catriona matched his tone. 'Not quite. And you? Any girlfriends?'

He grinned. 'Several! All stunners, as well! I only date beautiful women.'

'I'm flattered!' Catriona stroked the sculpture in her hand. 'I'll treasure this, Duncan. I've always wanted a piece of your work.'

They emerged from the exhibition into a cold, crisp November afternoon, and Fran left the pram to Jim, and put her arm around Catriona.

'Well, is that the past put thoroughly to bed? You didn't feel any new attraction? He's a good-looking man!'

Catriona shook her head with a smile. 'He enriched my life for a while, but I'm happy to have him in the past.'

'I'd say he could be complex to deal with,' was Jim's comment.

Catriona nodded and laughed. 'He could.'

'And your Pietrek?' Fran asked her. 'Is he complex to deal with?'

The answer to this was an emphatic shake of the head. 'Pietrek is nothing like him. He's not even handsome like Duncan. But he's just wonderful.'

Fran kept her arm around Catriona and squeezed. 'Well then, Sister-in-law, we just have to hope that he gets back to Scotland before we finally have to leave, because Jim and I can't wait to meet him.'

CHAPTER FORTY-SEVEN

Islay, January–February 1946

It was a full four months later that Pietrek finally came to Islay. A whole winter went by without him. All over Islay sons and husbands were returning from the war, but Pietrek stayed away. It was so much easier to persevere in patience when the country was at war, but now it felt as though it was time to begin a new life in peacetime.

The new year came and went, the first of the post-war, happier than for many years in this community, with old bottles of whisky unearthed to carry from home to home to celebrate. Even the wind and driving rain couldn't put people off. There was a determination to be happy.

February came, and with it Jim and Fran, now a civilian couple making their plans for the future. Jim had been offered the job in America, and now he broke the news to their father.

Fergus's only memories of people going to America were from before the turn of the century, when he was just a child. Emigration was a very final move back then, born of poverty, and the village would hold a wake for their departing youths, knowing that they would truly never see them again.

But Jim's job was a two-year posting in the first instance, and all of the villagers combined to convince Fergus that it was just as though his son was going away to sea. Boys from Bowmore had always gone to sea, and had always come home. It's a great opportunity, they told him. Your son will come back here with his pockets full and buy Islay House.

'Remember old Donny MacRae,' one of the fishermen told him. 'He went off to India for years, and we never thought we would see him again. But then he turned up full of beans, throwing money around like nobody's business. He'd made a packet.'

Fergus waved a dismissive hand. 'My sister already threw his case in my face years ago,' he retaliated. 'You'll not convince me by talking of Donny. He drank away his entire savings in the back bar, remember, and then he had to go back to work fishing like everyone else.'

'And you think your Jim would do the same?' the fisherman asked.

Fergus bridled. 'Certainly not! Jim is a man of intelligence and principle.'

'Well there you go, then,' was the uncompromising reply.

It didn't take away all Fergus's fears, but pride in his son began to win over his doubts. He approved of his marriage too. Fran's charm had worked a special magic on her father-in-law. She now had a huge bump, and Fergus treated her like a fragile flower to be protected from every wind.

'At least Father approves of one of our partners,' Catriona commented drily to Jim.

'He'll approve of yours too, don't worry,' was his reply. 'I'm working on him!'

Catriona shrugged. She no longer cared too much what her father thought, if only Pietrek would come back.

In parliament, Britain's Foreign Secretary Ernest Bevin told a tense House of Commons that terror had become an instrument of national policy in the new Poland. Opponents of the Communist government were being systematically murdered. The West's leaders demanded free elections for the country, but Poland's Russian masters, of course, took no notice at all.

For some weeks there was no letter from Pietrek. Catriona imagined him and his brother in long and hard discussions with their fellow Poles in the regiment, depressed, angry, so terribly let down by the West in whose armies they had served. He would be worried about his family, even more than he'd been last summer when she'd seen him. She fretted for news, but more than anything wanted to be able to talk to him, to comfort him, in as far as comfort was possible.

And then he came, just like that, without any warning. Catriona came home from work late one afternoon, hugging her coat around her against a cold wind, and as she turned up towards the cottage she heard him.

'Catriona,' he called, and she twirled round at the so familiar voice. He was moving towards her from the shore, and she ran towards him across the road. She heard herself giving out the strangest little miauling noises, and as she reached him she said his name in a howl, and threw herself into his arms.

He had been there for two hours, waiting in the cold.

How could he not have gone to the house? He had, he told her, and there was no answer, and then later he'd seen her father going inside, and had decided to wait for her. Her father had since left the house again, and Pietrek had kept watching, waiting for her. He was cold, and she dragged him with her to the cottage, hurling open the door and pulling him inside, bags and all.

'Come, come, my love, come to the fire.' And she took off his coat, pushing him onto the sofa, and rubbed his hands, and brought hot water.

'I'll heat some soup,' she said, and he protested, laughing.

'Stop, *kochanie*. I don't need anything, I only waited a short time. Come and sit with me rather, so that I can see your sweet face.' He pulled her down beside him, and held her close. 'It has been too long,' he said, simply, and for a moment they said no more.

'You didn't write,' Catriona said eventually.

He smiled. 'We were on the move, and I wanted to surprise you.'

'So your whole regiment was disbanded?' He nodded.

'And your brother?'

He frowned. 'Alfons decided to go home. We wrote to our mother, and she got a letter back to us telling us not to come, although she had to say it in a coded way, because mail is censored out of Poland. Supposedly the mail system has been freed up since Hitler fell, but letters only get out if the authorities want them to. Alfons and I agreed that he would go back, and if possible get my mother out, and in any case get fuller news to me somehow. I can't go back now, not after spending so many years in France. I'd be a marked man, and anyway, my love, I have my reasons for wanting to be here.'

'And they're going to grant you British citizenship?'

'So they say. Will you marry me, *kochanie*?'

'Of course.' She nestled closer to him on the sofa. 'And go wherever you want.'

'Wherever there's work for a doctor, I suppose.'

'Oh, there'll be work. There's a new National Health Service, remember. With all the changes there's a lot of demand for doctors.'

Pietrek touched his lips to the top of her head. 'And what will your father say?'

'My father can say whatever he likes, Pietrek. I am twenty-six years old, and it's time I led my life my way. Our father is fine now here on Islay. He has accepted that Jim is going to America, so he'll have to accept wherever I choose to go, and with whom.'

Pietrek smiled. 'I don't think we'll go as far as America. I like it fine here in Scotland – the people have been good to me. But if I were your father I would be wrong not to worry about my daughter marrying a forty-year-old man.'

'We'll make him some babies,' Catriona chuckled. 'He has gone gaga over my little niece Victoria, and Jim's wife is about to have another child next month. It has made Fran the perfect wife in my father's eyes!'

'Your brother is here?'

'Yes, and I assume that's where my father is just now. They have a cottage a few doors along. They'll head off for America after the new baby is born.'

'So if we get married quite quickly they can be with us for the wedding.'

He spoke with quiet satisfaction, and Catriona thought that after so much exile and heartache Pietrek just wanted a family, and failing his own people, then it would be her family. He would always yearn for the land he couldn't go back to, and for his brother, his sisters, his mother. It was her job to make that up to him, and it would be a privilege to do so. She nestled in closer to him.

'Soup, Pietrek. Let me give you some soup,' she said, and could hear her Aunt Sheila's voice, and her mother's, and that of every island woman she knew. Well if that was who she was, then so be it, because every one of those women had grit, and heart, and character, and enough personality to carry the world.

Pietrek ate his soup, and they sat together for an hour, talking and not talking, just hugging their closeness. Catriona didn't have to prepare food, for they had been invited to eat this evening at Jim and Fran's cottage. Fran was experimenting with local ingredients and producing some interesting dishes, if you were generous, but the welcome at their home was enough to compensate. Tonight they would have an unexpected addition to their numbers, and if necessary Catriona would add some rations to make the food stretch. But she thought they would be happy enough to meet Pietrek that nothing else would matter.

She talked to Pietrek about Jim and Fran. They'd told her just yesterday that if Fran had a boy they were going to call him Michael, after the brother Fran had lost, but if they had a girl Jim wanted to call her Catriona. It would be wonderful to think of a little Catriona in America, charming all those ex-GIs, but Fergus so wanted a boy that it seemed mean to wish for it.

After an hour the door opened and Fergus came in. He

stood for a moment taking in the couple on the sofa, and when she finally registered him Catriona rose to her feet to greet him.

'*Daidí*,' she said simply. 'Pietrek has come home.'

She knew that Jim had been working on their father and coaching him in how good his daughter's life might be with a loving man who had served their country, but she didn't know how successful his efforts had been. She stood for a moment just watching Fergus and he didn't move, but his eyes never wavered from Pietrek's. Then Pietrek also stood up.

'Mr MacNeill,' he said, and it dawned on Catriona that this was only the second time that the two men had met. 'I hope that it doesn't inconvenience you too much that I should come here. You see, I love your daughter.'

The simplicity of it was magnificent. Fergus MacNeill stood long enough without replying, and then just said, 'Catriona, where have your manners gone, my child? Has Peter come all this way after being so long in Germany, and you haven't offered him a dram?'

Catriona smiled at him. 'We were only waiting for you, *Daidí*. Only waiting for you.'

AUTHOR'S NOTE

This novel has involved so much intensive research that I could not mention every resource I have used. However, two books merit specific mention because they added not just facts but also wonderful colour. These are *Alexandria: City of Memory* by Michael Haag, which evokes the glamour and history of Alexandria in Egypt in the first half of the 20th century, and Dennis Royal's lovely, colourful book about the United States Naval Base at Rosneath in World War Two.

The history of the Free French navy on the Clyde during the war is legendary, as is their hospital at Knockderry Castle, which did wonderful work, although not much detail remains of how it was run. In contrast, Dunmore Hospital is entirely fictional, but the Clyde boasted a ground-breaking hospital at Erskine doing similar work. My accounts of my hospitals are based on many records of hospital management during the war.

The *Alexandria Journal* is a fictional newspaper, but is based on similar newspapers being published at the time.

In all else, the descriptions of events and places are as painstakingly accurate as I could make them, but all my characters are my creations, and I love them all.

ACKNOWLEDGEMENTS

As always, there are so many people I'd like to thank. Jenny Brown, for her endless support and advice; Jenne, Morag and Maureen, for reading this book for me so helpfully as always; Charles, for his insights on Islay; Kenneth, for setting me straight on naval matters; and the whole MacKenzie family, for allowing me to write what is not their story, but what is inspired by their story.

JANE MACKENZIE has always had a love of languages and speaks fluent French. Much of her adult life has been spent travelling the world, teaching English and French everywhere from the Gambia to Papua New Guinea to Bahrain, and recently working for two years at CERN in Geneva. She now splits her time between her self-built house in Collioure, France, and the Highlands of Scotland, where she has made her family home.

janemackenzie.co.uk